THE VINE CODA

S. P. DAWES

Copyright © 2020 by S. P. Dawes

All rights reserved.

No part of this book may be reproduced in any form or by any electronic or mechanical means, including information storage and retrieval systems, without written permission from the author, except for the use of brief quotations in a book review.

❧ Created with Vellum

INSPIRATION

One day, just like that...

You'll discover your light.
You'll embrace your inner warrior.
You'll snatch your power back.

And the whole game will change.

Quote unknown.

THE VINE CODA

"ARE YOU OKAY?" THE WHISPERED SIGN OF CONCERN CAUGHT HIS EARS and before he knew it he was looking up to find out where it had come from. "Are you okay?" asked the gentle voice once again. Squinting as though that might help his eyesight his eyes finally focused on a young woman with a heavy woollen coat and a brown handbag that she gripped tightly to her chest as though a gust of wind may blow it away; Peering down at him with concern reflected in her eyes, Rob couldn't help but feel visible once again.

Too many nights he had curled up with whatever material he could find to help keep him warm, or at least starve off the icing chill of the wind while he tried to get some shuteye. Not an easy feat when you had to keep one eye on your surroundings to ensure you weren't knifed in the back for the shoes on your feet, or the cardboard box you clung to.

After a few attempts to open his mouth speech failing him, he just nodded limply, before allowing the weight of his head to anchor his body. "I saw what happened, do you want me to call the police or an ambulance?" On the word police he sharply looked up, jolting his neck from shaking it frantically. "You need to be seen, you're covered in cuts and bruises." As if her words suddenly reminded him he was battered he looked down at himself half sat, half crouched on the dirty needle laden pathway under the bridge he'd been hoping to hide under.

"No." he managed to scratch out of his throat. Seeming to weigh up her choices, she continued to stare at him as though he might change his mind if she hung around long enough. Finally, giving up any pretence of strength, he slumped onto the floor. Leaning up against the grimy graffiti ridden wall, he allowed his legs some relief by stretching them out along the path, becoming an obstruction for anyone who might choose to pass.

"I'm Freya." said the lady who was still watching him intently. He nodded to acknowledge he'd heard but said nothing. If he ignored her long enough, she'd get the hint he didn't want to talk. "Why did they beat you up?" Looking back up at her he saw her sparkly eyes, he couldn't tell which emotion was more prevalent, fear or concern but the fact she hadn't walked away already told him she was more concerned than scared. He'd seen those eyes before, or not those exact ones, but they had been blue and they haunted him every night when he closed his eyes, memories of what he had done. If the woman stood before him only knew what he was capable of, she would run for the hills not making sure he was all right.

Letting out a slight gargled laugh, he watched her shrink as though she had been made a fool of. "Because they could" he answered wanting her to know he wasn't laughing at her more at what she might have expected him to say in response. Watching her look around herself as if to check she wasn't being set up for a quick purse grab he grimaced at how untrusting she looked, he'd seen that look all too often before, it was the look Hayley had on her face right before she had realised he was going to end her life.

"Look I don't normally do this, well... because it's too dangerous... but... but..." unsure what she was trying to say he just sat and waited trying to weigh her up. She was of average height, slim with wavy chestnut hair, big blue eyes with a dainty elfin face and a delicate nose. She wore a long woollen coat over jeans, a turtleneck jumper and what looked like brown leather knee-high boots. She didn't look exactly well off, but she didn't look short of a bob or two either. "Do you want to come back to mine? You can get cleaned up and you can use the first aid kit?" she asked while scanning his clothes, ok so she might have to incinerate his clothes and fumigate the house but she couldn't very well leave a man already down on his luck sitting on a dirty path after having been beaten up by a bunch of yobs for being just that.

"You want me to come to your house?" he asked thinking his ears were definitely playing tricks on him. That couldn't have been what she said. That was crazy. What kind of person would willingly open their home to someone like him, looking and smelling the way he did, and a young woman to boot. Was she not concerned for her own safety?

Shuffling on her feet, she had another scan around to check they weren't being overheard. Looking back towards him, she worried her bottom lip between her teeth before checking her surroundings again. "Sure. It's just a chance to grab a break." She answered as though she wasn't just offering her house, safety and sanity on a plate with all the trimmings. She'd keep her bag with her at all times, she'd have easy access to a phone and her bank cards and cash were not something she wanted to willingly flaunt under his nose.

"Are you stupid?" he asked, frowning at her. Taken aback she opened her mouth to answer only deciding to close it instead she stepped back. Glancing down to her own feet away from his scornful gaze, she suddenly felt embarrassed. "You don't even know me." He answered realising she was more insulted at being called stupid than grateful for the opportunity to withdraw her charity.

"Are you going to hurt me?" she asked looking back to him, watching his dark eyes turn a shade lighter.

"No, but..." answered Rob quickly.

"Then it's fine. I mean the offer's still there if you want it. No pressure." she said standing with her arms folded glaring down at him, which did everything to contradict what she was saying.

Smiling, "How do you know you can trust me?" asked Rob, amazed that a stranger was taking such a chance on him, no one had ever given him the benefit of the doubt before, even when he had done nice things for people they had always thought he had an ulterior motive. Okay, sometimes he did, but he'd always thought it was best to spare the stick and use a carrot, at least until that fateful day that had changed his life forever. "Rob."

"Pardon?" asked the woman, leaning closer to hear him.

"My name? It's Rob."

"Nice to meet you, Rob." smiled Freya, holding out her hand to him. Taking it, he worried about where his hands had been but gently shook her hand anyway so as not to appear any ruder. Gently heaving himself from the stench of the urine covered concrete floor he brushed himself down as though that might do something to make himself more presentable, which it did nothing of the sort, it just highlighted how shabby his clothes were. "It's not too far away; it'll take about 5 minutes." He tried to smile, but he was sure it came across as more of a grimace. Turning, she stayed beside him as he hobbled forward. The kicking might not have been the first he'd received while living on the streets, but it didn't stop them from hurting his already battered body. "Maybe 15." added Freya, watching his slow progress. When he chuckled, she couldn't help but laugh a little too. "Do you need to lean on me?" she asked observing how his left leg appeared locked and unable to bend appropriately.

"No, I can manage. Thank you." She doubted it, but she knew when to leave well alone, so she just kept pace with him and carried on directing him to her home. All the time a little voice in her head was screaming at her that this was an awful idea, but she was sure the voice belonged to her oldest brother so she shook it off and continued. She wouldn't tell him, simple.

Reaching the door she felt around in her handbag for the key, retrieving it she slipped the key in the lock turning it before pushing the door open. The scent of spiced apple hit him in the nose the second the change in air caught him. "Sorry, I was baking earlier. Stunk the whole house out."

"Smells amazing." said Rob, sniffing the air as if he could fill his stomach from scent alone.

"Are you hungry?" she asked, slipping her coat off before hanging it on the end of the banister in front of them. When he gave her a look, she reprimanded herself for the stupid question. Of course he was hungry, he was homeless. "I'll get you something to eat after you've had a shower."

"A shower?" asked Rob, shrugging off his filthy coat and laying it on the floor, it was too dirty to even contemplate placing on top of hers.

"There are some spare clothes in the bedroom first left off the bathroom, just wear whatever you like. Once you've cleaned up I'll look at taking care of those cuts, but I don't want them to become infected so you best clean up first."

"Oh." Rob was unsure what to say, the generosity she was showing him was astounding. He was fairly sure that she could knock him down with a feather if she wished.

"There're clippers in one of the bathroom cupboards too if you fancy a trim."

"Wow, I'm not sure what to say." answered Rob dumbfounded.

"Tea or coffee?" frowning at her, she smiled that beautiful smile, the one that lit up her whole face. "Would you like tea or coffee?" she repeated as though she was talking to a five-year-old.

"Coffee, please."

"Righto. First door at the top of the stairs." She said before skipping off down the hallway without a care in the world. Watching after her he shook his head, he couldn't work her out. Why was she being so nice to him, so trusting?

Hearing the shower running upstairs, Freya pulled two cups down before spilling milk into them from a fresh carton. He'd looked a mess, and she had never seen someone take such a beating before. No one deserved that. There had been a gang of them against a lone homeless guy, she'd watched them rip the rucksack from his back, rifling through it as though it was their possession before punching him to the ground and cheering each other on as they all took turns putting their boots in. Knowing she wouldn't be able to stop them, she had had to wait until they had finished before she could go anywhere near the guy to offer help. He looked broken, his eyes told stories of visits to hell, and his clothes said he'd been on the streets for far too long. Normally if she saw the homeless she could walk away, sure in the fact that they had somehow brought it upon themselves, bad choices, no economical background, drugs or alcohol abuse. But when she had witnessed six youths beating on one man, there was no scenario in her head that could allow her to just leave him.

Sitting the cups on the table, she sat down and waited, flicking through her phone on Facebook for something to do. When she heard the bottom step of the stairs, creak she knew he was downstairs, finishing a text to her friend to say she was at home and would phone her later as something had come up she looked up in shock to see a freshly shaved, clean man wearing her brother's navy t-shirt and dark denim jeans.

"Wow, you look different." she said lifting her jaw up from the floor.

"Thanks. Well, I hope it's a compliment, because I looked like shit before." He answered, trying to contain his smile.

"It was. Sit down, your coffee's getting cold." she said pulling out a chair, grabbing it he pulled it out further before sitting down. Wrapping his fingers around the cup, he brought it up to his lips, inhaling the scent before taking a sip. "Has it been that long?" she asked, eyeing him over her own drink.

"Too long." He answered, taking another sip, as the first warmed his empty stomach.

"How's the cuts?" she asked, pointing to his face.

"A little sore, especially as I caught them on the razor." Watching her wince, he laughed at her face. "But I've not been clean shaven for a while. I needed to see if I still looked like me."

"And do you?"

"Mostly." He answered sorely. Smiling, she stood before walking over to a cupboard to retrieve a small first aid kit. Coming back she laid it open on the table taking her seat again she looked at his face trying to decide which cut to tackle first.

"Do you think anything's broken?" Freya asked, opening a pack of sterilised wipes.

"No. It's just bruising." Nodding she dabbed the wipes to the cut on his nose, it was the longest and the scariest to look at, although it looked like his blood had done its job of coagulating, it still looked as though it wouldn't mind a couple of stitches just to support it. Every time he winced she mirrored him and soon he was wincing just to get a reaction. When she cottoned on she gave him a look to behave, before smirking and grabbing a bag of frozen peas.

"Here, put that wherever it hurts most." Taking it, he held them to his ribs, which had taken most of the force.

"Do they really hurt?" she asked watching him try to get comfy.

"I think they were getting some penalty practice in, with my lungs." He answered.

"Yeah, they got a few good shots in." she said solemnly. "I'm sorry I didn't stop them but I thought they might turn on me if I did." She explained. "That sounds awful, doesn't it?"

"Don't apologise Christ, if you hadn't turned up when you did I would probably still be sitting in last night's kebab." She smiled, silently thanking him for not being cross with her. "Wouldn't usually mind, but it wasn't even my kebab." When she looked back to him, she couldn't help laughing as he smirked at her.

"They're always best when you're drunk, anyway." she added.

"Totally." He laughed, moving the peas up a bit.

"So how come you ended up on the streets?"

"Long story." answered Rob.

"Sorry, I didn't mean to pry." A memory suddenly struck him, he remembered saying the exact same thing to someone before, only he hadn't meant it as innocently as Freya did, he really had been prying and biding his time. The memory only brought him shame; he'd been an idiot and made a grave mistake, one that would never leave his nightmares and that wouldn't allow him to escape the streets.

"No. It's not that. It really is just hard to explain." Nodding as though that was good enough she popped the lid off the Germaline before smoothing it over his hands. "I messed up."

"Don't we all?" She muttered, taking great care to cover each scrape and graze.

"Not like I did." Looking up at him she saw much sadness mixed in his eyes with great regret.

"I gather it's not something you can just apologise for?" she gently asked, while replacing the lid and depositing the tube back inside the first aid kit.

"It would take more than an apology." He confirmed watching her watch him.

"Then I'm sorry." She murmured, looking away. Once again Rob was left staring at her. She was unique. Soft porcelain skin and full candy floss coloured lips, her long lashes dashed her cheeks, and he was struck by how beautiful she was. "What do you fancy to eat?" asked Freya, glancing back towards Rob.

Rob shrugged, he wasn't sure what she had said at first but when it finally sunk in; he was glad to have not put her out any more by answering with something she'd have to make or order in. "Okay, well if you're not eating regularly then your stomach is going to be quite sensitive so how about something light like toast or a sandwich?"

"Whatever. Honestly. Anything would be good right now." He smiled watching her scan the full fridge, whilst worrying her bottom lip between her teeth again as she thought.

"Ham and cheese sandwich?" she asked, turning to him with a block of cheese and a pack of ham in her hands.

"Brilliant. Thank you." Watching her take the bread out of the bread bin and slather the slices with butter he couldn't help admiring her physique, she was trim but also seemed fairly contoured under her clothing, he wondered what she did for a living that could give her that body?

"What do you do for a job?" asked Rob, giving in to curiosity.

"Oh. Me?" she asked. Rolling her eyes once, she realised of course he was talking to her. "Sorry. I'm a gym instructor." That made sense, but if he said anything now he'd come over as a creep, so he just nodded dutifully. "Well, I do classes mainly, Pilates, yoga, that sort of thing."

"Wow." Again he bit his tongue.

"Did you have a job before?" she asked, flicking the knife his way.

"Yeah, I was a chef." He answered.

"Oh wow, now that is amazing!" she cheered. "I'm a simple cook, stir fry, beans on toast. Anything that doesn't take much skill. I'd love to learn how to make a proper meal." She beamed.

"Maybe I can show you one day." Rob offered. Once the words left his mouth he regretted them, she'd allowed him to shower and eat, she wasn't offering anything more and he shouldn't be treating her as though she should. "Sorry."

"No. That would be lovely." She smiled sheepishly.

"Not very practical though, since I'll be back on the street soon." He answered, wiping his hand down his face to rid himself of tiredness. The shower had helped clean him, relax his muscles, but the heat had dissipated and now he was cool enough to nod off.

"How will you get off the street?" she asked, going back to the task of the sandwich.

"I won't. You can't very well go for a job interview stinking of piss and if by some miracle they were nose blind and well.. just bloody blind, then I have no address so they can't very well set up wages for a bank account without an address can they?"

"I didn't realise. How is anyone ever supposed to get back up then?" she asked, genuinely concerned.

"We don't. There's no safety net unless you're lucky enough to find a charity that will help out, but honestly they have limitations too."

"Gosh that's awful, how is anyone ever supposed to get back on their feet if they can't get a job to be able to afford a home?" she asked as if appalled for him. Rob just shrugged. His Mum had a home, but he knew he wouldn't be welcome. He even had a home if it hadn't been taken back by the bank yet due to unpaid mortgage fees. But he couldn't go back. If anyone saw him, he would be immediately arrested and be serving the rest of his life behind bars. With the prospect of bed and three meals a day it sounded enticing, but he'd pissed off the wrong people and he knew he wouldn't last a day in there.

Passing over the sandwich on a plain white plate, he took it before lowering it to the table as she made one for herself. Biting into it, it felt like heaven. Even when the ham stung his split lip he couldn't stop from closing his eyes. His stomach had screamed for food for so long, he wasn't sure if it would know what to do with the foreign invasion.

"Slow down, you'll make yourself sick." Freya warned.

"Oh, my god it's so good." sighed Rob, suddenly realising he sounded like Sally in that film he'd watched once. Chuckling, Freya sat across from him before biting into her own. "I think this is the best ham and cheese sandwich I've ever eaten." Freya blushed at the compliment, even though she knew realistically that it was only because he hadn't eaten in so long. She remembered being on a diet for so long once that when she finally ate chocolate, she thought she'd missed an entire era of new delicious recipes, but no they'd been the same recipes and she was just acting like Augustus Gloop. She couldn't help laughing at Rob's sheer enjoyment made by her own fair hands.

"Would you like another?" she asked, eyeing his empty plate. Rob shook his head, but apparently he was unconvincing as she placed her second triangle on his plate. "Eat it; I'll make us both more." Deciding to take what was on offer, knowing he couldn't be sure where the next meal was coming from, he ate through it quickly.

After Lunch, Freya showed him through to the living room. "Anything you want to watch?"

"I should really get going, leave you in peace."

"You can't go yet. I've not put your clothes in the wash yet, and I can't imagine you'll want to put them back on in that state."

"It'll not take long to ruin, I assure you." He answered.

"Well, I can't let you get them back on, so sit." smiling at her bossiness he sat and when she handed him the control he flicked the large flat screen on, and started scanning the TV guide. When Freya had left him to it to fill the washing machine, he laid his head back and closed his eyes.

Peeling his eyes open, he looked around, wondering where he was. Scanning the room he could see it was comfortable and cosy, and then Freya came into his mind, his guardian angel. Looking around the room for a clock he noticed one on the fireplace, but being too far away and his focus not yet righted he stood up stiffly walking over to read the dials. Realising he'd been asleep for a couple of hours, he walked out the room in search of Freya. Noting how dark it was outside he couldn't work out what was going on, everything was so quiet. Glancing to the digital clock of the cooker, he read 02.04. But that would make it..? Panicking, he rushed back to the front room. But she still wasn't anywhere to be found. Why had she left him sleeping, it was the early hours of the morning, and where was she? Looking up the stairs he tried to listen, blocking out any other noises like the ticking clock and the fridge's humming. But he couldn't hear a thing. If she was home and in bed, he couldn't very well just let himself in to say bye, she'd be terrified before he was given a chance to explain. But the thought of just leaving felt wrong too, she'd done so much to put back his faith in humanity.

Suddenly his stomach grumbled, and he thought about feeding it from Freya's supply, but he had no idea what she usually ate and so didn't have a clue as to what wouldn't be missed. He didn't want to take something that she'd bought specifically, that would just be rude and ungracious. Coffee, he could do that; trick his stomach into feeling full.

Walking back into the kitchen, he filled the kettle and turned it on. Staring outside the kitchen window, he looked up at the stars whilst wondering about what was going on at home. He missed them, even his brother, in fact mainly his brother. He had spent the entire last year trying to get back at him, trying to relieve some stress and pent up anger, but when he had finally exploded all, he felt was horror and shame and he just wanted to go back home, feel the loving arms of his family, put right their wrongs and start a fresh, but he'd killed his brothers ex girlfriend and there was no coming back from an event such as that. Jesse would kill him. He knew how much she had meant to him and he'd use it against him. He was no better than them, no better than the people who had put the idea in his head to make Jesse pay. Hearing the kettle flick off, he made his drink, sitting back down on the chair he'd occupied earlier.

"Thought I heard you." said a quiet voice. Looking up at the door frame he noticed Freya dressed in a long silk dressing gown. "Is there enough water in the kettle for another?"

"Of course." he answered, jumping up to make her a drink. "Sorry, I didn't mean to wake you, but I wasn't sure what time it was."

"You were shattered." she answered, taking the chair out and sitting across from him. "Thought it was best to let you sleep."

"You shouldn't have, but I appreciate it." smiling she took the offered drink and sipped. "I can't believe I slept so long, I'm so sorry."

"Don't be and stop apologising. If I'd have wanted you removed, I'd have phoned my brothers." she answered, laughing at the shock of fear in his eyes. "I didn't phone them." relaxing a little, he sipped his coffee. "I have three brothers and then all their mates, and there are literally hundreds of them, so I'm covered, trust me."

"Good to know." he smiled. "Especially when you invite waif and strays into your house." Laughing she took another sip as he smiled back at her.

"Would you like to stay?" she asked. Rob almost choked on his coffee, setting it down before he spilt any more on her flooring, he tried to recover himself. "It's just you were telling me about jobs and work yesterday and I can't see how anyone can get back up when they need both at the same time, so I've been thinking about it and I have a spare room. You could have that, get a job and then either leave or pay rent?"

"Why would you do that? You don't even know me?" he asked, watching her face intently as she tried to put together what she wanted to say.

"Look. I've seen people fall and not get the help they need, not because people don't care but because they don't always know how to care. I know what you need and I have that, it's not costing me anything, but it could be the stepping stone you need to get your life back together. Therefore, it makes the room priceless, but it also means that any rent you pay later on down the line will be extra, it won't be because I need it, and so if you turn into a twat I can just call my brothers and get them to toss you outside, and I won't feel guilty because I would have done everything I could to help and it would be your fault for being a tool."

Unable to stop the spread of his smile, he laughed at her comments. "Wow, you really think this is a bad idea."

"Not necessarily, but I just wanted to get the worst-case scenario out there so we know we both understand." Freya advised.

"That's not the worst thing that could happen. You're putting a lot of trust in me when you don't even know me, what's stopping me murdering you in your sleep?" he asked watching her flinch slightly at the word murder.

"Will you murder me?" she asked, raising her eyebrow.

"No. But anyone could say that. I'm sure Fred West didn't drive round telling women to get in the car because he had a nice patio to build."

"Do you want the room or not?" asked Freya exasperated.

"Yes. I do. Thank you." said Rob humbly.

"Well then, no more talk of serial murderers, especially this late into the night. Gives me the Willies." She said shaking her shoulders animatedly. Laughing, he took another sip of coffee.

"Thank you, Freya." Once her name left his mouth, her spine tingled, and she saw the deep pool of his eyes. There was something comforting inside them, but it overshadowed them with darkness. He was not in a good place but he was trying to hide it, she could tell. Something inside of her wanted to be that person to help, encourage him to smile a genuine unadulterated, spontaneous smile, where just happiness shone through. He was capable of it, she was sure; she just needed to get inside to work her magic.

"Okay, well it's late or early depending on how you see it, but I need my bed because I've got work tomorrow, but the spare bedroom is up the stairs, second bedroom on the left. Mine is the first one on the left, don't get confused. I have a baseball bat under the bed and I know how to use it."

"I'm sure you do. Thanks, I'll finish this then head up."

"Okay. See you at a more respectable hour and we'll go through some ground rules and chores." Nodding he smiled watching her leave the kitchen. How had he gotten so lucky to have fallen into her path?

CHAPTER 1

"Hey baby." Smiling, she instantly felt her boyfriend's warm body against hers. Wrapping an arm around her waist bringing her closer to him while sniffing the scent of her neck he nuzzled her making her giggle.

"Morning." she answered, feeling his left hand lower to her pelvis. "And what do you think you're doing?" she asked, raising her eyebrow seductively whilst turning in his embrace.

"I'm trying to find the control." He murmured before kissing her bare shoulder. Smiling as she felt his hand between her legs she inhaled sharply as he entered her.

"Not sure you'll find it there." she argued, laughing.

"I dunno, I'd say I have complete control when I'm there." She could feel his smirk on her shoulder and bit her bottom lip as she relished the feel of his skin on hers. There was nothing else that made her feel quite as content as when she was in his arms. He was the balm to her skin, the oxygen to her lungs and the blood to her heart. He made her feel alive while also protected, and she was the best version of herself when she was with him.

"Daddy!" Groaning and lying down on his back whilst trying to hide his face with his hands, Jesse blew out of his mouth exasperated.

"You've got to be kidding me." Jesse sighed. "It's like the kid doesn't want a brother or sister." Laughing, Hayley watched Jesse leave the confines of their bedroom to go and grab Daniel. On his way back in, he dumped the toddler in the middle of their bed before lifting the covers back up to glide in. "Right Daniel, we need to talk man to man." Daniel nodded, watching his Dad talk to him with great importance while Hayley watched on wondering what patch of wisdom Jesse was going to pass on. "When a man loves a woman..."

"Jesse?" warned Hayley.

"You need to make sure she knows it." Hayley scowled at him. That was not what he was going to say, and they both knew it. "And in order to do that they've got to have a bit of personal time." Hayley shook her head, laughing as he glanced to her smirking. "So son the next time Mummy and Daddy are having a bit of personal time, let me do the deed okay?"

"Jesse!" scolded Hayley. "Don't say stuff like that to him."

"What? He doesn't know what I mean." assured Jesse. "Dude, just sleep in, okay?" he asked, turning to Daniel to plead his case.

"Daddy! Daddy! Daddy!" shouted Daniel, jumping on his knees, bouncing the bed.

"Yeah, that went in one ear and out the other." laughed Hayley as she grabbed her nightie off the floor from where Jesse had thrown in last night. It seemed after all their time apart, he was trying to make up for it and that meant with the least amount of clothes on as possible. "Anyway, you're going to have to get used to it, because we'll be having another jumping on our bed in a few months." said Hayley before exiting their bedroom. Hearing something hit the floor she smiled knowing how she had just dropped a bomb Jesse hadn't even suspected coming.

In the kitchen Hayley hummed along to the radio and placed bread in the toaster while filling up the coffee machine with ground coffee. Turning when she heard a noise she found Jesse stark naked in front of her down on one knee holding a navy velvet box out to her.

"Jesse what are you doing?" she asked laughing.

"What does it look like? I'm freezing my bollocks off to propose."

He answered. Biting her lip, she waited for him to start. "I told you that once we got out, I wanted to ask you to marry me. But it didn't seem appropriate back then because of my Dad. But I bought the ring and I've been waiting for the right time. So this is it. Hayley, will you do me the biggest honour of my life by becoming my wife?"

"How could I say no?" she asked, trying to stem the tears.

"Pretty easily if you could see how my nuts have shrivelled up, it's bloody freezing in here." Jesse complained.

"Jesse, you're ruining the moment." she said trying to act stern but failing miserably with a smile stretching across her face of its own accord.

"I'm ruining my chances of procreation." argued Jesse.

"Talking about procreation, I'm eight weeks pregnant."

"That's amazing, but seriously answer me before I get frostbite in my extremities." Laughing, she nodded. Before drawing him up in an embrace and kissing his soft lips. "That's amazing, baby. I can't believe we're having a baby."

"I can't believe we get to share it this time." she answered, watching the hurt flicker in his eyes, before he drew her lips to his and kissed them tenderly.

"You've made me the happiest man alive, and not just because of the baby." he said watching her face intently.

"You might want to get some clothes on. I think Mrs Parker from over the road is getting an eyeful." said Hayley, glancing to the window.

"It's okay; she'd need a frigging microscope to see anything. My jewels have gone into hiding until the heating comes on." Laughing, Hayley pushed him away, pointing to the door and silently telling him to get dressed, but he dragged her back into his arms for another kiss before finally leaving.

When Jesse was dressed and holding a content toddler in his arms he entered the kitchen to see Hayley looking longingly at the ring he had given her. It made him smile that she loved it, he'd spent hours deliberating over the kind of ring to get her. He wanted her to know how much he loved her, but it couldn't be too big because she'd hate it. She liked simplicity. So he had gone for a single stone on a rose gold band.

"I was thinking." said Jesse, placing Daniel in his high chair and strapping him in to secure him. "If you're eight weeks gone, then we must have caught while we were inside witness protection."

"Yeah, seems that way. So all that practice was for nothing." she smirked.

"I wouldn't say that." smiled Jesse grabbing her and wrapping his arms around her. "Right, I really need to go."

"I'll see you later. I'll do something special for tea, to celebrate."

"Las-"

"I am not doing Lasagne, so don't even ask." Hayley warned, taking the toast from the toaster and spreading butter on it, before slicing it into triangles.

"I wasn't going to say that, I was going to say I would really like..." when Hayley turned, she could see Jesse trying to work his way around the word he'd started, which was definitely Lasagne. "That last thing you did." Jesse drawled out as though that was the best thing he could come up with on the spot.

"Really? That's what you were going to say?" she asked, smirking. "It wasn't lasagne even though you'd eat more than Garfield if I let you?"

"Nope." said Jesse shaking his head unconvincingly. "I love whatever you cook."

"Hmm."

"Right I'm off, see you later." watching him leave she then turned to Daniel who was munching on the toast Jesse had slipped from behind her without her noticing.

"Your Daddy is a cheeky monkey." said Hayley, kissing Daniel's forehead.

"Daddy! Daddy! Daddy!" yelled Daniel, strangling the triangle between his fingers.

"Your sibling better be a mummy's boy or girl, just to even up the score." warned Hayley light-heartedly.

"Jesse! I've got those prints and the swabs have been taken, just waiting on the lab now."

"Brill. Let's hope they come back with something conclusive." watching Martin shuffle the files on the desk looking for one he needed Jesse contemplated how to ask him, when it seemed his demeanour had given off warning signs Martin turned to him to wait. "Hayley's pregnant."

"Oh my God, that's brilliant! Congratulations."

"Thanks."

"Why don't you look as ecstatic as I thought you would?" asked Martin cautiously.

"She's eight weeks gone."

"Ok." When Martin didn't seem to understand where he was coming from Jesse waited, while looking around to see if anyone was nearby, he didn't want to be overheard. "Oh shit! You think-"

"It's tight, isn't it? I mean it could be from when we were in witness protection, but what if it's not?"

"But she said nothing had happened." said Martin.

"I know she did, but what if she didn't know? They knocked her out, and they found drugs in her system, what if they-"

"Whoa, whoa whoa, just hold up. We found no evidence that they'd been there remember, they gave her a full body work-over." Martin assured him.

"I hope so." Jesse sighed. "I'd just hoped that the next time everything would be plain sailing, and she's really excited. I can see it in her face."

"Jesse, if she said nothing happened, and the tests back that up then you've got to let it go. They made you a mess last time with wondering whether or not Daniel was yours, this time don't let them take what should be a joyous occasion away from you." Martin advised.

"I know. I know you're right, it's just the timescale. Soon as she said eight weeks, my stomach dropped out. If it had been 9 or 7, I wouldn't even be thinking about it." said Jesse.

"They're not that specific, you know they'd have given her an estimate. Claire was adamant Oliver should have been born two weeks before her due date and she was right, he was well over baked when he came out, even the placenta had deteriorated."

"Oh Mate, that's gross." said Jesse, wrinkling his nose.

"Get used to it." laughed Martin. "So, when are you finally going to put a ring on it?"

"I wanted to ask you something actually." said Jesse, pinching the bridge of his nose. "Would you be my best man?"

"You going to ask Hayley to be your wife first, she might say no?" said Martin jovially.

"Already asked, and she said yes." When Martin looked back at him, he stared at him for a second too long to be comfortable. "What?"

"You're engaged?" he asked, shocked to the core.

"Yep, I asked her this morning." said Jesse, puffing out his chest.

"Oh, bloody hell, mate. Well done, congrats." Swinging his arms around Jesse's shoulders, he hugged him tight. "You could have led with that you fucker?"

"Dude this is getting awkward." laughed Jesse. "Mart people are staring." He warned.

"Don't give a crap, they can stare." answered Martin wiping his eyes. "I'd be honoured to be your best man." said Martin, finally stepping back. "I'm over the moon mate, truly."

"You crying cus I asked you to be my best man or because I asked Hayley to marry me?"

"It's hay fever." Martin dismissed him. "Sodding tablets don't work." Jesse left him to his work before entering his own office, still laughing at Martin's reaction.

∽

Hayley bundled Daniel into the pushchair, securing him in, as he enjoyed trying to escape far too much. Once he was safe she left the house and wandered up town. It was a beautiful day, and she needed some fresh air. She hadn't planned on telling Jesse just yet that she was pregnant, but when he'd mentioned about the bed, it seemed easy enough to just let it slip. She was more than aware eight weeks was a time period that would no doubt hold a lot of questions but she was sure that this time things had been plain sailing regarding the babies paternity, she couldn't remember her captures getting that far even though they'd threatened it, but with only days to spare, it meant their time in witness protection had been optimal. Jesse had taken the news better than expected, though. He seemed excited, but she wondered how much of a niggle he was getting at the back of his head. He wasn't stupid, and she was no longer naïve, they could have simply drugged or knocked her out, but then she had been tested and there hadn't been any sign of-, shaking her head she tried to rid herself of the thoughts, she couldn't spend her life what-iffing.

Sitting on their own in the booth Hayley pushed a straw into the carton of juice she'd bought Daniel, taking a sip from the over full carton she gently handed it over, telling him not to squeeze. Taking the packet of sandwiches from the tray she opened them up before transferring the ham in one triangle and folding it over, handing that to Daniel she did the same with her side, but with the cheese. Taking a bite she looked around to see if there was anyone that she knew, unsurprisingly she didn't know anyone. Life after the great escape had been pleasant but wholly isolating. She had had to walk away from her job to take care of Daniel. Jesse hadn't wanted her to go back, saying she wasn't ready and needed time to heal, but all she felt like she was doing was purely existing. When Jesse came back after work she was fine, someone to talk to, cuddle up with on the sofa, watch a movie, but it was those hours when Jesse was not around that seemed to stretch. Filling her time with menial tasks made the day go quicker, but it didn't bring much fulfilment.

"Hi. Sorry is anyone sitting here?" Looking up she saw an old lady, with a cup and saucer in her hand.

"No, sit, please." Hayley offered. Moving Daniel's coat away and putting it on her side.

"God bless you." Hayley inwardly cringed but smiled politely. "I was in such a rush to get a drink I didn't even check they had space to sit." said the lady laughing lightly as she undid the buttons on her coat to slip out off. "Well, aren't you a bonnie lad." she said, looking to Daniel as he watched her intently whilst chewing on his big mouthful of sandwich.

"A bonnie piglet maybe." Hayley laughed.

"Ah, what's your mummy saying about you?" said the lady to Daniel as he tried to grin through the sandwich which just made it look like he had a gum shield in his mouth. "He's beautiful. Treasure them while you can." advised the lady looking to Hayley.

"I intend to." she smiled back.

"I've got three boys and a girl. They're adults now, mind." said the lady, taking a sip of tea. "But you never stop worrying, even now. My eldest is 36, then I have a 28-year-old, a 27-year-old and a 25-year-old."

"What do they do?" asked Hayley.

"Oh my oldest Teddy, he runs his very own wine bar." Hayley smiled. "George is a teacher, he teaches in a junior school. William is a salesman and my daughter is a gym instructor."

"Wow, that must have been a busy house." Hayley smiled while taking a sip of her own drink.

"Yes, it certainly was. My baby girl was somewhat of a surprise. We thought I was going through the menopause, but when I found out I was having Freya, I was overjoyed, especially with having three boys." Hayley nodded. "So do you plan to have any more?" asked the lady.

"Well, between you me and the gatepost, I'm expecting." she answered, smiling sheepishly.

"Oh! Sweetheart, that's marvellous news, congratulations."

"Thank you."

"What does your man do?" asked the lady.

"He's a detective."

"Wow! Hard job."

"Yeah." Taking another sip of her drink before fidgeting in her handbag, the lady pulled out her purse, opening it up she peered inside. Hayley wondered if she normally wore glasses because she seemed to struggle to find what she was looking for, then after a few more seconds she pulled out a pound coin.

"There it is. Knew I had one in there!" she exclaimed proudly. Taking Daniel's podgy hand in hers, she prized his fingers open and placed the coin in his palm, closing his fingers around it. "Now that's to bring you luck kind sir, and also enables you to buy a bag of sweets, when Mum says it's okay." smiled the lady before winking at Hayley.

"What do you say?" asked Hayley.

"Tank too." he said in a quiet, unsure voice.

"You're very welcome, young man. Now, you be a good boy." Kissing him on his head, she rose from the chair. "Nice to have met you, sweetheart."

"You too." Hayley watched as the lady made her way out of the café, smiling. It had been one of the first times she had actually had an enjoyable conversation with a stranger, the thought was sobering but it also gave her hope, maybe she was getting better, those counselling sessions were working after all.

CHAPTER 2

Rob re-awakened to a stream of light beaming through the gap in the curtains. Moving away from the source that had woken him, he looked around the room to familiarise himself with where he was again. Spying a note on the side table at the side of the bed, he picked it up.

Rob,
I'll be back around 1pm. Make yourself at home, see you later.

Freya

Rob couldn't believe her generosity. Once again she had stumped him. Leaving him alone in her home was either a huge lapse in judgment or a tremendous leap of faith? He hoped she'd not regret giving him a chance, he certainly hoped he'd never give her reason to. Getting up, he went in search of something to cook. She had said she wasn't very good at cooking, so the best thing he could do to show her how much he appreciated her was by making her a meal.

Walking in the kitchen he opened all the cupboard doors so he could see in them easily and then opened the freezer to look for something to defrost. Finding a bag of mince he pulled it out and placed it in the sink, filling it with lukewarm water to help defrost it quicker he turned to finding the rest of the ingredients in different cupboards. Bringing it all together near the chopping board, he started preparing it by finely chopping an onion.

A few hours later, Rob was finishing off, tidying up and wiping down the sides when he heard the front door open. Smiling to himself, he waited patiently for her to enter the kitchen. Stepping in, she took a big lungful of air.

"That smells amazing!" she announced, throwing her handbag over the back of the dining chair and walking over to him at the sink. "But you didn't have to you know."

"I did. I wanted to say thank you, and besides you said you can't cook, so thought I'd help you out."

"I can cook!" admonished Freya. "Just not very spectacularly."

"Well, I'm not sure how spectacular you think Chilli is, but it's ready when you are."

"Oh, I'm ready now, I'm starving." Laughing, Rob opened the oven before pulling out the enormous stock pot. "Where did you find that?" asked Freya, not recognising the dish.

"It was at the back of the cupboard where the pans were." answered Rob, taking a dish and ladling a healthy portion of Chilli into it.

"Must have been Mum's." answered Freya nonchalantly.

"Why would your Mum have a stock pot in your kitchen?" asked Rob, ladling food into his own dish.

"It was my Mum and Dad's house. We bought them out of it and they went into assisted living to help Dad."

"Oh, I'm sorry, is he ill?" asked Rob.

"He was. He died a few years ago. Mum carried on where they'd stayed, said there was no point up rooting again and besides it's a nice little bungalow with a warden, so at least I know she's safe and not going to be falling down some stairs because she's too stubborn to wear her glasses."

"Sorry to hear about your Dad."

"Yeah, thanks." Taking the bowl he offered, she sat down at the table ready to tuck in when Rob carried over a pan full of white fluffy rice, placing it in the middle of the table. "Do you have family?" asked Freya scooping up a big spoonful of the rice before dropping it in her dish. When she looked at him he seemed far away and she wondered if she had just inadvertently put her foot in it. "I'm sorry, you don't have to answer that, sometimes I just speak without thinking and ramble on for hours, you might have to tell me to shut up sometimes."

"No, it's fine. My Dad died a few months ago. But I have a Mum and a brother."

"How did he die?" asked Freya, gently placing the spoon back on the table.

"He was murdered."

"Shit!" exclaimed Freya before holding her hands up to her mouth. "Oh gosh! That must have been awful?"

"Yeah. I found out through the paper." said Rob.

"Did no one try to tell you?" she asked. Shaking his head, he took the spoon from the table and helped himself to rice.

"Me and my family had a big falling out, we don't speak." he answered.

"Even so, you'd think they'd at least get in touch to pre-warn you of what to expect in the papers." she sounded mortified for him, but he couldn't admit to her what he had done to make them that way, she would be appalled and definitely kick him out. "That's awful." She conceded.

"So you said you had brothers." said Rob, changing the direction of their conversation.

"I do. Teddy, George and Will."

"Are they all older?" he asked, taking a mouthful of the Chilli.

"Yep. Mum and Dad had me quite late on; they thought I was the menopause." She laughed before taking a mouthful of rice. "But from all the stories I've heard apparently they really wanted a daughter, so they got their wish, just later than they expected."

"What do your brothers do?"

"One works in a bar, one's a teacher, and the other is between jobs at the moment. Well I say between, he's on a job now that's why he's not here, but it's temp work he wants something permanent but unfortunately he's not found anything yet."

"What does he normally do?"

"Sells shit." She laughed. "I don't mean like manure, I mean just regular shit, like Hoovers, cars, phones, that type of thing."

"I don't imagine many people could sell manure." He answered, smiling at her.

"I don't know. Its good fertiliser isn't it?" she laughed taking another mouthful. "This is delicious, by the way. You should make it when Will gets back, he loves spicy food."

"When does he get back?" asked Rob feeling a little apprehensive about meeting her brother, especially when they'd have to tell him how they met and that now he was bunking there for free.

"Next week, I think. He'll call first so don't panic." smiling at her he tried to hide his anxiety, but he was terrified of what her brother might think was going on between them, or what he thought his intentions might be.

Watching her eat made him happy, she was really enjoying it and he was glad to have finally done something for her, not that one pan of chilli could really pay her back but it was a start. After eating their meal Freya said she would take a shower and freshen up. While she left to go upstairs, he gathered all the pots and placed them next to the sink before wiping down the table and the stove.

A few minutes later Rob realised he'd have to change the water, he'd left the glasses till last but the water was filthy, so pulling the plug he waited until all the water had run out before taking a cloth to the sides to remove the grease and sauce remaining. Once the sink was clean again he turned on the tap and put the plug back in before squeezing more liquid in. Suddenly there was a high-pitched scream, wondering what an earth had made Freya scream so badly he bounded up the stairs to the bathroom, swinging the door open he thought he'd see her on the floor in a bloody mess.

Instead, she stood directly in front of him stark naked, screaming again he froze whilst she slammed the door in his face. Rob's breath had been zapped the minute he had seen her body. It had been a long time since he'd seen a woman naked and she was beautiful. Realising what an idiot he'd just made of himself, he tapped lightly on the door whilst trying to compose himself.

"Freya, I'm sorry. I heard a scream, and I panicked."

"Okay." She replied shakily. She was making no attempt to come out, and he wasn't going to go back in so he slowly turned and walked back down the stairs, as soon as the shock had worn off he heard water, remembering he'd left the tap on he ran to the kitchen and sprinted to the sink, quickly twisting the tap head to stop the water, having been too late to stop it from overflowing he grabbed a couple of tea towels off the side and placed them on the floor to soak up the sudsy water.

Sat at the dining table with a cup of tea in front of him and another across from him waiting, he contemplated how to handle the awkward situation with his new landlord. He'd messed up already, and it had only been a day. He was useless.

"That for me?" asked the kind voice. Looking up to her, he nodded. She seemed a lot calmer now.

"I'm so sorry, I heard you scream-"

"It's okay, it was the water." When he looked at her puzzled she continued. "The water pressure in here is a little temperamental; when you did the washing up it sent a shot of cold water on me. I was a little surprised." She smiled kindly but embarrassed.

"Shit, sorry."

"I should have warned you, my mistake."

"I... I..." not sure what he wanted to say, he took another sip of tea instead.

"Liked what you saw?" asked Freya, watching him intently. Watching him flap made her smile. He was more uncomfortable than her, and yet she was the one who had been compromised. It made her laugh. "I'm teasing."

"You're beautiful." He answered, deciding to own what he'd seen and stop acting like a teenage boy with a hormone problem. Watching her blush and look away made him suspicious for someone who seemed so direct he hadn't expected her to blush at his compliment so easily.

"I noticed you didn't use the clippers the other night, is that because you like the homeless look or because you couldn't use them?" she asked, veering the conversation away from her. Laughing, Rob pushed his hand through his longer than usual wavy hair.

"I've never used them, I always used to go to the barbers." he answered.

"Okay, well I can do it for you if you like?"

"You cut hair?"

"Not for a living but my mum did, and she showed me how to cut a bloke's hair." She answered. "I can even grade." She beamed proudly.

"Okay, let me just get one thing out the way with first though." Frowning, she waited. "That you're not going to take it out on my hair because I saw you in all your glory?" Laughing she turned another shade of pink before going off to get the clippers from the bathroom.

Putting the dining chair in the middle of the kitchen, she asked him to sit before placing a towel over his shoulders. Patting it down on his shoulders, she realised just how broad he was. Running her hand through the back of his hair, she pulled a little at the top as they got longer. His hair at least felt clean, but it was wiry and thick, different to Will's that she usually cut.

"What grade do you normally have on the sides?" she asked, scratching her nose.

"Two normally."

"And the top?"

"I just normally have it trimmed with scissors but I don't mind the clippers, whichever is easier for you."

"Well, I can do a five on the top if you're happy to go a bit shorter?" she offered.

"Fine by me." Taking the Wahl trimmers from the black pouch, she placed the plug in the wall before attaching a grading comb. Turning it on, he heard the buzz, and she approached him. Pushing his head to one side she started at the bottom and pushed up, going all the way around his neck, once she was happy with that, she took off the comb and added another, larger one, repeating the process but moving to the top of his head. Rob listened to her humming a tune as she worked, and he watched out the corner of his eyes as the hair dropped to the floor, he was hoping he'd have some left, but if she took revenge on him through his hair he'd take it on the chin. Running round again with a comb taking care to grade the two contrasting lengths effectively, she stood back to admire her work. Watching her smile turn to a grin, he wondered if he should be scared? Walking back out of the room, she re-entered with a mirror. Holding it out in front of him, he surveyed her handy work.

"You like?" she asked eagerly.

"It's great. Thanks." He said sweeping his hands down the back and sides.

"You sound relieved, did you really think I'd mess your hair up?" she asked laughing.

"I would have deserved it." he answered, watching her eyes soften.

"You actually look quite handsome with the mop-a-top sorted." She said gauging his response. He just smiled, and she smiled back, something was going on between them, something in the air but she wasn't sure what to do about it, she didn't know him and she didn't get attracted to men she didn't know, she'd only ever gone out with long-term friends. Looking away, she tidied the clippers back into their pouch while Rob gathered all the hair up with the dustpan and brush she'd set down on the floor earlier.

Placing the hair in the kitchen bin, he handed Freya the dustpan and brush back, unsure where she had gotten them from. When she took it, their hands brushed each other's, and they both looked at each other as if they'd both felt something, but dismissing it, they quickly looked away again and continued to tidy up.

"Right I'm popping out, I need to get a few bits, is there anything you need while I'm out?" asked Freya, grabbing her handbag off the chair.

"No thank you, I think I'm fine."

"Really? You don't need boxers, or toothpaste or deodorant or shampoo or condoms or vitamins or anything?" she asked sarcastically.

"I do, apart from the condoms, but I can't pay you back." He answered apologetically.

"I know. I didn't ask what you need so you can pay me back. I asked so I could get you things to make you feel more comfortable."

"Freya, you've done so much already." There was her name on his lips again. Why did a shiver run down her spine?

"And you cooked. So is there anything else you need?" she asked again.

"No, I think your list is sufficient." He smiled shyly, watching her's broaden. Watching her leave again, his heart tugged. He wasn't a prisoner, but he couldn't go out either. Even looking for a job would be problematic, it wasn't as if he could use his actual name, he'd be taken into custody in an instant. But he needed to get out. Looking out at the back garden he saw that it needed some care, it was looking a little overgrown and dry, so he went in search of the keys to the shed outside, he'd make headway with the garden and that would hopefully be another thing that could help pay back Freya's faith in him.

It was roasting outside and after pulling up as many weeds as he could and hopefully nothing that was actually a flower he started cutting the grass with the old electric lawnmower from the shed, stripping off the top he wore he threw it on the ground and continued. Bagging the dry cut grass he then went back over the lawn again with the rake, just to ensure he's got every last bit of cut grass. Turning, he saw Freya holding out a glass to him. Standing up surprised, he took it, downing it in one. He hadn't realised how parched he was.

"You've done a grand job, it looks amazing." she said surveying the trimmed garden. "I can see the swing chair." She laughed as though she'd not seen it in ages, although in reality the garden hadn't been that bad that the chairs hadn't been visible.

"Thank you." He said handing her back the glass.

"You looked hot." she said eyeing his naked chest, before realising what she was doing and looked away with a pink tinge. "I meant with the weather being so warm, because it's warm, because its summer, you know." She cringed, noting how much she'd just rambled. Laughing, he watched her try to gain her confidence again. It was like a cloak she wore, but now and then it would completely drop and it was beautiful.

"It's only fair you see me naked too." He answered, watching her eyes widen with shock. He should feel guilty for making her uncomfortable but he didn't, he liked that shade of pink on her, so he just wet his lips watching her try to swallow.

"From where I'm stood, you still have some way to go." she said eyeing his bottom half, and there was that sassy confidence he loved so much.

Taking her cue he slipped the buttons from the holes of his jeans, pulling down the zipper, watching her watch him was fascinating and he made sure to slow it down, putting his thumbs into the side of his jeans he pushed them down until gravity took over and they fell to the floor. Her eyes were at his feet so he pushed his boxers down to meet his jeans and her eyes slowly scaled up. Smirking she met his eyes, and he hoped he hadn't pushed it too far. "How about now, we even?" he asked, raising his brow.

Nodding slowly, dumbstruck by his sudden confidence, she scanned his body again. Suddenly feeling a lot more vulnerable herself, she rushed from the garden and ran back inside the house. Rob wasn't sure what had happened, maybe he shouldn't have done that, but the playfulness in her tone had spurred him on. Had he been foolish to be so brazen? He didn't know her, or her limits, and he already knew her confidence wasn't as bone deep as she liked to perceive. "Shit!" Pulling up his boxers and jeans, he cursed himself for being an idiot, especially to the only person who'd tried to help him.

Once he was dressed he walked back into the kitchen to find it empty, scanning the living room he decided she'd either left or hidden upstairs, taking each step slowly so that she could hear his approach he tapped on her bedroom door. No answer. Tapping again, he listened, but there was only silence, so he moved to the bathroom and stripped off. Standing in the shower, he lathered himself up with soap and rubbed some shampoo in his shortened hair. Facing the spray, he thought back to what he had done in the garden and promised to go and apologise to her before the end of the day. Suddenly the water turned icy, and he jumped back, letting out a squeal as he did so. Now he knew why Freya had screamed. That was freezing. Suddenly the door burst open and there she stood, a huge grin on her face as though she'd just won the lottery. "Now we're even." she beamed. Laughing, he pulled her to him until she was drenched under the cold shower too. Once their laughter had subsided, they stared at one another, feeling an intensity zap between them. Breathing heavily, they each took time to examine each other's faces, searching for emotions reflecting their own. "Freya…"

That was all it took, her name on his lips and she pressed hers to his. Once he tasted her his blood rushed, sending a heat wave to his core. Freya moaned as his hand slid under her top, groping her side. Sliding her hand into his hair, she pushed herself further into him until there was no space between their bodies. She loved the scent of him. Moving her hand lower she placed her hand on his rock hard length, but instead of turning things up he stopped, holding her by her arms and pushing her back.

"Freya stop." wondering what she had done wrong, she waited for him to explain. "We can't do this." Feeling rejected, she stepped back so her arms were no longer being held. "You'll regret this."

"I'll regret it, or you will?" she asked, stepping out of the bathroom.

Rob turned off the water and grabbed a towel, wrapping it around his waist as he made his way onto the landing where he could hear Freya in her room rummaging around. He shouldn't go in, but he couldn't leave it. She felt rejected, and he had to make her understand that she wasn't the reason he'd stopped. Knocking on the door he waited but when no answer came he slowly opened the door, she was on the bed facing the other way laid on her front.

"Freya."

"Go away."

"Freya." He tried again.

"I said go away." she answered firmly.

"I'm not going anywhere until I explain. I can't leave you thinking you did something wrong." When she didn't answer him he took that as a good sign so stepped closer to her, sitting on the edge of her bed. "I'm not a good man. I've done a lot wrong. Hurt people who didn't deserve it. I made stupid decisions because I wanted revenge. I made people I love, hate me."

Turning to her back, she shifted herself further up the bed to lean on her head board to watch him. "You've been the only person who has ever tried to help me. You've taken me on trust alone and you didn't have to do that. You've given me a chance to get out of the pit I've found myself in, but I couldn't live with myself if I hurt the one person who'd gone out her way to help me."

"Then don't." she offered.

"It's not that simple. If we got together and then a week or a month down the line we split up, I'd be homeless again, and I'd have hurt you."

"So because you think I'd be petty and throw you out like trash, you're not going to explore whatever this is between us?"

"It's not just that. Everything I touch falls apart. I couldn't bear to do that to you, you're amazing. You're vibrant, sassy, intelligent, you have the body of a goddess and I'm just not worthy." Hearing his words, she crawled along the bed to him, wrapping her arms around his still damp shoulders.

"I'm a big girl. I'm also more than capable of making my own decisions. So unless you're physically going to stop me, I say you let us go with the flow and see where this takes us." Turning to her, he watched her determining whether he really could take such a leap of faith like she was choosing to do. "I'm not asking for marriage, I'm just saying we see where this leads us and if we decide we don't like each other than we go back to being the landlord and the lodger."

Grabbing the back of her neck, he pulled her to him, and they shared another kiss, full of passion and promise. Feeling him finally give himself over to her, she pulled him down on top of her, making sure to not let go in case his conscience struck him again. "We have a problem." She whispered in his ear as he caressed her breast through her top.

"What?" he asked, stopping what he was doing, alarmed.

"I have entirely too many clothes on for this activity." She answered coyly, watching the flash of desire in his eyes. Smiling, he slowly unbuttoned her blouse but after the third button she growled, taking the job from him, she ripped it over her head and threw it on the floor, staring at him, as if to say enough of the slow business. Laughing, he helped ease her jeans down her toned legs. Taking in her skin and the feel of it on his fingertips she pulled at the towel still wrapped around him, tugging it, she threw that to accompany her blouse. "Are you trying to torture me?" she asked watching him take his time on her limbs as if he was trying to burn them onto his memory.

"I might be." He answered, watching her grow impatient. He loved being able to drive her crazy, the anticipation was building, and he knew that would only be better for her. But she was impatient, and he knew if he took too long she might completely turn off.

"Rob please I think I've waited enough." she begged, cursing how weak her voice sounded.

"You've waited barely enough." He reminded her.

"I think 24 hours is enough, don't you?" The second the words were spoken, her eyes closed as though if she closed them what she had just said wouldn't meet his ears and she could take them back.

"24 hours?" asked Rob, watching her face screw up as she refused to look at him. "Does the homeless look do it for you?" he teased.

Shaking her head, she gradually opened her eyes. "It was when you shaved." She admitted, running her fingertips along his jawline. "You look much nicer when you're groomed." Kissing her, she melted under him again and this time he didn't make her wait.

CHAPTER 3

Jesse walked in the house to the smell of something rich and sweet, sniffing the air as he made his way to find out what she was cooking. Wrapping his arms around her from the back, he kissed her shoulder as she peeled the potato in her hand.

"What are we having?" he asked, looking at all the vegetable peelings on the side.

"Well, I thought we could eat when Daniel's in bed, so it's not quite ready, but I've got prawns for starter, lamb shank for main and I've made a lemon tart for dessert."

"Wow, you didn't have to do all that."

"I know, but I wanted it to be special, especially since we're celebrating two things." When Jesse said nothing she turned to him, wrapping her arms around him. "You are happy, aren't you?"

"Of course." He kissed her head. Wondering whether he was telling her the truth, she rested her head on his chest. "Hey, it was just a shock, that was all." Nodding, she decided to let it go. Turning back to the potato still in her hand, she thinly sliced it before layering it in a dish.

Jesse walked into the front room to see Daniel playing with his trusty cars, lining them up and putting them into groups of colour.

Sitting down on the sofa, Daniel ran over, launching himself into his Dad's lap for a cuddle. Once he had had his fill he climbed back down to continue with his cars. Jesse watched him but couldn't take his mind off what had happened this morning. He wasn't sure how they'd cope if it turned out she was pregnant by someone other than him. They'd been through enough, too much, but they'd come out stronger. Their bond was unbreakable but he couldn't stand by and watch her fall apart if it turned out she'd been abused again without her knowledge and it landed her with a child. She hadn't coped well when there was a question mark over Daniel, and it had almost killed him in the beginning, not knowing whether or not to get close. If he spoke to her about his concerns, he would be handling her a poisonous chalice, on the one hand he would be being honest and open, communicating but the other was one of fear, fear that she would be thrown back into that nightmare if not physically, potentially emotionally. Martin was right, he was over-thinking it. When had anything just gone their way, he was anxious and waiting for the other shoe to drop like on every other occasion they were involved in? Maybe this was their chance to just enjoy?

Daniel went down quickly. The fresh air had knocked him out, and it meant they could finally sit down and eat around seven. Sitting down, he opened a bottle of wine, pouring liquid into each glass. When Hayley placed his plate in front of him, she frowned. Why was he pouring her wine? Was he trying to tell her something?

"Spicy prawns with mango salsa." she said, taking her seat at the table. Jesse tucked in, it was delicious and he ate every piece. Taking her glass of water, she took a sip, pushing the wine glass further away.

"I'm sorry; I completely forgot you can't drink." He said, eyeing the glass. Hayley just nodded. "Would you like something else, coke, lemonade?"

"No, I'm fine thanks." Eating her starter she realised how quiet they'd become, both thinking thoughts the other wasn't privy to. When a tear rolled down her cheek, she tried to rub it away by pretending her nose was running and covering half her face with a tissue from her pocket. But it seemed she'd failed when Jesse stood up and pulled her up out of the chair for a hug.

"I'm so sorry." With just those words Hayley began to cry. "It's just the timing." He admitted.

"Do you want me to get rid of it?" she asked trying to control her breathing as she listened for his answer with her head over his heart. When there was silence she pulled away. "You don't want it do you?" she asked shocked.

"It's not that." He said, shaking his head. "I'm just worried."

"About whether they did something before you got there?" she asked.

"Yes, but I'm more worried about the reality, about what happens if they did."

"What do you mean?"

"Hayley when you had Daniel you were all ready to adopt, you'd drawn the line in the sand and there was no budging you. You struggled to bond with him and even when we found out he was mine, you still struggled. What if we have this kid and find out he's not mine? What happens to you? Me? Daniel? What happens if you decide you can't bear to look at him, or you want him gone, where does that leave me and Daniel? Is he expected to bond with his brother or sister and then wave them off as though they didn't exist?"

"I love Daniel." she said meekly.

"I know you do. But I also know you wouldn't if he wasn't ours." Hayley swallowed. "That baby will grow; your belly is going to show how pregnant you are. There is nothing that will keep that news away from Daniel. So what happens when you have the baby? We get him tested and you find out your worst nightmare has come true? What will you do then?" Sitting back down, she filtered through everything that he'd just said.

"What if I end up getting rid of our baby?" she asked timidly. Jesse didn't answer, he couldn't. Silence over took the room and suddenly the mood to celebrate had evaporated. Hayley didn't know what to say and Jesse didn't want to force her in any direction so kept quiet. If she was going to go through with the pregnancy, she had to be sure, and he just wasn't convinced she would be.

Taking his glass off the table, he walked into the front room and relaxed into the sofa. They both needed time, they also both needed to talk, but he wasn't sure he could say any more tonight, he was exhausted. Hayley gathered the plates and washed them, whilst simultaneously wiping tears from her eyes. Turning the oven off before removing the food, placing foil lids on them, she also wiped the sides down then made her way to bed before climbing in. Laid on her back, she drew circles along her abdomen whilst staring at the ceiling. Could she love a child even if its father wasn't the man she wanted it to be?

When Jesse followed her to bed Hayley was already asleep, curled up on her side away from him. He felt dreadful for ruining their night, but it had needed to be said. He couldn't go through the pain of watching her bare another man's child and then be expected to just forget about it when she handed it over to someone else. His Dad had been right all those years ago, he loved completely, there was no half measures and if she gave a child away who he'd bonded with it would break him and he couldn't let her do that to him or Daniel. But it had to be her choice; he just hoped she wouldn't get rid of it before they found out. He wasn't sure which scenario was worse, bringing up another man's child or killing his own. No he did, he could see a child for a child, not an extension of its parents, but could she? Would she? He was asking her to decide without knowing the result? Was he being fair? Was he being too harsh on her? Was he asking her to make a decision that no matter the result he could stand by?

Crawling in beside her, he gathered her in his arms, hugging her close to him. He didn't want to put her in pain, and he never wanted to see her hurt ever again. Feeling her softness in his arms, he let the tears fall, wetting her hair. She'd been through so much, he couldn't be angry with the way she saw it, but he couldn't just let her carry on without thinking about the effect it would have on their family. Placing his open palm on her belly, he looked up at the ceiling. "Please God, let this be mine. I beg you." He pleaded.

"It's yours Jesse." she whispered. Turning over, she held his jaw in her hands. "I've thought about what you said and you're right. I have to make a choice and I have to stick to it. Jesse I know deep in my heart that this baby is yours, I can feel it. But if by some twisted turn of fate it turned out to be biologically someone else's then yes I'd be heartbroken, but it would still be yours. It takes more than just semen to make a child, and I've watched you with Daniel. This baby with whoever's blood running through its veins is still yours, it will always be yours."

"Do you promise?" he asked, hoping she could do what she was saying.

"When this baby is born, no blood tests, nothing." she said before kissing his nose. "Because we already know everything we need to know." Grabbing hold of her once again he pressed her to him, wrapping them up together they held on shaking as they sobbed and then laughed at the state of themselves.

"We're having a baby." exclaimed Jesse smiling down at her, while running his hand along her stomach.

"Yes, we are." Hayley said before passionately kissing him on the lips.

CHAPTER 4

Rob woke up in Freya's bed. Looking to the side of him, he could see Freya was still unconscious. Wiping her errant hair from her face, he admired her beauty, watching her eyelashes flutter before fully waking; he smiled when her eyes fell on him. "Hello Beautiful."

"Hi." She smiled back. "What time is it?" she asked, stretching.

"Err.." looking around he tried to locate a clock, seeing a digital radio behind her head he read it. "6.20."

"Wow, he really burnt up some energy." she answered.

"Certainly did," laughed Rob. "Are you hungry?"

"Ravenous." Laughing once again, he got out from under the covers, before leaving her room in search for some clean clothes. "I don't mind eating in bed!" she called out.

Popping his head back in the room, now fully dressed, he winked at her. "I know." Shock gasping, she threw the pillow from under her head at the door, missing him as he scurried downstairs.

Downstairs Rob looked around once again, trying to gauge what she might like for dinner. Deciding on something light but filling, he decided on Carbonara. He hoped she wasn't a calorie counting kind of girl because so far he'd been feeding her up.

Taking some cooked ham, he cut it into cubes before placing

cream in a pan to warm through and water in another for the spaghetti. Hearing the shower go on, he placed a tea towel over the taps to remind him not to turn them on while she was freshening herself up.

"Who the fuck are you?!" bellowed a loud voice. Turning quickly, he could just make out the sight of a man before he had him by the collar, pushing him back against the sink. "Why are you in my house?" Struggling to breathe and concentrate enough to answer, he managed to squeal out his name. "What the fuck are you doing here?" deciding, getting Freya's attention to be the only answer he quickly flicked the tap on through the towel, on hearing the scream the man lessened his grip looking up at the ceiling. Deciding to go in search of the noise instead of beating the man in front of him, he dashed off.

"What the hell are *you* doing here?" He heard her scream. The man said something but he couldn't work out what, it was too monotone. After another few minutes of conversation, the Man came back downstairs and entered the kitchen scowling at Rob.

Waiting for Freya to join them they stood on separate sides. Breezing in, she waltzed over to Rob, taking his hand in hers. "This is Rob, Rob this Neanderthal is Teddy." Rob might have laughed at the name had he not been facing a man who resembled more of a silverback gorilla than a teddy bear. Teddy just stared at him like he was about to die. "Teddy be nice!" scolded Freya.

"Who is he?" asked Teddy, ignoring Rob.

"Ask him, he speaks and everything. He's like a real life boy, Geppetto." said Freya, crossing her arms. Teddy looked Rob up and down, curling his top lip. "Teddy." warned Freya, which was meant to sound threatening Rob was sure, but sounded anything but with a name like Teddy.

"Are you sleeping with my sister?" groaning Freya dropped her head in her hands.

"Don't even answer that." warned Freya, turning back to her brother she pointed her hand to the door. "Teddy out."

"But I asked your 'real life' boyfriend if he was sleeping with you, you said talk to him?"

"I didn't say be a dick!" shouted Freya. "Get out and come back when you're ready to apologise and make sure it's with chocolate."

Huffing, he walked out the kitchen and back out the front door. Feeling as though he could breathe again he watched Freya staring at the door. "Wow, that was intense."

"Yeah, he always is." Freya said, turning back to Rob. "Anyway, he'll be back in a few minutes after he's visited the corner shop and bought me some chocolate."

"You're sure about that, are you?" asked Rob, stepping towards her to lace his arms around her waist.

"Yep, because he came here for a reason, and he didn't say what it was?" Freya confided while Rob untucked her towel from where it held together. "Did you put the water on?" she asked, eyeing him as he dropped the towel to the floor.

"It was either that or I'd have been unconscious on the floor." He admitted.

"Ape." She said regarding her brother. "Anyway, I'm going to finish off getting dressed." She smiled knowing that was not what Rob had been expecting, turning she grinned before walking naked up the stairs, very slowly so he could get a full look. Breathing out his mouth he realised there was no hope, he was under her spell.

When they got back downstairs some time later Teddy was sitting at the dining table with a half mug of coffee, and a box of black magic chocolates next to it.

"Ooh my fav!" said Freya, snatching the box up greedily and unwrapping the cellophane.

"So how long have you and boyio been together?" asked Teddy, thumbing the man over his shoulder who was leaning on the doorframe.

"None of your damn business. So what do you want?" Freya asked. Opening the box, she made her selection. Picking one she handed the box to Rob who heard a growl from Teddy so declined.

"I came to ask about Mum."

"What about her?" Freya asked while chewing on her confection.

"She's had a fall and I don't think she should be on her own for a while."

"Is she all right?" rushed out Freya placing the box back on the table and suddenly looking alert.

"She had a fall in town and after being discharged she's gone back home because she's a stubborn mule, but I don't think she should be on her own, she's getting fragile and won't accept help."

"So you thought you'd ask me to just turn up as a surprise and play nursemaid?" Looking at her, that was exactly what he thought. "Why me?"

"Because you're a woman." answered Teddy.

"Excu-" but before she could get out her retort Teddy held up his hand. "I'm not being sexist I just think Mum will feel more comfortable with a woman helping her in and out the bath and toilet etc." Freya stood with her hands on her hips contemplating his argument resigning that he was probably right.

"I'm going to need to book some days off work. I'll call them and let them know what's going on." Nodding, Teddy smiled to thank her. "Is there anyone else who can fill in if I need to cover some classes?"

"Yeah, I've already phoned George and Will, they said they'll do what they can, it was mainly the evenings we needed covered."

"Ok, well then that might work better; I can knock off some evening classes and still work in the day for a couple of weeks." Nodding again, Teddy pulled his phone out to let his brothers know the plan. Picking up her own, she walked in the hallway to call work and explain what was going on. Rob listened to both conversations playing out and admired how they all seemed to rally around to help their Mum. It was heart-warming, if not a little painful. Stood wondering how his Mum was getting on after his father's death he bowed his head, he should be there, she had always loved him, cherished him, stuck up for him and yet she was going through the worst thing that could have happened to her and he couldn't do a thing about it, he couldn't even send a card to let her know he was thinking of her.

"Ok, that's done." announced Freya walking back in the kitchen.

"Work, are letting me do seven till two every day for two weeks and they said if I need to extend to give them another call."

"Brilliant, Will's coming back tomorrow, so he will cover eight till just after lunch and George said he'll pop in as much as he can to relieve whoever's on."

"Good. Because if you were going to tell me he was too busy I was going to go all Kill Bill on his Ass." Laughing Teddy stood up. "I'll get my stuff together and be there in a few hours." Nodding again Teddy looked from her to Rob. "He'll be staying here, he's my new lodger. So make sure Will doesn't kill him."

"Is that what they call it now?" asked Teddy sarcastically.

"I mean it Teddy, I'm holding you responsible. No harm comes to Rob. Do you understand?" Looking Rob up and down again he leant down to his sister, kissing her on her head, even though she was still waiting for him to answer her demand.

"I understand." Leaving them, he let himself out.

Turning to Rob, she looked up at him shyly. "I'm so sorry, leaving you in the lurch like this but we all made a pact we'd do what we could after Dad died."

"It's fine, she's your Mum."

"It means my brothers will interrogate you, hope you realise that?"

"I guessed as much when you told him not to let them harm me."

"Yeah, I don't think they'd do actual damage, but sometimes they act like I'm ten and need rescuing." Rob nodded, but he wasn't looking forward to being drilled by three over protective brothers, especially if they all looked like him. "I wouldn't say how we met if I was you. I don't think they'll understand, just say we got chatting at the gym and you've just moved out and needed a place to stay and I offered."

"Ok. Will I see you at all next week?" asked Rob hoping he would but not wanting to be clingy, it was clear she needed to do this but they'd only just met and he really didn't want to be sharing the house with her brother.

"I'll pop in. Besides, it'll give you time to look for work. Right! I'm going to pack." Running upstairs, Rob stood in the kitchen thinking about what to do. He could just leave. She wouldn't be around to have to explain and he wouldn't have to go through the interrogation that was coming his way. Normally he wouldn't be bothered about standing up to her brothers but he had too much to hide and too many secrets to keep, if he let them out they wouldn't think twice about wrapping rocks around his ankles and chucking him in the canal.

∼

PULLING UP OUTSIDE THE COMPLEX, Freya shut the engine off before grabbing her suitcase from the boot. Walking in she was welcomed by some of the residents who had seen her around before, seeing the warden over the other side of the pond in the middle of a garden she rushed over.

"Hi Freya. Here to see your Mum?"

"Yep, I'm stopping for a few weeks actually just to make sure she's all right."

"Yeah, I don't blame you, that was a nasty tumble she took."

"Yeah anyway my brothers will pop in to take over when I work, but can you just let me know if you see them?"

"Don't trust them?" asked the warden, smiling conspiratorially.

"About as far as I can throw them but what can you do?" Laughing, the warden agreed to let her know before Freya found her Mum's apartment. Walking in, she was immediately hit with the smell of warm veg. The smell took her back to school days, but she wondered if her Mum had had someone over to cook, because her food had never smelt like that. "Mum!" she called out.

"In here, sweetheart." called back her Mum. Following the sound, she stood in the living room and saw her Mum's injuries. She was covered in dark purple bruises and wore a split lip. "Now don't look like that, it looks far worse than it is."

"What happened, you decide to join a Rugby team?"

"Ha! I wish! No, I just fell. I slipped and hit my head on the pavement. Went down like a sack of spuds I did."

"Well, I need to stop for a few days if you don't mind, we've got the electric people in and they're all up in my face and I need the peace." said Freya looking around the room to try to locate the smell.

"Teddy's already spoken to me so don't even think about telling me such porkies."

"Well, Mum, I'm damn right offended." She said faking shock and horror.

"He also told me you have a man living there." Freya grumbled a curse under her breath while she went back to the kitchen.

"Cup of tea, Mum?!" she called over her shoulder.

CHAPTER 5

THE ALARM CLOCK RANG OUT, AND JESSE HIT IT TO SHUT IT OFF. Wiping his hand down his face, he groaned. He didn't feel like he'd had a full eight hours by any stretch, but it didn't matter he had to get up and get to work. Laying still, he took in another deep breath before rolling out of bed and sitting on it to tug his boxers on from his side drawer.

"What time is it?" groaned Hayley.

"Seven."

"You mean he actually slept through?" asked Hayley disbelievingly.

"Unfortunately not. I got up with him a couple of times." answered Jesse, pulling on his trousers as he stood up to face her.

"Shit, I got my hopes up then." said Hayley, getting out of bed and grabbing her dressing gown to swing round her shoulders. Daniel hadn't slept through since their ordeal but she couldn't get cross with him for it, she barely spent a night fully sleeping without nightmares presenting themselves at some point. "You should have woken me. You've got work I haven't."

"You need your sleep too, especially now you're growing our tiny human." He said slipping his hands around her waist pulling her to him.

"Our tiny human is tiny. So wake me." she said before kissing him and leaving him to get changed.

In the kitchen, Hayley filled the kettle before putting bread in the toaster. Looking out the window she could see it was going to be a nice warm day again. The sky was cornflower blue and there wasn't a cloud in sight. Hearing the kettle finish she pulled down the cups and made their drinks, hearing Jesse in the bathroom shaving his day old stubble she placed the cups on the dining table before taking the hot toast from its tormentor and spreading butter on. When she placed the plate on the table Jesse was making his way into the kitchen while folding his blue tie in on itself.

Taking a seat, he grabbed the toast and took a huge bite. "What's your plan for today?" he asked while watching her take a sip of her drink.

"I've got an appointment with Ruth so that and then maybe I'll just do some window shopping before I pick Daniel up."

"Mum having him?" asked Jesse. She nodded. There really was no one else to have him, so he knew the answer before he asked it. "You going to tell her about the pregnancy?"

"You're Mum? No. I thought you might want to wait and do it together."

"That's fine, but no I meant your counsellor." Jesse never asked about her time with the counsellor, he always just left it to Hayley to talk if she wanted to, which she rarely did. When she still hadn't answered, Jesse continued. "I think you should." Hayley nodded, she hadn't made her mind up about what she was going to talk about today. Things had been spinning around in her head since her session last week and she still hadn't managed to pin anything down, she was hoping it would come to her when she got there. "Are you ok?" asked Jesse, watching her intently. Nodding, she got up to leave the table, but Jesse tagged her wrist gently. "Did I say something to upset you?" asked Jesse, concerned. When she didn't answer he could tell she was struggling, biting her bottom lip, her eyes filled with tears. "Hey hey.." standing up he enveloped her in his arms. "Tell me what's wrong."

"I don't know." she answered, her voice breaking. Pushing her arms out so he could scan her face, his brows furrowed. "I don't know what's wrong with me, I don't, I swear."

"So why are you crying?" he asked watching her try to wipe the tears from her face.

"I don't know!" she shouted, angry with herself more than him, turning round she ran to their bedroom and hid under the covers, letting out all her pent up frustration through tears.

A few minutes later she heard the door to the bedroom open, it had a slight squeak whenever it was opened slowly. She could just imagine him staring at the mound in the bed, dumbfounded. She was doing everything she promised she wouldn't. Hiding, crying and keeping him at bay rather than letting him in. She had to be stronger; she had to trust him. Pulling the covers from her face, she stared at him as he stared at her. "I'm sorry." she mumbled, knowing he didn't have a clue what was going on with her, because neither did she.

"Care to explain?" he asked, arms folded, leaning on the door frame to their bedroom. Watching him look at her like she was crazy or an irrational child, she had an overwhelming feel to hit him and scratch his eyes out. But she knew she was being irrational, he hadn't done anything, and the fault laid directly at her feet not his.

"Something's wrong with me." she cried, watching Jesse's face turn from pissed off to concerned once again. "I don't know what's wrong with me. I think I'm broken." she answered, holding her arms across her stomach. "I don't know what to feel. I don't know how to not feel like this."

Once it seemed like Hayley would not be feeling better any time soon he quickly dug out his phone from his pocket and walked out of the room. Watching him leave made her cry even more, had she finally pushed him away, made him regret ever being with her, she was a mess; he didn't need it. A few minutes later he walked back in the room and untied his tie, slipping it from his collar before throwing it on the floor and loosening his top two buttons, then pulling it over his head. Wondering what he was doing, she stiffened. Slipping his trousers off, he threw them on the floor too. Feeling panic rise in her throat she backed up the bed unsure what to do.

Grabbing the covers he threw them wide revealing her, before taking her hand and pulling her to him. Reluctant, she looked at him wide eyed.

"Wh.. what are y.. you doing?" she stuttered.

"Showing you something." He answered calmly. Thinking she knew where this was going, she scrambled to the other end of the bed, to get off from that side. "Hayley." When he said her name, it sounded like a command and she froze. "Turn around and look at me." Still feeling paralysed, her eyes leaked silently.

Watching her shake made his stomach clench. Someone had done that to her. Made her believe that there was no genuine goodness left for her, that people would always try to hurt her, but it stung to think after all this time she still thought that way about him. He'd hoped he'd done everything he could for her to trust him but it seemed he still had a way to go if she thought he would make her do something she didn't want to. "Hayley, please. Listen to me; I'm not going to hurt you." Watching her shoulders drop slightly was some comfort, but she still wasn't facing him. "Look at me, please." Slowly turning her head he could see how terrified she was, her eyes were certainly windows to her soul and her soul had been turned dark by people who should never have been allowed near it. Trying to discard the broken pieces of his heart, he tried to soften his feature. "Lay down." Watching her swallow, she did what he said, never taking her eyes from his.

Getting on the bed beside her, he placed his hand on her stomach, running his thumb around her belly button. "Is it the baby?" he asked, not looking at her face even though he could tell she was watching him. "Is it me?"

"I don't-"

"You do. Something is sending you into these rage episodes and I want to know what it is." Hayley sighed, looking at the ceiling, feeling her body let go of the tension.

"I don't know, I swear. I don't understand it myself."

"So talk to me, talk shit if you have to. We'll work it out, just talk." He said looking back up to her, this time she caught his eyes, and she looked back at the ceiling, if she was really going to do this it would be much easier without looking in his eyes.

"I'm scared." When he said nothing just kept running his finger around her belly button lightly she carried on. "I just feel overwhelmed sometimes, like there's so much going on around me but I can't pin anything down. I can't concentrate and then I make mistakes or forget things, sometimes I can't even remember whole conversations. It scares me, it makes me feel broken and then that makes me angry because I feel like I should be able to bounce back, this shouldn't be bothering me still. I should be able to look at my life differently, I'm free, I'm happy, I have you and Daniel and I'm pregnant. It's everything I ever wanted but I have this black cloud that just descends and all it does is remind me I'm not worthy, that I'm living on borrowed time. That someone up there will allow me some happiness, but only so they can whip it away again. I feel like I'm waiting for it all to go wrong so it won't come as a shock and it won't hurt as much, but it will. I know it will, it'll kill me." Jesse didn't know what to say to that. It was a lot to take in, and he felt useless having not realised what she was going through before now. She had looked like she was coping on the outside, to anyone else she had been, but only because she'd been hiding it, this pregnancy had brought out more feelings than she was letting on. She had only recently learnt about her daughter's life, having made herself believe her own story that she had died she'd been confronted with a picture to show how she looked and that she was happy, but the girl had looked so much like Hayley it had broken his heart to know she'd had to give her up to keep her safe. Then they'd had Daniel who she'd been resigned to thinking was going to meet the same fate until they had realised he was Jesse's and now she was pregnant again with a huge question moreover it. "I know when you touch me, you feel me tense first." Jesse looked up to her face, but she was still staring at the ceiling. "I hate that I do that, but I can't help it. I'm sure you think it's because I don't trust you, but it's not. It's just a response, like muscle memory. Everything reminds me of him, everything triggers me, everything has him in my head even when I beg him to leave I hear his voice, feel his touch before yours. I hear a door slam and I shake. A loud voice and I cower, and I thought I'd got it all under control. I was clawing back my life and then he came back, and now I just wait.."

"He's not coming back this time." said Jesse. "You killed him."

"But Frank's still alive."

"He's in prison, he's never coming out."

"Then there's Alexi."

"I don't think he wants to hurt you." Hayley shook her head. She didn't either but it seemed someone was always sneaking round the corner ready to pounce, so who could she trust, really? "I wish I could take all those feelings from you." Hayley looked up at him and realised he was telling the truth, he really did and she smiled slightly knowing that he truly loved her. "But you're not half as broken as you think. I know you tense, and I know you do it subconsciously, I know you can't help it, but I know once you know it's me and your brain gives you the go ahead you soften, because I know you trust me and I know you love me. I'm not going anywhere and nothing will change the way I feel about you. You getting angry at how you react is normal, and it's all about being on the correct path to recovery, because you can see it, you feel it and now you're trying to understand and overcome it. None of that is easy, especially when like you say, everything makes you think thoughts you don't want in your head. They'll fade with time. Because we'll make new memories and they'll take over their space in your head. You'll never forget but you'll be able to live without them being at the fore front of your mind. Just don't ever be scared of telling me the truth, ok. I'm a big boy, I can handle it."

"What about sex?" asked Hayley, watching his eyes hold hers in place.

"What about it?"

"Sometimes my head takes over and I think things I don't want to, but I can't help it. I feel like I'm not completely present and I hate that."

"So tell me what triggers you and I'll not do it."

"But then that stops us from having a healthy sex life."

"How?"

"Because you'll have a checklist of do's and don'ts, I don't want that. I want to be able to just be with you, in every way. I just want to let go." Jesse nodded. He understood her drive to want normalcy. If he veered away from things, it would only amplify their importance. She needed to feel him love her so that the memory of them both together would override the abuse she had sustained.

"Ok. But if we do this, you have to tell me to stop if it gets too much, or if not stop, slow down."

"Slow down. I like that better." She nodded.

"That way I know to take extra care without making you feel uncomfortable but without giving those bastards the power you think they gain from stopping." She nodded again, being flooded with relief that he understood. "Thank you."

"What for?" asked Hayley, confused.

"For telling me, for talking to me and for trusting me, I know that was hard for you." Smiling, she gripped his chin and kissed him on the lips deeply as though to suck some courage from him. When they let go, she watched him looking at her with all the love he possessed.

"Why did you get undressed?" she asked.

"To put myself in the same state of undress as you. It was to make you feel more comfortable, but I saw the look of horror on your face, as though you thought I was going to make you do something."

"I'm sorry."

"I'm not. We needed this talk." smiling. She kissed him again and suddenly she felt lighter, the dark cloud having disappeared. "Right I best get to work. I just called Mart to cover for me." Nodding, she watched him get dressed again. "If you go into town, can you get some oranges?"

Frowning, Hayley nodded. "Why?" Tapping his nose, he walked out the room and she laid back into the covers of the bed with a contented smile on her face.

When Hayley left the counsellors room, she felt so much lighter, as though a vast weight had been lifted from her shoulders and suddenly the warm sun on her face made her feel free and alive. She'd told Ruth everything that had happened that morning, from her fears that had gripped her to the conversation she'd had with Jesse. The counsellor confirmed to her what Jesse had said about being more self aware; being the footpath to a brighter future. She'd seemed proud of her too when she'd said she'd opened up to Jesse, she knew how much it meant to her to be able to do that, as she'd spent many sessions just saying she wished she could speak but found it incredibly difficult to open up. It seemed she was on the road to recovery and she liked that feeling, as though she'd just jumped a huge hurdle. Taking her phone from her pocket she quickly tapped out a text smiling before she placed it back in her pocket to go and have a look round the shops.

∼

Taking his phone out, he opened it up to a message from Hayley. Smiling, he typed a quick response before picking up the paperwork on his desk. Martin across from him noted the smile and wondered what had changed his boss's demeanour so quickly. He was suddenly more relaxed and happy.

"Everything all right? You never said why you were late." pried Martin, watching Jesse quick scan the words in front of him.

"Yes it was Hayley, and yes that's why I was late." said Jesse without taking his eyes from the document. Martin tried to stifle a laugh but failed.

"She ok?" asked Martin, turning serious. Jesse nodded absently. Still trying to read the information in front of him, Martin waited.

"Yeah she's good. Had a session with the counsellor. She was getting herself worked up this morning, so I stopped a bit longer to calm her down." answered Jesse, flipping the paper over to read the rest. "She just sent a message to say she was ok."

"Good. Claire wants me to invite you both to lunch at ours on Sunday."

"Claire does? Do you not want us?" said Jesse, laughing light-heartedly.

"I'm happy to say you can't make it if you don't want to come." said Martin. "If Hayley's not ready I'll make up an excuse."

"She doesn't want people pussy footing around her Mart." warned Jesse, eyeing him over the document. "I'll ask her and let you know tonight."

"I haven't told Claire about the pregnancy." added Martin.

"Good, because it's too early, we'll get the scan out of the way first. Besides, I need to tell my Mum first."

"So you're keeping it?" asked Martin cautiously. Jesse huffed, throwing the document on the desk unceremoniously.

"Mart, get to the fucking point, I'm trying to concentrate." ordered Jesse.

"It's none of my business." answered Martin holding out his palms.

"You're damn right it's not, but you're gunner be a stick up my arse until you come out with it, so you might as well get whatever it is off your mind now."

"I'm just concerned about her mental stability. Having a kid changes things and I'm just wondering if maybe this step's coming a bit too soon."

"Ok. Now you've said your piece, I'll say mine. I know that you feel something for her-"when Martin tried to interrupt Jesse held up his hand to stop him. "I know it's not sexual, I know you've put yourself as some kind of older brother to her. I know you care about her and that you feel a connection, probably through when you were liaising with her when she was under surveillance and you saw her at her lowest point, and I genuinely get it. I probably wouldn't be able to get those images out of my head either, especially when you have to see her on my arm and you can't just shake her off as you would any other case. But listen here, if you ever try to tell me how to handle Hayley and her condition again, you'll be finding yourself on another team. This is my line, you cross it again and we're done. Do you understand?"

Feeling suitably chastised and a little embarrassed at being called out, Martin nodded solemnly. Standing up from his chair, he pushed it under the desk. "We good?" asked Jesse, watching Martin open the door. Turning to him, Martin nodded before exiting.

Jesse sat back in his chair. He felt like crap, but he needed to shut that shit down. Martin felt responsible for her and that wasn't healthy, especially since he knew he wasn't being asked to be. Martin might be taking it as a scolding now but he hoped sometime in the future he would see what Jesse was trying to do for him, which was to set him free of his responsibility. Martin needed to step back like they had to with every other case, he understood how difficult that was when you were made to be around them for the rest of time but he'd be forever up Jesse's arse if he didn't put him straight now. He needed a friend, not a father or brother-in-law. He certainly didn't need to be told how to look after Hayley, that time had passed and he would not be letting her go anytime soon.

CHAPTER 6

Rob sat across from Freya's three brothers, thankfully a table sat between them but he wasn't sure how much of a barrier that would be if they decided they didn't like what they heard.

"So, how did you meet her?" asked Teddy, the oldest and more dangerous looking of the bunch.

"At the gym." answered Rob, looking from one pissed off brother's face to the next.

"How did you get to move in here?" asked Will, the younger of the brothers, with dark black hair and a thinner frame he was the only one who wore glasses.

"Freya and I got speaking, and she knew my rental contract was coming up for renewal, she offered her room. The room. The other room." Stumbling, Rob watched their eyes narrow on him. "The spare room."

"How long, you known each other?" asked George. A mix of the other two brothers, he looked more like Freya, with chestnut-coloured hair, blue eyes and the same shaped face. He looked the less annoyed, and far more like he couldn't really be bothered to be here, but the other two had insisted.

"A few months." Rob lied.

"How many?" asked Teddy.

"Two."

"How long you been sleeping with her?" asked Will.

"Bro! I do not need to know that shit!" shouted George. "Don't answer that!" he said pointing to Rob.

"They're definitely banging." said Teddy, raising his brow to Rob. "I heard."

"Ted! Shut the fuck up! I don't need that in my head!" shouted George, thumping his brother in the arm.

"You going to marry her?" asked Will, ignoring his brothers.

"What?" coughed out Rob. "No!" when they all looked at him as though he'd asked them to start a war, he whiffled his head. "I don't mean I never will, just that we've literally just met."

"Thought you'd known her, two months?" asked Teddy, watching him intently.

"We have, but we've not-"

"Dude, I get it!" said George holding up his hand. "Where you from?"

"Err.."

"That's not a place." said Teddy sharply. Rob wondered if he could effectively swallow his tongue to be a good enough reason not to answer them. "You shouldn't have to think about it."

"Lincoln." answered Rob.

"Where?" asked Will.

"Close to the supermarket on the main road in."

"What was the name of the road?" asked Teddy curiously.

"Honeysuckle drive?" said Rob, but it came out more as a question.

"How should we know, you should know what road you used to live on?" said Will, leaning forward.

"Yeah it was Honeysuckle drive." said Rob swallowing whilst praying to god there was such a drive somewhere around there.

"Number?" asked Teddy.

"Eight." When they all glanced to one another, he wondered what he'd said for them to silently speak to each other.

"What do you do?" asked Will.

"Nothing." answered Rob before seeing Teddy move forward on his chair. "I mean I'm out of work at the moment, but I'm looking."

"What do you do?" asked George, seemingly interested.

"I'm a chef." answered Rob, hoping that telling the truth might lower his heart rate a fraction. They all seemed to consider that.

"What's your last name?" asked Teddy. Rob had been waiting for that since Freya had said she was leaving, so whilst being prepared he still didn't feel entirely comfortable saying it.

"Holden."

"Age?" asked Teddy.

"Twenty seven."

"I can probably find you a job." said Teddy. Rob felt his heart sink. He should be happy but he couldn't accept it, especially now he'd told him a fake name, he couldn't very well come up with new identification and the second his real name was put in the system the police would descend.

"Freya said you work with computers." said Rob hoping it was an empty threat to find him a job.

"I do, but I also part own a bar and we serve food." Shit! Rob grimaced. "We could probably get you a few hours to start you off." This was not something Rob had been expecting but then he thought how clever Teddy was being by offering him a job he was getting in Freya's good books whilst also being able to keep a close eye on him. Smart.

"I'd take it because you ain't slumming here for nothing for much longer and I don't care what Freya says." said Will holding his arms across his chest and leaning back in his chair as if to say he'd said his piece and that was all he offered.

Nodding, Rob looked back to Teddy and tried to smile, but it came out as more of a grimace. Banging the table loudly as if to end the discussion Teddy stood up. "Well, that's sorted then. Come by the bar tomorrow and we'll set you up. Be there for ten." Rob nodded again, watching the other men standing in front of him.

Once George had left and Will had disappeared upstairs Teddy came closer to him, blocking out the sunlight from the window. "I'm going to warn you once. If you ever hurt my sister, I will break your legs and feed them to you whilst simultaneously shoving your teeth up your arse. Do you understand me?" Nodding, he looked into the deep depths of Teddy's eyes and believed him. Somehow he would do exactly that and he'd make sure he felt every break. "If you even think you run the risk of doing that, you will pack your things and get out, you will leave no communication and you will not turn up to my pub tomorrow. But if you turn up tomorrow I want you to know I'll be watching you and you'll regret ever having known her if you so much as look at her the wrong way."

"I'm not out to hurt anyone." answered Rob. "I like Freya."

"Ok then." Walking away from him, Rob watched Eddie walk out and then heard the front door slam shut behind him. Letting go of the air in his lungs he deflated, feeling like his legs had turned to Jelly he fell into the chair Will had left pulled out from the table.

Rob held his head in his hands. He had a choice to make, but he just wasn't sure if he could pull off the one he wanted to choose. If he started working for Teddy, he needed his new name to mean something; he needed a new national insurance number, a new account, a new life but he had no idea how to do that. If he left, he would have to leave the most beautiful woman he had ever seen and potentially hurt her, something he'd just promised Teddy he wouldn't do. Something he had no intention of doing.

CHAPTER 7

Jesse walked in, throwing his blazer over the back of the chair in the kitchen diner. When he couldn't hear anything he went upstairs to investigate. Opening the bathroom door, he watched as Hayley sat in the tub with Daniel between her legs washing his hair. For a few seconds Hayley didn't seem to notice he was there while talking to Daniel about when Daddy would get back what story he might read before bed. Daniel shouted, "Cuffy Bufferfeed!"

"Yes, Daddy might read Cushy Butterfield. I'm sure he'll be over the moon to read it for the hundredth time." Jesse scoffed, and she turned to him, smiling.

"I'm going to burn that book." Jesse joked.

"It wouldn't matter, I'm sure you know it by heart now, anyway." Laughing, he nodded. "Here grab him will you, I just need to do my hair."

"Sure." Jesse grabbed a towel, wrapping it round Daniel once Hayley lifted him up. Pulling him to his chest he rubbed the towel all over him while he squirmed giggling.

Once they'd settled Daniel in his bed and eaten some dinner they decided on an early night. Checking Daniel was sleeping soundly Jesse grabbed the string net of Oranges, pulling a hole in the material he cut three into quarters before placing them in a bowl and taking them through to the bedroom while Hayley undressed. "What are they for?" asked Hayley eyeing the bowl he put on his bedside cabinet.

Tapping his nose, she frowned, but then shook her head before crawling into bed as she waited for him to undress and follow her. When he got in, she cuddled up to him as he wrapped his arm around her shoulders, bringing her in closer. Having flicked the television on, they watched the film start.

"So you going to let me in on your little Orange fetish?" laughed Hayley who was unable to smell anything else in the room as they were so strong.

"I'm going to show you." Looking up at him, she wondered what an earth he meant. "Lay down." asked Jesse. Looking at him with confusion, she decided to do as he asked. Watching him take an orange quarter from the bowl, she watched him dribble some juice on to her stomach, giggling as she leant up on her elbows.

"What are you doing?" she was intrigued more than anything else, he'd never done anything like this before.

"Smell is one of those things that trigger memories really well; it also makes those memories quite strong. You said you didn't want to remember some things and unfortunately I can't take them away but what I can do is give you new memories and the odds are that if we hit as many senses as possible at the same time then they will override the bad ones."

"So what are you going to do?" asked Hayley warily.

"Nothing you don't want to, okay?" nodding she carried on watching him squeeze the orange so the juice ran onto her stomach. "I want you to tell me to slow down if you need me to, but I also want you to tell me to stop if you want to, I need you to be completely honest with me."

"Okay." Laying back down, she tried to steady her breathing.

"Look at me." Looking at him, she watched him wink at her making him smile. "You need to look at me all the time baby, okay?" nodding she puffed the pillow up beneath her head. "No closing your eyes, no looking away, eyes only on me."

Having squeezed all the juice onto her still flat stomach, he watched it congregate in her belly button and around as though it was a pond. Taking his tongue he dipped it into the juice and touched Hayley's stomach hearing her take an intake of breath made him smile, but he carried on. Making trails of juice all over her rib cage with his tongue he took another quarter of orange dripping juice onto her nipples before taking them each in his mouth, twisting them to peaks, when her eyes closed and her back arched he mouthed her name around the flesh until she opened them again. When she was obeying him he raised her arms above her head, tightening one hand around both her wrists, something he knew she didn't like, when she stiffened he looked down to her, with a raised brow, waiting for her to tell him.

"Slow." She said quietly, nodding he ran juice down her arms, collecting it on his tongue. All she could smell was oranges and all she could feel was his skin tenderly touching hers, and while she just wanted to close her eyes and savour every bit she knew he didn't want her to, she needed to watch. Lacing his fingers through hers, he brought her hands back down, kissing her wrists as he did so. Whispering how much he loved her close to her ears, her eyes almost closed again. Popping them open, she watched his hand lower to her thighs. Freezing again she said "Slower." Nodding as he kissed her clavicle he picked up another orange after tossing the old one before sitting up and dripping juice on her thighs and her mound, when the juice hit her clit she leapt from the bed, she hadn't realised how turned on she was until that point, but now it was obvious, her heart rate had increased her breathing was sketchy and erratic and every nerve ending she possessed tingled with anticipation. Lapping the liquid up, he trailed his thumb on her thighs, feeling her quiver and shake. Exactly what he'd hoped for. She wasn't shaking from fear, but from passion. When his head went between her legs, she almost bolted from the bed, but he gently pinned her legs, leaving her open for him while he drove her crazy. Thrashing and trying to contain herself, she closed her eyes and all she could feel was the twisting in her stomach. A feeling rising from Jesse's tongue matched the coil as they entwined, finally bursting and raising her from the bed as her body and mind shattered.

Gently laughing, Jesse climbed over her body, kissing her lips and neck then her breasts while she tried to come back down from whichever stratosphere she'd just entered. "Are you ok?" asked Jesse lightly.

"Oh, my god. I have no idea." Hayley chuckled. Completely boneless and more satisfied than she'd ever felt, Hayley just lay still while Jesse chuckled at her. Wrapping her body up with his, he held her tight, and she melted into him as though they belonged together.

Once she'd calmed down again, she looked up to Jesse. "I love you."

"I love you too." answered Jesse, smiling. "That was amazing." This time Jesse flushed a shade of pink. "I think Orange has become my new favourite fruit." Laughing, Jesse kissed her head, holding her to him until she fell asleep.

∼

A WEEK later Freya was paying for her and her Mum's drinks at the till of an old coffee shop in her Mum's town. After arguing with her about stopping in, she had relented with a visit to her Mum's favourite weekly pastime. Her Mum was finding somewhere to sit in the busy café and so while she waited for the assistant to count out her change as if she was a six-year-old she scanned the room to make sure her mum was getting by people safely and not tripping over people's feet or discarded handbags.

"Hello sweetheart, where is he?" asked the old lady.

"He's just gone to the toilet with his Granny." smiled Hayley registering the woman as the lady she had seen a week ago who gave Daniel the pound coin. "He'll be back in a minute, do you want a seat?"

"I would but I'm with my daughter."

"That's fine, there's plenty of room." said Hayley, smiling, leaning over the table to remove Daniel's change bag and Marie's coat.

"Oh thank you, that would be lovely." said the lady sliding into the booth. "I had a fall last week, so I'm being babysat." said the Lady rolling her eyes. Hayley couldn't help but laugh, she hoped she was as lively as this lady when she was that old. When another lady approached the table with a tray, she looked up smiling while the older lady patted the seat. "Freya, this is the lady with the little boy I was telling you about."

"Oh Hello. I'm Freya." she said, resting the tray on the table.

"Nice to meet you. Hayley." Once they'd all been seated and Marie and Daniel had come back, they all started chatting about the weather and other day-to-day pleasantries.

"How long do you have til the little one's due?" asked Edith. Looking to her left where Marie sat, she hoped she hadn't been listening too closely. Swallowing, Hayley thought about how to get out of this fix quickly.

"Have I really put that much weight on?" laughed Hayley hoping she was coming over as convincing.

"Oh, Mum!?" admonished Freya. "I'm so sorry." Edith looked on gob smacked as she tried to work out what she'd said that was so wrong.

"But I thought you-"looking at Marie, where Hayley's eyes had wandered, the shoe suddenly fell. "I'm so sorry. It's this old age, it's sending me senile."

"No worries. We certainly want more, we'll just have to see when that happens, maybe that's what you remember me saying." said Hayley smiling timidly, hoping the woman saw it for the apology it was.

"Must be. Like I said, it's this old age." said Edith, giving her a knowing look. Hayley relaxed a little. Marie looked on, smiling politely while she glanced at the pair of them.

∽

BACK HOME AFTER her shift at the gym she showered and dressed before walking in the kitchen to start preparing dinner.

"You're here?" said Rob, surprised.

"Yeah Mum's much better, says she doesn't need me cramping her style so I'm home now, but I think Will's going tonight and then it's the weekend so the boys can chip in." Nodding approvingly, Rob dumped the spare house keys in the bowl on the table that Will had reluctantly given him before starting his first shift with Teddy. "So it's a wine food and movie night."

"Sounds good." said Rob, wrapping his arms around her waist. "I've missed you."

"You mean you had to put up with my brothers busting your balls." scoffed Freya.

"That too." laughed Rob.

"How have they been?" she asked suddenly concerned.

"Like a bunch of bears with equally sore heads." Laughing, Freya turned the stove off, turning in his arms to kiss him.

"Well, I am their goldilocks."

"Maybe you should give them back their porridge then and they might lighten up?" laughing again, she swatted him on the arm.

"How's work been?" she asked, bending down to retrieve two bowls that she then poured baked beans into.

"It's ok."

"You mean Teddy's not had you cleaning floors and taking rubbish out?" asked Freya, feigning shock.

"No he has, but it's ok, it's my job." Taking the toast from the grill, she buttered each before cutting into triangles. Sticking a corner of the toast in both bowls she turned passing him one before sitting at the table. "The guys at the bar don't call him Teddy."

"No, they don't, they use his old tag name."

"What?"

"He was a soldier, went to Iraq and everything so they call him buy the nicknames they've all crafted for one another."

"So why's Teddy called Jaffa?" asked Rob who had been curious since he'd heard it, but he was never going to ask the guys, it seemed Teddy had told them all to keep a close eye on him and with them watching him he was trying to give them no reason to take umbrage with him.

"Apparently they used to get treat boxes and there would always be

Jaffa cakes in them, but whenever anyone went to get one my sweet toothed brother had already filched them." She laughed, shaking her head. "So he became known as the Jaffa cake thief. Now whether that's actually the accurate story I'll never know, because if there's one thing those guys can do. It's keep secrets." Taking a mouthful of toast, she chewed. "And make shit up," she added. Rob nodded, knowing they were all ex-military now made sense; they all looked at him like he was an unstable live bomb or an enemy within their ranks at least. It also meant Teddy was a genuine threat to his survival, and he'd unwittingly stepped into a minefield.

"So what did you get up to today?" asked Rob, deciding to think about something else.

"I went uptown with Mum. She always gets her shopping on a Friday and likes to pop into the local bakery come café, so we did that then I took her home, unpacked her shopping and went to work."

"Sounds nice. You're Mum alright now?"

"Yeah, she's still a little bruised, but she's not as stiff as she was last week. It seems she's made friends in the café anyway so I'm not sure even a fall would put her off seeing that young man."

"Young man?" Rob asked, choking on his toast. Laughing, Freya nodded, suddenly excited to tell him.

"There's a woman who comes in with her little kid, seems a bit of a charmer if you asked me. Mum's smitten with him, and his Mum told me she already slipped him a pound coin last week."

"Bless her." Rob laughed before taking another mouthful of beans.

"I think she dropped the woman in it though because she mentioned her being pregnant and the woman sat next to her seemed to be surprised, but then the woman said that she must have misunderstood. But Mum told me on the way back that she definitely hadn't."

"Ooh so she's giving away secrets now." Rob smiled conspiratorially.

"I think so. Anyway, Daniel's a charmer and will keep her in cuddles for a while I'm sure." Looking at Rob, she saw he'd frozen.

The spoon that was midway to his mouth stood stationary as he seemed to process something.

"Rob are you-?"

"Where does your Mum live?" asked Rob placing his spoon back down in the bowl.

"Gladstone House."

"Where?" asked Rob, irritated. Freya stared at him, wondering what was going through his mind. "Freya where does your Mum live?" Still watching him, she refused to answer, unsure why he needed to know so much. What had she said to make him change so quickly? Looking at her face, he could tell she was unsure of him and he hated himself for making her wary. "Freya I'm sorry. That name means something to me, so if it was the same place it might be the same person."

"What? The boy?" asked Freya.

"Yes. I know a Daniel." cursing himself for being emotional and showing his hand he looked away unsure what to say next. "I'm sorry, there's no way it was the same kid. I'm just being stupid. There must be thousands of Daniels." He said laughing, trying to lighten the mood. "Forget I said anything."

"Oh." said Freya, holding her hand up to her mouth. "Do you have a son?"

Rob shook his head. "No. He was my nephew." answered Rob.

Unsure what could have spurred on such a reaction, Freya leant forward. "Was she your girlfriend?"

"No! Nothing like that." Freya seemed to weigh up what he'd said with his reaction before leaning forward again on her chair.

"Newark." answered Freya finally. When the word hit him, he visibly tensed. "The woman's name is Hayley." seeing Rob's face visibly pale, she watched his shoulders crumple. "Is she the same person?" asked Freya gently.

"What did she look like?" he asked through heavy tear-filled eyes.

"She was about my height, my stature, blue eyes I think. Brown shoulder length hair, pretty in a not at all trying to be kind of way.

Her son's around two I think, brown hair, blue eyes; she said he looked just like his Dad."

"Did she mention his name?" asked Rob, hoping he'd hear what he wanted to.

"Yeah, it was a funny name. Not one I thought was for a boy, jay, no jee something. I'm sorry I can't remember."

"Jesse?" asked Rob desperately.

"Yeah that's it!" said Freya thankful for him getting the answer so she could let it go. "So do you know her?" Rob wiped his eyes before nodding and then started to cry. Freya just sat stock still, she wasn't used to seeing men cry, she had three older brothers who'd rather cut their own limbs off before letting themselves get emotional. Deciding to let him get it out, she just sat uncomfortably waiting for him to compose himself.

A few minutes later he wiped his face on his shirt whilst trying to control his breathing so he could explain to a very bewildered Freya. Placing a glass of water in front of him, she sat back down. Thanking her, he emptied it. "So what's going on?" asked Freya kindly.

"I thought she was dead." Freya nodded. "I thought I'd killed her." Watching her eyes widen and her back grow stiff, he placed his hands out in front of him as if he was talking to a small child and trying to show he meant no harm. "It was a mistake. I didn't mean to. But I thought I had, anyway."

"So it was an accident?" asked Freya warily.

"Not really." There was no easy way to say this, but she deserved the truth and it was only a matter of time before her brothers found out anyway, he'd been keeping Teddy at bay saying he'd find his N.I card and his P45 but he wasn't going to be able to stall him forever. Holding his hand out to her on the table, she ignored it but kept watching his face. "She was my brother's girlfriend. She was part of a sect and when she ran away, they eventually tracked her down. They used my fiancé to get to her. They threatened her with my life and that of her cousins, so she did it. She got Hayley to go with her and then they abducted her. Hayley was held and abused by them for six months."

"Oh, my god!" gasped Freya. "She looks so put together."

"He raped her and when Jesse eventually got her back eight months later she gave birth to Daniel."

"Holy shit! Is Daniel from then?" asked Freya.

"We didn't know for sure but later she did a DNA test and it seems Jesse had strong swimmers, she was pregnant when she was abducted, she just didn't know it yet." Freya sighed with a lungful of relief. "I was messed up. I was angry, and I was hurting but no one seemed to understand how it all affected me, it was as though I didn't matter." Freya sat listening. "Caitlyn was sent down for her part in the abduction but while she was in there, she lost our child and I snapped. I wanted revenge, and when I met one of Demy's men outside the gaol, he convinced me it was all Hayley's fault. If she'd have just done her job in the first place, none of this would have happened. He offered me some coke, said it would take the edge off and I needed something. I knew Mum and Jesse wouldn't understand. They were still trying to bring Hayley out of herself. She was a wreck when they got her back and I couldn't stop feeling responsible for that, just by association. I loved Daniel to bits but every time I looked at him all I could see was my son and how unfair it was that Jesse's has lived and mine didn't and that he wouldn't even try to understand why I was upset. He just kept saying she deserved it, but she didn't, she was just trying to protect me."

"What did you do?" asked Freya quietly.

"I kept using, the bloke outside the prison kept in contact with me and he always had a stash. We would talk and he seemed to understand how I felt. He said I needed to show Jesse how it felt, to make him understand and the only way of doing that was to show him that Hayley wasn't what he thought she was."

"Rob, what did you do?" asked Freya again but this time with added concern.

"I set about to destroy their relationship, sow the seeds of doubt. I thought if he could see that she was no better than a two-bit whore he'd realise that she was the one who'd created this divide not Caitlyn." Running his hand back over his face again, he sat back in the chair. "I followed her, made myself welcome in her house, I even had a key cut so I could enter and leave when I wanted. I tried it on with her, tried to get her to sleep with me so I could get evidence. I even set up scenarios that I knew she wouldn't handle well just to tip her in my direction. I was out of my mind with grief and coke and I just wanted to make her hurt." Taking a look at Freya he could tell he'd scared her but he needed to cleanse his soul, he'd been walking around with the grief of his actions for over two months and the responsibility had weighed heavily on him. "We were invited to a wedding and when I managed to get her alone, I made it look like we were making out. I watched Jesse's heart be torn apart, and I was glad it was victory, but even when he walked away I still had this rage I needed to expel. So I tried to force her and when she wouldn't let me touch her, I told her I was going to kill Daniel. When she tried to scream I panicked, and I held my hands around her neck to stop the sound, but right at that moment the guy from prison turned up, saying he was ready for delivery, you see I'd promised to deliver her back to Demy in exchange for Jesse and Daniel's life. But when they came, and she saw them the fear she had in her eyes from me strangling her was nothing to the fear, she held when she saw them and that's when I decided I couldn't let them take her. I couldn't live with myself if they treated her like last time and she was beaten on the regular, so I applied pressure and when they tried to stop me I pushed harder, until she went limp and fell to the floor. They all went crazy saying I was a fool and Demy would kill me, so I ran. They'd already booked me tickets to Italy where they said they were going to give me a job but I didn't go, I couldn't. So I parked up and took a taxi and went as far as I could to just process and make my next move, but I thought she was dead. So I couldn't go back, ever."

"So you're wanted by the police?" asked Freya. Rob nodded.

"If they find me, I'll go to prison. No questions asked. The fact she's not dead means I might get back out, but I'll still be tried for attempted murder or GBH at least."

"But you work with Teddy; all they have to do is trace your employment history."

"I know, that's why I told your brother a fake name. But it won't last me long."

"What are you going to do?" asked Freya.

"I've no idea."

"Well, do you want forgiveness?"

"Do I want the impossible, sure?" Rob smirked, before dropping his smile from shame. "Look, the best thing I can do is to remain on the run." Looking at Freya's still shocked face he just wanted to hold her but thought better of it, he'd just confirmed to her that she should be wary. "I can't bring this to your door, it wasn't fair of me and I shouldn't have done it. I'm sorry. You're amazing and I wish things were different."

"So you're just going to run?" asked Freya. Nodding, Rob continued to watch her. "I can't say what you've told me isn't horrific because it is. But if you're truly sorry, maybe you should go back and try to make amends."

"Freya I can't. They'll arrest me, I'll be put in prison and they'll still hate me even if I get out."

"Maybe, but what's worse, running and having the weight of the world on your shoulders or owning up and taking the punishment you deserve?" she asked.

"I'm scared. I'm a coward, a pathetic human being." He admitted hating how pitiful he sounded.

"You're a man who made a bad choice fuelled on anger and drugs. I can't condone what you did, but I can understand up to a point. You were hurting, and you lashed out."

"I really thought I'd killed her." He admitted painfully.

"But you didn't. She's still alive, which means there's still hope." answered Freya.

"Jesse would kill me as soon as look at me."

"The way I see it, you have a choice. You either man up and own what you did, take responsibility for what you did and take your punishment or you're running for the rest of your life, checking over your shoulder and never really living because all you'll actually be able to do is survive, barely." Rob knew she was right, but the thought of going to prison was horrific. "If you choose to be the better man, I'll stand by you, but if you run, we're over."

"You'd stand by me? Even when I've told you what I just told you?" he asked, astonished.

"Rob I've not met a single person who's not made a mistake and while yours is bigger than most I'm prepared to stay with you if that's what you want?" she answered, rubbing her thumb along the side of his hand on the table between them.

"You can't be serious?" he said, enveloping her hand with the other.

"I'm not saying I'm ready to go back to what we had straight away, but I am prepared to be your friend and your landlord." Nodding, Rob understood, but even with just one friend he was better off with her than without her. "We cool our jets as far as us, goes. I'm not happy to continue with that right now. But you still have a home and you still have a friend and I will help you anyway I can, but if you are stopping, you have to promise to go back and to put things straight."

"It's going to take time. I can't just rock up." Freya nodded. "Are you going to tell your brothers, because they might just save me the hassle and murder me?"

"I don't keep secrets from them. At least not ones that could come back and bite me on the arse, anyway. And your confession has all the hallmarks of a grenade going off." Rob hung his head. They would kill him. "But I can stop them killing you. They won't hurt you as long as I'm around to stop them."

"So what should I do?" asked Rob.

"We'll have a family meeting tomorrow, and you're going to have to attend. It's going to be ugly but if you want my help, then you have to get them on side."

"I'm fucked!" said Rob.

CHAPTER 8

JESSE OPENED HIS EYES AS THE ALARM RANG OUT, SQUINTING HE SAW that it was indeed seven o'clock. Groaning, he hit the radio to shut it off. Moving from Hayley, he looked down at where their skin pinched together, then realisation dawned. It was the orange juice they'd not washed off. Laughing quietly, he peeled himself away before standing up. Looking down at her she was sleeping peacefully, a smile still on her face, a flush to her cheeks and a glow to her skin.

Deciding to be mischievous he grabbed the edge of the covers before whipping them off, waking up startled she glared at him, which just made him laugh. "What did you do that for?" she complained, wiping sleep from her eyes.

"You looked too delicious to leave like that." Laughing still unsure whether or not to be annoyed, she made a grab for the covers but he held them fast, admitting defeat she laid back down.

"Fine, have the covers." Leaning on the bed, he leant down and kissed her pouty lips.

"You're adorable when you're grumpy." said Jesse. Unable to stop the smile, she closed her eyes. Feeling him lower his hand down her body, she revelled in his touch. "Oh, shit!"

Eyes popping open, she looked to Jesse to see what was wrong. As

Jesse held up his hand, she could see the blood on his hand, as if to make sure her mind wasn't playing tricks she sat up looking between her legs and the small patch on the bedclothes. "Oh god!"

"Get dressed, I'll get Daniel and we'll drive to the hospital." said Jesse, suddenly serious.

"Oh God, Jesse!" cried Hayley with tears in her eyes, still sat motionless.

"Hayley, we need to go. Get dressed." assured Jesse whilst he tugged on his trousers from yesterday. Scrambling from the bed, she hurried while Jesse darted out of the room.

∼

ONCE THEY WERE SAT on the plastic chairs of the waiting room at the hospital Jesse's phone rang. "Sorry that will be work, I'll be two seconds." Nodding, Hayley watched him leave to go outside before accepting the call. Hugging Daniel close to her, she kissed his head.

"Miss Timpson." called out the nurse as she held a clipboard scanning the room. Looking to the window, she could see Jesse was still on his call. Standing up, she adjusted Daniel on her hip before making her way over to the nurse, where she turned and led them down a corridor. Just as the nurse opened the door, she felt Jesse's hand at her back.

"Sorry. I rang off as soon as I saw you stand up." Trying to smile but knowing why they were there, she took the door from the nurse and walked in.

After explaining what had happened, the doctor took her behind a curtain and examined her, Jesse sat hopelessly with Daniel sitting on his knee. He knew that the doctor was only doing his job, but he wasn't sure how Hayley was handling the intrusion so he was keeping his ear out for any sign of discomfort. Once she was dressed again, she pulled the curtain and appeared looking pale and anxious, Jesse just wanted to wrap her up, holding his hand out she took it before sitting across from the doctor as he tapped on the keyboard.

As the doctor turned to them he tried to smile but it seemed more strained that genuine so Jesse tightened his grip on her hand and she squeezed back without looking at him, her focus solely on the doctor. "Ok, well I've had a good look and felt around and everything looks as it should. It's quite possibly just spotting, could have been brought about by many things but many women have it at some time throughout their pregnancy, it's absolutely normal. Just take it steady, no heavy lifting, plenty of rest and no strenuous exercise or too rough sex."

Breathing out a sigh of relief, she wasn't sure if she'd just deflated her lungs entirely, because she crumpled up in the chair and broke down. The doctor looked to Jesse, who tried to smile again as he rubbed her back in circles. "I'd also say try to keep the stress levels down but I know that's easier said than done." smiled the Doctor sympathetically.

Once she'd regained the skills to breathe and sit back up, she wiped her tears before thanking the doctor and leaving. In the corridor Jesse grabbed her and tucked her head under his, angling Daniel in his arms to make room. "It's ok, baby. Everything's ok."

"I was so scared." admitted Hayley.

"I know." Squeezing her shoulder, he guided her to start moving, so they weren't blocking the corridor. Outside, Hayley sat in the front while Jesse clipped Daniel in his car seat. Getting in the front, he started the ignition before taking Hayley's hand again and kissing her knuckles. "You ok now?"

"Yep." said Hayley, nodding.

"I'll drop you both off and then get to work." Nodding, Jesse let go of her hand and pulled out of the hospital car park.

∼

WHEN THEY ARRIVED Jesse pulled up before jumping out to get Daniel while Hayley stepped out and made her way to the front door. Opening it, she flicked the kettle on and turned to see Jesse placing Daniel in the high chair. When he was clicked in and munching on a rich tea biscuit, Jesse walked over to Hayley to give her a proper cuddle. "I thought we'd lost it." She cried.

"I know. I know." soothed Jesse. "But he's all good. He's just making sure we're all taking notice." Hayley tried to laugh. "Are you going to be ok if I go?"

"Yeah of course." She nodded, wiping her eyes.

"If you need me just call." Nodding again she watched him leave before preparing Daniel's breakfast.

∼

BACK IN THE station Jesse rushed into his office, there was no telling what he'd missed and how much time it would take to get back in front but he dialled his phone quickly to make sure the DCI knew he was back at his desk and apologised for being late. Once that was over, he powered up his computer and scanned through the files on his desk, when the door swung open he didn't even look up, there was only one person arrogant enough to just waltz in without knocking first.

"Mart."

"Jesse." With the formalities over, Martin took a seat. "A kid's gone missing over night, fourteen, female. Last seen outside a gym talking to a regular there. I've got Bobbies round their now taking a statement from the guy and Adam's rolling the CCTV now."

"Great. I'll take a look in a second. Anything suspicious so far?"

"No. Other than the expected. We're going over her social media now too, but she seems like just an average Jo. No trouble as far as we're concerned and Rosa's at the school talking to the teachers and any pupils she knows well."

"Sounds like it's all in hand. Keep me posted. I'm just going to get this sent off, then I'll be across." said Jesse, tapping on the screen. When Martin didn't say anything or make any mark to move Jesse looked at him across the desk to see what was wrong. "What's up?"

"Jesse I need to apologise to you."

"You don't." said Jesse, holding out his hand. "It's been said. End of."

"No, it's not. I have to say this or it'll just eat away at me." Jesse sat back in his chair, he didn't need this but apparently Martin did so he waited. "Yesterday you were right to pull me up. I was acting like I was responsible for her and I'm not. I know better than to get emotionally attached, but somehow Hayley's managed to worm herself into my heart. I don't mean-"

"I know." said Jesse to save his embarrassment.

"You didn't see the state she was in when I found her and normally I'm not around to see the aftermath, obviously that's different with her and I've grown to consider her a friend. But I overstepped yesterday and what's worse is that I didn't even know I had until you pointed it out. I've felt like shit all night, not least because I know you're a good man, and I don't doubt your intentions with her for a second but I just worry about her and I can't help it. But I need to back off and so I'm going to, I just don't want this to become between us."

"Are you shitting me right now?" asked Jesse. When Martin reeled back Jesse laughed. "Have you got this on Candid camera or has Claire finally lopped off your balls and made you sit through pride and prejudice?" When Martin sat back shocked, Jesse laughed again. "Jesus Christ, Mart. I forgot it as soon as you walked out the door, you didn't need to grovel and come blow smoke up my arse. I'm actually offended you thought you needed to."

"I was... I just..." stuttered Martin.

"Mart find your balls and fuck off!" laughed Jesse. When Martin had walked back to the door, he opened it and turned back to Jesse.

"Can you smell oranges?"

CHAPTER 9

Rob sat on a dining chair that had been strategically placed in the living room. He wasn't sure whether it was to pen him in or give him an exit out of the window, but he took it anyway. Freya sat next to him with Teddy in the armchair, taking it up as though it was a child's and the other two on opposite ends of the sofa.

"So you're probably wondering why you're all here for a family meeting?" started Freya taking a deep breath before scanning the men in the room.

"If it's telling us he's got you up the duff, then I'll give him a five second head start before I pull his balls off and chop hi-"

"Seriously Will, shut it! It's nothing like that. In fact, we've decided to just be friends for the time being." Freya assured him.

"Thank fuck for that, because I was starting to admire the shit face I wanted to hate." Rob glanced at Teddy not sure if he'd been complimented or further insulted. "No offence." stated Teddy when Freya glared at him.

"So what's this about Freya cus some of us have shit to do?" asked George.

"Rob hasn't been completely honest." Freya sighed, as though she was starting a bedtime story.

"No shit!-What you done?!" asked Will, eagerly. Rob shifted in his seat, glancing at the men waiting expectantly so they could be rewarded with being set free to maul him.

"Cool your jets!" snapped Freya, seeing them wind themselves up. "Look Rob can't give you his P45, because he didn't get given one."

"Ok, just phone the tax-" started Teddy.

"No, you don't understand he didn't get one because he just left without giving notice." explained Freya.

"Ok, he can still phone-"

"No, he can't. If he phones them and gives them his name, he'll be flagged."

"By who?" asked Teddy suspiciously?

"The police."

"Why?" asked George, moving forward on the sofa, not looking quite so relaxed anymore.

"Because he did something stupid and regrets it immensely." answered Freya.

"What are they looking for him for?" asked Teddy, almost growling.

"Attempted murder." As soon as the words came out, the room erupted and Rob didn't know where to look first, which threat would be the more efficient and costly.

"I want him out now!" shouted Will on his feet.

"I'm calling the police." said George, grabbing his mobile from his pocket.

"I'm going to fucking kill you!" growled Teddy, stalking towards him. But with Freya in the middle of them, she stood directly in front of him, refusing to let him past.

"Sit down and shut the fuck up!" shouted Freya above everyone. Once they'd stopped shouting they all stared at Rob while she looked from one to the other. "Sit down." She warned. "All of you."

Watching the men re-take their seats, she stayed standing just in case. Hands on hips, she flashed a glance from one to the others as she spoke. "Now listen to me. I told him to stay because he needs our help. He didn't mean for things to go that far, and thankfully she's still alive or at least we think so, because Mum met a woman in the café with the same name and with a boy who sounds like it could be her son, Rob's nephew."

"You tried to kill your sister-in-law?" asked Teddy, curling his top lip.

"No. It's not that simple. In a strange way, he was trying to save her." responded Freya tentatively.

"Are you fucking kidding me right now?" chuckled Will rubbing his chin. "Save her?"

"Look it's a long complicated story, but if he's going to tell you, you all need to shut up and wait until he's finished." When they all glanced to one another, then back at Freya, they all reluctantly nodded, leaning back in their chairs to settle in. "Good. Now Rob." said Freya, giving him the floor space. Rob watched as her brother's noses flared and their jaws stiffened as though they were being made to sit through it, before they could exact their revenge.

"Hayley was a runaway, she started working with me in the kitchen and we became friends. After someone trashed her house, I offered her a space at my Mum and Dad's while they renovated her. Anyway, my brother lived there too because he was going through a divorce. They got close and after a while they started going out."

"If this-"asked George. But Freya glared at him to shut up.

"The thing is Hayley had been brought up by some sect and they had signed her up for an arranged marriage, which was why she ran in the first place. Her partner was violent towards her and she had a miscarriage." Freya looked to her knees, tightening her hands as she listened to him continue. "We didn't know any of this until my fiancé was told to get her to a warehouse so her partner could pick her up. Caitlyn didn't know what to do, but when they threatened to kill both me and her cousin, she agreed. They abducted Hayley, and she was with them for about eight months. When she got out she was heavily pregnant and went into labour almost immediately. Everyone thought it was her partners, but it turned out it was Jesse's, my brother. They had conceived before she was taken. The police arrested and convicted my fiancé and while she was in gaol she miscarried through stress, I lost my baby and my fiancé and I went out of mind with grief. I took it out on Hayley. I blamed her for it all and I shouldn't have. I ended up getting in with some heavy people and started taking drugs, and then I met her ex and he told me he wanted her bringing back or he'd kill Jesse and Daniel and probably the rest of my family until I did as he said. The plan was to get her on her own and then deliver her to him. But I couldn't go through with it and my anger took over. I strangled her and until yesterday I thought I'd killed her." When the room sat silently, he looked to Freya who had tears in her eyes. He'd never felt so ashamed in his life, but retelling the horror of what he'd done made it even worse when the surrounding men looked anywhere between wanting to kill him and wanting to vomit. "So I ran."

"What the hell are you doing with this chump?" asked George, pointing to Rob but calmly directing his question to Freya.

"So you tried killing a young mum who had gone through being kidnapped, tortured and I presume raped if they thought this kid was his and now you want our help? To do what?" asked Teddy.

"To get his family back" said Freya as though it was obvious.

"Are you for real? I wouldn't let him in the same county as my girlfriend if he'd tried to kill her. How the hell do you prescribe getting his family to even consider taking him back?"

"I want to get close to them, do some groundwork and then ease the way so to speak, for him to go and speak with them." answered Freya. "Ask for forgiveness."

"Freya you've lost your goddamn mind! If any of you lot tried to kill my wife I'd shoot you in the head without a second thought." said George.

"Cheers, nice to know." said Will.

"Don't try to kill my wife and you'll be fine." snapped George.

"Fair enough. I like her anyway." answered Will honestly.

"Good job." George looked back at Freya. "What makes you think we should help him?"

"He's got no one else." pleaded Freya.

"That's his problem. He should learn to keep his temper." answered George.

"He made a mistake!" shouted Freya.

"No! Making a mistake is leaving the milk out the fridge, not closing the back door or forgetting your purse. It's not murdering someone." answered Teddy.

"Who are you to talk?! You've murdered loads of people." exclaimed Freya with both hands on her waist.

"I'm a fucking soldier! It's in the job description and I do it with the full backing of Queen and country. I do not get pissed off about mundane shit and then try to kill a young Mum." Teddy bellowed.

"He's right, it's not the same at all." added George. "The Taliban had guns and IED's. What kind of threat was a young woman?"

"You trying to say women can't threaten?" asked Freya.

"You're missing the point. He put his hands around a woman's neck and tried to take her life. If a dog bites someone they put it down. What's saying you don't burn his toast and he snaps?"

"You're being ridiculous. He lost a baby. He was in pain." answered Freya.

"I don't give a shit how much pain you're in, if you can't stop yourself trying to commit murder you need a bullet." said George. "Get your shit together and get out!" said George turning to Rob.

"No! He's not going anywhere, and it's my bloody home not yours." said Freya holding her hands out to stop anyone thinking they could move.

"Actually, it's ours and I don't want him here either." said Will.

"He's staying or I walk too." said Freya sternly, glancing from one brother to the other.

"You wouldn't dare?" said Will.

"Try me." warned Freya. Watching the boys breathe heavily as they looked to each other, she realised they regarded her threat with merit. She wasn't known for backing down, in fact she was well known for sticking to her guns and digging her heels in. "He stays and we help him."

"I'll drive him to his Brother's. Watch his brother kick his arse, I'll even give him a hand if he likes then I'll help bury the body. But that's about as much help as you'll get from me." resigned George folding his arms.

"You know we could just call the police. Do a citizen's arrest and wait for them to come and cuff him." said Will. "In fact that would brighten my day right up." He smiled.

"No one's phoning the police. I'm asking you for your help." Freya reminded them.

"No, you're asking us to help a criminal who deserves to be behind bars." said Teddy. "I'd even pay good money to watch his brother kick seven bells of shit out of him."

"Mum is friends with Hayley. She's pregnant." said Freya. The men all looked to each other as though they were trying to work out what that meant.

"Even more reason to leave her the hell alone." said George.

"Even more reason to bring a family back together." argued Freya.

"Not when he's done what he's done, they're better off without him." answered George.

"Says you." said Freya.

"Says a warrant for his arrest." Intercepted Teddy.

"Look, we get why you're trying to bring them back together but it won't work." said George.

"Do you?" asked Freya, unconvinced.

"Yes. You know how it feels to lose a child and you empathise. But you didn't try to kill someone." Rob suddenly felt like shit and held his head in his hands. Freya tried to pull her shoulders back as though she could bounce that comment off, when in reality she knew that would kick around in her head for a while.

"You mean other than myself?" Looking at her brothers as they lowered their heads in shame, she knew she'd hit home. They felt guilty for not being there for her in her darkest hour and she felt like a bitch for manipulating their pain but she needed them to listen to her and a bit of guilt right now was exactly what she needed. "I know how it feels and I remember the empty feeling it left me with, the utter devastation of knowing there was nothing I could do. I hated myself and everything around me. So yes, I can see that a cocktail of drugs, self hatred and a dead baby can make you do things that you'll live to regret, because I do. You all saw me go through hell and I know you all felt responsible, so don't you dare sit there and tell me otherwise because you'll be a bunch of bloody liars. I'm asking you to help him make amends. If it turns out that his brother can't forgive him then he'll do the time. He'll take his punishment, but don't you think he deserves to try to make it right first?"

After a lengthy silence and a few awkward looks, finally Teddy broke the macabre atmosphere "How?"

"By doing as much as we can to make their lives easier." answered Freya.

"How?" asked George, not seeing where she was going with this.

"I want to use the gym and help build Hayley's confidence up. Maybe even show her some martial arts. Make her more capable and give her confidence so that when she finally meets Rob, she doesn't feel at a disadvantage. If she's not intimidated, she won't make a decision based on fear, I'm hoping she'll make one based solely on what she believes is the right thing to do."

"And what if that is to kick his ginger arse under a lorry?" asked George.

"Then I'll have to sit back and let that happen." said Freya shrugging as if she could handle that.

"No, you won't." smirked Teddy.

"I'm hoping it won't come to that." she admitted.

"It's not her you have to convince. It's his brother." answered Teddy.

"That's where you come in." lifting his eyebrow, he waited. "You have a bar. I want to get them there somehow and I want you lot to befriend him, gauge what will work and what won't." she said looking at her brothers hopefully.

"This won't." said George.

"Men don't do that. He would see something shifty coming from a mile away." said Will.

"Not if we can create the right atmosphere." she answered.

"She's lost her freaking mind." said Will, shaking his head. "She's actually lost her marbles."

CHAPTER 10

Jesse opened the door to the bar, looking around at the dark wood panels behind the optics and up at the steel tubes above his head. On the walls were images of boats and landscapes, of the sea and lighthouses. The naked bulbs hung from the ceiling whilst spot lights were fixed around the bar in the far corner. They had situated tables around the edges of the room with a platform in the middle showcasing a large silver disco light that reflected little squares all over the room.

"This place looks posh." whispered Jesse close to Hayley's ear.

"She said it was nice." answered Hayley, taking his hand as he guided her to the bar so they could get a drink. "I love the walls. The timbre really makes it feel warm."

"Alright, Llewellyn Bowen." Jesse laughed whilst taking his wallet out, scanning the room and leaning on the bar. "Don't get any ideas."

"Can I help you?" asked the barman.

"Yeah, can I have a Bod and an orange juice, please?"

"Coming right up." As the barman poured their drinks Hayley saw Freya coming towards her.

"You came!" shouted Freya.

"Of course. This place looks amazing." gushed Hayley.

"Don't let Teddy hear you say that, his head's big enough." laughed Freya. "Are the rest of your lot coming?" asked Freya this time, looking to Jesse.

"Sure are. I think the whole station might be coming. It's not very often bars put something on for the police, normally we're only brought in when someone's thrown a fist or a glass."

"Yeah well Teddy knows all about service, I suppose he wanted to give something back." Nodding, Jesse took a sip of his beer before paying the barman. Besides, he's got a mean menu, he can't wait to pull out, so you'll be his guinea pigs."

"Ha! New there was a catch." said Jesse laughing. Hayley nudged him, glaring. "Sorry, that was a joke." said Jesse, looking back at Freya.

"I know, stop panicking." she smiled. "I'm going to go and see if he needs a hand, I'll leave you to enjoy your night."

"You ok?" asked Jesse, frowning at Hayley as she watched Freya walk away from her.

"Yeah." she answered, smiling tightly.

"Thought we were being honest with each other?" He whispered in her ear as he watched her scan the room.

"I will be." She corrected.

"What's wrong?" he asked, turning her to face him.

"I don't know. I just feel off." she answered, shaking her shoulders as though that may help alleviate the sense of dread she'd picked up in her spine.

"What do you mean?" he asked, unnerved.

"I can't explain it." She answered. "Maybe it's just nerves." Stepping in front of her, he pulled her to him, so she had to look up at him.

"I'm here, I'm not going anywhere. If you want to leave we'll leave, if you want to sit we can go and find a seat in a dark corner. I'm happy to do whatever makes you happy ok?" Nodding she tried to smile as though she meant it, but something was making her uncomfortable and she couldn't work out what.

She'd been getting better in social situations. Maybe it was because it was his work friends who all knew her story. She couldn't hide who she was when they all knew. Taking in a deep breath, she felt it quiver on its way out. Jesse noticed too, and cupping the back of her head, he brought her lips to his. "I love you." Making her smile first, he kissed her gently and hoped she was gaining some confidence from it. "Tell me when you've had enough." Nodding, she wrapped her arms around his waist and tucked her head under his chin for comfort.

"Hey! Leave the smooching for the dance floor." Turning, they both saw Martin walk towards them, Claire by his side. "I see you've already got a drink."

"That's why you're a detective." smiled Jesse. "Claire." He nodded, while Hayley took a step back from Jesse to retrieve her orange juice from the bar. "How are the kids?"

"Whining because they can't go out." answered Claire. "Any way talking about children I hear baby number two is on the way?" When they all looked to Martin, he just shrugged apologetically.

"It's like living with the Gestapo, I swear." answered Martin whilst trying to wave down the barman and turn away from the glares boring into his head.

"Any way, congratulations." said Claire looking to Hayley.

"Thank you."

"What, you having?" asked Martin over his shoulder as the barman poured the pint he'd ordered.

"White wine, please." When he looked at her to continue with an order he could actually use, she rolled her eyes before replying "any, you pick." while flicking her wrist.

"Bloody women." Martin huffed, looking at the bottles at the back of the bar. "Give me that one with the crappy label."

Laughing, they all looked to the door as more people entered. Hayley could feel her nerves getting worse but pasting a smile on she tried to take notice of what those around her was saying. After half an hour, the place was heaving with police personnel and war veterans. She assumed other services were in the room too, but without knowing them or it being obvious it was anyone's guess. The music was now blasting out, and the room had darkened, lights flickering all around them as the establishment turned from just a pub to a nightclub. The bar area was fully lit and Hayley chose to stay around there.

Thankfully, no one seemed like they wanted to move, anyway. Claire was chatting about her children and the boys spoke about work, albeit office politics and gossip, but she could tell they were enjoying the ease of it. Hayley didn't quite feel so at ease and after another half an hour she needed to find a quiet space, just to compose herself and settle her nerves, she didn't want to flake out yet and she didn't want to give Jesse a reason to worry; he hadn't been out in ages and she knew he needed this.

Excusing herself she walked to the toilets, pushing the door open, her ears were assaulted with cackling, stepping back she looked around and saw an office further down saying private. Touching the door gently she noted it was unlocked so slipped in, when she walked in the lights automatically came on and she saw that it was the office for the club. A big desk with different-sized piles of paperwork stacked on it and a computer angled to the side. Filing cabinets were stacked at the back and a small spirits bar sat at the side with a coffee machine on top. Knowing she shouldn't be in there but just needing five minutes, she pulled the chair from the visitor's side of the desk and sat down. Holding her head in her hands, she leant over trying to steady her breathing whilst trying to work out what had her feeling so anxious. After a few minutes she realised how cold she suddenly felt and rubbed her bare arms. Although it was still warm outside, she felt distinctly colder after sitting for a period of time. Just as she was thinking about going back the door opened and in stood a hulk of a man. Jumping up abruptly, she apologised profusely.

"Calm down. It's fine. What's wrong?" asked the man concerned.

"Nothing." She answered, eyeing the door and hoping to escape, but the large man in front of her wasn't moving and she felt penned in, making her nervous all over again.

"Sit down." Doing as she was told she took the seat she'd just fled from as though it was on fire.

"I'm really sorry. I only came to get some peace, and the toilets were really loud."

"You struggle with loud noises?" he asked

"Not usually no. It's just really busy tonight." Nodding as though he understood he watched her look at him as though gauging whether he was a threat.

"It's not normally this hectic but my sister wanted us to put on a do." he answered.

"Freya?" asked Hayley.

"Yeah. You know her?" he asked.

"Yeah, well no, not really." When she could see he didn't understand, she wet her lips again before speaking. "I've not long known her, but she seems nice." Nodding, he looked her over again.

"I'm Eddie." He said offering his hand for her to shake.

"Hayley." Stopping momentarily when he heard her name, he then continued to shake.

"Nice to meet you. So you're Hayley?" Nodding, she bit her lip wondering what he thought he knew about her. "Freya's mentioned you, said you've had a rough time." Looking away, Hayley wished he'd stop looking at her. "I'm sorry, that was crass. I just meant I understand why you might be in here now." Nodding, she still couldn't look him in the face. "That wasn't much better was it? I'm not used to seeing pretty women in my office, you've got me flummoxed." Seeing her tense up, he wanted to take it back, in fact start all over again. Why was he getting so tongue tied? "Would you like me to go and get your fella?"

"No." said Hayley too quickly, holding her hand out as though that alone would stop him.

"Ok." He said suspiciously.

"Sorry. I just don't..." when she wasn't sure what else to say she just lowered her hand, placing it back on her lap.

"Are you in trouble?" he asked cautiously.

"No." she answered, shaking her head. "Have you ever been in a situation where you don't feel comfortable but you don't know why and if you bring it up you're going to come across as neurotic or better still everyone's just going to think you can't cope and give you sympathetic looks all night?"

"Sure. But what's worse? Trying to pretend everything is ok or admitting they're not?" Hayley didn't answer him but thought about what he was saying. "I suppose you have to decide what's more important, the illusion of being all right or actually being all right."

"At the moment I'd go for the illusion." answered Hayley, trying to laugh. "I just haven't got time to work out how to get better."

"Why not?" asked Eddie. "What's more important than feeling better?"

"My relationship, surviving." She murmured, not facing him, but wringing her fingers together in her lap.

"Do you think that will work if you're not being honest with him?" asked Eddie after a brief space of silence.

"I don't want to spend our whole time together with me crying on his shoulder or telling him all my woes." she answered trying to smile. "Who wouldn't get fed up with that, right?"

"Someone who cares about you." Hayley nodded. He cared. She knew that, so why did she find it so difficult to talk to him, explain how she was feeling. He would walk over hot coals for her, he'd lay down his life for her and she knew that, but she couldn't open her mouth to speak. The words were lodged in her head and no amount of coaxing made them move. She'd stuffed everything so far down she struggled to pull them back out, but the back of her head was getting full and it was weighing her down, she couldn't think straight and her head just felt so full she was sure she'd tip over soon. "Look I don't know your fella, but I know that if you were my girl, I'd want to know what's going on inside your head. Maybe you need to try to find a way to sit him down and just talk. Even if things don't make sense, sometimes off loading just works."

"I can't." she said so quietly that Eddie wasn't sure if he'd imagined it.

"What's stopping you?" He asked calmly.

"Me." She laughed, humourlessly. "*I can't even make sense of stuff.*"

"You, speaking with anyone?" he asked. "A professional, a counsellor or something?"

"I have a counsellor, and I've told her what happened."

"Then maybe that's all this is, you've begun the process and you're in that funny stage of not understanding what's going on whilst trying to make sense of it. Realising the importance of being open, but not knowing how to start."

"That's exactly how it feels. I felt really good coming out the other day, but now I feel..?"

"Overwhelmed?" asked Eddie. Hayley nodded.

"Have you been to counselling?" she asked suddenly aware that he seemed to know what he was talking about, and not just in that sympathetic manner people did as though they felt sorry for you because you had to talk about your problems with a professional.

"Yep. I was ordered to. I lost a friend of mine when we hit an IED."

"That's a mine thing they use in a war, isn't it?" asked Hayley. Nodding, he looked down at the picture on his desk. It was of him and the rest of his team before they were deployed on their last fateful mission, before their lives had all changed forever.

"I was diagnosed with PTSD soon after, so I left the army." He admitted looking back to her.

"They've said that's what I have but I've not been to war." she answered, shaking her head.

"Not all battles are fought on the front line." said Eddie acutely. Hayley looked up to him, seeing that there was something in his eyes that said he understood. She nodded. "So crowds are your trigger?"

"Sometimes. I seem to gain more by the day." she said, trying to laugh through her turmoil.

"You're just becoming more aware. I bet most of the time you don't even think about them other than the second you realise you've straightened up or tensed your jaw." he answered, watching her intently.

"Yeah, most of the time I can just shrug them off, but everyone's really close out there. I felt like I was going to detonate."

"Ok, well that's easy. There are booths over at the far side; would you feel better being in one of those? You might not feel so surrounded." asked Eddie, standing up.

"There are people already in them." she answered, hating how her voice betrayed how she had already considered that.

"Come with me." said Eddie flicking his head to the door and holding out his hand to her. Ignoring his hand, she followed him back into the bar area. Seeing Jesse conversing with Martin and some other work colleagues, she watched Eddie stroll over to the already full booths. Picking the one closest to the door, he leant over the table and spoke with the occupants. Once they'd acknowledged him, they all got up to leave, emptying the booth. Standing back up straight, he looked over to Hayley, beckoning her over. Once she was next to him. He watched her look mystified at him, as though he'd created a magic trick. "Take a seat and I'll get your guy. That him over there?" asked Eddie pointing to the small group laughing. Nodding, she took a seat whilst Eddie strolled over to Jesse.

"Hey mate, your girl's over in the booth by the door." Looking over, he could see she was sitting on her own.

"Thanks. She okay?" asked Jesse.

"Yeah, she just needed to sit down." answered Eddie before walking behind the bar.

"Thanks." Grabbing his pint from the bar, he walked over to Hayley. "You ok?"

"Yeah, I had a bit of a wobble so Eddie got me a booth."

"Eddie, eh? Should I be worried that you're fraternising with the locals?" asked Jesse, raising his brow mockingly.

"Idiot." answered Hayley, they both laughed. Martin, Claire and two of the guys from Jesse's work all seated themselves around the table as a young girl in a black pencil skirt and white blouse walked over with two serving dishes full of food. Placing them on the table, she whipped her pad out whilst hovering her pen over it.

"What would you like to drink? This rounds on the house." Looking at each other, not sure whether to believe it, they turned back to the waitress for confirmation. "Boss sent some food over and said this table gets a round of drinks, so what would you like?" As she took their orders Hayley tried to look through the crowd to see if she could see Eddie to thank him, but he was nowhere to be seen. Smiling, she turned back to Jesse as he placed a spicy battered prawn in her mouth.

Being in the booth worked, she could see everything without being in the middle of it and with Jesse grabbing drink refills she could just sit and enjoy the atmosphere and the music. She was thankful for her chat with Eddie, he'd made her feel comfortable and he hadn't disregarded her issues even though she was sure he had gone through and seen much worse than she had. He'd been right when he said not all battles were fought on the front line and she mulled the sentence over, she'd come through a lot and there was no wonder she was left with residual effects. Maybe she should cut herself some slack? Even the thought made her smile. She was alive, Daniel was safe at home with his grandma and Jesse was laughing with his work colleagues at the bar, everything was good.

"You look better." said the familiar voice, looking up to the visitor her smile widened.

"Yes. I feel better, thank you." said Hayley.

"No problem." answered Eddie, grabbing the empties off the table before taking them to the back of the bar.

When Jesse looked over to Hayley she was talking with that man from earlier, with a huge smile on her face, they'd been rare occurrences recently. Watching the man walk back behind the bar he kept an eye on him while he changed out dirty glasses for a clean one, placing the clean ones above his head so they were easily accessible for the bar staff. Now and then he would glance behind his shoulder to Hayley, who was busy watching the antics of the patrons dancing in front of her. Narrowing his eyes, his stomach clenched.

"Mate, you ok?" asked Martin, watching Jesse as the others carried on gossiping.

"Yeah." Although he knew he wasn't convincing anyone, least of all himself. "Who's the guy behind the bar?" asked Jesse.

"Why?" Martin shrugged.

"Nothing." answered Jesse, shaking his head. "I'm just being paranoid."

"If it's about him, keep checking out your missus, then you're not. I caught him earlier." Jesse took a deep breath in. The last thing he needed was to make a scene tonight, but no one was going to take Hayley away from him. Letting out all the air in his lungs, he swiped his hand through his hair, turning his back on the guy. "What you thinking?"

"I'm thinking there was far too much in the papers for people not to know about her and Freya probably knows more than I'd like." answered Jesse cautiously.

"You think she'd tell her?" asked Martin. Jesse shrugged. "Besides, maybe he just fancies her?" When the look of abject horror crossed Jesse's face Martin just laughed slapping his back. "People are going to look. She's a good looking girl. Get used to it." Jesse wasn't sure he could ever get used to that. Maybe he should have bought her a bigger ring after all, so everyone could see it and now they had no right to look.

"Where's Claire?" asked Jesse, scanning the room.

"Bogs. She'll be out in a minute and can go back to sitting with your girl." Martin smirked, knowing where Jesse's mind had wandered. "Better still you could just go over yourself."

"I might have a word." said Jesse, looking back to the man behind the bar as he pulled someone a pint.

"Don't. Just leave it." warned Martin. "I'll say something, least you won't appear a jealous prick then. I'll just be a concerned mate." Jesse nodded absent-mindedly.

Walking over to Hayley, suddenly the room grew even darker, the lights had gone down and the disco ball sprayed a silvery light around the room instead of the multi-colours that had been turning all night. When the music faded out, James Arthur's dulcet tones sounded into the air around them. Holding his hand out when he reached her, she looked from him to the other people. Urging her to move, he took her hand, pulling her up as they made their way to the dance floor. Holding her to him, he wrapped his hands around her and swayed to the music, glancing around the room as they turned. Everyone seemed to be having fun and even Hayley felt pliable in his arms. Lowering his head, he rested it on her head, closing his eyes as he took in her scent and her warmth.

CHAPTER 11

Rob sat waiting every time he heard a noise. He wondered if someone had ratted him out and Jesse was on his way to take him out. He'd seen everyone arrive, and he'd watched Hayley clinging onto Jesse for dear life when they'd entered. But then Eddie had made him leave, if they caught him on the premises with a room full of coppers on site not only would he be arrested but Eddie's business would probably be shut down. Even though he didn't officially work there or get paid Eddie had kept him on, voluntarily hoping he would be away from Freya and in part payment for the room she was offering him.

Sitting on the sofa, he waited until the gang was back to tell him what had happened and what they were all going to do next. Hearing the rattle of keys in the door and voices chatting while others laughed, Rob waited for them to appear in the living room.

"How did it go?" asked Rob, looking from one to the other as he turned off the television.

"The party was a success, god knows how much we took in, but if there's one thing the services can do, its drink." laughed Will, knowing exactly what he meant but refusing to be bated. Waiting for them all to catch on Eddie took the armchair again while the others blocked him in on the settee.

"She's fragile." answered Teddy. "And her fella is very protective of her." Rob nodded, he already knew that. He had every right to be.

"He got warned off." laughed Will. When they all looked at him he reddened and swallowed before looking back at Teddy who was patiently waiting for him to explain how he knew. "I wasn't far away when I heard that guy come up. Said he'd seen you staring at his mate's girl and you best think twice before going there."

"You were hitting on her?" asked Freya accusingly.

"No." answered Teddy. "No." he reiterated when they all looked his way sceptically. "I found her in my office. She was trying to catch a breather. I think she was starving off a panic attack. So I moved her into a booth to help and she was fine after that, but I kept an eye on her, seems they were keeping an eye on me too."

"What did you expect?" asked Rob.

"I don't know. But I wasn't expecting her." answered Teddy.

"What's that supposed to mean?" asked Will.

"She just wasn't what I had envisioned." Teddy explained.

"So what now?" asked Rob, looking at them all?

"She's not strong enough to see you." said Teddy.

"You've known her five fucking minutes and you think you know what she's strong enough to deal with?" asked George, astounded.

"I can see pain. Him being near her isn't going to help." answered Teddy, pointing to Rob.

"You do realise that the longer he stays away, the longer we have to put up with the prick?" asked Will.

"So we do my option. Get her in the gym in a M.A class." answered Freya triumphantly.

"She's pregnant." said Teddy.

"She confirmed it?" asked Freya.

"Her outfit did. She wasn't hiding the bump." Freya nodded. "Which means she can't train to fight?"

"She can still train, I just can't hit her."

"What do you want to hit her for?" asked Rob.

"To train her." she answered in a tone that suggested she wanted to add 'duh'

"Well, she can't fight properly till she's had the kid." said Teddy.

"No fucking way. That means he's here for months!" shouted Will.

"No, he's not." When everyone looked at him for an explanation, Teddy rubbed his thumbnail along the bottom of his lip as if considering his next move. "Would your Mum rat you out?"

All eyes on Rob, he looked from one to the other until he rested on Teddy. "I've no idea, why?"

"Because if you have any chance of getting into the family fold you're going to need her on side, which means you need to make contact and try to build up your relationship."

"I can't. I step foot back in Newark and every cop in five miles will bang down the door." answered Rob.

"They're not sitting outside your Mum's house 24/7, or I highly doubt it." scoffed Will.

"No course not." snapped Rob.

"Then go and stay with *her*." advised Will.

"I can't. My brother will kill me!" answered Rob.

"How would he be able to keep undetected living at home?" asked Freya, wanting them to be reasonable.

"His problem. I've had enough of coddling him." answered Teddy.

"Teddy you promised to help!" she screeched.

"Well, I've changed my mind. He needs to go home, beg for forgiveness and take the punishment he's due. Like a big boy." When Freya looked at her other brothers in disgust, they either lowered their heads or looked away from her gaze.

"This is bullshit!" she shouted, flinging her arms in the air.

"No! What's bullshit is that we're harbouring a criminal who tried to kill a young woman all because someone hurt his feelings and after witnessing her tonight he did a lot more than that. So, I'm not happy with him being near you and I'm certainly not helping him hide any longer. He needs to grow a pair and confront his brother." Screaming with frustration Freya stamped her foot and clenched her fists before storming to the door, opening it wildly till the handle cracked on the wall and then storming out.

While silence descended in the room, Rob held his head in his hands.

"I just need time." he hissed.

"No. You don't." Teddy argued. "You've had a month, and nothing's changed. I met her tonight, and she's struggling. I can't be party to keeping you safe when you're probably the reason she can't move on."

"If I'm found, they're going to want to know where I've been, what do I tell them?" he asked looking up at Teddy.

"You keep my family out of it." he answered coldly. Nodding, Rob stood up before walking to the open doorway and going in search of Freya.

"Man, that was cold." said Will on a sigh. "What changed your mind?"

"He's too chickenshit to do anything, he needs a push. Freya needs to stop meddling, and that girl needs to be able to move on. I can't sit here thinking I'm aiding that pussy to do nothing."

"You do realise he could just tell the police he's been living here and working in your bar, then we'd all be screwed."

"He can tell them what he wants; he's going to have to prove it. As far as Will and Freya are concerned they could just say they threw him out once they realised he couldn't pay, and I'll say he was on a trial period as a volunteer but he didn't cut the mustard."

"Was she pretty?" asked Will smirking thinking he'd worked it all out.

"It's not that. I've not been happy about this for a while, but I wanted to see what he was up against first."

"And?" asked Will.

"His brother is high in the police and from what I could gather he's well respected. If what I've seen tonight is anything to go by, he's also very protective of her and I wouldn't doubt for a second that the first thing he'll do when he gets back to the station is run a check on me, if he does that then I don't want him finding anything to do with his brother. He'll assume I'm an adversary and be a pain in my arse. His friend and I assume, a colleague warned me off tonight, he's already marked my cards."

"So this is about your club?" asked Freya from the door, leaning against the door frame.

"It's about doing the right thing." Teddy confirmed, looking straight at her. "He needs to Man up."

"He needs help."

"Freya, he's not a lost puppy, he's a grown man who tried to kill his brother's girl. What do you think would happen if this was any of us?" he asked, twirling his finger around in a circle to show who he meant.

"You'd fight it out."

"I'd kill any one of you." He answered standing. When his brothers stared at him in disbelief, he looked down at George. "If anyone hurt your wife, what would you do?" Nodding slowly, he understood. "Exactly."

"So we hand him over to his brother." said Will.

CHAPTER 12

Jesse lay in bed staring at the ceiling, he couldn't sleep and something felt off but he couldn't think what it was. The man behind the bar concerned him though and he couldn't be sure whether it was a cop thing or just a jealous lover thing. He'd seen the way Hayley seemed to speak with ease to him and it was like a knife to the gut. She was usually so sceptical of people, unsure and almost standoffish until she witnessed something to relay her fears, but with him it had been almost instant. Which meant she knew him or something had happened? Or was he being jealous? She was speaking to a man twice his size and didn't seem at all frightened, but seemed to enjoy his company. Was he just going back in his mind to a time when his ex wife had betrayed him, was it making him see things that weren't there? He trusted Hayley, she'd never do anything like that, but he didn't know him. Maybe that's what he needed to do.

Glancing towards Hayley he watched her chest rise and fall as she slept soundly, with her hand on her stomach he gently moved her hair from her face to take a good look at her. Her pouty lips begged to be kissed, so he did so, watching her smile as though she was conscious. Getting out of bed, he walked to the kitchen and filled the kettle.

Once he had a drink in front of him he flicked through one of the folders from work, he could take a glance at that while sleep eluded him, maybe he'd see something different.

"How long have you been up?" hearing Hayley's voice, he turned to see her walking towards him in her dressing gown.

"Not long, I couldn't sleep." He answered, taking the hand she offered.

"Come back to bed." She pleaded.

"Oh, yeah?" laughing, she bent and gave him a kiss on the lips.

"I might make it worth your while." She answered coyly. Grabbing her, he spun her so she sat across his lap. Taking the belt at her waist he undid it, opening up to see her properly he nodded as if he was happy with what he saw. Hayley laughed, swatting away his hand, looking down at the paperwork he had splayed out; she noted the gruesome murder pictures.

"Sorry." Realising where her eyes had wandered he placed them all back in the folder before closing it up and placing it back in his bag.

"Looks nasty." she said.

"It is." He answered. Looking back to her, he pulled her closer to him, kissing her; he led her to their bedroom.

∼

ONCE JESSE WAS AT WORK, Hayley decided to spring clean the house. She was bored being at home all the time but she had promised Jesse she wouldn't even attempt to go back to work until long after the baby was born, so she wanted to make the most of being at home and clean and tidy things up. She wasn't earning, but she wanted to make sure she felt worthy enough to be using the house and eating the food Jesse's wages provided. She'd never liked feeling beholden to anyone, and it didn't matter that he told her she was being silly, it was part of her, part of how she felt and nothing was going to shake it.

Grabbing the cleaning fluids from under the sink and the dishcloths that sat beside them, she turned on her heel and made her way to the bathroom. On hearing Daniel wake up and call out to her, she placed the bottle on the floor before wiping the sweat from her brow.

Standing, she made her way to Daniel's room and picked him out of his cot. Kissing him on the forehead, she made her way back downstairs to the kitchen and popped some bread in the toaster before placing Daniel in his highchair close to the table. Spinning back round, she filled the kettle before turning it back on.

Sitting at the table with a cup in her hand, she watched Daniel munch his way through two slices of buttered toast. Hearing her phone chirp she looked around for it, spying it over near the sink she walked over to pick it up.

Opening it, she saw a picture of a child. A young girl with flowers in her hair was staring directly at the camera with an enormous grin on her face as she held a melting ice cream at the beach. Hayley wiped a stray tear from her face. Her father had sent pictures of her daughter twice since they'd returned home. She had sobbed for hours seeing the first one, not knowing whether it would be the last and her only keepsake of a child she gave away at the tender age of 16. Getting this one now brought it all back home. She had a daughter. One that had a life she couldn't be part of.

Staring at the photograph she recognised her own eyes and hair, but her chin and nose were all Frank. She wasn't sure whether seeing these pictures were helping or hindering, but she assumed they were much like what people thought watching a car crash play out might mean. Emotions flooded her system and memories bounced around her head. But she could see her daughter and she was happy. There was no point messaging back, he never replied, so she blacked out the screen and turned to see Daniel tipping his juice cup upside down, spraying liquid all over the table, grabbing it she tutted whilst cleaning it up.

A bang on the door pulled her up short. Deciding to leave Daniel in the high chair she made her way to the front door, opening it slowly she could see a young woman.

"Freya?" opening the door wider she allowed her access walking back to the kitchen so she could follow her. "What are you doing here?"

"I have a confession to make." Hayley started to laugh but the look on Freya's face told her this was no laughing matter. Taking Daniel from the chair, she watched Freya stand uncomfortably in front of her. "I know Rob." Hayley sat down, while she tried to process what Freya had just said. "He's been hiding with me." Hayley suddenly felt sick and she struggled to make any sense of what she was being told. "I met him a month ago and I've been helping him but he's stuck because he can't work or use his name because of the police." Hayley nodded, still dumbstruck. "I'm coming here to ask the impossible."

"What?" asked Hayley.

"I'm asking you to withdraw your statement and say you can't remember or that you were mistaken."

"Has he told you what he did?" asked Hayley. Freya nodded before looking to the floor. "And you want me to let him off?"

"No. That's not what I'm saying. I'm just asking that he doesn't go to prison. It was a mistake, one he greatly regrets."

"Get out." said Hayley calmly. When she didn't move, Hayley said it again and again, getting louder each time until Daniel started to cry and she soon followed, by which time Freya had already gone.

Shaking in her chair, she clung to Daniel. Why did it always feel like everything came at once? If she told Jesse, he would go nuclear. But she had to talk to someone, or she'd go crazy. Grabbing her coat and bag, she slung them on the table before taking Daniel to his bedroom to get changed.

Once she had passed Daniel over to Marie. Hayley rushed to the train station near the castle. Once on it, she sat down tapping her fingers on the table. Not knowing whether or not she was doing the right thing, she bit her bottom lip while looking out the window as all the trees and fields pass by. When the train arrived, she darted off the train showing her ticket to the machine before letting her through. Once on the outside she made her way down the main street and pushed open the door.

"Hi, can I get you anything?" asked the barman as he collected glasses from a nearby table. It was still only early afternoon, but their regulars had come in early to wet their whistles.

"Eddie, please." she asked, folding her arms over her chest. The man looked apologetic and then rushed round the back of the bar. When he came back a few minutes later Eddie was following close behind looking annoyed, but when he saw her his face changed to one of curiosity.

"Hayley, what can I-?"

"Don't Hayley me!" she shouted, almost surprising herself with its intensity. When he looked at her dumbfounded stopping at the bar as if it would protect him she stepped closer, seeing the first guy watching them from her peripheral vision. "You knew all about me, didn't you?" When Eddie looked to his colleague, he rubbed his chin with embarrassment. "She told you everything."

"Look-"

"Don't look at me! How long has he been here?"

"Who?" asked Eddie.

"Rob!" she shouted. Watching Eddie's face flush with resignation made Hayley's heart stop, for all the bravado she had mustered, she'd hoped she'd been wrong and that someone had finally understood what she was going through, not playing her, so he could laugh at her behind her back.

"Jesus Christ-"started Eddie.

"You knew?" she asked breathlessly.

"Hayley please, come and sit down. Let me explain." Eddie answered, showing her the way to his office.

"No. No way am I going back there with you." She said, defiantly shaking her head.

"Ok, no, of course. Take a seat. Do you want a drink?" when she didn't answer he caught the barman's eye and nodded. Walking over to a table at the back that looked out onto the street, Eddie watched Hayley try to compose herself before he began. He could see she was struggling and trying to put a brave face on. When a pint of cola and a gin and tonic were placed in front of them, Eddie leant back in his chair. "How did you find out?"

"Why?" she asked, ignoring his question and facing him.

"What are you asking?"

"Why did you pretend like you gave a shit?" she asked, trying to keep the tears at bay.

"I do." he admitted.

"And you just so happen to be harbouring one of the people who's tried to kill me?" she asked indignantly.

"I'm not. But Freya was. I was never happy about it." answered Teddy.

"Well, that makes two of us. "

"How did you find out?" asked Eddie

"She came round, asked me to withdraw my statement against him."

"Fuck-!" Eddie stood up, pacing in a tight circle while he held his hands in his hair. "I told her to stay out of it." He answered when he looked back down to her, as she took a sip of her drink. "What did she say?"

"I told you." She answered through gritted teeth. "You know what pisses me off more than knowing he's that close, it's that I actually liked Freya and I confided in you."

"I know, I'm sorry." he said genuinely.

"So why? Why not tell me you knew him?" she asked, wanting to understand what he was gaining from her humiliation.

"Because you looked like you needed to talk." he answered.

"Fuck you!" shouted Hayley, slamming the glass down on the table before standing back up. Rushing to her, he placed his hands on her shoulders before seeing her shrink away.

"I'm sorry." answered Eddie, watching her pale in front of him. "I didn't mean to-"

Feeling herself shiver, she wrapped her hands around herself as though she was cold and just trying to warm up, but she was neither kidding herself nor him. "Please sit down and I'll explain." Pulling the chair out and away from the table, she lowered herself without taking her eyes from him. "The other night I found you in my office. I didn't know that you were *her,* until you started talking, by which time I couldn't have very well told you what I knew, and I thought it was more important you off load before you went into a full-blown panic attack. I've had them myself and you feel like an idiot afterwards, I was just trying to save you some embarrassment."

"Well, that's works." answered Hayley sarcastically. "Because I feel like an idiot right now. I told you things… things." Leaving it there, she looked away. She didn't want to remember what she had told him, but she knew she'd been open with him and that it felt vulnerable then but it made her feel almost naked now.

"I know." Eddie nodded empathetically. "If it's any consolation, I'm not in the habit of gossiping."

"No, just harbouring criminals." Hayley snapped.

"I met him at my sisters when I went round there to sort out our mum. I didn't exactly gel with him straight away, well actually I never have." Looking back at Hayley, she was watching his every move and listening to every word intently. "She told me they'd met at the gym she works at; he needed a place to stay, so he was renting out her spare room. Later I found out that was a load of crap and he had actually talked her into giving him a room free of charge whilst he worked out what to do about you."

"About me? What about me?" asked Hayley, alarmed.

"Well, more his brother I think. From what I can gather he regrets what he did and wants to make amends but if he steps foot near his brother, he knows he'll arrest him."

"Cuffs will be the least of his worries." Hayley scoffed.

"I've no doubt. Well, anyway, she held a family meeting to get us brothers to back down and give him time to sort his life out. Not something I was altogether happy with, especially as Will's not home half the time and if he'd strangled one girl, I didn't want Freya being the next. Anyway, I installed CCTV throughout so I could monitor things, and he's not so much as raised a voice to her from what I've seen. But I told him I wanted him gone the night of the party. Freya did her nut but Rob looked like he understood and walked off to pack his bags, according to CCTV he left a few hours later."

"Why is she trying to protect him?"

"I wish I knew. But I've not seen her look at a guy the way she does him in a while so I think it's a case of rose-tinted glasses."

"Rob always was one for the ladies." she said taking a sip of her now still drink.

"He told her about his girlfriend and how she'd lost her baby."

"Yeah, he told me the same, before he strangled me." she answered flippantly.

"Hayley I'm sorry."

"It wasn't you." She answered, tipping the glass to empty it.

"Rob told me some of what you've been through." he said, watching her still.

"Jesus." Whispered Hayley wishing she had more to drink.

"That can't have been easy." He said empathetically.

"You, a shrink now as well as a barman?" when he looked away she instantly felt guilty. "I'm sorry that was uncalled for."

"Does your fella know you're here?" asked Eddie.

"No." answered Hayley, rubbing her finger up and down the spine of the glass, as if she was weighing up whether or not to throw it. "If I had, your bar would be being ripped apart by police."

"He's not here." admitted Eddie.

"That wouldn't stop him."

"He's protective of you, I get that."

"If he gets his hands on Rob he'll kill him." answered Hayley "And Marie will not only lose her husband because of me but she'll lose a son and the other one will be in gaol, and he's a cop how long do you think he'd survive in there?"

"Not long I'd imagine."

"Precisely, so no, I can't tell him." Eddie took a sip of his coke and watched her over the glass as she struggled with the new information she had. "I don't even know why I came here."

"Because you're trying to get in front of it." He guessed, "You're protecting those you love."

"I'm doing a shitty job of that." Hayley replied. "Where is he?"

"I genuinely don't know. I'd tell you if I did."

"But Freya will." Watching him take another sip as if to give himself some time before answering, she watched him swallow, licking the coke from his lips and rubbing his stubble covered chin.

"Possibly."

"Can you set up a meet?" asked Hayley.

"You want to meet him?" he asked in disbelief.

"No. But I want there to be an end to it, so if he wants to speak with me he can, but he's not to go near Jesse." Nodding, Eddie watched her, waiting for him to answer.

"If I set up a meet, I don't want you in there, on your own." answered Eddie.

"Just be outside the room." said Hayley, not ready to allow him to protect her.

"Ok, give me your number and I'll set something up."

Chapter 13

Hayley took large confident strides towards the house, she wasn't feeling confident but the extra height in her heels and the pencil skirt made her feel more in control. She'd purposely clothed more business like to give herself more confidence, knowing internally she'd be lacking. If she could create a facade, then that was the best she could offer. Fake it till you make it, she thought. Lifting the knocker on the door, she tapped it down three times before taking a step back to wait. Breathing in and out steadily, she cursed her heart for beating so rapidly.

"Hayley." Freya opened the door looking Hayley up and down, as if to check it was really her, she'd never seen her out of jeans, and she looked so in control it took a second for Freya to gain her bearings. "Come in. They're in the kitchen." she offered, holding her arm out to show the way to the back of the house.

"They?" asked Hayley, trying to contain her alarm.

"My brothers and Rob." Hayley nodded, confidence waning she hoped she wasn't walking into a trap, after all she didn't know these people and she was walking into their territory. Taking in a deep breath, she stepped towards the open kitchen door. Hayley was in the doorway within seconds, looking around she saw one man stood with ankles crossed and arms folded, leaning back on the sink, two at the dining table with arms outstretched whilst leaning on the table for support and one foraging in the fridge. Then there was Rob. He was one of the guys at the table, all eyes on her, she tried to smile towards the others, but it barely passed as a grimace. Looking back to the door she'd just entered, she contemplated running back out, but she didn't want to give him the satisfaction of knowing he scared her.

"Hayley." Looking up, she realised the man in the fridge was Eddie. "Come with me." Holding his arm out but not touching her, he showed her through to a sitting room across the hallway. Once the door was closed behind her, he turned looking at her as though he could see something she couldn't.

"What?"

"Are you sure about this?" asked Eddie tucking his hands into the back pockets of his jeans so as not to be tempted to hug her, she looked so lost he just wanted to comfort her but he knew that would be a bad idea.

"No." said Hayley on a shaky breath, "But what other option is there?"

"I'll stay in here with you." assured Eddie. "I'll not say a word." He answered by holding his hands up.

"No. It needs to be me and him." she answered shaking her head hoping that he understood, after a few seconds of watching her he conceded.

"I'll be right outside the door." Hayley nodded and Eddie left to get Rob.

Once Rob walked in, Hayley's confidence took a further nosedive and she wished she hadn't rejected Eddie's offer of a chaperone.

"Hi." Rob said nervously. He sounded exactly the same. She wasn't sure what she'd expected, but it wasn't that he would sound or look like he used to before the wedding. Before she knew he truly hated her and wanted her dead.

"Sit down." said Hayley. Rob looked down and took the nearest seat to him, which was the sofa. Hayley continued to stand; she needed the height and wanted the authority that came with it. Rob sat forward with his legs parted and his hands clasped together between them while he waited for her to speak. "I've come here to find out what you want, but that's it. I don't want Jesse being dragged into this." nodding, Rob rubbed the back of his neck. "So tell me and then I can get out of here."

"I wanted to say sorry." said Rob, looking up at her.

"Sorry?" she asked, gob smacked.

"I owe you an apology." he said.

"I'm not changing my statement." she answered, crossing her arms. "You tried to kill me."

"I know. I know. And trust me when I say I'll never forgive myself for that." he said shaking his head.

"Trust you. Trust you?!" shouted Hayley. "I trusted you and you hurt me. I thought you were my friend and then you tried to... tried to make us into something I didn't, and then you told Jesse we were having an affair knowing full well how that would destroy him after Rihanna. You threatened my little boy and then you —"losing all composure she suddenly didn't care but she refused to get any closer to him as she shouted at him.

"I know. Hales I'm so sorry." said Rob, moving forward as if to stand.

"Don't call me that!" shouted Hayley, backing up. "You don't get to call me anything but my name. You lost that right." she blurted, wiping a stray tear from her cheek. "So hurry and explain, because I want to go home."

"I was a mess after I found out about the baby, it tore me up and then Caity wanted nothing to do with me, and I just flipped. Something disconnected in my head and the next minute this bloke's offering me coke to take the edge off, make me feel human, superhuman. It made me feel immortal and strong and made me even more determined and destructive because it made me paranoid too. I was on a slippery slope and once I was on it I couldn't get off, not until I thought I'd killed you. Then I realised how much of a mess I was and I've been trying to stay clean and get better ever since."

"Am I supposed to feel sorry for you?" she asked, having walked over to the window.

"No. I know what you've been through is much worse and you've never tried to kill anyone, I know I have no excuse." Hayley looked away for a second; she could still feel the blade in her hand, the movement of it as it struck Demy's throat and the sound that it delivered before puncturing his artery and she was showered in his blood. It was a memory that would never leave her, and whilst she knew it was to save her and Jesse's life she couldn't get the idea out of her head that there was something dark inside of her, something that had made her capable of taking another human being's life. Even Rob hadn't achieved that, who was she to condemn him when she had blood on her own hands. "Are you ok?" Looking back to him she realised he must have seen something on her face. Taking a deep breath in and allowing it back out, she took a shaky step to the armchair before sitting. "You look really pale."

"I killed Demy." she answered, looking him directly in the eyes.

"Wha-When?"

"After I was released from hospital, I went to live with Jesse to recuperate, while I was there I was stabbed and then at the hospital I was knocked out and moved from the hospital to a warehouse where Demy was going to-" stopping herself she looked around the room again to gain some composure.

"I can't believe you killed him." said Rob, astounded.

"He stabbed Jesse, I thought he'd –"Rob nodded, realising that she had done the one thing he hadn't. She'd protected those she loved, and even though it was clearly not something she revelled in, she'd done it to protect those she cared for.

"How did that feel?" he asked watching her turn back to him.

"Not as good as you might think." She answered, looking at the carpet beneath her feet. "But they had Daniel."

"Is he ok?" asked Rob quickly.

"Yes. Martin got him out. Apparently their DCI had put someone under cover and he came through." Rob nodded again, wishing he had been there to help. "He's not been sleeping very well, but he's physically all right."

"Jesus, Hayley, I'm so sorry."

"Jesse will never forgive you." said Hayley, watching her words sink in. "You tried to take away everything he loved, and you might not have had anything to do with me and Daniel being abducted but you were a catalyst, an enabler. Jesse won't see the difference; he'll blame you for it all, you played your part."

"I know. I just want to see him. Apologise and then he can do what he likes." offered Rob.

"How about you just go?" When Rob just stared at her, she bit her lip. "Start a new life, leave, become someone else."

"I can't, what about Mum? What about Dad?" asked Rob.

"Michael died." answered Hayley, quietly.

"I know, but I've not been able to risk going to the cemetery."

"You were there the day of the funeral." It wasn't a question as much as it was an observation, but Rob nodded solemnly. "Jesse saw you while he was reading the eulogy."

"I needed to say bye." answered Rob.

"Then you've done it." said Hayley.

"Not just to Dad but to Mum and Jesse. I need them to know I'm sorry." explained Rob pleadingly.

"It won't make any difference. Jesse hates you." Rob nodded despondently. "I wish I could tell you this was a good idea, but if Jesse knew I was even here speaking with you he'd do his nut." rubbing his neck Rob looked around the room, trying to ease the tightening of his jaw. "If you need forgiveness to move on, then I forgive you." Rob quickly looked back at her in shock. "I can't imagine what losing a child must feel like, but I'd have gone out of my mind if anything had happened to Daniel, so I'm giving you the benefit of the doubt that you were temporarily insane because once we *were* good friends. I wouldn't have even met Jesse if it wasn't for you, so I owe you for that."

"You don't owe me anything Hales, Hayley." He corrected. "But thanks, and I know you *do* know what it feels like to lose a child. I know that Demy took that from you too." Hayley looked away, nodding; she couldn't tell him the truth. Hardly anyone knew the entire truth as that had been the only way to protect her. Telling him would do nothing anyway, so she shook that idea out of her head straight away. "He really did a number on you." Nodding, Hayley looked around the room at the photographs of the children in the frames. They looked happy, and she felt that familiar pang of loss.

"So Freya?" asked Hayley.

"She's amazing." He smiled; when he couldn't stop himself he looked away, not wanting to appear facetious.

"You really like her, huh?" she smirked, seeing a flash of their old relationship, the ease they'd once felt with each other.

"Yeah, although I think her brothers would rather hang me up by my knackers." He admitted. Laughing, Hayley held her hand over her mouth; the last thing she expected to happen was her sharing a joke with him. "I'm fairly sure they've measured out the rope already." Looking embarrassed about laughing, he watched her look around again.

"Yeah, I don't think I'd want to get on her brother's bad side." She answered.

"No, I think Teddy' already weighing up options on the best way to kill me." Hayley didn't know which one was Teddy but she wouldn't have put it past any of them. "Freya reminds me of you." When she turned to him with a raised brow, he rubbed his neck before looking away.

"She reminds me of you in the kitchen. Fun, genuine, feisty and pretty."

"Rob-"

"I'm not hitting on you. That's just what you were. Well still are, I suppose. I just stopped seeing it." Hayley smiled tightly. "I could say I'm sorry till my last breath, I know it won't change a damn thing, but I do need you to know that if I could take it back I would. If I could do everything over I would." Hayley nodded. "How's Danny? Sorry, Daniel."

"He's good, growing every day. Eats almost as much as his Dad." Rob laughed.

"I hear you're pregnant." Hayley nodded, pinching her lips together as he lowered his eyes to her stomach. "Congratulations."

"Thank you. We've only just recently told people."

"I bet he's over the moon." Hayley nodded. "Am I to have another nephew or a niece?"

"Rob-"warned Hayley kindly.

"It's ok. I know." Placing his hands on the sofa, he stood up before walking over to the mantelpiece and leaning on that. Raising her hand, she went to place it on his back but then thought better of it before lowering it again.

"Bye Rob." Nodding he let her leave without turning to watch her go, when she reached the door she turned back but again thought better of saying any more and opened the door to Eddie who was leaning on the opposite wall.

"You ok?" he asked as soon as he saw her. Nodding, she closed the door behind her.

"Can you take me to your bar, I need a drink?"

"My car's outside. You go ahead, I'll be out in a sec." Walking out of the house, her stomach felt like a lead weight had landed there. Even taking the steps towards the car felt heavy. Once she heard the click of the door, she watched Eddie round his side of the car before opening the door and getting in, doing the same her side she pulled the seatbelt across, before resting her arm on the window and her head on her knuckles. "Are you all right?" he asked, watching her glaze over.

"I have no idea."

"Did he do anything?"

"No. Other than apologise." Leaving her to mull over what had happened in the room he drove across the city towards his bar pulling up behind it, he parked and pulled the brake up before turning back to Hayley.

"Ready?" smiling timidly she opened the door, stepping out and following Eddie into the back of the bar, once he grabbed a bottle of whiskey from the bar, they made their way to the window seat they'd shared before. Hayley sat down while Eddie poured generous amounts of whiskey into each glass. Handing her one, she took it, taking a mouthful and almost regretting it when it burned her throat. "Steady." Coughing, she took another sip. Eddie laughed a little at her amateur drinking. "So what happened?"

"He apologised." she shrugged. "He wants Jesse and Marie to forgive him, but he's not going to get it, least not off Jesse."

"What about you?" asked Eddie.

"I already told him I did." she admitted.

"Do you?" he asked, taking a sip.

"There's not much point not to, is there? What's the point of holding a grudge; it doesn't help anyone, least of all me."

"That's very mature." admired Eddie.

"I'm not 10." answered Hayley.

"Sorry, I didn't mean to sound condescending."

"No, I didn't mean to snap, it's just been a long day." She sighed, taking a sip of the warming alcohol.

"So what now?" asked Eddie, watching her twirl the liquid around in her glass.

"That's the big question." said Hayley, widening her eyes. "I have no idea." She answered before tipping more liquor into her mouth and swirling it around. "That stuff warms your stomach." Hayley observed. Eddie laughed before sipping his own.

"Yeah go steady it's not all it does."

"Oh, yeah?" she asked, raising both her eyebrows before smirking. Eddie looked away; he did not need to be accused of hitting on a copper's missus. "I'm joking, sorry don't look so worried. I'm a one man kind of gal."

"Yeah well don't go making those eyes at other men or you'll be a one man in gaol kind of gal." laughing she emptied her glass.

"He knows I'd never-"

"What the fuck is going on here?!" shouted Jesse.

"Oh, shit." said Hayley, panicking. When Teddy turned in his seat, he was almost face to angry face with Jesse.

"What the hell's going on?" asked Jesse, staring at Eddie.

"Nothing. We were just having a drink." answered Eddie steadily. When Jesse just stood staring at him, Teddy stayed seated, he did not need to be showing any type of aggression at this time, he knew as soon as he did Jesse wouldn't waiver in either punching him or flicking hand cuffs on just for shits and giggles.

"Jesse I was just having a drink, we were chatting." answered Hayley standing up. Jesse didn't take his eyes from Teddy's.

"I'm taking you home." He answered. Deciding it was best to just leave rather than cause a scene, she thanked Teddy for the drink and took Jesse's hand that he held out to her. Half pulled out the bar, he rounded the corner, so they were out of site before dropping her hand and turning on her. "What the fuck was that?"

"I was having a drink." She answered as though it was obvious.

"You're pregnant!" he shouted. When her face dropped, she looked away.

"I'm sorry, I didn't think."

"You didn't think? You didn't think that drinking while pregnant could be a problem?"

"No, of course it is, I just-"

"Forgot?" asked Jesse, nose flaring. When she nodded gently he started walking in circles, running his hand through his hair. "I was worried about you. Mum called to say you had dropped Daniel off, but she hadn't heard from you, said you were due back two hours ago. Then I called and I couldn't get through. So I tracked your phone here. And I find you having a drink with the barman."

"Jesse, I know how this looks, and I'm sorry about the drink, I really am, I just forgot I swear."

"Why are you here?" when she glanced away unable to answer, Jesse quelled his rage to hit out. "I'm going to fucking kill him!" storming off back the way they'd come, Hayley ran after him snagging his arm and pulling him back.

"Jesse I swear, nothing's happened."

"So why are you here?"

"I can't-"

"Fine, we'll see what the barman says." shrugging her fingers off he stormed back round to the bar almost pulling the door off its hinges before stalking over to Eddie who was filling the cabinet behind the bar with citrus slices. "Do you want to explain to me why my pregnant fiancé is in here with you drinking whiskey in the early afternoon, because it seems my fiancé has lost the power of speech?"

Turning round he glanced from Jesse to Hayley who was trailing behind, almost tripping over the entrance step. "Jesse, stop please." said Hayley when she was only a foot away from his back as he leant on the bar.

"I apologise for the drink, I didn't think. But we were just talking." answered Eddie calmly, holding Jesse's gaze.

"Why? What did you have to say that was so important?" When Eddie glanced at Hayley, she was gently shaking her head. "Eyes on me!" shouted Jesse, slamming his hand down on the bar.

"Jesse-"but Jesse held up his hand to stop her, and she bit her bottom lip watching Eddie try to come up with something believable.

"Well?"

"She needed someone to talk to. Someone who's been through PTSD. Someone who understands what it's like to live through." Teddy immediately saw the hurt in Jesse's eyes, before he turned to Hayley for confirmation.

Hayley took a heavy swallow; the look in Jesse's eyes tore her up, not least because she knew how much it was hurting him to think she'd sought solace with another man but that she had lied about her recovery. Not that the truth would be any less painful, but this was too close to the bone not to be real. "Jesse I-"

"Stay away." said Jesse, turning back to Eddie. "Stay away from Hayley or I'll have environmental health breathing down your neck and the Inland Revenue sniffing up your arse, do you hear me?" Eddie nodded watching Hayley look at him with an apologetic look written all over her face. "If you so much as come within 50 meters of her I'll have you arrested quicker than you can pull a pint." Grabbing Hayley's hand he pulled her out the bar and marched to his car, pulling the door open, Hayley stepped in before Jesse slammed the door shut and made his way round to his side. Once behind the wheel Jesse pulled away and emerged onto the main road leading to the dual carriageway to head back home.

"Why?" asked Jesse, almost desperately. "Why did you go to him?"

"I didn't." she answered pathetically.

"Hayley I just saw you in a bar with another man drinking and laughing, and then he tells me you've spoken to him about your PTSD. Something you barely even speak to me about, so again, why him?"

"I don't know. He understood, I suppose."

"But how would you even know unless you'd both spoken about having it?"

"I let it slip the night of the party. He told me then that he had it due to his army days." she answered, feeling more comfortable bearing the truth.

"So you arranged to meet up and didn't think to tell me?"

"No, it wasn't like that."

"Hayley he lives in Lincoln, you didn't just pop to the shops and he invited you back, although I'd be pissed enough with that, you actually made the trip to be there with him." Hayley felt effectively scolded and stared ahead out of the window at the road. "And why the hell are you all dressed up if it wasn't what it looked like?" Looking down at her clothes, she cringed.

"He said if I ever needed to talk, I could pop in. So I did. That was all."

"You arranged for Mum to look after Daniel, you got transport there, you didn't just pop in." Hayley could almost see his carotid artery throb under the pressure it was being put under.

"He didn't know I was coming though."

"Well, that sure makes everything better." answered Jesse sarcastically. "So he just thought his luck was in when you walked through the door looking like that and he started plying you with alcohol, and suddenly his charm made you forget about my baby in your belly."

"He wasn't charming me. I made a mistake. It was my mistake, not his."

"And what mistake is that Hayley?" turning to her she could see the rage in his eyes and it scared her, for the first time his anger towards her scared her and she wasn't sure what to do with it. "Do you want to shag him?"

"What?" she screeched.

"You heard." He answered, knuckles whitening on the steering wheel as he overtook a Vauxhall in the left-hand lane.

"No!" Hayley folded her arms defiantly over her chest, looking out her side window at the family in the car beside them. "I'd never do that, I told you."

"Things change." answered Jesse.

"Not that." she answered stubbornly. "I can't believe you think I'd do that."

"I can't believe I found you in a pub with an ex soldier swigging back whiskey, but it seems we're both in for a surprising day."

"Oh, my god! I'm sorry ok? I'm sorry." When Jesse said nothing else Hayley turned the radio on, but when tainted love played out she quickly turned it back off.

"Why do you do that?" he asked sharply

"What?"

"You turn the radio on and then straight off again." When Hayley didn't answer he looked to her, deciding that she needed to give him something if he was ever going to trust her again she let out a sigh before pulling the visor down to stop the glare of the sun in her eyes.

"He used to play it, repeatedly, after he... you know." Hayley watched Jesse's shoulders suddenly drop before he placed his hand on her knee. "It's just that one song."

"I'm sorry, I didn't realise." why would he she thought, she'd never told him, he was right, she barely opened up and when she did, it was like opening a flood, everything came out at once and he struggled to understand it all, of course at those times it was more about comforting her than gaining information so he probably didn't understand half of what she blubbered. For some reason she had been able to open up to Eddie without the water work and she wondered why?

"Jesse I swear to you nothing's going on between me and Eddie. I'd never do that, and he's been nothing but nice." watching Jesse's jaw twitch, she decided to leave it there.

Pulling up outside Marie's Jesse jumped out, before heading up to Marie's back door. Waiting for him to come back out she pulled her phone from her back pocket, realising her phone was on silent she went to the settings to change it, but before she was finished Jesse pulled her door open, staring at her phone. Feeling guilty, she tucked it away into the back of her jeans. "It was on silent, that's why..." but before Hayley could finish Jesse was buckling Daniel into his car seat behind her. "Hello cheeky, did you have a good time at Grandma's?"

"Grandma!" shouted Daniel excitedly.

"Bye bye sweetheart, see you soon." she waved from the doorstep. When Hayley smiled at her, Marie simply looked away and she wondered what had been said between Marie and Jesse.

CHAPTER 14

That night Hayley bathed Daniel while Jesse washed the pots from dinner, they'd barely spoken since they'd been home. He'd commandeered the bedroom as a makeshift office while he worked from home, and she wondered if he was doing it purely to monitor her. Hayley felt washed out, she'd had confrontations with him running through her head since he'd picked her up and she was exhausted from just playing them out, no matter what she said or how she phrased it, it looked bad. She'd run to another man for comfort and she'd hurt Jesse in doing so, something she'd never have done if it hadn't been for the secret she was keeping. Rob was coming between them once again and Jesse didn't even realise he was there. If she told him he'd blow up and she'd be in the midst of world war three but if she didn't, she would be continuing to lie to him and deceit wasn't something she knew Jesse could handle. Even if he didn't know what it was she was keeping from him, he'd know she was hiding something and now he thought it was an affair with the barman, having been hurt like that before it wasn't going to be easy convincing him otherwise.

Wiping a tear from her cheek, she tried to smile through her sorrow whilst washing Daniel's back with a soapy cloth. Not realising

Jesse was even there, he watched her bathe their son. He'd not seen her that sad in quite a while, not even with everything they'd been through. Feeling guilty for being the person who'd upset her, he knelt down next to her, taking the cloth from her. Looking at him, she wondered what he was doing.

"I'm sorry." Jesse whispered.

"No, you were right." when he snapped his head up to hers, she shook her head. "Not about what was going on, but that I shouldn't have kept it from you." nodding, relieved he took her hand in his.

"I was terrified something had happened to you. The last time I couldn't find you, you were being sold on the dark web."

"I'm sorry, I didn't think." she answered.

"I worry about you constantly; they're always in the back of my head. I only have Alexi's say so that you're safe and to be honest it's hardly reassuring." admitted Jesse, watching her look at him with sorrow in her eyes.

"I didn't mean to worry you."

"I know you don't, but you do. I don't think you realise how much I worry and that hurts. I care about you and I can't bear to think that something has happened to you. When I saw you in that pub, I just lost it. There you were talking to some ex squaddie about things you can barely speak to me about. We're supposed to be a team. You're supposed to be able to speak to me."

"I can't."

"Why?"

"Because you have an opinion on everything, you're emotionally attached and because you just want to make me feel better."

"What's wrong with that?" asked Jesse dumbfounded.

"Nothing, but sometimes I need to talk to someone who's not going to try to gloss over it or tell me everything's going to be ok, because it's not. I'll always have these quirks, these fears, these things I can't explain. They're just part of me and they can't be fixed, but sometimes I just need to vent. My own head drives me insane, it's my own torture device and you just want to fix, but I'm not fixable Jesse."

"You're not broken." Jesse assured her.

"Well, I don't feel whole either." she said desperately.

"I thought that was why you were seeing a counsellor, to discuss these things?"

"I do. But she doesn't answer my questions, she just nods and asks how I feel and do I think there's anything I can do to feel better, yes I can vent but she doesn't tell me what to expect. She doesn't say whether I'll have these feelings for the rest of my life or whether I can get over them. Eddie's been through this, he's been through seeing horrific things and he's done counselling. He's been where I am and when he speaks it makes sense. He can say one sentence and it just resonates, I can't do that. I can't vocalise coherently how I feel, it's garbled and I'm not even sure I make sense anymore, but he made me think that maybe I'm not as messed up as I thought and if he can get through it and come out relatively normal then maybe so can I?"

Hayley watched her words affect Jesse, and while he processed it she bit her lip, wondering how he would take it, she had effectively told him she needed someone else because they understood her better, but that's not how she meant it, she just needed those things to be separate. She wanted to share her life with Jesse, not pull it down by being depressive and the constant drain on their relationship. "Jesse I love you, but I can't share everything with you."

"You can't keep pushing me away either." He answered looking at her. "If we're going to be a team, husband and wife. We need to be able to rely on each other, be honest, and communicate. You can't go running off to some other guy just because you're worried about how I'll take it. That's just part of marriage we have to work with each other not against one another." Hayley nodded solemnly. "I don't mind you talking to your friends, we all need other outlets too, but I don't want you talking to him." Looking back up to his face sharply, she wondered if she'd miss-heard. "I don't trust him."

"Don't trust him or don't trust me?" she asked.

"Hayley I don't like it. I don't like you taking your problems to him, I don't know him but something seems off. I don't trust him."

"And I'm incapable of making that decision, am I?" asked Hayley defensively.

"Hayley I don't want him knowing things about us, and that's final." Feeling suitably chastised she stood, leaving Jesse to sort Daniel out as she walked out the bathroom making her way to the kitchen. Telling her not to do something felt wrong. How dare he forbid her, and who the hell did he think he was? She could talk to whoever she liked; she was going to be controlled by anyone, least of all him.

Once she'd made her coffee, she stood in front of the large window facing the back garden. She didn't even realise Jesse was there until she felt his arms slink around her waist, dropping his chin on her shoulder, she stood, stock-still. She was still mad with him and refused to bend.

"You coming to bed?" he asked, kissing her shoulder.

"No." Jesse stopped kissing and looked at her reflection in the window.

"What's wrong?"

"I'll not be told what to do, Jesse. Neither by you nor anybody else." she stated firmly.

"I've never-" realising what she meant he stopped, removing his hands he walked out the kitchen slamming the door behind him, the next thing she heard was the front door and then his car engine.

CHAPTER 15

JESSE WAITED, HAVING KNOCKED ON THE DOOR HE WASN'T SURE WHAT kind of reception he'd get but he needed to speak with someone. Knocking again, he stood on the doorstep looking around at the front garden and up the street. As the door opened, he saw two weary eyes looking back at him.

"Jesse!" exclaimed the excited boy, bouncing up and down.

"Hi pal, where's your Mum?" leaving the door open the boy ran off down the hallway. Stepping over the threshold, Jesse closed the door behind him before following the boy. Once in the kitchen he was attacked with a plastic sword, shielding his face he grabbed it, whipping it out the boy's hand and turning it on him, when the boy giggled everyone at the table turned round.

"Jesse?"

"I wondered if you had a spare bed for the night, or a settee?" asked Jesse hopefully.

"Always, but what's up with home?" asked Claire, standing up from the dining table. When Jesse looked away, Martin looked to Claire before nodding and curtailing Oliver, his son, around the breakfast island to sit with his mother.

When Martin and Jesse were in his living room with the door

closed Martin watched Jesse pace around looking unsure of himself. Waiting, he took a seat.

"The guy from the bar, Hayley went to speak with him today." admitted Jesse.

"About what?" asked Martin.

"Everything." answered Jesse.

"Why?"

"No idea." Jesse sighed. "Apparently there's stuff she can't talk to me about, but apparently she can to him." Martin stayed quiet, it wasn't too long ago Jesse had told him to keep his nose out. "I don't trust him."

"So what do you want to do?" asked Martin.

"I want to get in touch with Lincolnshire police and tell them to look into him."

"On what grounds?"

"No idea." answered Jesse exasperated. "He's ex-military." Martin nodded; he wasn't sure what he meant by that, but it seemed Jesse had an idea. "Apparently he has PTSD."

"Ok?" Martin said, frowning.

"Who has PTSD and owns a bar with flashing fucking lights and a sound system like that?" asked Jesse.

"I don't know enough about-"

"He's lying, I know he is. He's up to something and I don't like her being around him."

"Have you told Hayley this?" when Jesse looked at him as if he should know better, it suddenly dawned on Martin why Jesse was there.

"So you put your foot down?" asked Martin, already knowing the answer.

"Wouldn't you?"

"What, you think I'd get away with pulling that shit with Claire? You've got to be joking; she'd string me up by my short and curlies." Martin laughed.

"So I'm the bad guy, am I?" asked Jesse defensively.

"I never said that. But how you word things might have something to do with how she's reacted." He said holding his hands out as if to fend off an attack. "Has she kicked you out?"

"No. I left."

"Then take a pew and think about everything before you go back, you want a drink?" asked Martin standing up before making his way to the door. "Coffee, beer?"

"Coffee will be fine." Leaving Jesse, he walked back into the kitchen where Claire was cleaning up. Checking the kettle for water, he flicked it on before resting his back on the countertop. Raising an eyebrow, Claire waited for Martin to tell her what was going on.

"Hayley went back to the bar to speak to the barman from the other night."

"So?" asked Claire.

"She's opened up to him about stuff. Jesse's not very happy."

"Why? I thought he wanted her to start talking?" asked Claire.

"He did, but not to some random." answered Martin, spooning instant coffee into three cups.

"Oh. So he's jealous?" asked Claire.

"Not the way I'd put it."

"Who cares who she speaks with as long as she speaks?" when she looked back at Martin, she read something on his face before forming an o shape with her mouth. "He thinks she's..?" Martin just shrugged. "Well then, he's an idiot, because that girl loves the bones of him, anyone can see that."

"I'll be sure to tell him Mystic Meg." Martin laughed, before kissing her on the cheek and finishing the coffees.

"Well, I'm going up, I'll see you later. Don't be too long." winking, he kissed her again before she retreated to the stairs.

"Hey coffee!" he shouted.

"Bring it up with you." she called back.

When he reached the living room Jesse was sitting on the sofa with his head between his legs propped up by his elbows. Placing the coffee in front of him, Martin took his chair back.

"Thanks." said Jesse, lifting the cup to his lips. "I'm sorry. I shouldn't have dumped this at your door."

"You need to talk to Hayley, you know that right?" asked Martin, before watching Jesse nod forlornly. "Tell her how you feel."

"She knows." snapped Jesse.

"That you don't want her talking to another fella." said Martin sipping his own drink. "Yeah, I can imagine how well that went down."

"He's trouble."

"And you're jealous." answered Martin.

Jesse hung his head, almost growling. "I can't fucking help it. All I can think about are those morons putting her in that auction and the sick fucks making bids to see her hurt." Martin nodded. "Dressed up like a sacrificial lamb, waiting to be degraded in front of thousands of men with hands down their pants." Martin kept quiet, taking another sip as he watched Jesse come apart. "All I can remember is his hands all over her, looking at her like she was his possession."

"Do you really think Hayley would willingly put herself in that kind of environment again?"

"No, but who's saying this guy isn't leading her like a lamb to slaughter?"

"No one." answered Martin.

"Exactly, and Hayley just trusts him. Opens up to him and sits there laughing like…"

"Like what, Jesse?" asked Martin scornfully.

"Like… like…" sighing, Jesse leant back in the sofa staring at the ceiling. "Like we used to." when Jesse looked to his friend he saw him sitting with a smug grin on his face like he'd worked it all out as soon as he'd seen him.

"There's a garage round the corner, flowers aren't too shabby. Click the latch on your way out." Standing up, Jesse listened to him walk back to the kitchen before walking up the stairs holding onto his and hers cup of coffee.

CHAPTER 16

When Jesse stepped back into the house, it was in total darkness. Pushing his key into the lock, he turned it after pushing the door closed behind him. Walking into the dining room, he switched the lights on to find Hayley sat on the sofa in the open plan living room.

"Why are you sitting in the dark?" asked Jesse.

"Where did you go?" asked Hayley, ignoring his question.

"To clear my head." answered Jesse.

"It work?" Jesse just shrugged. Placing his keys on the dining table that separated the living room and kitchen he went to the kettle, filling it with water he placed it back down before grabbing two cups down and adding coffee.

The silence grew thick between them and neither knew what to say to disperse it. The boil of the kettle lent some relief, but it was soon back after Jesse twirled the spoon round in their cups. Carrying them over to the sofa, he placed them on the coffee table before sitting on the settee furthest away from Hayley. Looking at his feet whilst trying to come up with something to break the ice, Hayley scrunched up her dressing gown belt, rolling it up and unrolling it.

Sighing Jesse sat back rubbing his hand through his hair before looking back at her. "I was jealous." Jesse admitted. "When I walked in, you two looked so happy, laughing and chatting, it made my gut hurt."

"I didn't-"

"No." holding his hand up, he stopped her from saying any more. "I seem to get moments with you where we're ok, but they're filled with gaps of desperation. Like I'm only getting parts of you, you feel I should be privy too. I feel like I have to keep earning your trust daily and it's tiring. But I'm ok with that because I understand what you've been through, well I can imagine. But then I saw you with him and there you were. The real you, the happy you, but as soon as you saw me you were guarded again. I just don't understand why I get the guarded version, what am I doing wrong?"

When tears fell down her cheeks, it took all his effort not to wipe them away, but instead he sat still, waiting while she pulled herself back together. "You're not doing anything wrong." she sniffed.

"So why?" asked Jesse desperately.

"I don't want to keep falling apart on you. I don't want to be your project and I don't want you to be my carer. I want you to be my husband, a partnership, but I just feel like all I do is take. Because I need something."

"What?"

"I need to feel worthy." she cried, letting the tears flow.

"What are you talking about?"

"I don't feel worthy of you. I feel like I need you more than you need me. I feel like you'll get bored with me falling apart and walk away and I won't be able to cope, because I'm barely hanging together now." cried Hayley.

"I'd never do that."

"Because you feel responsible, but I don't want you to be with me because you feel responsible for me."

"Hayley I love you. That means I worry about you, I care about you and yes sometimes I feel a little possessive over you. I want you in my life because I can't think of how that would be without you in it. I don't care what happened to you, only that it never happens again, and that if you need to talk about it that you know I'm here."

"But you're not." argued Hayley. "Whenever I mention something your jaw tightens, you clench your fists and you speak through your teeth. I know how hard you find it so don't sit there and lie to me. The only reason I spoke to Eddie was because he didn't judge or have an opinion, he just listened. I didn't have to worry about his reaction."

"I don't like him Hayley, he's hiding something." when Hayley looked away Jesse scowled at her. "What is it?" Hayley wiped her nose and cheeks with a tissue from the box in the middle of the table. "What are you hiding?"

"I'm not-"

"Don't fucking lie!" shouted Jesse, standing up. Hayley watched the vein in his neck pulse and his fists clench, she'd never been scared of Jesse hurting her before now but she jumped up and made her way to the door for a quick exit if she needed it. "What are you hiding Hayley?"

While Hayley tried to control her racing heart and steady her breathing Jesse stepped closer and she felt her joints stiffen and paralyse. Leaning up against the door, she watched Jesse plant his hand on the door next to her head, while leaning into her, effectively barring her from moving. "Tell me or so help me God."

"It's Rob." she squeaked out, panicking. As if she had slapped him, his head rolled back in shock before looking back at her. "He wants me to withdraw my statement." she shivered. Grabbing hold of her shoulders, he enveloped her in his arms, pulling her towards him until she fully broke down. Jesse's blood was raging, rushing through his veins at a ferocious speed, but he needed to kerb his reaction, as he comforted Hayley. She'd been protecting him again by not telling him things; he needed her to break that habit. But right now she needed to know he didn't blame her. Feeling her tremble, he wished he could take it away, holding onto her until she calmed back down again before letting go. He looked down at her glossy eyes and puffy face.

"I need you to tell me everything." nodding, she wrapped her arms around his waist, resting her head on his chest while she tried to compose everything in her head.

Once they had sat back down and held hands Hayley relayed

everything she knew. When she was finished Jesse took her by the neck, pulling her towards him so he could kiss her. As soon as their lips touched things became far more desperate. After shedding each other's clothes, they gave each other what they both craved. Their love.

CHAPTER 17

"Better now?" asked Martin, dropping a take away cup of coffee in front of Jesse on his desk.

"Depends what you mean by better." Martin stood waiting. "We talked when I got back and she told me everything." admitted Jesse.

"Oh shit, that doesn't sound good, what's up?" asked Martin watching his friend struggle.

"Rob's been putting pressure on her to change her statement." he answered.

"Rob?" asked Martin stupidly. "I thought he was in the wind?"

"As far as I knew he was, but this girl Hayley's been hanging around with apparently she's been renting Rob a room, and she knows all about what he did."

"Shit! I did not see that one coming."

"No, me neither. This Eddie bloke from the bar is the girl's brother and apparently he's been trying to get rid of Rob."

"So what he thought he could use Hayley to frighten him off?" asked Martin.

"No, he thought he could put Hayley and Rob in a room to sort out their differences." scoffed Jesse.

"Hope she told him where to go?"

"No, she went." said Jesse flatly.

"What? She met with him?" asked Martin, astonished.

"Yep." Martin grabbed the seat nearest to him, wheeling it over to sit directly across from Jesse as he came to terms with what he'd just been told. "What did he say?"

"Nothing more than we already knew other than he was hooked on drugs, given to him by someone outside the gaol. Seems he was being whispered to, and the plan was to deliver Hayley to Demy, but he snapped and almost killed her."

"What did Hayley say?"

"That she forgave him." answered Jesse. Martin blew out his mouth, exasperated with disbelief.

"She's a better person than me." he admitted.

"Yeah and me." answered Jesse. "She says she feels sorry for him. He lost his fiancé; baby, Mum, Dad and me."

"You know we've never found any evidence to prove Caitlyn was pregnant." reminded Martin.

"I know I told Hayley, but she said that didn't mean he didn't believe it." Martin nodded, that was true enough.

"So I gather we're not just kicking the shit over a latte, what's our move?"

"You're being drafted to be directly under Walker again, he's taking the case. As far as I know they're raiding the bar and going to each of the sibling's houses in search for him then they're bringing him in for questioning."

"What happens to the barman and his sister?" asked Martin.

"No idea, that's up to Walker. I really don't give a shit." He said, shaking his head, exhausted.

"Does Hayley know what's going on?" asked Martin wearily.

"No. But she's not stupid."

"No, she's not." Martin mused. "Which means she's probably already warned them?" When Jesse went into his pocket, he pulled out a mobile, dropping it on the desk. "Is that Hayley's?"

"I must have picked it up by mistake." said Jesse, resisting a wink.

"I'll get Claire to set the bed up for you in the spare room." said Martin woefully.

"You don't have a spare room."

"No, I don't, so make sure you get that back with a descent apology otherwise I'll be kicking one of the kids out of their beds and if I have to give up my sexy time because you think you can get away with that shit, well let's just day, you'll have bigger things to worry about than which divan you sleep in."

Chapter 18

"Edward Masterson." When Eddie looked up an army of police greeted him, the one with stripes on this shoulder held out a piece of paper to him. "We have the authority to search these premises-"

"What for?" asked Eddie, taking the slip of paper, scanning it quickly. "What illegal activity?" When no one answered he watched the one in charge order his troops around the premises, watching as they roughly turned things over in search of whatever they were looking for.

When his cook came running out like her kitchen was on fire, he shrugged his shoulders at her, and then two more employees joined them with equally confused looks. Dragging the low chairs out, they all sat down watching the surrounding chaos.

"What's going on boss?" asked one of the younger men.

"No idea. Just do what you're told." nodding, he watched as the officer behind the bar shifted glasses out of his way to check at the back.

Once the pub had been suitably ransacked the officer in charge waltzed up. "I see you have CCTV." He said pointing to the camera behind him.

"We do." Eddie confirmed.

"I need to see it." glancing at his employees who gave him a faint smile of compassion he hauled himself from the low chair and strode across the drinking area into the back. Opening his office, he could see they had been in there too. Although it hadn't been totalled, it had seen better days. Flicking on the computer and bringing up the feed, he angled the screen so the officer could see it. "How long do you keep footage for?"

"About a week." answered Eddie.

"Can you find me the furthest back and then we'll move up from there?"

"Sure." He answered while scanning the desktop for the correct file, finding it, he flicked it on and stood back while the officer watched it, speeding it up and slowing it down at different times, once he'd done with that days he clicked onto the next. "Can I ask what you're expecting to see?"

"Sure, we have reason to believe you've been harbouring a fugitive." Eddie nodded as though he was thankful for the information, but nothing more. He'd been right; Hayley had cracked under the pressure and given him up. He couldn't really blame her, but that's why he had destroyed all tapes of last month where Rob could have been clearly seen walking around and working in the kitchen. He'd gone through all rotas, shredding them and he'd pre-warned his brothers and sister to make sure all evidence of them knowing him was destroyed just as a precaution. His sister had refused to give up his location saying she didn't know, but he wasn't entirely convinced, he just hoped she'd heeded his warning and got rid of anything liking them. "And you keep nothing longer than this?"

"No, afraid not." He lied.

"Ok well it looks like we may have been misinformed." Eddie nodded calmly as he escorted the officer back out into the bar area. "Sorry to have ruined your day, we'll be out of your hair now." when they had all left, all his staff crowded round him.

"What was that about?" asked the young Chef.

"Did they ask you anything?" asked Eddie.

"They gave us pictures of Rob to look at."

"What did you say?" he asked, kicking himself for not pre-warning them, but a part of him had hoped he was overreacting.

"Just that we didn't recognise him." answered the woman, who would definitely have recognised him as she was the one who had worked beside him for nearly a month. "I'm gathering that was the best thing to say?"

"I'm sorry I should have warned you." he sighed.

"What's this about?" asked the older man.

"It's best you don't know, but if you ever see him round here again, let me know." nodding, they all retreated to work. Taking his phone out of his back pocket he scrolled down his contacts until he was met with Hayley's name, tapping on it he held it to his ear.

"Hello." Eddie looked around him, that wasn't Hayley's voice. "Sorry were you expecting Hayley, she can't come to the phone right now."

"You're a prick do you know that?" when all he heard was a laugh on the other end, he wandered to the glass door to look out over the street. "So she told you?"

"Told me what, Edward?" asked Jesse.

"That she enjoys riding on my hard cock." stated Eddie.

"You piece of shit, if you ever-"

"I'd be careful now, officer. That could be deemed a threat." goaded Eddie. When he heard Jesse take in a deep breath he smiled. "I think we need to speak face to face don't you?"

"Where?" asked Jesse.

"Anywhere except the cop shop."

"Ok, I'll meet you in the castle grounds at 2pm."

"It's a date." answered Eddie before hanging up.

∽

OUTSIDE THE AIR was warm and the people walking in town were happy to be in shorts and T-shirts, licking ice creams or downing cool drinks. Eddie had been sat on the bench for twenty minutes now, just so he could gauge whether anyone had been purposely placed to listen to them, he couldn't see anyone who had, but that didn't mean he shouldn't be careful. Jesse hated him and he clearly didn't trust him, that was a bad combination and sometimes attack was better than defence but he didn't want Hayley to be at the brunt of it and he'd regretted goading him earlier, wondering if Jesse would take it out on her, he didn't look like a man that would but then what did he know?

Seeing him walk towards him, he could see he'd rather be anywhere but here. Good, the feeling was mutual. Taking a seat on the bench, Jesse looked around as if to do the same thing Eddie had earlier.

"So what did you want to talk about?" asked Jesse.

"Well, we could start with you sending the boys in blue round, but I think we both know why you did that, or we could just clear the air so we both understand what's really going on here?"

"Which is?" asked Jesse.

"I'm not trying to move in on your girl." when he saw Jesse compound his back teeth he knew he'd hit the mark. "I can see you're protective of her but I'm not a threat."

"Really?" said Jesse sarcastically, while still looking around the park.

"But Rob is right?" When Jesse looked at him he knew he'd hit the nail on the head once again. "She told me what happened."

"I know." Bit out, Jesse.

"That pisses you off?" Jesse looked away. "Look I get it, well sort of. I've never had a brother try to kill someone I love, but if I had I'd be pretty miffed about it too."

"Good to know." said Jesse.

"For what it's worth, he seems genuinely cut up about it. I mean I can't stand him, but I can't lie and say I don't believe him."

"Great, he's sorry." said Jesse sarcastically as he stood up. "I don't need you to tell me how to deal with my family. If I find him, I'll kill him and nothing you say will change that."

"The thing is, my sister kind of likes him."

"Too bad." answered Jesse.

"I can get you two in a room together." said Eddie standing up to be at the same height as Jesse. "You can deal with it like men, or I can take him to the cop shop, you're choice." when Jesse scanned his face to see what angle he was going for he only saw honesty. "I'm an ex army. If we have beef with each other, we knock the shit out of each other, we don't call cops. If you want time with him, I can give you that, but you keep my family out of it. We didn't ask to be part of this shit fest."

Rubbing the back of his head, Jesse watched Eddie watch him. Eddie had a scar running from his chin down under his t-shirt and another creeping out under the arm to his wrist. Hayley had been right about the IED, he'd clearly been involved in some sort of accident. A white scar lay under his left eyes too. This guy had seen things, and he probably knew how to take him out without notice, something that he'd neither attempted nor looked like he'd even contemplated. "Ok."

CHAPTER 19

Walking into the bar Jesse wasn't sure what to expect, but a slight woman in gym gear and three varying sizes of males with the same genetic code were not it. Leaning on the bar sipping beer, they all watched as he was ushered in before Eddie locked the door behind him. When Jesse glared at him, Eddie just shrugged before making his way over to the bar to complete the Russian doll set.

"So this, his brother?" asked George, flipping his fingers towards Jesse. Eddie grunted before pouring himself a whiskey from behind the bar into a heavy tumbler.

Jesse felt like a spare part as they gazed over him, he wasn't weedy but he certainly wasn't as broad as them and every one of them looked like they'd be at home in any fist fight, even the woman looked built. Wetting his lips he looked from one to the other deciding what to say, but he was relieved when Eddie knocked Freya on the arm. "Go and get your cowboy."

Her eyes shot back to Eddie, and he realised she had no idea about what was about to go down, which made him feel a little more confident. Standing up from the bar stool, she flicked her gaze to Jesse before disappearing into the back.

"So how's this going down?" asked George, turning to Eddie.

"However, the sheriff wants it to."

"You know they ransacked my house today, right?" asked the smaller of the men pointing his finger to Jesse who was clearly unhappy about the situation.

"Cool your guns." said Eddie, stopping his gripe in its tracks. Just then Freya came back into view and Jesse saw Rob closely behind her.

Rob was dressed in too loose jeans with a too large checked shirt opened up to reveal a pale blue t-shirt, his hair was cut shorter and more strict than normal but his face looked washed out. Jesse couldn't remember another time where he had looked so withdrawn. His eyes reminded him of that of a bloodhound. An overwhelming feeling to hug him after so long unnerved him. He wasn't here to welcome him back, and he quickly reminded himself of the way Rob had tried to not only ruin his life but take Hayley away from him. Once Rob was a few meters away from him, Freya leant in kissing him on the cheek before retreating back to the bar with her brothers.

"Jesse." looking at his brother, his stomach turned acidic, and he suddenly wanted to vomit. The brothers watched on, glancing to one another as if to ask what they thought was going to happen. Eddie moved round so that he was only a few steps to the side of Freya, who hadn't taken her eyes from Rob or Jesse since she'd returned, looking ready to pounce, he wanted to be able to take her down swiftly.

Coughing, as though uncomfortable. Rob shuffled awkwardly, glancing from Jesse then back to the window behind him and then his feet. "I want to apologise." when Jesse said nothing, Rob took that as an invitation to carry on. "I'm sorry for what I did to Hayley, and for what I tried to do to you." glancing back to Freya she gave him a reassuring smile. "I'll never be able to make it up to you."

"Damn right you won't." said Jesse.

"But I'd like-"

"I don't give a toss what you'd like!" shouted Jesse, sending Rob a step back. "For all I care you can go and rot in some stinking, junkie squat, where you belong." when Freya moved Eddie slammed his arm against her chest, before shaking his head, trapping her. "You think I buy all that crap about Caitlyn. I don't. She wasn't fucking pregnant and even if she had been, I'd still want to knock you out." when Freya looked to Eddie with watery eyes he squeezed her shoulder. "It's all been a sodding sympathy story, brought about to make you sound like the victim in this. You stood there and lied to me, telling me you and Hayley had been together when all the time she's been keeping you at arm's length on her own, because she was too scared to tell me in case we fell out. Then you rip my heart out like its nothing by crushing her windpipe." When Rob looked away, he tried to blink away the tears that gathered in the corners. "Don't you dare cry!" shouted Jesse. "You don't get that right." When Rob looked back to the floor, one slipped, and he wiped it away quickly. "How could you do that? How could you take Daniel's mum away like that?" asked Jesse in disbelief. "How can you care so little for someone else's life?"

"I wish-"

"You know what I wish? I wish that Dad hadn't died in a pool of his own blood while looking after my son. I wish my son hadn't been traumatised by the barbarians that kidnapped him. I wish I didn't have to watch my girlfriend being paraded on some dark web channel being auctioned off like a piece of sodding meat while sick Neanderthal's sat there typing what depravity they wanted her to be put through first!"

When all the boys at the bar heard what Jesse said they each took a deep breath in and looked at one another as if to confirm what they'd just heard. Freya stood with her hand over her mouth, blinking back tears. "But you know what I wish most of all?" asked Jesse, stalking towards Rob. "I wish you'd been the one on the floor bleeding out, or the one being sold for parts or even the guy that Hayley dug a penknife into, because you're no brother of mine and I don't think you ever were."

"Jesse I-"but before Rob could continue Jesse floored him, punching him straight in the face. Rob's nose exploded while his whole body fell back, landing on his hip on the floor covered in blood while he held his nose. Freya screamed, lunging forward, but Eddie held her back. Suddenly Jesse straddled Rob across the waist, raining fists in his head, sweat and blood spraying everywhere while Rob held his arms up before lowering them and just taking it. When it seemed Jesse had finally worn himself out, he sat back on his heels and looked down at the groaning mess below him.

"I wish you were dead" said Jesse, wiping his own tears on his arm before standing back up. Once it looked like he'd had enough, Freya ran over, kneeling down to Rob to cradle his battered head. Eddie grabbed the whiskey bottle before heading over to Jesse and handing it to him. Taking a huge gulp, he took another before turning back to look at the bloody mess his brother was in. Shaking from adrenalin, Jesse grabbed hold of the nearest chair and collapsed into it as his legs gave way.

"George Will, take him out back and get him cleaned up." nodding they left the bar and crouched down to lift Rob from the floor, each taking an arm they practically dragged him round the back of the bar out of sight as Freya followed crying. Sitting back in the chair next to Jesse, Eddie watched as he tried to pull himself back together. Jesse sat shivering, covered in blood while he stared off into space. Once Jesse seemed to focus on things again and breathing a little steadier Eddie moved the bottle towards him again which he took up greedily.

"Thanks." answered Jesse after a while, although he wasn't sure if it was for the drink or the chance to beat up Rob. Sitting silently as they let thoughts run through their heads, they almost forgot each other were there. Only the sound of passing cars and people outside broke the silence up, Eddie could still hear Freya crying out the back but even that stopped after a while.

"We were drafted out to do cons on an old warehouse. When we got there, we expected some resistance, but we didn't get any. When we made our way in, we were faced with something that no amount of training will ever prepare you for." Jesse looked at him; his eyes were glassed over as though he was back there again staring at the same things he had all those years ago. Eddie took the bottle, filling his own mouth. "We walked in and saw women, girls laid out like some sardonic harem. I've never seen such dead eyes as those of them girls. It didn't take much imagination to see what they'd been put through and even though we tried to help them they couldn't handle it, they thought we were there to hurt them. I've seen men fight for their lives, I've seen children grieve parents but the look in those girls's eyes will haunt me forever, they were broken. Irreparably broken, and it felt like the only humane thing to do would have been to give them what they wanted, they wanted to die. They wanted the pain to end. They pushed their foreheads to our guns and waited, begged us. But none of us were there to kill them and we couldn't. Instead I had to call for assistance and get them out of there, but with the way everything was I often wonder if we saved them or just past them on to some new horror, more torture, more men thinking they somehow had the right to degrade them like that. It's not the men I've killed that keep me awake at night, it's not even the mates I've lost, it's those women, not knowing whether we actually saved them or just moved them on. The women that needed more help than anyone but were herded out just so we could carry on with our job and retrieve the asset. It was then I questioned why I'd joined the army. If I couldn't protect them, or give them refuge, what was the point?" said Eddie despondently before swigging the whiskey again.

"I had to watch them place their bids and send in their requests for hours, because we didn't know where they were. I had to watch her, knowing that if we didn't get there, I'd be seeing her ripped apart for entertainment, raped and tortured. I don't think I could even imagine the things they would have done, but even seeing the equipment in that room made my stomach clench. Every shred of her was going to be torn apart as though she was nothing. As though they had every right to. By the time I got in there she was almost past caring, as though she knew that was how her life would end."

"I can't imagine what seeing someone you love go through that can do to you." said Eddie shaking his head.

"They sent me a text once I got her out of that room, I thought it was Martin but it seems they had taken his phone. They told me Daniel was going up for auction and when I told Hayley she ran into that room with no regard for her own safety."

"What happened?"

"He wasn't there, they'd lied, and they knocked Hayley out. I pulled a gun on him, but I hadn't heard Hayley's sister come up behind me. When I came back round I was stuck in a storage room and they'd set it on fire. I had to prise myself out of there with a piece of metal I found, but Hayley was gone." Taking another sip, he swirled it around his mouth while he looked at his bloody knuckles. "I genuinely thought I was too late but when I ran around the warehouse like a rat out a drain pipe I was taken down by his henchmen. Then they chucked me in the room with her and told us we were taking part in a snuff movie."

"Jesus!" said Eddie, unable to comprehend what he was hearing.

"I thought I'd seen the worst of mankind until that day." stated Jesse. Eddie turned his glass around as if admiring the simple pattern. "I was once on a case where a man was sending us body parts in the post."

"Christ." Eddie sighed in disbelief.

"It's what got me fast tracked, so to speak. He was mutilating women while they were still alive and then drying out their skin to make a type of paper. On that, he'd give us clues to the next victim. But every time we got close she was already missing and the next part was on its way to us. He was always one step ahead, because he already had the victim by the time they sent the clue. We were catching our tails."

"How did you get him?"

"We spoke with psychologists, realised he was following a pattern and then placed a trained officer in an environment we believed he must have frequented."

"Like a honey trap?"

"Yeah, similar. Only he went for the wrong woman." admitted Jesse. "By the time we realised it she was already disfigured." Jesse looked far off, as though remembering every detail. "He knew we were on his tail, so he'd gone to my DCI's home and attacked his 15-year-old daughter. We didn't know at the time, but there were two of them. One would get the girls and the other would do the work, we'd followed the one we had seen on CCTV. But the other had been following us. Not long later she killed herself; she couldn't live with what he'd done to her and my boss resigned. After we realised there were two, the psychology changed, we thought he'd got too cocky, and made a mistake by leaving behind information at the crime scene, it was nothing really but it meant we could trace it. When we did it led to the DCI's wife, she'd been having an affair, and the bloke was the one collecting these women. She of course didn't have a clue, she helped in every way she could but when it came to it, all the information she gave us was false. The bloke had made everything up; there wasn't a single thing that fitted. When their daughter committed suicide, she followed suit not long after. So I've seen what the job can do to a family, and how we put our lives and those we love on the line. But nothing prepared me for finding out my DI was the culprit."

"Holy shit!"

"He was masquerading the whole thing. The bloke he'd gotten to seduce his boss's wife was a confidence trickster he'd come across in an old case, he'd paid him to sleep with his wife and gather evidence that she was having an affair. His daughter had recently been threatening to go to the police, he'd been sleeping with her too, and he'd used the same man to disfigure her, which was why it was different to that of the others. She was too scared to tell us anything, and the man who should have protected her was the one who destroyed her. The DCI's wife clearly couldn't live with what she found out, and no doubt thought he'd get away with it because of his job. The women he killed were nothing to him, just part of some elaborate game to him, so he could feel powerful, and working his own case, he was able to manipulate the investigation. When I started to have my concerns about him, everyone told me I was wrong, I was letting the job get the better of me, I didn't have enough experience. But I knew something wasn't right. I knew I couldn't trust him and I risked everything to find out the truth."

"So you trust no one?"

"No. I trust, just not those that let me down. If they can do it once they can do it again." said Jesse.

"You're not going to forgive him, are you?"

"No. He might not have been solely responsible for everything that happened, but he played his part." Eddie nodded resolutely. "Keep him away from me and my family. If I see him again, he'll not be getting back up." with that Jesse stood, making his way to the door. "I suggest you find a way of separating your family from him too." said Jesse before catching the keys Eddie threw to him. "He's bad news." slotting the key in the lock, he twisted before pulling the door open and leaving.

Eddie slumped forward in his chair, digesting everything that Jesse had told him. Hayley wasn't just the love of his life, she was his salvation.

CHAPTER 20

WHEN JESSE ARRIVED HOME, HE NOTICED HAYLEY WAS IN THE KITCHEN from the front window. Looking down at himself, he contemplated whether or not to allow her to see the mess. He could always say it was someone else's blood, but he didn't want to lie if he didn't have to. Taking his keys from his trouser pocket, he flicked through to find the key for the other door that led straight up the stairs. Finding it, he took a few steps to the left out of view and quietly slotted the key in the lock, turning the handle quietly and stepping inside; he pressed the door shut attentively.

Running upstairs on his toes, he pulled his shirt over his head before pushing it to the bottom of the laundry basket in the bathroom. Turning his hands over, he noticed all the blood from Rob's nose had dried brown. Pushing his trousers down and slipping out of his boxers, he flicked the shower on, knowing the water pressure would change downstairs and if Hayley was washing up, she'd notice instantly. Grabbing the liquid soap dispenser, he quickly stepped in the shower and rubbed his hands together to create a foam before rinsing them and then grabbing the shampoo to coat his hair.

On opening the door, Hayley looked shocked to find him through the glass of the shower door. Folding her arms across her chest, she smirked, admiring him.

"Like what you see?" asked Jesse, cocking his jaw towards her.

"Might do?" she answered coyly.

"Come and join me if you like?" he asked, rubbing himself with shower gel having gotten all the shampoo out of his hair.

"I might just do that." said Hayley, unbuttoning her top. "Daniel's taking a na-"suddenly a cry came from the adjoining room. Rolling her eyes, she looked at Jesse apologetically.

"I'll be quick." He promised, almost pleadingly. Laughing, she shook her head. "Me and that kid need a talk!" scoffed Jesse watching her leave after re buttoning her shirt. Leaning on the shower wall, he thought back to the pummelling he'd given Rob. He didn't feel half as good as he thought he would.

∽

ONCE JESSE WAS BACK down stairs Hayley was building up block towers for Daniel to crash down. Stood watching them until he was finally at peace. He'd seen Rob and dished out what he'd wanted to ever since he'd found Hayley lying on the floor that day at the wedding reception and even if it hadn't given him the satisfaction, he thought it would at least he'd done something. Her captor was dead; her abuser was in prison and unlikely to ever see the outside of a prison. Hayley was recovering and her old self was flourishing. She was bright and happy and now he could definitely recognise the glow of a pregnant woman. His woman, his to love and to take care of and his children to watch grow. Her bump was barely there, but it was visible if you knew to look, and he couldn't help looking. The thought of his child wriggling around in there was what kept a permanent smile on his face. He had everything he'd ever wanted right in front of him and no one would ever take that away from him again.

"What are you smiling about?" asked Hayley, looking up at him.

"Just you." He answered before bending to give her a kiss, reaching up she let him plant his lips on hers. "I need to pop out for an hour. You going to be ok?"

"Of course" answered Hayley. Kissing her again, he ruffled Daniel's hair before leaving.

∼

STANDING outside the office he took a deep breath in before releasing it, tapping on the door as he waited to hear his DCI hail him inside. "I need a word." said Jesse peeking through the door, hoping his boss had 5 minutes to spare.

"Ok, come in." said DCI Walker leaning back in his chair to straighten out his back.

"I've done something really stupid." admitted Jesse, pulling a seat out from the desk.

"Okaaayyy?" said DCI Walker, dragging it out as if he was unsure he wanted to hear this. Watching Jesse sit down, he waited for him to spit out whatever it was he was he wanted to say.

"I found Rob." When the DCI's eyes widened he realised that was one thing he hadn't been expecting him to say. "You know I told you he's been living with some bird, well it seems her family doesn't like having the police trample throughout their property that much and I was allowed access to him."

"So they had him hidden." Jesse nodded, "and you've brought him in?" questioned DCI Walker.

"Not exactly."

"What do you mean not exactly? You either have or you haven't."

"Then I haven't." admitted Jesse.

"What the hell!-Why the hell not?" shouted DCI Walker.

"Because I might have made a promise to keep them out of it for access to him." answered Jesse, knowing full well that was exactly what he'd done.

"So you've seen him? Spoken to him? What's happened?" asked DCI Walker eagerly, scratching the back of his neck after running his hand through his hair.

"He's going to need a couple of days to recover." when the DCI eyeballed him he nodded solemnly, before looking at the door, wishing he could escape whatever was going to be coming next. Watching Jesse, the DCI thought about his own family and what he'd be prepared to do to protect them. Just about anything was the answer, but he had a job to do and he wasn't known for turning a blind eye.

"Jesse, I want you to stop right now. Go home, have a meal with your lovely fiancé and your son, sleep on it and then come back in the morning. In the meantime we didn't have this conversation, and if you still feel as strongly to be honest and righteous then my door will be open tomorrow for you, but right now it's closed." watching in disbelief at the life belt being thrown to him by his boss, he nodded before standing back up. Reaching the door he went to pull it open but DCI Walker made a noise in his throat and Jesse turned back to him. "Can I give you some advice?" nodding Jesse waited. "Think about what you've lost already, what you're likely to lose and whether it's worth it?"

"And if I decide I've lost enough?" asked Jesse. Rather than answer, his boss just shrugged. Believing he had his answer, Jesse left the office and made his way back home before anyone saw him and asked him for anything. He needed to be at home with Hayley and Daniel. Mull over his options and set his conscience to rest.

∽

JESSE AND HAYLEY pulled up outside the house. Glancing to their new baby who sat in the carrier snuggled up in a blue cardigan, wrapped over at the wrists with dungarees that needed turning up at the ankle, he looked tiny, but content while he slept.

"He's beautiful." said Hayley, gently touching one of his clenched fists.

"You going to keep staring at him or should we get him inside?" asked Jesse, laughing at her. They had stayed in the hospital overnight and he wasn't sure that she'd slept a wink, every time he caught her awake she was just staring at their new son as though she was making the most of every second. He couldn't reprimand her. He understood her need to bond. After Daniel had been born in such dire consequences, her bond with him had come late and only after they had done a test to verify his parentage, it had been the only time she had been able to look at him, but it had cost them both dearly. "Come on. I'm sure Daniel will want to see his little brother, and I know Mum does." laughing, Hayley carefully climbed out of the car while Jesse unbuckled the car seat and carried it to the door.

Once inside Hayley walked into the living room and sat down on the sofa, just walking from the car to the sofa had worn her out, the pregnancy hadn't been easy and Daniel had become more difficult; they were sure it was due to the impending birth and the change to his routine but his tantrums had kicked up a gear and as such had run Hayley ragged by trying to pacify him. When Jesse placed the carrier on the floor, he asked her what she wanted to do, but she just shook her head and waved her hand as though to tell him to leave the baby asleep. "Tea or coffee?"

"Can I have a tea?" kissing her on the forehead Jesse walked into the kitchen to fill the kettle, it wasn't long before his phone rang and he was talking on that, leaning back on the sofa Hayley closed her eyes. Walking back into the living room brandishing a cup, he passed it to Hayley before seating himself on the other sofa. "That was Mum; she's on her way over. Apparently Daniel tried taking his clothes off just before they were meant to leave and then decided to hide them around the house."

"Oh god." groaned Hayley, lolling her head back, she had been so looking forward to seeing him, but if he was in one of those moods, she would end up crying.

"He'll be fine." Jesse assured her. "He's probably just playing up because he's missed you?"

"No. He's missed you." Hayley said sternly to him. "I just hope he's good with him?" she said looking down at the sleeping baby.

"He'll be fine." said Jesse reassuringly. "Stop worrying." Jesse smiled.

A few minutes later they heard the door click open and a thunder of tapping feet on the wooden floor. Once the floor swung open Daniel dived forward landing on Hayley full throttle, being shocked she groaned as his knobbly knees hit her in the stomach but when Jesse went to pick him off her, she shook her head and held Daniel closer to her, smelling his hair and feeling loved by his sudden burst of need for her. Jesse watched as tears formed in Hayley's eyes and he hoped she finally saw what he did, that Daniel loved her very much and he'd clearly missed her like crazy. He sat back down, happy to be the observer.

"How was he Mum?" asked Jesse once she'd discarded her coat and followed Daniel into the living room.

"Oh, well." Marie sighed. "Much like you used to be."

"That bad?" Jesse laughed.

"No, not really, he's just full of energy isn't he?" said Marie laughing as she took a seat further up the settee. "Little monkey's like a whippet."

"Drink?"

"Ooh please, if you don't mind. Then I can get my hands on this cheeky cherub." she answered, smiling down at the baby still sleeping in the carrier.

6 Month Later

After Jesse had made yet more drinks and Daniel had gotten bored with having a cuddle from Hayley and climbed into his Dad's lap, they nodded to each other conspiratorially. "Mum, do you want me to get the baby out so you can have that cuddle?"

"Do I?" laughed Marie. "Come on. Pass him over." she urged them, placing her cup on the floor before flicking her fingers as she laid them on her lap. Laughing at her eagerness, he unclipped his new baby son from the carrier and placed him in her arms. Hayley and Jesse watched her coo over their baby while Daniel poked his nose in to see what was going on. "Look Daniel" said Marie "your baby brother." still looking but not really giving anything away about how he felt about his new tiny brother, Jesse cleared his throat of emotion.

"Daniel this is your brother Michael Darren Hallam." as soon as Marie heard his name her head popped up like a Meerkat and then her eyes filled with tears. Shaking from emotions she was trying to suppress, she held Michael closer, kissing his soft light hair.

"Thank you. Thank you so much. He would have loved that." Marie beamed.

"Well, we wanted him to be proud of his name and he's got his granddads and his uncle's who helped save him in some way." When Marie looked up to see Hayley she could see she was full of emotion too.

"Thank you Hayley, he'd be so proud." Hayley smiled whilst she tried not to cry. "I wish I had known Darren, but he'll live on through this little one now. I promise you."

"I hope not." laughed Hayley wiping her eyes. "He was a monster as a kid. He'd undo everything just so he could work out how it worked, but nine times out of ten he'd never be able to figure out how to put it back together again." laughing they all watched Daniel watch in awe as his brother stretched and yawned.

"So now you just need to get ready for the wedding?" asked Marie, eyeing them both seriously.

"It's already booked, we've just to pay for it." answered Jesse.

"I'm not sure about the being ready bit, but we'll be there." said Hayley laughing.

"Are you going to get Michael a suit?"

"He'll be tiny." answered Jesse, scoffing at the suggestion.

"We'll get him a suit Marie, don't panic you can take all the pictures you want." said Hayley, watching Marie smile widely.

"It's going to be a tall order getting ready for a wedding with a baby, are you sure you've not bitten off more than you can chew?" asked Marie concerned suddenly.

"Mum-"

"Marie. Yes, quite frankly, we've taken far too much on." Jesse looked at Hayley, suddenly worried and a little concerned himself that she was going to pull out. "But that's why we need your help and your experience and I'm giving you full rein to do whatever or however much you like."

"Are you sure?" asked Marie, reservedly flicking her eyes to Jesse and back.

"Absolutely. We can tell you what we do and don't like and then you can just crack on." answered Hayley.

"Oh." Marie exclaimed in shock.

"Or not, you don't have to." Hayley assured her, thinking she'd somehow offended her.

"No, I'd love to. I just expect you to ask for my help."

"Well, why not? It's not like I have any parents to ask, is it?" explained Hayley. Although Hayley's father was alive, on paper he was declared dead years ago and he had to stay that way due to his connections in the underworld. He occasionally contacted her through text but the one and only time she'd seen him was when she and Jesse were in a safe house trying to protect themselves from the sect they had taken her to as a child.

"Don't go all Bridezilla on us mother, we just want small and simple." warned Jesse, watching the cogs turn around in his mother's head.

"Oh, don't be silly," said Marie, waving him off. "What colours are you thinking?"

"Well, I'd like cream and pinks." said Hayley, pointing to herself before looking at Jesse. "But we've not really spoken about it."

"It's up to you. As long as you walk down that aisle to me I'll wear a sumo fat suit if required." laughing at his suggestion, she turned back to Marie.

"Not that." said Hayley.

"Ok, we'll do cream and dusky pink." said Marie confirming, Hayley nodded.

"Well, that's settled then, I'll start having a look." Jesse shook his head. Now Marie was on task, there would be no turning back. Not that he wanted to. He couldn't wait to have Hayley be his wife, but he could see his Mum running with this like a professional wedding planner.

"What about your dress?" asked Marie, concerned again.

"I'll get one, don't worry. I'll just wait for my belly to flatten down a bit first and my bum to not resemble the size of a bus."

"Don't leave it too long. You might need work doing to it and the longer you leave it the more difficult it's going to be to get it altered on time." warned Marie.

"Mum." warned Jesse.

"I'm just saying, it's not like picking out a dress for a party."

"I'm sure Hayley realises that." smiling tightly he was glad when his Mum took the hint and closed her mouth.

"Don't panic Marie I've already spoken with Sam from work and she's a seamstress as well as a chef, she's already said she's going to help." nodding but looking less satisfied than before, she dropped the subject.

CHAPTER 21

Martin walked through the gate of the old stone walled church. Being back here was eerie. The last time he'd walked through the doors of the church it was to a nervous vicar who was trying to hide the true identity of the church. Whilst materials had been taken away to be tested, and they had found blood droplets and other bodily fluids, tying people to the building had been a lot more difficult and finding witnesses willing to speak out had been near impossible. Now, a new vicar had taken over and Martin only hoped he had more genuine approach than his predecessor.

"Ah, you must be DS Wells?" said a man in jeans and a brown cable knit jumper. Looking to the man's out-stretched hand, he shook it before smiling. "They told me to expect you."

"Please call me Martin. I hear you've found something we might be interested in?"

"That I have." said the man showing Martin his way to the back of the church. "I was tidying out the old offices and while I did, I must have knocked an old lever for the bookcase, once I found it again I was able to reopen it, as it's on a timer I assume. Once I was able to look inside, I pulled out an old chest and well. You'll see what I mean." Opening the door the vicar led Martin through the office and pulled a lever under the table, when the bookcase crept away from the wall Martin realised what the vicar was talking about, it opened for no longer than five seconds before it slowly closed again.

"I'm surprised our officers missed the lever." said Martin.

"It had been tucked away, when I was under the table my jumper snagged on something and the hidden plate fell away. Now I can just access the lever without removing the plate first. Martin nodded, that made more sense. "This is what was inside." said the vicar lifting an old chest onto the table between them. Once he pushed in the key he had on his belt, he clicked and then opened it all the way up.

"Where did you get the key?" asked Martin

"It was handed to me with all the others, I just tried my luck and it paid off thankfully."

Taking a step closer, Martin peered in the chest. Old documents, tinged brown and yellow, filled the chest. Not wanting to contaminate them, he reached into his pocket to pull out a pair of vinyl gloves. "Have you touched them?" asked Martin.

"I only took out the big file, as soon as I saw what was in it, I replaced it." answered the vicar. Looking at the extensive file the vicar pointed to, he pulled that out first, laying it on the desk. If it was already contaminated it was better to look at that one and just take care not to destroy any more potential evidence. Opening it, he instantly saw what had made the vicar so quick to call. In front of him laid a black-and-white picture of a young girl tied to the altar, naked and bound with rope around the ankles and wrists. She looked terrified as a hot branding iron was being held above her. "Pretty intense isn't it?" Martin nodded as he moved that away face down on the opposite side of the folder and stared at the next picture. A young baby, clearly screaming at the top of its lungs while someone held a knife above it. Moving that one, he was faced with even more forms of torture and murder.

Making his way through them all, the vicar had turned away, taking a seat. They were clearly too much for him to stand as he watched Martin flick his gaze over them without showing much emotion. "I don't know how you do it?"

Looking at the vicar, he waited for him to continue. "Look at those and not flinch?"

"I hate to say it, but you get desensitised."

"You must." nodded the vicar solemnly. Martin went back to the photo's and flicked through them a little quicker, he'd call the forensic team to come and take them back with him, it was clear the vicar was having a hard time seeing them. Getting to the last one he saw a colour photograph of a young girl.

The girl was dressed in a summer dress with a braid in her hair, laughing at someone out of shot while she held a dandelion. Something about her looked familiar, but he couldn't place what or where he may have come across her. This photo was completely different to the others. It wasn't taken in the church but in a field and she looked wonderfully happy, whereas the others had all been full of pain and anguish. "Do you know that girl?" asked Martin, picking up the photograph and showing the vicar.

"No. Can't say I do, but then I've not been here long. Should I ask around?"

"No, not yet. But thanks." answered Martin. "I might take you up on that."

"It doesn't look like it belongs there, does it?" said the vicar.

"It's certainly very different."

"I know this church has been used for Satan's work but I'm hoping that now I am in charge I can bring it back to how it should have been used. I hope you'll ask should you need anything. I'll be more than happy to help." smiling, Martin nodded before putting the file back in the chest. Taking his phone out, he called through to the office and asked for assistance with removing the box so they could go through it in a more appropriate and sterile environment.

Once the lab technicians turned up, they carefully wrapped the chest with its contents and placed it in their van to take back with them, after firstly photographing its contents and the secret cupboard they had retrieved it from.

BACK IN THE lab they lay each individual piece out on to the plastic and gloved technicians went through every piece with tweezers and brushes. Under a microscope they identified new areas to test and imprints to cross-examination. The job was painstakingly difficult and every minute detail was being shown great care as they catalogued it. Martin wasn't sure if the evidence they had would just strengthen the case already being prepared for court or if it would bring about new lines of enquiry, new culprits, new people of interest, but there was no getting away from how important the find was and how it could cement convictions.

After everything that had happened he wanted the case to be watertight and if this new piece of evidence yielded any results, he would be more than pleased to skip his lunch break at his desk. The lengths of depravity some people would go to, would never cease to amaze him, but the vicar had been right, the more he saw the less shocked he was by it and he wasn't sure that was such a good place to be.

"What have we got?" asked DCI Walker coming into the room to stand next to Martin, as he observed the documents splayed out on the table.

"Everything. There's a log book, dates, initials, amounts, comments, pictures that range from the sixties to present day, certificates such as births, marriages and deaths. There's paperwork and documents detailing a dedicated and brutal organisation of torture and murder for monetary gains."

"Something we already know, but it's nice to have backup." commented DCI Walker. Martin nodded.

"It's going to take an age to get through, there's just so much of it, but at least it corroborates what we already know."

"Have you seen anything of interest, apart from the obvious?" asked DCI Walker, scanning the paperwork further up the table.

"There's a girl." answered Martin, walking back to the other table near the door. Pointing to it, DCI Walker moved to be next to him again. "It's just one single picture, but it's not like any of the others.

She's clearly outside, it's recent and she looks happy, like it's just a family snap."

"Yeah, so why would it be with the others?" asked DCI Walker, scratching his chin thoughtfully.

"That's what bothers me." said Martin. "She must be important, but I don't understand why?"

"So we need to find out who she is?" Both looking at one another to agree that they were both on the same path, they looked back at the photograph. "Why do I get the impression I'm not going to like this?"

CHAPTER 22

"Freya!" Looking up from the table, she saw Hayley approaching. Feeling suddenly on edge, she smiled tightly, hoping she was coming across as friendly. "How are you?"

"Good." answered Freya wondering what Hayley wanted; they hadn't really spoken outside the gym since Hayley had walked into her house to see Rob. "I hear you're doing really well in class." when Hayley looked confused Freya waved her to sit down. "I help out at your gym sometimes, they're sister companies, I saw your name on the list and asked Scott. Sorry, but he said you were doing well."

"Yeah, well, I was until I had to leave." answered Hayley taking the seat across from her.

"Oh, my god! You've had the baby!" shrieked Freya, suddenly realising. Laughing, Hayley nodded. "Where is he?" she asked looking around them hoping she'd just missed him being put down.

"He's with grandma, this is my two hour weekly break." laughed Hayley. "It's the only thing that keeps me sane." She answered, rolling her eyes before sipping her steaming hot coffee.

"Does she have Dan too?" The shortening of his name made Hayley bristle. Thinking only of Rob, Hayley looked away before she made a fool of herself, then nodded.

After a few minutes of awkward silence where they either looked at one another like they wanted to speak or looked around the room for a distraction they both tried to break the ice at the same time and then laughed when they both apologised at the same time too. "Go ahead."

"I was just going to ask if you were doing ok?" asked Hayley.

"Yeah, I'm good. But that's not really what you wanted to know, is it?" asked Freya. Smiling shyly at Freya's bluntness, she took another sip of her coffee while she chose what to say.

"How is he?"

"Wow, that's not what I was expecting either." said Freya

"What were you expecting?" asked Hayley. "Me to jump down your throat?"

"I was expecting you to rip me a new one to be honest. I lied to you."

"Yeah you did, but I kind of understand why you would." answered Hayley taking another sip of coffee. "I don't know what he's told you-"started Hayley.

"Everything." answered Freya.

"Okay." said Hayley, feeling a lot more uncomfortable, his perspective would no doubt be incredibly different to hers. "I never meant to cause any trouble. I wish I'd never-"

"Hayley he told me. He's not proud of it, the way he acted, what he did and I struggle to see that man he describes to me, because to me he's nothing but thoughtful and loving and kind. But I'm not naïve, I know he's done some horrific things, and you showed great charity in retracting your statement. You didn't have to do that." Hayley nodded before taking a sip again to coat her dry throat.

"I think Jesse misses him." said Hayley, looking directly at Freya. "He seems to have the whole world on his shoulders, and I'm sure this thing with his brother is causing him stress."

"Jesse knows where to find him if he wants to speak." advised Freya. "He wasn't slow in coming forward last time, and he left nothing to the imagination. I really don't want Rob to see Jesse until I know he can keep his hands to himself." When Hayley looked back up at her confused, it suddenly dawned on Freya that she didn't know what had happened between the two brothers all those months ago. Realising she had said too much she filled her mouth with coffee whilst Hayley looked at her for an explanation.

"What do you mean?" asked Hayley. "When did Jesse see Rob?"

"I thought you knew." said Freya finally. "I didn't say it to bring it all up again."

"Freya, when did Jesse see Rob and what happened?"

"Not long after the party Jesse walked back into the bar with Eddie and called Rob out. Jesse beat the crap out of him." admitted Freya awkwardly.

"I can't believe he didn't tell me." said Hayley dazed.

"Yeah well maybe he didn't want you to know he acted like a bloody animal." when Hayley looked back to her for confirmation of what she meant Freya looked around to make sure they weren't being overheard first. "He beat the shit out of him, Hayley. He refused to go to hospital because the police would have found him, but he should have been heavily medicated. He was in agony. It looked like he'd been mowed over by a bus. Jesse beat him until he fell unconscious." Hayley couldn't believe it; she'd never seen Jesse raise a hand, ever. "They were both covered in blood; you must have seen his shirt?"

When Hayley thought back she remembered seeing a bloody shirt and when she'd asked Jesse about it, he'd said some drunk had gotten handy and made his nose bleed, and because the guy had been in a fight already he'd transferred most of his own blood onto him when they'd wrestled him to the ground. She'd accepted it. She knew how dangerous his job could be and he'd not looked alarmed to tell her, more apologetic about that fact that she'd probably not be able to get it out.

~

MARTIN HAD BEEN INFORMED about everything that had been found within the chest and while it helped tie up a lot of loose ends and corroborated a lot of what they knew already, adding weight to their investigation, and the mystery of the girl still needed unlocking. It seemed to stick out like a sore thumb and wouldn't let him rest. She must be important or she wouldn't have been locked in that chest, thought Martin. But with no name it was impossible to find out who she was, they'd been through all the databases concerning lost children and nothing had confirmed her identity. He only hoped she was safe.

Information had confirmed the involvement of the church parishioners and all their illegal deeds, the photos had confirmed the means in which they instilled fear and held others accountable using them as blackmail. More arrests had come from it and they had uncovered more secrets, including all the missing children who Hayley had helped to disappear over the years. It seemed she hadn't gotten away with as much as she had thought though and when push had come to shove the people who knew of her exploits had used them to strike fear in her heart and make her run. Everyone had assumed she'd run to rid herself of the life Demy had forced her into, but with more information coming forward, the more Martin realised she'd had bigger problems than a heavy fist meeting her jaw. She'd been found out, and someone had wanted to make her pay. He just couldn't work out who or what they had threatened her with. It must have been something strong if she was able to endure the life she had been thrust into but ran at the fear of having her secret exposed. He'd have to speak with her, but he couldn't tell Jesse, not yet. There was a distinct possibility that she was still holding out on him too. The last thing they needed was any more interruptions, especially as they seemed to be finally getting it together.

~

KNOCKING ON THE DOOR, he waited patiently. On opening it, Hayley smiled, seemingly happy to see him. Noting the icing sugar swiped across her cheek, he smirked. "Making the cake by any chance?"

"How did you guess?" asked Hayley, opening the door wider to let him in. Martin just laughed at her until he walked in to the kitchen and saw the cake she'd been constructing.

"Wow."

"You like?"

"Impressive." He admired the piping going around the top and base of the cake with icing that resembled curtains wrapping itself around the sides. She had partially constructed flowers sitting on the table, looking as though they were waiting to be painted and finalised. "You sure it's not bad luck or something to make your own cake?"

"Ha!" laughed Hayley, taking a seat at the dining table. "I think even we deserve a break." Taking a seat across from her, he watched her pick up a rose and start to press the petals between her fingers and thumb. "So what's up? I doubt you came here to learn how to ice a cake." asked Hayley, flicking her gaze up to him. Seeing him look far more serious that she'd expected she dropped her hand and waited.

"I went back to that church a while ago." Hayley's face drained itself of blood and she suddenly felt very light-headed. "There was a chest. They had hidden it in the church and the new vicar found it, he reported it to me and the team have been going through it." Hayley couldn't speak so she just waited, feeling suddenly very sick. "There's a picture of a girl. We don't know who she is, but it's recent and we're concerned for her safety." watching Hayley, she just nodded. "Hayley we've found evidence to suggest you helped get children out of the cult." sweating, Hayley felt like she was under the microscope again. "It seems someone knew what you were doing, and they kept a log. Every child who ended up dead last year is on that list, but that girl doesn't seem to be there. We have checked the other children on the list on over the last few weeks and none of them are alive, or at least not with their given name, which makes finding this girl very important."

"They were killed?"

"We're not sure, but their investigations are being reopened because of this find. Some were in accidents or caught in crossfire or they've simply disappeared. They're all over the country so no one made a link between them until now, now that this list has come out it makes all those cases rather unlikely doesn't it." Hayley nodded.

"Am I under arrest?" asked Hayley.

"Should you be?" Hayley just stared at him, she wasn't sure. "Did you kill anyone?"

"No. Only Demy."

"That was self defence." argued Martin. "How did you get the kids out?"

"It was different each time."

"Ok, give me some examples."

"Sometimes the woman would come to me and ask to get the baby away, so I'd organise for someone to drop the baby at a hospital. Other times I told them to contact family and say they couldn't cope and then abandon all contact, others would ask me to leave them somewhere they would be found like a train station or a post office or something."

"But how did anyone else know you were doing this?"

"Because I'd rely on other people's help. I couldn't possibly have done it alone. My absence would have had my cards marked."

"So you had to let someone in on your plan?"

"Yeah, it was a security guy, his name was Liam, but he'd let me out and then cover for me."

"Why?"

"Because he saw what we all had to go through?"

"But why go against them? He would surely have been killed if they found out he was helping you do that?" asked Martin.

"No, when they found out they killed his wife."

"When?"

"When they found out he'd helped women get rid of their babies, I don't know the exact date."

"And he didn't betray you?" shrugging, she looked away. "Hayley what aren't you telling me?"

"They beat the shit out of her and then made him watch, made all of us watch to put the fear of god in us."

"And he still didn't rat you out?" shaking her head, she bit her bottom lip.

"They had children. I got them away. I promised him if we were ever caught I'd take care of his family. But I was too late for Alice. I was in the house when they took her. I hid the children in the attic and then led the men out with her; there was nothing else I could do. I went back for the kids later and I got them to a man who owed me a favour. He took them."

"Who's he?"

"His name was Charlie Brent. He was a farmer; he took the cattle to the abattoir and hid the children in the lorry."

"Why? Why would he risk detection?" Looking away, she covered her mouth with her hand as if to stop anything from leaking out. "Hayley it's really important, someone knew about you helping those women, someone kept a tally, and then years later they've gone down it and used it as a target list. We need to know who knew, so we can find out who killed them and why?"

"You know all this; they did it to stop the reign of blood. Anyone within the Sect could campaign for leadership, but only if all the bloodlines above them were eradicated." she answered, ignoring his earlier question. Charlie had helped her because she'd found him trying to undercut Demy, he'd begged for forgiveness but instead she'd struck up a deal, he'd help her when she needed it and his secret would be safe.

"So for that many deaths, it had to be someone fairly low?" asked Martin, trying to understand.

"Or on the same level, yeah."

"So who could that have been Hayley? You know who you helped."

"I helped all those that asked." she shrugged.

"All?" asked Martin, astonished. "Weren't you fearful of being found out, someone using you to confirm their suspicions?"

"They didn't know who they were dealing with."

"I'm lost." said Martin, shaking his head as if to rid himself of fog descending on his brain.

"They went through Liam, he then came to me. I helped get them away but the only person they saw was him well unless I had to see them."

"I'm still lost. Why would Liam risk everything to help you help others?"

"He was Frank's illegitimate son." answered Hayley. "He was raised as a soldier but he was treated badly, I took care of him after one particularly bad beating and we got close."

"So he would be our first suspect in trying to eradicate anyone above him?" explained Martin. "Get his own back; take their place at the table."

"No not really, he was illegitimate. They were the lowest, which was why he was a soldier. If you were female, you were one of their whores if you were male you did their fighting for them. Union between families had to be validated, and the only way to do that was by being married in their church with witnesses, and a signed declaration by the parents that they supported the union. It also meant the men could do whatever they wanted, but they ostracised any woman who happened to fall pregnant. Their baby would mean nothing and the women would be set to work, they were no longer upstanding, so they were no longer cared about."

"Set to work?" asked Martin.

"In the private clubs." answered Hayley despondently. "Any woman who lay with another man and found themselves pregnant because of it were publically shamed, humiliated but sometimes the women had had no choice in the matter."

"So if anyone wanted to take someone out of the running all they had to do was impregnate one of the women who were being raised for baring another founding member's kid?" said Martin piecing it together. "If they took out the competition and held on to the one pure woman, then they'd be effectively placing themselves at the top."

"Yep, that's pretty much the long and short of it. That was why I was kept under house arrest until I was pregnant. So no one else got the opportunity."

"Only you weren't under house arrest if you were helping these women?"

"No, Liam was my guard." Martin looked around himself and noticed the picture of Daniel smiling a toothy grin at whoever had taken the picture. "So someone knew what you and Liam were doing, kept a log and then seemed to do nothing with it until these last few years, why now?" when Hayley opened her mouth to answer he continued. "And how did these women hide their pregnancies?"

"They didn't always, sometimes they weren't very visible, especially under the old-fashioned dresses we had to wear. Other times their husbands sent them away knowing full well what had happened but without wanting to lose their own privileged places they'd hide the women away before they gave birth then act as though nothing happened. That was when I had to rely on Darren to get them picked up as soon as they gave birth. Those kids were normally placed in children's homes, as we had more time to organise things. Some women went to Liam only after they'd given birth, they'd probably hoped the baby was their husbands and then decided that the baby definitely wasn't or they could take the risk when they'd have to be tested. They tested all babies at birth." As she said it, she thought back to what Alexi had said to her, that he'd thought she was Franks and as such he'd beaten her mother in a rage and her mother had ran with her to protect her. Something suddenly didn't feel right. Why would he have thought that? All babies were tested it was part of the celebrations that took place within the church, so she'd have been tested too, if that was the case Alexi would have known right from the start and it wouldn't have mattered what Frank had said, the blood test would have been proof enough and she'd have been brought up knowing her role instead of being thrust into it when her mother died.

"What is it?" asked Martin, concerned.

"Nothing." waved off Hayley. When he watched her intently it was clear, he didn't believe a word she said. "The sect was all about keeping up appearances; the families in power had to be spotless, beyond recrimination. The women had to be whatever their husbands wanted, but if they stepped out of line, the whole family would come into question, which was dangerous for the kids too."

"So did these men ever protect their wives?"

"Rarely, some used them as bargaining chips. As soon as they had their first child cementing their legacy they were up for the group's consumption. Some men shared them round like sweets, often to bargain deals or smooth past miss-demeanours, sometimes just because they wanted to swap, others sold their wives to make money. You've got to understand the women in the sect were only there to do one thing and that was to bare children. As far as anything else went it was up to their husbands and the women had to go along with it."

"Which they did?" said Martin thoughtfully. "But what happened if they kicked up a fuss?" Hayley looked at him as though he already knew the answer to that. "The brand?" Hayley nodded.

"How many other women did you see get that?" asked Martin.

"None. I'm not sure the women ever did, I think it was only the council members who were allowed to watch, and they were all men obviously."

"But if it was meant to be a deterrent?" asked Martin.

"Yeah I know, you'd think they'd want as many people watching as possible wouldn't you, but then maybe Demy was embarrassed by my behaviour." shrugged Hayley. "I mean it was because I didn't want to marry him. That must have been hard to swallow in front of his peers."

"Yeah, I can imagine it was." nodded Martin. Men like Demy wouldn't have taken kindly to being ridiculed. "Hayley Baxter mentioned to Jesse before he died that they had paid him money for you."

"It's more than possible." admitted Hayley. "He'd racked up enormous gambling debts; it wouldn't surprise me in the least if he used me to get out of paying, or maybe even gambled me away."

"Jesus." sighed Martin. "No wonder you ran." Hayley tried to smile but instead looked away, she'd told no one about that night or the ones leading up to it and she didn't want to talk about it now either. "It still doesn't answer the question of who or why someone kept a log." said Martin, eyeing her.

"I don't know. I certainly don't know why it would be kept at the church, that indicates they would have known about it, and if they did, why didn't they stop it?" asked Hayley.

"Usually people don't stop things if it benefits them." answered Martin.

"So you think someone knew about the missing children at the time, let me do it, kept a log and then wanted to use it to blackmail me?" she asked.

"It would make sense to have something on the woman who was supposed to conceive the most important playing piece on the board." Hayley sat back, casting her mind back to the time when she had been heavily involved in the women's life who belonged to the church, Martin was right they had trusted her and she couldn't really remember doing anything to encourage that. The first person who had asked her for help had begged her not to say anything and if she refused to help to just forget she'd ever said anything, but she'd listened and her story was as dark as the ones that followed. She'd felt great empathy for the women and once she'd taken charge of watching the men and detailing their every movement she'd grown in confidence with finding an escape route, then she'd just had to make sure there was someone on the outside who could pick the children up and that's where Darren had come in, being male he was allowed anywhere he liked without an entourage and he'd been the one to find safe homes and have collections made when they'd gotten them away. She had never asked for details on that, he could follow through without being caught, she didn't want to be the reason for him losing his life but it seemed him being so young was mistaken by those around him as being naïve. Darren had never been naïve, he was incredibly switched on. He knew things only Hayley could dream of but he was also quiet, he watched everything and everyone to the point people would forget he was around. She was sure that was what kept him above suspicion, age and silence.

Darren had lost his father to drink just as Hayley had, but rather than sit and get depressed about it he'd thrown his head into books and computers, she wasn't sure where his first computer had come from but the battered old thing had turned up one day looking as though it deserved to be in a skip and a few weeks later it was taking up much of his bedroom with contraptions Hayley had no idea about. When she'd questioned what he was doing he'd just replied that he was messing about but it was clear to her even then it was much more than that.

She hadn't been surprised when a few years later Frank and Demy had taken him under their wing and had him working for them; she knew whatever it was, was illegal, but she had just hoped Darren was smart enough to cover his tracks. While he sat quietly tapping away Demy and Frank had rubbed their hands with glee, and a shiver had descended on her spine. Darren never divulged to her what they had him doing and after he told her it was better, she didn't know she never asked again. Not long after her marriage to Demy, they sent Darren to London, and she rarely saw him after that, but he always kept up his deal to help her extricate unwanted children. Thinking back now he must have relied on others to keep up his part of the deal there's no way he could be in two places at once but she had no idea who he'd asked for help, but why would they have kept a log, that seemed like a dangerous thing to do.

"But I was never threatened with exposure, no one ever came to me with that." explained Hayley.

"None of this makes sense. If the children meant nothing, I understand the women getting rid now, to help their families but why would someone go after the children if they weren't a threat? And why would they keep a log of it?" looking away Martin knew she was hiding something, but it was like getting blood out of a stone. "Hayley, please explain to me why someone would watch you and keeping a log."

There was only one reason someone was keeping tabs on her and that was because they didn't trust her. The thought made her shiver, had someone known all along what she was planning to do. Had she been set up? "Maybe they wanted to keep track of them in case one of them was the real McCoy. If a baby was sent away possessing the blood of a founding mother *and* father, then that child would be very important."

"So you're saying they killed the others just to ensure no nasty surprises came back and bit them on the arse?" asked Martin. "That's a lot of effort to try to cover something up."

"Exactly." Hayley nodded, hoping he'd leave it there. Her stomach and head were whirling with all the possibilities she'd missed.

"So they were looking for a particular child?" shrugging, Hayley bit on her bottom lip again. "So the picture we have of the girl who could she be?" Hayley shrugged, but Martin wasn't convinced. Unable to probe more, he heard the front door swing open and Jesse walked in a few seconds later carrying shopping bags.

"Mart?" Placing the bags down on the kitchen floor, he started to empty them onto the counter worktop. "What are you doing here?"

"Thought I'd pop in, see if you were getting on all right with the wedding stuff."

"Really?" asked Jesse, unconvinced. "Well, if you're thinking of wrangling out of your best man speech forget it, you're committed now."

"As if! I can't wait to tell Hayley some stories I know about you." laughed Martin. "In fact, it's a good job, the ceremony is after the vows or she might change her mind." winked Martin towards Hayley.

"As long as they're clean my mum's going to be there remember." warned Jesse jokingly.

"I'm making no promises."

"Coffee?"

"No thanks, I'll leave you to it, I need to get back, anyway." nodding, Jesse carried on unpacking while Hayley followed Martin to the door. Once they were at the front door Martin turned to her. "I need to know why a girl's photo is in amongst all that other stuff." Hayley opened the door.

"If you can find her, then so can they." answered Hayley.

"What happens if they find her first?" shrugging she looked down to the hall where the kitchen was and Jesse was busy with shopping.

"Then I'll know a promise wasn't kept." she answered.

"What's that supposed to mean?" Martin hushed, wary that Jesse could hear.

"Martin you need to leave it. Take what you need from that chest to conclude your investigation but don't open anymore." Stepping back Martin surveyed her face to try to gauge what she was talking about but she was giving nothing away and he was even more confused than when he'd entered. "Let it go, Martin." she begged. When he made no attempt to move, she looked back down the hallway again before looking back at him. "The girl's safe while no one is looking for her, whoever kept that chest and wrote them logs are probably already dead or inside." when Martin continued to stare at her as though she'd just landed, she drew up closer to him and whispered in his ear. "If you start this crusade to find her, you might not like what you find."

"Hayley you're scaring me." whispered back Martin. "What's going on? And does he know?" he asked, thumbing towards the kitchen.

"He knows what he needs to, to remain safe." Blowing an exasperated breath from his mouth, he looked from her to the door back to the entrance to the kitchen. "I know what you're thinking, but you don't know what you're dealing with."

"That's what scares me. I thought I knew you and now I'm not so sure."

"No one ever really knows anyone Martin." answered Hayley. Watching Hayley walk away from him, he opened the door to exit the house and clicked the door shut behind him. His head felt foggy. What on earth was going on? What was she hiding?

∽

JESSE GLANCED at the wedding cake she was lovingly pulling together and his gut twisted, with the wedding round the corner Jesse was getting nervous, he'd been married before and that had all broken up in a matter of a couple of years, they'd never had to endure what him and Hayley had but who was to say that they could be successful in marriage. They still had their ups and downs, still had arguments that seemed to go nowhere, they certainly didn't seem to come to a resolution most of the time. Hayley was still living with nightmares and even though Daniel had settled down now they had a baby to contend with, and he wasn't sleeping through, in fact he was disturbing their sleep more than Daniel had.

They'd booked everything they needed, which wasn't much, neither of them wanted a huge party and they certainly didn't have that many people they wished to invite. With no family on Hayley's side and only the intention of inviting his mum, they had a handful of friends they wished to attend. Having looked at a stately home in which to have their wedding, so they didn't have to attend a church, the only thing Hayley was adamant about they had temporarily held it when a letter came through a few days later thanking them for their payment and confirming their booking for the orangery, the gardens, the dining room and the honeymoon suite along with five rooms for guests with the potential for more. When they thought a mistake had been made they called the function only to find out a man had paid in full saying he was a friend of the bride. They had known instantly that that friend had been her father. After much deliberation they had decided to keep the reservation and let him pay for it, from Jesse's perspective she was due a lot more than that from the man who should have protected her, but Hayley didn't want to be held in debt, something they decided wasn't how her father intended it, it was a peace offering, compensation, a present to his daughter who he'd been unable to be present for.

Having gone for another look around, they had taken pictures for Marie who had given herself the job of flower arranging. Hayley was doing the wedding cake to keep costs down and also to keep her sane, as she said. She needed something to do that wasn't revolving around nappy changes, breast feeding and cleaning. Jesse and Martin had been to the bridal shop to hire suits as they had no intention of buying some just for one day and the bridal shop had offered them a deal as Hayley's dress was coming from the same place. While Sam Hayley's friend had said she would help out with her dress once Hayley had walked past the bridal shop the dress had caught her eye and her heart and there was no going back. Jesse didn't care how much it cost as long as that was what would make her happy, it would be her first proper wedding but there was no getting away from the fear of the makeshift wedding she had been put through as a teenager in order to keep her under their control.

She had walked in on her own and tried it on. Once she had told him, he felt totally deflated for her. He knew most women fantasised about the day they would get married, dressed in the gown of their dreams with friends and a mother who they could share the excitement with. She had no one. But the thought hadn't seemed to have caused her much concern as she'd practically bounced into the house excitedly telling him that she really liked a dress and would she be able to stretch the budget to include it, how could he have said no to that? So there she was making the cake and preparing card placements and doing anything for the wedding that she could to bring down the cost. Sam had agreed to make the boy's suits, so that was one less job.

CHAPTER 23

THE WEDDING

Hayley looked into the full-length mirror. Her white lace dress stood a few inches off the floor revealing her white strappy heels, the neckline was wide but tasteful and she loved how Freya had designed her hair. Admiring her reflection she smiled today was the first day of the rest of her life and she was going to enjoy every second of it.

Taking lessons with Freya had helped tone her body up after having Michael and she loved the strength in her arms, it made her feel strong and the feeling was a welcome one. After they had gotten over their initial awkwardness Freya had gotten in touch to apologise again and offer her an opportunity to learn some martial arts, something she'd always wanted to do. Not wanting to lose any more friends she'd spoken to Jesse to see what he thought, and he'd agreed that it could be good for her so she'd taken her up on the offer and in doing so they'd gotten close.

Flattening her dress down, she removed her engagement ring, putting it on her side table in the honeymoon suit at the expensive stately home they were being married in. Having looked around and pencilled themselves in they'd then concluded they couldn't afford it so had cancelled, only to have a card in the post a week later thanking them for their booking and paying up front. When Jesse had enquired as to who had paid, he was told it was a friend of the bride. Knowing there was only one man who could afford it and who wouldn't want to be identified, they determined that it was Alexi, Hayley's father, who had surprised them.

At first they'd been unsure whether to accept such an offer but when Jesse explained he probably felt guilty for not being there for her over the years and it was his way of saying sorry she accepted that and looked forward to arranging everything around it. Jesse said how much she deserved the wedding of her dreams and if he couldn't afford it, who was he to stop her father giving her it?

She only wished she could hold his arm down the aisle, but when he had to remain anonymous, that wasn't something she could have, not if she wanted others there too. Looking at the earrings Marie had left her as her borrowed item she put them in. Looking at her watch she realised she was cutting it thin, so she gathered her bouquet and made her way downstairs to the made up aisle outside in the garden. As soon as she appeared the music came on and her heartbeat picked up.

Making her way upstairs with a baby sitting on her hip and a toddler clutching her hand as though he was hanging from a skyscraper, she simultaneously juggled her bouquet. Having listened to her mother-in-law about keeping it safe instead of doing the obligatory throw she wanted to get it out of the way before a well-wisher or helping hand decided to move it to a safe place, she knew all about safe places, her husband laughed at her efforts to keep things safe on numerous occasions, undoubtedly forgetting where that special place was and would find something from the previous search instead.

"Come on Daniel." she urged hoping the muscle in her arm would spring back once he let go. "One more step, then we'll be at Granny's room." On reaching it she shuffled her baby in her now numb arms and placed the bouquet on the floor at her feet, as she clutched the round knob of the door and twisted it open. Daniel pushed the heavy door open, almost swinging it off its hinges as Hayley bent down to pick up her bouquet. Sensing Daniel freezing still next to her, she looked up.

Sitting on the windowsill with his hands entwined she stood in shock as the man dressed in a grey suit with a white shirt open at the top smiled at her cautiously as he took her and the boys in with his gaze.

"Thought I could catch you before you put them down." smiled Jesse jogging towards her, wrapping a hand around her waist he pulled her in for a kiss, but she was frozen to the spot looking off into the room he'd just watched her open. Glancing inside to see what had gripped her interest, his smile instantly dropped and was replaced with a frown and tight jaw. "What the hell are you doing here?" shouted Jesse. "Get out!" when the baby suddenly wailed at his father's angry voice they all turned to it as Hayley bounced, trying to soothe away the baby's anxiety, whilst pulling Daniel towards her, wrapping his body around her legs.

"I didn't come here for trouble." said Rob, raising his hands in the universal surrender stance, watching Jesse effectively stand in front of Hayley and the boys as protection. "I just came here to see Mum, I didn't think you'd come to her room." added Rob apologetically.

"Are you deaf? Get out!" shouted Jesse once again sending his youngest son into a wailing fit.

"Jesse, calm down. You're scaring Michael." warned Hayley calmly. Turning to her with an inconsolable baby, he saw that she was right and bent down to Daniel. Scooping him up in his arms, he held him to his chest, no doubt transferring the sticky residue of his dessert onto Jesse's own attire, but he didn't care. He couldn't leave them with Rob and he wasn't about to leave Rob on his own.

"You named him after Dad." observed Rob smiling at Michael as he began to settle. Ignoring Rob's comment, he turned to Hayley.

"Take the kids downstairs and get Martin." Jesse whispered.

"But Jesse..?" sensing she knew exactly where he was going with that, he just nodded, eyeing him to make sure she'd received the information loud and clear she made her way out of the hallway and back downstairs, almost dragging Daniel behind her.

"I didn't come here for any trouble I swear, I just came to see Mum and get a glimpse of the happy couple." Rob answered steadily.

"Seen enough?" snapped Jesse.

"You look happy together." Rob continued.

"We are. No thanks to you." answered Jesse as he stood stock still in the doorway. Rob let his gaze slide to the floor, and Jesse realised how suitably ashamed he looked. "I don't want you here."

"I know. I'm sorry."

"Sorry for what? Turning up or trying to kill my wife?!" shouted Jesse. "Did you come to finish the job?"

"Of course not." answered Rob staring into his brother's eyes, hoping he saw how honest he was being. "I was going to ask Mum to set up a meeting; I need to speak with both you and Hayley."

"You're going nowhere near her." seethed Jesse, pointing to Rob as if to stress his point.

"Understandable."

"Oh, I *am* pleased." scathed Jesse sarcastically.

"I want to draw a line under everything that happened." admitted Rob.

"I'm sure you do. Tell you what; draw it in the yard at the local gaol."

"Jesse!" turning his head, he watched Martin jogging up the stairs to get to him. "He in there?" Nodding, Jesse turned back to Rob who looked a lot less comfortable than before. "Well well well, the local wedding crasher." mocked Martin; on seeing Rob, he folded his arms before leaning on the adjacent door frame. "What are you doing here?"

"I'm trying to talk to my Mum."

"Well, I'm sure they'll let you have one call when they take you in, you can either call a solicitor or Mum, your choice." answered Jesse. When Rob glanced from Jesse to Martin, bewildered, Jesse noticed how uncomfortable Martin suddenly looked as he gazed at the floor.

"You can't take me in." answered Rob shaking his head.

"Why?" asked Jesse, suddenly interested.

"Because she retracted her statement." answered Martin looking back up to Jesse's shocked face.

"What?!" shouted Jesse, unable to stop his feet from moving as he drew closer to Rob, who was leaning back as far as the window sill would allow. "When?"

"It was a few weeks ago, she told me she was going to tell you herself." Martin answered, still leaning on the doorframe. Glancing from one man to the other, he couldn't help but feel intimidated. But if the last year had taught Rob anything, it was that people could smell fear.

"What did you do to her?" asked Jesse, grabbing Rob by the scruff of the neck.

"Nothing I swear." answered Rob holding his hands out.

"I did it for you." when they heard Hayley's voice, they all turned. "I didn't want you to have his death on your conscience. If he went to prison, we all know he'd never last more than a day, especially after pissing off the Richards'."

"I couldn't give a flying f-"

"Jesse, calm down, please. You've lost enough, I couldn't be the cause of you losing someone else." explained Hayley. "I'm not saying you have to forgive him, or even talk to him, but at least you'll know he's alive if you change your mind."

"That wasn't your choice to make!" shouted Jesse.

"Then whose was it?!" she shouted back. "Yours, Martin's, your bosses?" when Jesse let go of Rob he looked straight at Hayley as she entered the bedroom. "He hurt me. No one else, just me. So it's my choice what kind of punishment he gets."

"What bloody punishment is he receiving when you've retracted your statement?" asked Jesse.

"That he can't come home, he has no relationship with his mother or brother and one nephew doesn't even remember him while the other hasn't even met him."

"And whose fault's that?" asked Jesse.

"His, of course it's his. But I don't need him to be in gaol." when

Jesse lowered his head he shook it gently before massaging his forehead.

"I can't fucking cope with this." walking past Hayley and Martin, Jesse hurried back down the stairs.

"I'm sorry, Martin. I should have told him sooner." Martin nodded before looking back to Rob.

"I didn't come to cause trouble, I genuinely just wanted to get in contact with Mum and Freya was already coming, so she dropped me off."

"You've been here since this morning?" asked Hayley. Rob nodded. "I thought you and Freya-"

"Split? We did for a while."

"So you thought the most sensible thing you could do was turn up here on their wedding day?" asked Martin scoffing as he shook his head in disbelief. "Are you both intentionally trying to fuck with his head?"

"I'm sorry, Hayley. I didn't come to cause any trouble." Hayley nodded while glancing back at Martin, as though he might be able to help in some way but only seeing resentment for not being honest with him about Rob in the first place.

"So what happens now?" asked Martin, slapping his hands down by his sides. "Jesse's probably going polar downstairs where your missus is" he said pointing to Rob. "and we're all up here staring at one another."

"Go downstairs, get a drink. Have a dance with Freya and then have an early night." said Hayley, looking at Rob.

"I don't think that's a good idea." said Martin, stepping in cautiously. "Jesse is not going to rollover about this." he warned.

"Then what do you think we should do?" asked Hayley, placing her hands on her hips. "Forget this ever happened, walk away from one another and never speak of this again or pull our big girl pants on and start acting like grown-ups?" Martin held his hands up backing away, he wasn't going to be a willing participant to the reunion and the quicker he got downstairs the better to help extinguish the inevitable fireworks.

Watching Martin leave, they then both turned to each other. Being alone in the same room again with the same uncomfortable feeling settling between them, they looked around themselves at the decor.

"He misses you." said Hayley finally.

"He really doesn't." argued Rob.

"You hurt him." she answered. "You tried to take everything he loved away from him, that's not easy for anyone to forgive."

"But you did." He answered, wondering if that was still the case.

"I did it for him, besides being angry with you takes up too much energy and I'm quite frankly sick of trying to win a war." answered Hayley. "Right now I've got bigger concerns."

"You've been through a lot." admitted Rob. Hayley nodded. Leaving Rob to think about his entrance she left in search of her own soul mate hoping she hadn't completely destroyed their marriage before it had even begun.

∽

FINDING JESSE at the wedding table, she tentatively took the seat next to him. Picking up his pint of beer, he finished it before looking at her. "When were you going to tell me?" he asked calmly.

"After we got back." she confirmed. They hadn't been able to book a honeymoon, straightaway due to Michael being too young to leave, but they'd managed to keep the honeymoon suit for the entire weekend so they could have a break and enjoy their new marital status. Marie was due to take the boys with her tomorrow, which was why they were going to sleep in her room overnight.

"He doesn't deserve it." said Jesse, shaking his head.

"It wasn't for him. It was for you." looking at her, he tried to see where she was coming from. Staring at one another intently for a while, he nodded, accepting what she'd done was done out of love and nothing else. "I've told him to come down and have a dance with Freya. I don't want her to feel awkward around me about going out with him."

"Jesus Christ Hayley." Jesse sighed, running his hands down his face. "I'm barely keeping my temper now."

"I told him to make sure he had an early night. You don't even have to speak to him." she assured him.

"I really don't want to see him." he admitted shaking his head.

"I know." said Hayley, taking his hands in hers. "You've nothing to feel bad about. He was in the wrong and he knows it. If anyone should feel awkward, it's him. Let us enjoy our wedding day." she said smiling, hoping she was coming over as convincing. "This is our day." smiling, Jesse nodded before kissing her. "I love you Jesse Hallam."

"I love you Hayley Hallam." laughing, she kissed him back. "I do like the sound of that."

"It sounds like you've got a mouthful of marbles." she laughed again, before mimicking him. "Hay wee Hay yam." she said playfully trying to sound as though her mouth was full.

"You're an idiot." laughed Jesse, before kissing her again. "Come on." said Jesse standing up whilst offering his hand "Mum's putting the kids to bed and I want to have a dance with my wife." Hayley beamed.

CHAPTER 24

The next day George was slumped over Freya's kitchen table whilst he cried his heart out. All his brothers, his sister and Rob looked at one another with concern and worry etched on their faces. Freya had cried since the moment she'd found out, but having managed to control herself a little in order to try to offer some kind of support to George, she'd stood taking in big deep breaths. Whilst they were all grieving they all knew that George had been hit the worse, and it was him they needed to help get through this. They just had no idea how.

"Do you need a lift to the hospital?" asked Will quietly.

"No." answered George, wiping his nose from the tears that were coating it. "There's nothing I can do right now, and I was there all night. I just needed to get away from that place."

"Understandable." answered Eddie, clapping him on the shoulder as he took out a chair next to him.

"She's gone." cried George, struck with another fit of sobs. Rob watched as the brothers and sister offered support to one another in just their looks and demeanours. He'd never felt that level of support and he didn't feel comfortable encroaching on theirs. Slipping behind Will, he left them to it, deciding to go and sit on the sofa in the living room. He was still in pain from yesterday when his own brother had looked at him like he wanted to kill him. After being reunited with his Mum he'd found the whole experience bitter sweet but he'd promised to stay in touch. Yeah, he didn't really get family support; she'd immediately scolded him for how he'd behaved rather than showing any type of relief that she knew he was safe. Easing down on the sofa, he was glad to take the weight off and be cuddled by the soft material. His head was throbbing from the stressful night at his brother's wedding. Although Jesse hadn't spoken to him once he was downstairs it hadn't stopped him giving him the evils for most of the night "Hey" looking up Rob watched Freya's tired looking, pale face try to smile.

"How's your brother?" glancing back to the kitchen, she decided to step in the living room and gently close the door behind her.

"I just can't believe it. I'm not sure how he's going to cope." Rob held out his hand, and she took it before sitting down next to him. "She's just so lovely. I don't get to see her much but when we do meet up, we always have such a laugh."

"I'm sorry Freya." nodding, she bit her bottom lip in an attempt to stop the tremble and make her cry anymore. "They got kids?"

"Yeah. Angel and Connor." she answered.

"How are they?" asked Rob.

"Angel was kept in overnight for observation, but Connor didn't make it." answered Freya whilst her voice broke. "The impact of the lorry hit Arianne's side and Connor was behind her. Angel was in the back on the passenger's side. She was incredibly lucky to get away with what she did. But poor Connor, he was only 11 months old." cried Freya.

"Shit!" Grabbing hold of her, he wrapped her in his arms to absorb her pain.

"He's got to go back to turn off the life support." she said against his chest.

"Why haven't they already done that, if she's not coming back?" asked Rob.

"She's a donor, they have to keep her organs going to use them." she answered.

"Jesus. That's rough." nodding she turned to the door as she heard the boys shuffling in the hallway. Tapping on the door, Will opened it to see his sister in Rob's arms.

"The hospital's just called, they're ready." nodding, she stood up to follow them out. Turning back to Rob, she offered him a tight smile before closing the door behind her.

∽

WHEN THEY ALL got to the hospital, they crowded round the bed where Carianne lay motionless except for the machine pumping her chest up and down. Watching George kiss his wife's lips for the final time had Freya shielding her eyesight in Eddie's chest while he rubbed her back. When each had said their final farewell it was Freya's time to say hers. Stepping closer to Carianne's head, she slouched down and whispered her goodbye.

"I'll look after Angel and George, I swear. We all will. You keep Connor safe, okay? Make sure you hug him for me. Plenty of kisses and don't scrimp on the sweets. I'll make sure Angel gets a healthy balanced diet so don't worry, she'll want for nothing other than you." Barely able to speak through the swelling of her throat she hoped Carianne understood, looking back up to the boys she witnessed them all trying to breathe through their own emotions and glassy eyes, turning to George she noticed how old he suddenly looked. His whole world had come crashing down around him. It would never be the same. Holding Carianne's hand, he nodded to the doctor who proceeded to turn off the machine. When her chest failed to inflate the line went flat and George had to let go while they wheeled her away. Eddie grabbed George and forcefully hugged him as though he could absorb all the pain for him. Will took Freya and they all broke down together.

When George had managed to pull himself together after a coffee break and a walk around the hospital grounds on his own he walked into the cubicle Angel occupied. Smiling to his sweet daughter, he kissed her forehead while pushing back her damp hair from her face.

"Where's Mummy?" looking at Freya, she gently shook her head while taking one of Angel's hands in her own. George took the other before sitting down on the free seat next to the bed.

"She's not very well sweetheart." answered George trying to smile as though that alone would relay her fears. "You were in a really bad crash." As tears dripped down the young girl's face George looked back to Freya as if to hope she would tell him he didn't have to do this. "Mummy didn't make it, sweetheart." As he said it, he broke down and tears cascaded down his face, as he held her hand up to his lips.

"What do you mean?" asked Angel with fear in her eyes, glancing from her father to her auntie.

"Angel sweetheart. Mummy died." answered Freya as gently as she could.

"What about Connor?" asked the girl, crying.

"Him too." Freya nodded whilst trying to remain stoic. When Angel lunged forward, it was to Freya and the shock of it took Freya by surprise, but wrapping her arms around the young girl gave her comfort and she hugged tighter hoping she felt it too. George just watched, distraught and hopeless.

CHAPTER 25

3 MONTH LATER

Rob threw his tea towel on the chopping board. "Dave, I'm going!" he shouted.

Popping his head out of the walk-in fridge, he waved to him while he held a roll of sticky labels in his mouth and a black marker between his fingers.

Once outside Rob took his phone from his pocket and typed out a quick message. "Hey, get in." looking up he saw George waiting in a parked car with the window down on the passenger side. Opening the door, Rob slid in, pocketing his phone. "Freya's asked me to pick you up; she's had Angel all day."

"How is she?" asked Rob

"Which one?" asked George, pulling out into the traffic.

"Both." laughed Rob.

"Freya's knackered, she's had an eight-year-old running around all day, and Angel's ok. Least she was when I left her this morning." Rob nodded. He'd spent quite a lot of time with George over the last 3 months, bizarrely they had become firm friends under the grief of his wife, it was as though George could finally understand how Rob had done what he had done and in knowing that, he'd opened up to him about what he'd like to do to the driver of the lorry who had taken out his wife and son if he ever got the chance. Rob had just listened without trying to placate him and they'd gotten close.

Not long after Jesse had beaten him up, he received a text to say Hayley had been to the station to retract her statement and as such no one was looking for him anymore. After being able to get back into his savings accounts and sort his home out, that he'd shared with Caitlyn, he sold it to pay off the last mortgage payments, fees and to put towards a little flat in Lincoln close to the city centre. Thankfully, he'd managed to get a company to empty it and move everything he needed to his new home while getting rid of everything else so he hadn't had to step foot back in Newark.

Pulling up outside the door, Rob climbed out and made his way to the front door, pushing his key in to open it. Stepping inside, George followed. Throwing his keys on the side in the kitchen, he went in search of the girls. George had told him that Freya had said to pick Angel up from Rob's as she wanted to spend the night being pampered by her boyfriend after having the whirlwind that was his daughter. Rob had laughed, but there really was nothing more he wanted. Running upstairs, he stopped on the landing when he heard giggles. Looking down the stairs he caught George's concerned face, flicking his finger towards upstairs George followed quietly. Once they opened the door they were accosted with the smell of nail varnish. On the bed Freya laid in her bra and jeans with a green mud pack on and cucumber covering her eyes. With scrunched up tissue stuffed between her toes, he could see where the smell was coming from. Angel lay next to her with an equal amount of gunk and cucumber on her face. Laid in a vest and leggings, she had tissue stuffed between her toes too. Rob and George shared a look before bursting out laughing. Once the girls heard them they shot up, cucumber dropping on to the bed covers.

"Oh, don't worry Angel it's just the chuckle brothers." said Hayley scowling at them.

"What have you done to my daughter?" asked George, still laughing.

"We've had a girl's pamper day. Haven't we Angel?" she said

turning to Angel. "You boys wouldn't understand." she said glaring back at them. Sharing another look, they laughed while walking down the stairs to the kitchen. Having boiled the kettle and made drinks they waited for the girls to join them after hearing them in the bathroom giggling while they tried to wipe the muck off their faces.

"How's work?" asked George.

"Not bad. It's easy enough and the staff are friendly."

"Can't ask for much else then." Rob shook his head.

"I hear you're trying to move up here."

"Yeah well we're here already, but at least Will will get some of his space back. The house has been emptied, and it's in storage at the moment, just got to wait till it actually sells now."

"Should be quickly down there, surely."

"Yeah, the estate agent seems to think so, so hopefully. I couldn't stick another day in there and I know Angel is going to miss it but I just can't survive in that house, it was choking me."

"Understandable." Rob reasoned.

"I just hope it doesn't cause Angel too much stress, she's had enough to deal with."

"She'll be fine, kids are resilient. Besides, she got her uncles and crazy auntie up here."

"True. Don't tell Freya, but I don't think Angel would be doing half as well if it wasn't for her."

"She's a good egg." agreed Rob. He'd seen how much time she dedicated to Angel, she helped with her schooling, taught her to cook, showed her how to use a washing machine and he even caught her doing a demonstration on how to use a sanitary towel. She was certainly doing her bit to make Angel feel grown up whilst still being cared for. They had even come up with an eating and exercise plan that they sometimes video chatted each other with, it was crazy but it was like Freya had muscled her way in to make sure Angel would never feel like she was without a mother figure in her life, and it made Rob love her even more.

Once George had decided he couldn't live alone with his daughter back in Bournemouth, they had decided that Freya and Will would take them in. Angel stayed in Freya's room while George had Rob's old room. Once Freya had manipulated her brothers into helping Rob again he'd been passed onto Eddie who begrudgingly put him up until Rob's finances had come through and he was able to buy his own place. While Eddie had been pleasant, they were never going to be good friends so he was glad to be out of there. Will still looked at him as though he wasn't worthy to walk the earth while George softened but the only person he really cared about was Freya and since she'd been able to move in with him, they'd gone from strength to strength.

CHAPTER 26

Hayley opened the door and was taken back to see Martin on her doorstep. Looking down at her, he shifted his head to indicate his desire to come in. Pushing the door wider, she stepped back to let him through. Once they were in the kitchen Hayley made them a drink and sat down at the dining table where Martin joined her. Looking around the room, he smiled at the bottle steriliser in the corner.

"How is he little monster?" seeing where he was looking she smiled.

"He's good. He's a lot better at sleeping than Daniel is." she answered.

"He still struggling?"

"A little." she shrugged. "I'm not sure if it's just habit now rather than anything else."

"Probably." nodded Martin taking a sip of the coffee. "They're sneaky little devils." she smiled again waiting to find out why he's suddenly decided to visit her.

"Martin why are you here?" asked Hayley noting how uncomfortable he looked.

"The chest." answered Martin. Looking away she took a drink before settling back down, seeing her hand shake Martin knew he was in the right place for some answers. "I've looked at that photograph until I'm blue in the face and I just can't shake off something Jesse told me before you both went into witness protection." Hayley kept her gaze transfixed on the cup as Martin leaned forward in his chair. "Hayley, Jesse told me you didn't miscarry, he said that you gave birth, and that you gave the kid away." when a tear slipped down her cheek she quickly swiped it away before looking back at Martin with glossy eyes. Taking out the photograph from his pocket, he showed Hayley it.

"I don't know how the photo got there." answered Hayley.

"I didn't think you did. But you do know more than you're letting on." he answered. "Like who she is."

"You're right she's my daughter but I don't know where she is." Hayley answered, taking the photograph in her hand.

"Who does?" asked Martin calmly.

"My father." when Martin sat back in shock, she took another sip of her drink.

"Frank?" he asked finally, looking even more confused.

"No. Alexi or Castor or whatever name he chooses to use."

"Castor is your father?" asked Martin to be sure he understood. Hayley nodded confirmation. "When... but... how... who?" stumbled Martin trying to work out what she was saying. Why was this the first he was hearing of it? Why hadn't Jesse told him? Did Jesse even know?

"We found out when we went into police protection. He managed to slip past security and get in. He told me then he'd been behind moving her and as such he'd kept an eye on her. That was when he showed me a picture of her. That's how I know who she is, but she's been kept away from this. She has a normal family with a Mum and Dad who love her and I want to keep it that way."

"But someone put her photograph in that chest. Someone other than just you and him know about her." said Martin gravely.

"I don't know how the picture got in there but Darren was the only other person who knew."

"What about Lynnie?" asked Martin.

"Not unless Darren told her but I can't see it, he knew even then we couldn't trust her, besides she was too young at the time."

"But then your brother was tortured." Martin reminded her. "He might have-"

"Oh shit! Frank knows." admitted Hayley suddenly panicked. "He told me he'd find her. But I thought he was bluffing because he said how brave Darren had been before he killed him." explained Hayley. "And then he was arrested."

"So he could have had people out looking for her?" asked Martin. "People we don't necessarily know about."

"Alexi promised me she was safe. That's why I told you not to go poking around; if they saw where you were going and what you were doing they could get to her first."

"Hayley, they have her picture."

"No! You have her picture." said Hayley.

"Someone knows she exists or this picture wouldn't, and if there's anything I know about that sect it's that they don't leave things to chance. Now is she a threat to them or is she a requirement?"

"I don't know it would depend on who wanted her." answered Hayley trying not to lose her mind.

"Who could want her?" asked Martin leaning forward. "Think Hayley, who needs her the most?"

"Martin I swear to you I don't know. It wouldn't make sense to go after her now everything's been destroyed."

"What if it hasn't? What if we only have part of the problem? What if there's more that Darren didn't give us?" Hayley knew there was but she didn't know enough about it to explain, all she knew was that her father had explained it metaphorically using a tree, she didn't understand specifics and she hadn't wanted to at the time. She had just wanted to know if her daughter, Jesse and Daniel were safe, and he'd assured her of that.

"Hayley I need you to be honest with me, I just need to find this little girl." explained Martin holding up the picture. "I need to put protection on her until we know what we're dealing with."

"Do you not think that's what I want too, but I need to know she'll be safe if I try?" urged Hayley. Hearing the door, Martin quickly put the picture back into his pocket and stood up from the table as he awaited Jesse's arrival.

"Hiya, did you need something?" asked Jesse, slinging his keys on the worktop before filling the kettle from the tap. When Martin looked from Hayley back to Jesse, he just shook his head before clearing his throat.

"No, just thought popped in for a coffee, I didn't realise you hadn't finished yet."

"Yeah well, I did but then I popped to the shops, it's a mare for Hayley on the bus with the kids." answered Jesse. "Stopping for another?"

"No, I best get back, Claire'll be cooking up a storm no doubt." said Martin tipping the remnants of his drink in the sink before clapping Jesse on the back and leaving.

"I'll get the shopping from the car." said Hayley, standing up.

"No, I'll get it in a sec sit down, where are the boys?" asked Jesse.

"In Daniel's bedroom playing." answered Hayley looking directly at Martin hoping he wouldn't say anything in front of Jesse.

"Right well I best get off, see you later." said Martin before leaving. Once they heard the door shut, Jesse turned to Hayley.

"Well, that was weird; he didn't mention he'd be popping by at work today." Hayley tried to smile as she shrugged her shoulders nonchalantly. "He didn't even moan about Claire's cooking." said Jesse observing Hayley as she walked around the kitchen apparently tidying. Wrapping his arms around Hayley's waist, he pulled her back towards his chest before lowering his lips to her right ear. "Why was Martin really here?" asked Jesse coldly. The thought that he might think something was going on between her and Martin sliced through her, he'd had that done to him once before and she hated keeping things from him but the idea that he thought she would willingly hurt him in that way caused her to bristle.

"He's found a picture in a hidden chest at the church; it's of a young girl."

"Do you think it's-?" started Jesse.

"It is." interrupted Hayley. "He showed it to me." when she felt him prop his head on her shoulder she raised her hand to run it through his hair, leaning her head against his.

"But who would have put her picture there?" asked Jesse.

"That's what I need to find out?" answered Hayley. Turning her in his arms, she faced him. Both his arms resting on her shoulders, he brought his lips down to her.

"How are we going to do that?" asked Jesse.

"We're not. I am." warned Hayley. "I need to go back."

"To the church?" asked Jesse stunned. "No way." He answered, dropping his arms from around her and taking a step back.

"I don't have a choice. I doubt that chest has just been uncovered due to luck, something more is at play and while she's still out there, she's in harm's way. If it was someone's intention to uncover her identity, then I need to make damn sure that doesn't happen."

"Why would they do that, Hayley? I thought your Dad said this was all over?" asked Jesse.

"Seems he was overconfident, doesn't it?" said Hayley sarcastically.

"Are you still in touch with him?" asked Jesse. Turning away, Hayley picked up the car keys to collect the shopping. "Hayley?"

"He sent me a picture of her a while ago." she admitted not daring to look at him and see the disappointment she knew would lay there.

"Why didn't you tell me?" Hayley shrugged. "Why is he sending you pictures?"

"I'm not sure, possibly to prove she's still ok." answered Hayley quietly. "Or that's what I hoped."

"This isn't over is it?" sighed Jesse leaning back on the worktop with his head in his hands. Turning around, she watched his shoulders tense and his back tighten, grabbing onto the worktop for some much-needed strength she watched him turn around and lean over the work top then step back and hang his head, standing back up he grabbed a spare pan off the stove and threw it with such force it hit the other side of the wall with a clunk before bouncing off and clattering to the floor. Hayley stepped back with her arms up as if to protect herself while she cowered in the corner, looking at Jesse with shock in her eyes as he kicked the pan on the way out.

Reeling from Jesse's outburst, her heart was beating out of her chest as she stood silently trying to regain her composure. Looking at all the pots and pan sitting on the worktop she decided to finish putting them away before anything else, Jesse needed time to calm down and she didn't want to be anywhere near him while emotions were so high.

After half an hour or so she heard Jesse making his way down the stairs with a suitcase thumping on the stairs with each step. Walking to the bottom, she glanced up. He had Michael in his arms while Daniel trailed behind him with a small holdall. "What are you doing?" asked Hayley.

"I'm going to my Mum's." answered Jesse.

"What are you doing with the boys?" asked Hayley anxiously.

"They're coming with me."

"What?" asked Hayley looking from Jesse to Daniel who was shrugging on his coat that had been strategically placed at the bottom of the stairs. "You're leaving-"

"We need some space."

"You're not taking the boys." said Hayley.

"If you think I'm leaving them here with you, you've got another thing coming."

"What?!" shrieked Hayley. He'd never so much as uttered a concern at her parenting of their boys. Why on earth would he think she wasn't capable of caring for them now?

"You keep your secrets Hayley, but don't expect me or the boys to be around when it all blows up in your face."

"Jesse!"

"Daniel go and get me the baby change bag from the kitchen, please." Listening to Jesse, Daniel trundled off happy to help. "You've been keeping shit from me for long enough, you've had plenty of time to come clean but you'd rather keep your secrets than let me in and actually be my fucking partner. I'm not playing second fiddle to your secrets, Hayley. You either tell me everything or I walk."

Gob smacked, Hayley watched Daniel re-enter the hallway with Michael's bag, looking at Jesse pleading him to stop she watched him look away. She couldn't lose anyone else, especially when they meant everything to her. "Ok Daniel we're taking Daddy's car, come on say bye to your Mum." wrapping his arms around her legs she bent down and kissed his cheeks, realising her own were wet, she wiped them. "You know where to find me when you can, be bothered to talk to me." nodding she watched her life walk out the door and slam shut with a finality she'd never experienced before.

She'd failed.

No, she wasn't going to let this happen; they weren't going to take away the only thing she ever wanted. Swinging the door wide open, she watched as Jesse lowered Michael into his car seat before clipping him in. "Don't make a scene, you'll scare them." warned Jesse without looking at her.

Looking down at her bare feet, she suddenly felt the cold from the pavement creeping up on them. "I'm being blackmailed." she admitted wringing her fingers together.

Turning to her, he closed the door to the car so their voices wouldn't be so clear to the boys inside. "By who?"

"I've no idea. I thought at first the pictures were coming from Alexi, but they weren't."

"How do you know?"

"I asked him, he phoned the other night. He told me my daughter lost her mother. She's dead, and he was pretty sure they'd tried to kill my daughter too." explained Hayley.

"Why?" asked Jesse.

"He has no idea. He says they took everyone who was involved into custody and they're either awaiting trial or they're dead, so he hasn't got a clue who could be trying to find her."

"So how are they black mailing you, what do they have on you? What do they want?" asked Jesse.

"A video."

"Of?" looking away, she bit her lip before folding her arms over her chest. "Of?" repeated Jesse. "Hayley what are they blackmailing you with?"

"They have a video of me with a politician." Jesse's stomach contents curdled. "I was there as a honey trap, I was to lure him into sex so he could be bought, but things went wrong and he worked out why we were there and tried to kill us."

"What?" said Jesse, astonished. Deciding he didn't actually require her to repeat herself, she looked into the car and saw Daniel falling to sleep with his head lolling forward and then back as if it was on a spring. Running his hand through his hair, he took a couple of strides away from her before turning back to her. "You said they wouldn't let you be touched." argued Jesse.

"Ordinarily no, but it was part of my punishment for running the first time, he wanted to show me what would happen if I didn't conform. He said they wouldn't allow it to go that far, but we had to give them enough for the tape to work, or next time I wouldn't be so lucky."

"How did you kill him?"

"One of the other girls used her stiletto." answered Hayley. "We were told they would run in when they had enough but he overpowered her and I was scared he was going to kill her, I screamed and it was enough to distract him when he hit him with her shoe, he was dead before we could think straight."

"So the video shows it as self defence?" asked Jesse not seeing the problem. "He attacked you and you tried to defend yourselves."

"Not the way it's been edited." answered Hayley shaking her head. "They made Darren chop and change it. He told me they'd completely distorted it, making it look like we tricked him into the room before we murdered him in cold blood."

"So who's had this footage all this time?" asked Jesse.

"I don't know." said Hayley, going paler by the second. "But that's what worries me. If someone has it, they could tear my life apart."

"What happened to the other girls?" Hayley shrugged. "Why him in particular?"

"He was a politician. They needed him to let some deals go through, have his backing," answered Hayley. "They wanted projects that they'd put forward to be rubber stamped because legislation was holding them up and causing problems."

"So they were going to blackmail him?"

"Yes. He was married and an upstanding part of society. The last thing he would have wanted coming out was a recording of him having sex with three underage girls in his hotel room after a conference on protecting vulnerable people in society."

"What sort of legislation?"

"I've no idea, they didn't discuss the project in front of me, but whatever it was, was worth millions."

"So you girls cost them millions of pounds in a deal that were supposed to go down?"

"What happened after that? They couldn't have been very happy about you culling their cash cow?"

"They weren't. They bludgeoned Callie and Amie to death in front of me. They tore them apart in front of me." Hayley looked away, ashamed. "they left me to Demy." Jesse instantly realised what had happened and covered his face with his hands while he tried not to think about the unthinkable.

"So someone kept the video to have something on you?" asked Jesse, lowering his hands from his face. "And they're using your daughter to threaten you?" Taking a step up to the car, he leaned on it, while bowing his head to look at the ground where his feet still stood. "That only leaves one thing." He said lifting his head whilst he looked intently at Hayley. "They have dirt, they have something to threaten you with, but what do they want?"

"I wish I knew."

"How do you know it has anything to do with this video?"

"I don't, but it's the only thing I can think of that I was involved in."

"How do you know you're being threatened, if no one's mentioned the video?"

"The photographs came from an unidentified number; Alexi didn't know who could have sent them. Why would someone send me pictures of her if it wasn't a threat?" Jesse didn't know, but his head was spinning, he couldn't think straight. The barrage of information was making his head fog up. Grabbing the door, he pulled it open before stepping in the car.

"So let me get this straight you were told to Honey trap a politician for extortion, and then one of the women you were in the room with killed him?" nodding she tried to sniff back tears."How old were you?" asked Jesse still leaning on the car door.

"16." answered Hayley. Jesse swiped his hand down his face, trying to take it all in.

"Then there's no way that video doctored or not could substantiate you being in that room for anything other than what happened. It still doesn't make sense. The video can't show something you didn't do, if you didn't actually kill him then you'd not be done for murder, you'd be-"

"An accessory." answered Hayley glumly. Nodding solemnly, he realised her predicament. She'd hidden vital information on a high profile murder.

"We still have no idea this video is even something to worry about, if they've not mentioned it, then maybe this is all to do with finding your daughter?" asked Jesse, when a look flared up on Hayley's face she tried to disguise it by looking away quickly. "Hayley?" When she didn't answer he took his foot back out of the car, slammed the door shut before making his way round to Hayley's side.

"Hayley talk to me, this is us being honest, remember?" he asked, holding her shoulders in his hands. "Why do you think it relates this?"

"Alexi found out where the number was coming from." answered Hayley watching his face intently while she delivered the blow she knew would shake his world.

"And?"

"The messages came from Rihanna." answered Hayley.

"Rihanna?" asked Jesse, confused. "What's Rihanna got to do with this?" Rihanna was Jesse's ex wife; they'd met at university and married after she achieved her first job as a lawyer in London. It wasn't long before he found out she was having an affair with his best mate and they'd split and divorced not long after.

"She was instrumental in organising the entire thing." Jesse stood stunned.

"You said you didn't know her?" asked Jesse, stepping back. "You said you'd met her due to an interview that went a bit awry."

"I knew who she was. Her Dad worked for the sect; he was a friend of Franks and was paid handsomely for covering things up. Darren had told me I could trust her, he said she could get me out but something happened and she didn't turn up, that's why I was left in that hotel room. She'd helped set the whole thing up but when Darren had told her he didn't want me involved, he said she'd set up a plan to get me out, get me out the whole thing, but she never showed and I had to go through with it. Darren was furious at the time because we didn't know why she hadn't done what she'd promised."

"But there was a picture of you and her later."

"No, they took the picture while I was in London trying to snare the MP. Rihanna was the one who set up the meet with Campbell. She knew what was going down, but she was also supposed to stop it."

"Why would she do that?" asked Jesse, trying to remember anything that he could from that time period to corroborate anything she was saying.

"We think Campbell found out about what she was planning, and he played her. His hotel room was switched last minute, and we thought the order had come from Frank or Demy, but it hadn't. We still don't know who ordered the switch or why, but we think that might be why they never entered, we were in the wrong room to begin with."

"But you said they were watching?"

"They were, but the room was identical. They didn't know we were in the wrong room till it was too late."

"But if he knew, why would he go ahead and risk being blackmailed?"

"Because he wanted to show Demy and Frank who was boss, I don't know." shrugged Hayley. Jesse looked in the car to see the boys were fast asleep and then looked around suddenly realising how dark it had become. "When was this?" asked Jesse wanting to know the exact date.

"She was married to you." answered Hayley, knowing what he really meant by the question.

"Did you know?"

"Know what?" asked Hayley.

"Did you know who I was when we met? Was I all just all part of some plan?" asked Jesse, astonished.

"No." said Hayley, tears streaking down both their faces, quickly wiping his away without looking at her, he tried to think back to anything that might enlighten him. Looking away, she let her own tears make their way down her face. "Did you play me?" When Hayley looked back at him shocked he continued. "Was I just your way of getting back at Rihanna?"

"I didn't know you had anything to do with Rihanna until I saw your wedding photograph in Demy's attic. I had no idea you even knew each other until then." Hayley took a breath and wetted her lips. "I think he tried to use her to hurt you. Demy would have known about you and Rihanna, I have no doubt. He looked into everyone he was associated with. I don't think Rihanna was having an affair, I think he found his only way to hurt you without you seeing it coming and he staged it."

"You weren't there Hayley, you didn't see what I saw." said Jesse shaking his head.

"If they exposed what Rihanna had done, where do you think she'd be now?" asked Hayley. "There was nothing more important to her than her job. If that was threatened, who do you think she'd have turned to?"

"Her father."

"Exactly, and who did he work for?"

"Demy and Frank." Hayley stood in front of him, letting it sink in.

"There's no way they would have wanted it to get out that she was dirty or that she set up the Campbell's murder. If they gave her an ultimatum, she'd have chosen her career, and in the process they got double points for ripping your heart out after you'd arrested Anatoly." Anatoly was Demy's younger brother and he's been arrested by Jesse for assault, it seemed while in prison he couldn't take any more and he'd committed suicide. Since that day, Jesse had been an enemy to be eliminated by Demy and Frank.

"Her Dad hated me." said Jesse as he came to terms with the fresh information and thought about the way her parents had always treated him at family gatherings. "I don't know what to say." said Jesse looking into the car. "You've known all this for so long and yet you've said nothing."

"How could I?" asked Hayley. "And I've not known all of it, just pieces. I still don't know why she would send me photographs of my daughter."

"We have two boys and I have no idea who you are anymore." Suddenly a crack of thunder blasted across the sky, followed by a flash of the brightest light before the rain threw its force down on them. Within seconds they were soaked but still stood there as though nothing had happened, getting wetter by the second. Jesse finally walked round to the front driver's side, opening the door he looked back at Hayley still stood soaking wet on the path with no shoes on and just a flimsy summer dress that was looking more like dish rag with every minute that passed. "You've held stuff back from me Hayley; even when I've asked you, even when I've begged you to be straight with me, tell me everything. And you've stood facing me and looked me in the eye and told me there's nothing else. You've lied to me and kept secrets; you've misled me and divulged only the things you aren't quick enough to spin. I can't live like that. I have to know I can trust you, and right now I can't trust a damn thing that comes out of your mouth." Slipping down in his seat, he slammed the door before igniting the engine and pulling away from the kerb into the road. Watching him drive off down the street she stood in the rain until her legs gave way and she knelt down sobbing, her whole life ripped away from her.

She didn't know how long she had spent kneeling outside crying, but when she came back in her body was shivering. Seeing the rest of their wedding cake on the table sent her into a furious rage and when she'd taken out all her frustrations on it, having smashed it to pieces she lay down on the floor hugging her knees whilst she sobbed what was left of her heart out.

CHAPTER 27

Her phone hadn't stopped ringing, but each time she looked it was never Jesse calling her and he was the only person she wanted to talk to right now. She had finally told him everything, and he'd left her, just like she knew he would. Whilst he deserved the truth, she just wished she'd have kept her mouth shut. Spilling her guts had finally made him realise how screwed up she really was and who could blame him for walking away from her?

She wasn't sure how long she had been on the floor but when the door finally opened to the kitchen; she woke up. Trying to prise her eyes open to see who was in her house glaring at her, she struggled to refocus her eyes. "Hannah, are you okay?"

"Don't call me that." snapped Hayley defiantly.

"Habit, sorry." said the gravelly voice, as he bent down wrapping his arms around her to lift her up off the cold floor. "Have a shower, you're absolutely freezing. Or better still, a bath to warm your bones up." Nodding dully she made her way upstairs and flicked the taps on, when there was enough water in the tub to partially cover her she stepped in and left the taps running. After a while her fingers and toes started to get painful so she rested her feet on the tub and held her hands behind her head. She was sure it was because her body was trying to acclimatise, but she didn't have the energy to sit back up and pour more cold in. When a light tapping came on the door, she called out to come in, as he opened the door she realised she was only partially covered with water, her guest looked away after handing her a mug of tea.

"Thanks." said Hayley, taking a sip.

"Where's Jesse?"

"He's gone." she said looking up to her father's concerned face. "I told him about Rihanna and London. I told him everything." she said, willing herself not to cry anymore.

"Why?" asked Alexi.

"Because he needed to know, and I was sick of keeping things from him." she answered. "He deserves better."

"I've no doubt that he does, but there're ways of telling people stuff like that." Alexi advised.

"Yeah well evidently my way sucked." said Hayley sarcastically. "Because he's taken the boys and gone." Nodding, he looked around the bathroom. "What happens when they find her?"

"I don't know. I wish I did, but without knowing Rihanna's intentions it's hard to say." answered Alexi.

"I just can't understand why Rihanna would want to hurt me? It wasn't me that went after her, it was Demy or Frank. Why would she want to blackmail me, I don't have anything." asked Hayley desperately.

"Is there anyone else who could have known about her?"

"Do you not think I've wracked my brain?" asked Hayley, sipping her drink. "There was only me and Darren at the hospital. I had a midwife that obviously knew and a few others, who just came in to check on me from time to time, but Darren was the one who phoned you and you were the one who changed the documents and placed her in the care of the other family. I walked out that hospital with no baby and I didn't tell a soul until Jesse."

"You don't think-?"

"Jesse? God no, he'd never do anything to hurt me." Alexi walked over to the toilet and after placing the lid down he sat, looking around the room. "What about his partner?"

"Martin wouldn't-"just then she remembered the conversation she'd had with him earlier, what if his digging around had alerted someone. "Martin's found a chest."

"A chest?"

"Yeah at the old church. He said it had documents in and that's where he found a picture of a young girl that he hadn't been able to identify."

"Why did he think you might know?"

"I'm not sure but he's pretty sure he knows she's mine, he knows I'm not telling him everything."

"Which means he'll keep digging." said Alexi thoughtfully.

"I can't believe we're going through this again." Hayley sighed.

"We need to stop him." said Alexi.

"How?" when he gave her a look she shook her head vigorously. "No, you can't hurt him." She sat up quickly in the bath, spraying water down the side. "He saved me, he helped get me out. Besides, he's Jesse's best friend."

"He could put you back in." warned Alexi

"You told me all this was done with." she reminded him.

"Gemini won't let it go, they know what went on with the vine cross but their rules stay the same. Any child of founding parents has to be reared within the confines of the circle. They have to marry those they are bestowed to; it keeps the circle strong and pure."

"They can't have her; she's part of another family. She has no idea about this."

"Then you know the other option." Alexi warned her, raising his eyebrow.

"I have Jesse and the boys and I'm spoiled goods, you know they won't want me." she pleaded.

"It seems he doesn't anymore." when tears leaked from her eyes and her bottom lip trembled she looked away so he couldn't witness her falling apart. "There is another way, but I've never known anyone actually do it." Looking back at him, she waited.

"You can buy yourself out of the circle."

"How?" she asked expectantly.

"I'm not sure. Like I said, I've known no one do it, and if I look too eager to find out they'll cotton on."

"So how do I find out?" asked Hayley.

"You can ask?"

"But then they'll know I'm alive." she said cautiously.

"Someone already does, it's only a matter of time until they tell the circle. If you got in front of it, you'd be taking away their momentum."

"They could still tell them about her." she warned.

"They could but I think they'd find you a lot more useful at the moment." The thought sent a shiver down her spine. But then what did have to lose anymore, Jesse had taken the boys and gone. Her life was already in pieces. If she had to sacrifice herself to save her daughter, then that's just what she'd have to do.

"It's at the moment that I'm worried about." explained Hayley.

"If you buy yourself freedom, then your offspring has that freedom too. You remove the entire thread."

"Not if they find out who her father is?"

"Think about it." Getting up off the toilet, he made his way to the door. "I'll wait downstairs. I can have a car pick us up and take us to the airport in ten minutes." nodding Hayley watched her father move towards the door.

"Hold on, if they see me with you, won't they think you hid me and went against them?"

"You worry too much, besides I will not let you go in on your own am I?" explained Alexi. "You're my little girl after all." smiling she watched him leave.

How had this entire thing gotten so out of hand, why was she back within it all when she had been promised it had all been disbanded? Just when everything was going right, she'd married Jesse, she had two beautiful boys and now she'd have to beg some maniacs to let her leave without causing her to give up her daughter. How could she be expected to give up one child to save the other two, and could she do it after sacrificing her own happiness?

Heaving herself out of the bath she wrapped a towel around herself, feeling as though she had been battered but no longer susceptible to pneumonia she quickly got dressed in a fresh pair of jeans, a t-shirt and thick jumper, pulling on her woolly socks she made her way downstairs to the kitchen where a mug of coffee sat waiting for her. Taking a seat, she sat down and watched her father clean the slides down and put plates and cups away. It was bizarre to say the least, but her mind just wandered to Jesse in the rain, looking as though she'd stabbed him in the heart. She'd really done it this time, she had broken his heart, and he'd never forgive her.

Hearing the front door open, they both looked up and waited for Jesse to enter the kitchen. Still looking like a drowned rat, he didn't look particularly surprised to see Alexi in his kitchen.

"Jesse." said Alex, lifting his chin slightly.

"Alexi." Hayley watched her father and Jesse stare at one another before Jesse walked over to the stairs and ran up them. When he came back down, he was in clean dry clothes with a towel wrapped around his shoulders. Picking it up, he ruffled his hair with it before throwing it down by the washing machine. "The boys are at Mum's for the night." Hayley nodded. "Someone going to explain what the hell's going on?" asked Jesse, raising his eyebrow as he looked at them both, after sharing a look Alexi pulled a chair out and sat down.

Jesse made no attempt to move while Alexi stared at Hayley as if to ask her where to start. "Gemini has found out I have a daughter with a founding member. They want to know where the child is and why she's not been brought to the council." Jesse looked at Hayley who kept her head down, seemingly taken with the veneer of the dining table. "Someone has found evidence that I have been keeping her from them and they're not happy, in fact they've threatened to cut me out entirely."

"So?" said Jesse. "Walk away, I'm sure you have enough to live off."

"Only I wouldn't be living, when they say cut you out they mean it. Literally."

"So you don't want to die, to save your daughter's life?" asked Jesse wondering what kind of man would put his own life first and above his own child's.

"If it was only that simple. They'll kill me and still take Hayley."

"Alexi says we need to buy my freedom." chirped in Hayley.

"How? With what?" asked Jesse.

"That we don't know." said Alexi. "Not until we stand before them."

"At which point the cost could be too high and they just not let her leave?"

"Pretty much." conceded Alexi.

"Then that's not even in the realm of possibility, that's suicidal." answered Jesse before looking at both Alexi and Hayley. "You can't be serious?" he asked, watching them both look at each other awkwardly. "If she walks in there, they could do anything and she'll not be walking back out again."

"They'll never leave us alone either." answered Hayley. "And they'll go after my daughter."

"They'll go after her, anyway! You think these pieces of shits will care that you don't want her involved, when have they ever given a toss about what anyone wants, they take Hayley, that's it."

"They will want something from her." answered Alexi.

"Yeah, I bet they will." said Jesse sarcastically; he knew exactly what the dirty perverts would want. "You said this was over, you said you'd dealt with this. We'd still be in police protection if you hadn't assured our safety. This isn't keeping your promise."

"I had no idea they had evidence at the time."

"What evidence?" asked Jesse.

"They have a video of Hayley. In it, she's easily identifiable."

"What video?" asked Jesse, looking at Hayley, he knew what video he just wanted Alexi to confirm details. When she hesitated Alexi shuffled in his seat uncomfortably. "What video?!" shouted Jesse. Watching Alexi stare at his daughter while she seemed to shrink made him feel like shit, but he was sick of being sidelined. He needed to know what they were up against.

"They needed Hayley to extract information from someone, so they forced the girls to play along. He was an important asset to help with import and export, but he found out what they were planning and he created a USB stick with information on about Frank's export business. I've no idea what was on it, but it was supposed to be his insurance that kept him alive, Rihanna got hold of it and Darren copied the stick. The stick went missing, and all evidence was lost. It meant they had no reason to stop his death."

"But Hayley said they need him to help them?"

"Not when they already had his replacement in their pocket."

"So what's their problem? They had him taken out, had something to threaten both Rihanna and Hayley with. They still pushed their business deal through, I assume, using the stand in. Why are they still coming after her?" asked Jesse.

"He was the chancellor of Gemini and a very wealthy MP who was profiteering off the back of the sex trade, namely trafficking." answered Alexi. "You've got to remember Gemini and The Vine Cross are two separate entities, Frank had tried making something just as powerful as Gemini so he could one day take over, but in doing so he had to show them how weak they were. According to Gemini Hayley belongs to them, she should never have been with Demy, she was destined to someone else. The pact still stands, she's betrothed to someone else and she'll not be free until she takes her place at the table." Jesse rubbed his face in his hands. "She escaped the Vine Cross, you beat them, but you didn't destroy Gemini and I had hoped to convince them to let her go, but with so few women of her standing left they've declined my offer."

"Where's Rihanna now?" Hayley's head sprang up to hear Jesse ask after her.

"No idea, she's been missing for a few days." answered Alexi. "My guess is that she either has the girl already and is hiding or she's lying low and trying to put herself in favour with the counsel."

"What was on the USB?" asked Jesse.

"Payments to offshore bank accounts. The Vine cross would have needed it to blackmail people on the list. Keep them quiet. It was leverage for them to turn their backs on Gemini and do the Vine's bidding." answered Alexi.

"We think that's how they rallied so much support, basically insurance that if anyone went against them they had something to discredit them." answered Hayley.

"Rihanna was a top shot lawyer, and she was turning against them and they knew it, that's why they needed the video. At the time Hayley was just collateral damage, but they took out insurance, which meant identifying her to the men in the room." answered Alexi.

"That's why I changed my last name. If my other name had come across their desk at any time, they'd have known who I was and they'd have informed Demy or Frank." explained Hayley.

"Why didn't you tell me all this before?" asked Jesse, leaning on the worktop with his arms folded across his chest.

"Because I thought they had destroyed everything." explained Hayley. "I didn't think anyone would ever know."

"Hayley why didn't you tell me this before?" repeated Jesse. "Regardless of whether I'd find out, why didn't you tell me?" Looking at her father then back at the tabletop, she shrugged, digging her nails into the wooden tabletop.

"Because I was ashamed." said Hayley quietly. "I didn't want you to think of me as some two-bit whore. It was bad enough when you knew about Demy but if you knew he'd used me to entrap people, I thought you'd see me in a whole different light."

"So you made a decision for me, you kept things from me even when I asked you to tell me the truth, the whole truth?" Looking away, she tried to stop herself from crying.

"Jesse I think-"

"I don't give a shit what you think!" shouted Jesse, eyeing Alexi. Alexi bit his tongue, there weren't many people who he'd allow speak to him like that, but he understood Jesse's predicament more than most, the person he loved was being manipulated and there wasn't a damn thing he could do about it. Breathing heavily, Jesse turned around, so he didn't have to look at them.

"We need to go. Ask them for the conditions of release." said Alexi softly, knowing he was treading through a minefield.

"And what do you think they'll be?" asked Jesse not turning, but anxiously gripping the worktop as he leaned over with tense shoulders.

"It won't be something easy, and it quite possibly will be illegal and incredibly dangerous, something that will benefit them in some way but that won't identify them. They'll want a reward for breaking the terms of the contract that was set in stone generations ago. Whatever it is they won't make it easy or that would just entice others to use it, the circle's only powerful if they all provide for it and if they don't need to provide for it, odds are they'd think they could be richer, more independent. Who wouldn't want that, especially when they have to run everything by the board before they move?"

"They must have enemies, no one with that much power doesn't tally up a group of over achievers wanting more?"

"You're right, they have many enemies, but they're all separate, that's what makes Gemini so strong, we unite against them and they're crushed." answered Alexi.

"You must have sway on this counsel though?" asked Jesse, turning to face him.

"I do. Which is the only reason she'll be allowed to even enter, but I have no power over what they'll decide? It will be a vote. Everyone will have their time to discuss but then they vote and I'm only one person."

"But you must influence some over the others, right? Have allegiances?" he asked eagerly.

"It's not that easy, I can state my case. But then it's all secret. I'd have no comeback on anyone as I'd not know who voted for what, unless they all voted one way of course." The answer rang in the air and they all looked at each other for a few seconds, weighing up their options.

"She married out of the sect, she's already broken their rules so what chance does she have of them seeing her point of view?" asked Jesse.

"I'd say it was incredibly minimal, near to impossible." answered Alexi.

"Then you're not going." Hayley shot her gaze at him but before she could ask him he interrupted her. "You're not going. If we have to up sticks, change our name, live in another country, we'll do that. I'm not sending you anywhere that could cause you your death."

"With respect it's not your choice." answered Alexi.

"With respect it's none of your fucking business!" shouted Jesse. "You think I'll let my wife walk into some unknown with a bunch over privileged arse holes who think they rule the earth like some sardonic game of fucking thrones, fuck that!"

"No. I mean I'm here to collect her." when both Hayley and Jesse looked at him shocked he had the sense to look ashamed. "They have sent for her and I must deliver." When silence fell once again, Hayley watched the man she barely knew, her father look at her with sorrow in his eyes.

"So all this, this was to make me think I had a choice?"

"I wanted you to make the right decision. Things need to be dealt with."

"By lying to me?" asked Hayley incuriously.

"It would be easier if you came along as a compliant member, rather than a prisoner."

"Get out." said Jesse. "Get out!!"

"I'm not going anywhere without Hayley."

"Get out of my fucking house right now!" seethed Jesse.

"Phone your friend." demanded Alexi.

"What?" asked Hayley.

"Phone your friend, Freya isn't it?"

"Why?"

"Because then I think you'll understand that you have no choice." Looking at Jesse, she picked up her phone and called Freya. After a few seconds it was picked up.

"Hayley?"

"Hi, are you ok?"

"Not really, this is a really bad time. Actually, are you with Jesse?"

"Yeah why?"

"We all might need some advice, we can't find Angel, and she's gone missing."

"Missing? That's your niece, right?"

"Yeah, she's only 8. She was taken from school this afternoon. If I send you a picture can you pass it to Jesse, see if there's anything he can do?"

"Sure."

"Great, I'll send it now, thanks Hayley. I'll speak later." Ringing off she held the phone in her hand and waited, she didn't have to wait long before her phone pinged and a photo shone up on the screen. When she saw it all the blood drained from her face.

"What is it?" asked Jesse.

"Oh, my god, no. No. No." Hayley dropped the phone on the table as tears leaked from her eyes. "No!" Jesse rushed over to her, picking up the phone. Unsure what he was looking at, the girl looked familiar but he couldn't work out what was going on. "You bastard!" she shouted, launching herself across the table to reach Alexi, who only moved back slightly to stop her from grabbing him, suddenly the door flew open and an army of men entered the kitchen dressed in black with combat gear and balaclavas on. Taking Jesse roughly by the shoulders they shoved him back until his back hit the sink, holding him upright he watched two others pull Hayley out of her chair, holding her arms down by her sides as she squirmed, trying to release his own arms he was thumped in the stomach by a third man. Bending over to absorb the blow, he tried to hold his stomach contents in, while gasping for breath. "No!" screamed Hayley, watching his face redden as he looked up at her. "Leave him alone! Why do you have her?"

"Because she's needed. I tried to grant you some freedom, but the board just didn't agree. They need you back Hayley, where you belong doing what you should have been doing all along, running your part."

"I don't want it. She certainly doesn't." she said looking at the screen while tears rolled down her cheeks. Hearing Jesse trying to breathe through the assault, she turned back to him. "We don't want this life; you promised you'd get me out." She cried, turning back to Alexi.

"It's out of my hands. I pleaded your case, but I was voted against. We have to go."

"No." said Jesse. "You're not taking her." Looking up to meet Alexi's eyes, he threw as much anger across the room as he could. "You're not taking my wife."

"You have no choice. Look after your boys."

"Fuck you!" Another punch to his stomach winded him, bending him at the waist. While Hayley screamed the men holding onto her arms gripped tighter, pulling her towards them. "Hayley." coughed Jesse. Before he could say anymore the man who had hit him before punched him in the face, sending his head flying back with a crack the skin under his eye split open, spraying the floor with blood. Screaming, Hayley tried desperately to free herself but when she was forced to the ground; her legs gave way underneath her as they tied her hands behind her back, still watching Jesse, barely conscious whilst being restrained. Boot after boot connected with either his torso or his face between sobs she screamed until a gag stifled the sound she was making. Finally, Jesse's arms were let go of and he fell to the floor, like a boxer in the ring, blood pooled around his face, both eyes closed but already ballooning, Hayley couldn't take her eyes of him. Feeling her stomach lurch, suddenly her gag was doing more than muffle her cries, it was suffocating her.

"Shit. Get the gag off, she's choking!" said Alexi, watching her body spasm. Spluttering and trying to cough up the chunks stuck in her throat, she pushed her body over to Jesse as the restraints on her arms loosened just enough.

"I love Jesse." She cried. "I love you so much." When he didn't stir, she rested her forehead on the cold floor that was covered in his blood. "Please forgive me."

"Pick her up, get her in the van." nodding the men who had restrained her earlier picked her up by her arms and dragged her out of the kitchen. The other men followed, and she was thankful they hadn't done any more damage to Jesse while he lay on the floor, and she only hoped he was still alive.

CHAPTER 28

Martin sat at his desk, rifling through the evidence and the notes that had been taken over the course of the last few months. Something was eating at him, but he wasn't entirely sure what. He knew now that Hayley and Jesse had kept information from him, and while that stung, he also knew there must be a decent reason for it. He was just lost as to what that was? Knowing now that the man known as Castor or Alexi was the same person helped, but working out how was another thing entirely. Remembering he'd seen information on both, he wanted to tie them up and get a clearer picture of the man who was her father. If he really was, then why had he stood back for so long before offering any help, he must have known what was happening to Hayley for all those years, how could anyone, let alone a father stand by and watch that happen?

Glancing towards the phone he contemplated calling Jesse, he needed to talk to him, something had come between them lately and he wasn't sure what it was but now he understood how much Jesse had been keeping to himself he realised that might be the answer he was looking for. They knew each other too well to keep secrets, but that's exactly what Jesse had done. He'd pushed him away when he'd needed help. Placing his hand on the phone, he tapped it with his fingers. Looking at the time displayed on his computer, he realised how late it was. But when had that ever stopped him before?

Leaning back in his chair he wiped his face down with his hands, his eyes were sore but it was the worry about Jesse that was taking its toll, exhausted he clicked off the computer and stood up grabbing his jacket to leave, just then he saw a name, moving the other paperwork out of the way he picked it up, Castor had money transferred to him, and something with the date rang a bell. Throwing the jacket back on his chair, he scanned his notes to work out why the date was singing to him.

Finding it, his blood ran cold. Grabbing his jacket, he ran from the room. He had to talk to Jesse now.

∼

PULLING up outside he ran up the drive and banged on the door, when the door slid open he looked around for something to use as a weapon, being unable to see anything that would remotely cause harm he ran back to his car and pulled out his jack from the boot, levelling it in his hand so he was ready to swing he stepped inside gingerly listening out for any noises to confirm inhabitancy. Rounding the corner into the kitchen, he dropped the jack as soon as he saw Jesse lying unconscious on the floor. Kneeling on the blood-spattered floor he pressed his fingers to his neck he could feel a tenuous throb. Sighing with relief, he took out his phone and dialled the station.

"This is DS Wells I need an ambulance dispatching to-"

"No." groaned Jesse. Raising his hand, he tried to flip the phone but missed. "No." he repeated. Ignoring his protests, he continued to relay Jesse's home address and the condition he was in. Hanging up, he swiped blood from Jesse's eyes. "Hayley." croaked Jesse, coughing at the effort to speak. Holding his stomach while he still lay on the floor, he tried to embrace his sore ribs from his coughing fit. "They have Hayley."

"Who? Jesse who has Hayley?"

"Alexi." answered Jesse, trying to prise his eyes open to see Martin.

"You mean Castor?" asked Martin knowingly. Jesse just nodded before lying down on his back. "Why didn't you tell me?"

"I'm sorry."

"I don't want your fucking apology; I want to know why you didn't trust me?"

"It wasn't that simple." said Jesse trying to sit up once he'd gotten to a sitting position he spat out any remaining blood from his cheek and leant back on the dining chair legs. "I didn't exactly enter that encounter very well."

"What and you think I'd give a shit about that?" asked Martin in disbelief.

"No, but you would have been an accessory after the fact." answered Jesse wiping his mouth. When Martin waited for him to explain he rolled his eyes and then instantly regretted it. His head was still thumping as though it was being used as a base drum. "I bought an illegal gun. I used that website we'd found."

"But we closed it down." answered Martin, when Jesse looked at him with a 'like that ever stops them' look. Martin nodded.

"It was easy enough to find when you know what you're looking for." Scrambling over to the freezer Martin ripped the door open and came out with a bag of peas, throwing them to Jesse he caught them one handed before shoving them on the side of the face that her the most. "I was sent a message to meet, so I didn't want to go unarmed, but when I reached the destination, it had been a setup. I ran back and there he was inside the living room with Hayley and Daniel. He told us he'd dealt with it all but he had to remain under the radar, or he'd be arrested or killed or whatever, I couldn't find it in me to try to take him in, besides I got the feeling that that wouldn't have happened anyway, he was powerful Mart. You could smell it, but with him being supposedly on Hayley's side I let him leave, he promised that in 72 hours we would be free to go back home, and when we got the call to tell us exactly that it seemed he'd kept his part of the deal." Martin nodded.

"But he knew about Hayley's pregnancy and apparent miscarriage that never was?" asked Martin. Jesse looked at him stunned for a second but then nodded dutifully. "You were telling me about Hayley when we were interrupted but you never filled me in after about what you'd meant." explained Martin.

"By the time I got back I thought any information what cause you to dig deeper, Hayley didn't want anyone to know about her, as far as we knew she was safe whilst she was unknown."

"How long have we known each other?" asked Martin angrily.

"I know, ok." bit back Jesse. "I know." Looking around himself, Martin tried to restrain his temper.

"So what happened to have you in this state?" asked Martin. "Where's the boys?" asked Martin, panicking, quickly standing up.

"Not here, sit down. They're at my mum's." nodding Martin sat back down on the floor.

"Alexi was here when I got back, we'd had a row. Not long after Alexi called his goons in and they beat the crap out of me, then they took Hayley."

"Why?" asked Martin. Jesse shrugged and then cried out when he jolted his ribs. When Martin's gaze didn't waver Jesse knew he'd have to be honest with him, lying was destroying their relationship and it was everything he'd called Hayley out on, he couldn't sit and be a hypocrite now.

"They have dirt on her." When Martin sat listening to everything Jesse had to tell him about what had been said that night, he started to piece together the puzzle he'd left back on his desk. By the time Jesse had finished the paramedics had turned up, while they saw to Jesse's injuries and tried their best to clean and patch him up Martin called their boss.

∼

IN THE VAN Hayley sat down on the floor awkwardly while the soldiers all stacked in and sat on the side benches. With no room, she leant up against one of their legs, while her toes rested on the one across from her. The smell of vomit was strong round her neck where they'd pulled her gag away and she hoped they didn't want to reuse it. Glancing up, she saw her father enter the front cabin and instruct the driver. Airport. She was on the way to the airport and they were taking her out of the country. She'd never see her boys again. Trying to hold on to her tears, she bit her lip and rested her head onto her knees. Feeling as though her throat had a ragged stuffed in it, she tried to think of anything but her boys but her mind only reminded her of them and Jesse lying lifeless on the floor in a pool of his own blood. She'd finally killed him. She knew she was dangerous, and she'd been stupid enough to think she could have it all. Without permission tears rolled down her face and her nose ran, wiping her nose along her shoulder now and then she tried to ignore the silent men around her.

After what seemed like an age, the ground under the wheels on the van began to change and crunch. Looking up, she saw the men seem to shift in their seats as if they were getting ready for something. Once the van stopped they all piled out and the man whose legs she'd used as a backrest pulled her out across the floor. Once she was on the edge, her father walked into view and she looked up at him.

"I didn't want it to be like this." He said calmly.

"Bull shit!" spat Hayley.

"You'll understand one day. Get out." He ordered. Looking down at her feet she jumped from the van and landed awkwardly, being cramped into one spot for the best part of an hour had done her limbs and joints no favours and when her feet were still bare, each sharp stone underneath them dug in. Taking her arm roughly, he guided her to the waiting plane. Walking up the steps she was greeted with an expensive looking elegant if not small space with only six seats, but with enough leg room to be adequate for a baby giraffe. Taking a seat, she watched the men that entered after her fill the others while her father sat across from her. When a lady in a tight hostess outfit walked forward, she offered Alexi a glass of something dark and then turned to Hayley.

"What can I get you Miss Lebedev?" when she glanced to Alexi she watched him lift his glass to her before smiling. Who the hell was

Miss Lebedev? Shaking her head, the hostess walked away after curtseying.

"That's your name." said Alexi leaning over his arm rest towards her. "Hannah Lebedev."

"My name is Mrs Hayley Hallam." she snarled.

"Hannah means 'favour' or 'grace', meaning God has favoured me with a child. It's said that Hannah is the mother of Samuel. Hannah was barren, so at a temple she prayed that if god gave her a son, she would give him up to become a priest. So after making her promise to the lord she returned to her husband and conceived a son who she named Samuel." Taking a drink he returned to his story. "Once she had weaned him she gave him to Eli, who did indeed raise him to be a priest."

Hayley really needed that drink now, if she had to sit here and listen to him spouting god's work she was liable to try to take him out herself. Turning away, she looked out of the circular window at the angry sky.

"You made a promise and then you tried to break it." said Alexi.

"I made a promise because I had no other choice." she answered sharply.

"You always have a choice."

"To promise or die isn't really a choice." answered Hayley. Alexi shrugged as though he didn't really care either way.

"This was always going to happen. You've never been free." said Alexi, sounding as though he suddenly felt sorry for her. "I created you into a world that would never let you leave."

"You could have gotten me out." stated Hayley still watching the sky.

"Like you said, promise or die isn't really a choice." answered Alexi throwing her words back at her.

"You didn't have to kill him." said Hayley.

"Would he have stopped?" asked Alexi. "Would he have ever let you go?" pressing her lips together she already knew the answer, he'd never have given up on her. "Then I think you have your answer."

"My boys." She cried, damning herself for breaking in front of him.

Watching the tears run down her face he leant forward and gently wiped them away, whilst staring into her eyes.

"You're beautiful, do you know that?" Pulling her face away she leant up against the window whilst staring at him with hatred flaming in her eyes. "You'll make lots of new beautiful babies."

Suddenly her blood flared, and she vibrated with anger, gathering as much saliva as she could in her mouth she spat right at him, watching it drip down his pristine suit gave her some satisfaction as she watched him wipe it away on his hanker chief. "You're going to have to learn some manners if you're going to survive in this world." warned Alexi.

"Are you not listening? I don't *want* to survive in your world. If I can't live with Jesse and the boys, then I'd rather die."

"Then you'll get your wish soon enough." answered Alexi, sitting back in his own seat as thought that was all he was prepared to say. Hayley sunk back in her own chair, wishing she'd made different choices.

CHAPTER 29

"WELL, THAT WAS WEIRD." STATED FREYA.

"Isn't everything?" asked Eddie. She shrugged as if to say 'yeah', putting the phone back down she picked up her cup of lukewarm coffee. Rob laid his hand on her shoulder and she leaned into it while they watched Eddie's friend tapping away on his computer, who was trying to find any local CCTV that might have picked up Angel being abducted.

"Ok I've got something." said the guy known to them only as T, who wore a stained black t-shirt and ripped jeans that looked to be from wear rather than style. Pressing play they all leaned forward to watch the grainy footage of a man getting out of a car with a roll of gaffer tape and a balaclava, putting the balaclava on, he shielded his face from the footage but T had already "snap shot it and was running a match on another program which flicked through faces at speed on the left. Watching the man, he pushed the tape into his right pocket of his dark jacket and rushed away to the left at the end of the street.

"Give me a sec." tapping away again, he brought up another feed that caught the guy just approaching from said corner. Watching him look around and remain in the shadow as much as possible they weren't surprised to know nobody had seen anything, and it certainly made it premeditated instead of just an opportunist, not that that made them feel any better.

"Where's he going?" asked Rob

"He's looking for an entrance." said Eddie.

"So they didn't know where to go?" asked Freya.

"It depends, they could have been given instructions or they could be hearing something we can't and he's reacting." Freya nodded, she wasn't sure she totally understood any of what T had said but she didn't need to as long as Eddie did. If anyone was going to bring their baby girl back, it was him and his 'retired security' team. She's always thought it bizarre that an ex squaddie ran a bar, especially one who didn't particularly like crowds or drunken idiots, but she supposed maybe the money was good. To find out he was actually in some security group that did special ops, she was now more convinced her brother was a spy than she ever was.

As the footage flicked again, they saw the same man dragging out something that resembled a body but that was wrapped in a quilt. Freya immediately recognised the quilt and felt punch drunk.

"Ok keep watching, tail him as far as you can and give me coordinates, I'm calling the guys and getting them on the ground."

Freya wanted to ask so much, but with Angel's life in the balance she didn't want to be the person to hold them up. Watching him grab a bag, already prepared, she saw him take ammunition from it before filling the barrels of his guns, strapping the harness on his chest and another on his leg, he lifted his trouser leg before attaching a nasty-looking knife before folding his trouser leg back over to conceal it.

"Stay here, keep the phone to hand and do anything and everything T asks of you." Watching Freya look from him to T she nodded before looking back to Rob. "You too, stay with Freya." nodding Rob agreed but when he reached the door to leave Rob was behind him.

"If I can do anything else to help, I will. Angel means a lot to me too." Looking across to Freya who was hanging over T to try to get a better view of the computer screen in the kitchen, he looked back to Rob.

"Freya's going to need you."

"T's here. I'd rather be doing something useful, anything." Looking back to Freya he saw her stiffen before standing up straight to see what was going on between them. "If you're coming, you need to listen to me and the guys, do everything we say and repeat nothing you hear."

"Absolutely."

"They're not going to like it." said Eddie, shaking his head. Looking Rob up and down, he noticed the trainers and bright T-shirt with his jeans. "Ok, go and get into some dark clothes, dark shoes too, boots if you have them, and hurry up." Running off to the bedroom, Rob quickly got dressed.

"What's going on?" asked Freya, pointing to the bedroom.

"He's coming with me."

"What?"

"He wants to help." said Eddie, holding her shoulders. "Might do him some good."

"You mean you might actually start to like him?" Freya smirked.

"I wouldn't go that far. But he does have a copper as a brother, he might be useful."

"A brother who doesn't speak to him." Freya reminded him.

"Bloods thicker than water." answered Eddie, giving her a quick kiss on the forehead. "What did Hayley want, anyway?"

"I dunno." shrugged Freya "Just rang to see if I was ok I think?" Turning, Eddie watched Rob zip a black hoodie up.

"Ready." Clenching her shoulder one last time, Eddie walked to the door and Rob followed. Taking her phone from her pocket she decided to ring Hayley back, it was odd for her to call at that time of night and she hadn't really thought anything of it because she was so worried about Angel, but now they had T going through footage and Eddie and his security team on the scene she was a lot more confident about getting her back. Holding the phone to her ear, she waited as it rang.

Brrm brrr brrr brrr brr, the phone vibrated on the dining table and Jesse groaned the sound made his head ache. His head was full of rocks that rattled against his skull each time he tried to move, even in the slightest. His throat was dry while his skin felt wet and clammy. Finally, the phone stopped, and he thanked it for shutting the hell up. His head couldn't take the sound, it was as though someone was drilling on his head with a compactor. Using one hand, he flattened it onto the floor before trying to push himself up again. The paramedics had laid him down, but his side was screaming in pain. He couldn't remember ever feeling this bad, every bone in his body felt like it weighed double what it had the day before and his face was swollen to bursting point. He just wanted to curl up and cry, but even achieving that would have been a stretch. Feeling his back pocket vibrate, he realised it was his own phone, and he clambered to slip it out without moving too much.

"Hello?" said the voice. "Hello?"

"Hrr."

"Jesse is that you?"

"Roh." The paramedics glanced to one another while they finished off packing their gear.

"Jesse?" Jesse wished he could answer, but not only was his lips unable to move his head felt as though knitting needles were poking his brain every time he tried. Jesse tried once more to make noise, but that's all it was noise, and he flopped his head back down exhausted. "Jesse?" Once the phone call had been cut off he had the overwhelming feeling to cry but he couldn't, not till Hayley was ok. Realising he couldn't do this on his own he decided to call Martin, Shouting was impossible with a sore head and a battered jaw so one of the medics walked away to get him.

"Jesse, what's up?" asked Martin, rubbing his eyes to wake himself up.

"Someone rang." He managed, holding out his phone, Martin took it.

Looking at the screen, he brought it back to life. Flicking through to calls, he noted the number down in his notepad. "Any idea who it was?"

"No." answered Jesse.

"Ok, give me a second." Walking back out of the room, he called the office to do a check on a mobile number to see if it was registered to anyone. Waiting on the line, he paced the hallway when one of the medics passed him. Grabbing hold of him, he moved the phone from his ear. "How is he?"

"It looks worse than it is, but he could do with a stay in the hospital for observation."

"He refusing?" asked Martin. The male, older, paramedic nodded before continuing on his way to the ambulance with a heavy looking medical bag. Placing the phone back to his ear, he confirmed that he was still there while he made his way back to the kitchen. "You need a stay in the hospital."

"I'm not going. I need to find Hayley." answered Jesse, looking up from the floor.

"What and you think you're in any kind of state to do that?" choosing to ignore him he took the hand the female paramedic offered him to help him get back on his feet. After much protest and groaning he was up, unsteady he reached for a dining chair before lowering himself onto it. "Yeah, you're gunna be quick as a whippet." narked Martin. The Paramedic tried to stifle a laugh but failed.

"Ok we've got everything, I've left you some paracetamol but if the pain gets any worse, you really need to make your way to a hospital or a GP at least. We've found no broken bones, but that doesn't mean you're out of the woods and should your injuries or symptoms worsen seek advice. You should be in a hospital bed being monitored, but I can't force you." Jesse thanked her for her concern but assured her he would be fine. "No problem, I'll go and get the paperwork you'll need to sign to say you refuse medical care." Jesse nodded again and then the paramedic left to retrieve the relevant paperwork.

"Yeah, I'm here." Cut in Martin listening to his phone. "Ok got it, thanks. Yeah, I appreciate it, cheers." Placing his phone back in his pocket, he turned to Jesse. "The phone belongs to Freya Jefferson. Do you know her?"

Shaking his head, Jesse tried to rack his throbbing brain. "Hold on, yeah maybe. Hayley's friend's called Freya." Sighing as realisation dawned on him, he looked back up to Jesse. "She was seeing Rob."

Grabbing his phone back out, he quickly called the number and waited.

"Hello?" asked the shy female voice.

"Hi this is DS Wells of Nottinghamshire police I'm calling to speak with Miss Freya Jefferson please."

"Yes, that's me."

"I've just come across a phone at an incident and you were the last person to call. Can I just ask what it was you were calling about?" When he heard the receiver being muffled and two voices underneath it, he tried to listen more intently, more he couldn't work out what was being said. When she came back on the line, she was coughing.

"Sorry about that. Whose phone do you have?"

"I was hoping you could tell me that, you rang no more than two minutes ago." More muffled noise he looked back to Jesse who was waiting for the outcome. Moving out of the way for the paramedic to speak with Jesse, he watched Jesse sign the paperwork to say he was refusing care and smiled at the young woman as she left.

"I'm sorry officer but I can't be certain who I'm speaking with so I don't feel comfortable giving out that kind of information over the phone." Someone was clearly feeding her what to say in response, and he wondered why they'd feel the need to do that?

"That's perfectly understandable, I'll have an officer run round to you now and take the information, can you make sure you stay where you are until they get there?"

"Er… yes.. er… actually." more muffled noise and Martin smiled at Jesse, he was going to get what he wanted. "It's ok I believe you, I'm kind of busy at the moment. I rang Hayley Hallam; she's a friend, is she alright?"

"Can I ask if you've called anyone else?" Just then he spied the mobile on the floor under the table shoved up against the wall. Pointing to it, Jesse spied it and leant down to pick it up. Mouthing that it was Hayley's he flicked it on, showing Martin the screen saying missed call from Freya. "I called her husband, but he didn't pick up, is he ok? I was just trying to speak with one of them."

"Can I ask what you wanted to speak with him about?"

"Is he there, can you pass him on?" asked Freya. Holding the phone out, Jesse took it.

"Hi Freya."

"Jesse are you ok?" asked Freya, panicking.

"Where's Rob?"

"He's out at the moment, why?"

"Hayley's been taken." When silence was met on the phone, he wondered if she'd hung up, but when he checked the phone, the call was still live. "Freya, you sent her something, what was it?"

"It was a picture of my niece."

"Why?" asked Jesse.

"I asked her to see if you could help, she's been…" a muffled noise came over the phone and when she came back she sounded funny, as though she was being careful with what she divulged. "She's been and had her hair cut, I just wanted to show it off to Hayley." Shaking his head he looked to Martin as if to tell him they weren't going to be getting anything. "Jesse, who's taken her?"

"I don't know." Jesse lied. "Ok, I've got to go." Disconnecting the phone he swiped through Hayley's until he retrieved the message Freya had sent Hayley, it was indeed a picture of a young girl. Showing it to Martin, Martin paled. "This is the picture Freya sent." Jesse, do you know who that it?" when he shrugged. Martin slipped his hand into his jacket pocket. Once his fingers clasped the photograph, he pulled it out.

"Snap." said Martin, showing Jesse.

"What's going on, why do you have a picture of Freya's niece?"

"Because she's your step-daughter." answered Martin. "And my guess is that both Mum and daughter have been taken and Freya was asking for Hayley for help."

"But I was just on the phone-"

"Someone's there with her, someone's coaching her." replied Martin.

"Then we need to get there." said Jesse, standing up. Holding his side, Martin looked at him sceptically. Giving in, he nodded before walking out the house and opening his car door.

∼

"Is this because of what we found in that chest?" asked DCI Walker over the radio. Looking around them to check what kind of area they were heading into. Martin glanced to Jesse, who looked like he was struggling to remain upright in his seat.

"I think so, boss. I think they've finally found her and made a play, sir. The fact that Hayley's gone missing too suggests they're up to no good."

"Ok I'm going to call the team in and get on this straightaway; we can't afford to lose any more time on this. How's Jesse handling this?" when silence descended in the car Jesse coughed his throat clear.

"I'm fine, Sir."

"What the bloody hell are you doing in that car, you should be in the hospital!" bellowed DCI Walker. "You cannot be on this case DI Hallam!"

"With respect Sir, I cannot sit in a hospital bed while my wife is out there somewhere." answered Jesse.

"With respect Jesse, I'm your fucking supervisor, get your arse back in bed and stay away from my investigation or I'll have your fucking badge!" shouted DCI Walker.

"Sorry Sir, the radio seems to be cracking up, we didn't quite catch that." answered Martin smirking.

"Don't even think about trying that bollocks, I'll have your badge too. Get him home now!"

"No problem Sir, we've just pulled up outside Freya Jefferson's, we'll be on our way back ASAP."

"DS Wells! DS Wells don't you dare-"cutting of the radio they both made their way up the path to Freya's home address. Knocking on the door they stood back and waited for it to open, when a young man faced them in black suit trousers and a pale pink shirt with his hair looking as though he'd spent a lot of time with his hands in it, Jesse recognised him as one of her brothers.

"You're Dick weed's brother." said the man, seemingly recognising him too.

"Can we come in?" asked Martin. Looking from one to the other he finally nodded allowing them entry; walking down to the kitchen, they all took seats as the man drank from his own coffee cup.

"So what do you want?"

"Firstly who are you?"

"You're in my house and you don't even know who I am?" asked the man.

"We're looking for Freya Jefferson. We had it on record that she lives here."

"No. Not since she moved in with her boyfriend, his brother. My brother and his kid moved in here." looking back at Jesse. "What happened to you?"

Ignoring him, Jesse leant forward onto the table. "Do you know anything about what's happened to your niece?"

"Is that why you're here?" asked Will. Looking from Martin back to Will, he decided to lay out some of his cards on the table. "Look, we think there might be a connection with another abduction."

"They rang you?" asked Will, mystified.

"Why are you so shocked?" asked Martin.

"Well, because normally-"spying them through his eyelashes, he clammed up. "Why are you looking for Freya if they rang you?"

"Where's the girl's parents?" asked Martin.

"What the hell is going on here?" asked Will, sitting up in his chair and clearly getting defensive. "Why are you in my house looking for Freya and now George looking like you've been in a car crash with a monster truck?"

"Where's George?" snapped Jesse.

"Here." Turning, they all watched George walk into the kitchen looking like he'd been on a graveyard shift for a decade or more. "What do you want?" he asked, grabbing a glass of water.

"We have reason to believe that your daughter has been abducted."

When George only watched them they shared a look. "You don't seem to be shocked by that, so can I ask why you've not contacted the police?" asked Martin.

George looked to his younger brother and when he looked away again, there were tears in his eyes. "If someone you loved was taken, who would you ask for help, the police who are more wrapped up in red tape than an Amazon parcel or the guys you know who will break every law of the land to find her?"

"And who would they be?" asked Martin.

"None of your business." answered George, taking another mouthful of water.

"If we know she's missing we can send out photographs to ports and airports, we can have policemen on the street doing door to door-"

"And you can have my daughter behind said door, gaffer taped to a bed but without a reasonable reason to enter and search you'd walk right on by, so don't tell me to trust a bunch of plods to get my daughter back when you have so many rules you have to abide by. I'm not interested in keeping other people's human rights intact, only hers. So shut the door on your way out."

"You know if someone is acting as a vigilante we'll have to arrest them and that will only hinder your search?" said Martin.

"Like I said red tape."

"I could arrest you now, you've pretty much admitted allowing an unauthorised search for your daughter."

"Yeah, you do that and then at the same time I can explain how I saw him kick seven shades out of his brother." answered George pointing to Jesse. When Martin bit his bottom lip and refrained from answering, George nodded. "Thought so."

"Hayley's gone missing." admitted Jesse.

"Is that what happened to your face?" asked Will. Jesse nodded before looking back to George. "We think both abductions are linked."

"Why would they be linked?" asked George.

Jesse took a deep breath and looked from one man to the other before landing on Martin and silently saying sorry for what he was about to do. "Hayley is your daughter's biological mum." When George stood up straight to move towards Jesse, Martin stood in his way.

"You best explain yourself pretty sharpish." explained Will.

"Hayley gave birth to a little girl 8 years ago, but she was unable to keep it. To protect her, she and her brother sorted it so that she could be swapped with another family. The daughter of the family died whilst in NICU and because they looked so similar they replaced her. I'm sorry to tell you this, but I don't think your daughter is biologically yours."

"That can't be true. Angel can't be…" George laid his head in his hands and cried. Martin looked to Jesse, who kept his eyes on the grieving George. Will sat silently with his own tears while he leant up against the wall and bit down hard on his lip that trembled furiously. "She did go to NICU, she was struggling, and I stayed with Carianne." They all watched as he tried to piece things together. "I barely got to see her before they took her. I was so worried about Carianne that I just let the nurses deal with Angel. It seemed when we got her back she'd fought like a trooper because there was nothing wrong with her. They called it a miracle. That's why we called her Angel. She was our rainbow baby, and she fought to stay alive."

"She's still your daughter, but someone very dangerous has found a link, they'll use it to get whatever they want." explained Jesse.

"What could they possibly want with an eight-year-old girl?" once the words left his lips he shivered as though he'd already made up his mind about exactly why they'd want her. "If they touch a hair on her head, I'll fucking kill them." roared George standing back up.

"Listen George, we both have people missing, we both want the same outcome. Tell me what you know and we'll do everything to find them." Jesse pleaded. "Who have you got out there now, we'll work with them?" When Martin shot him a look, he chose to ignore it. "George!" shouted Jesse, slamming his hand on the table to garner his attention. "Hayley is my wife and I love her just as much as you love Angel. If we're to find them before the worst happens we need to work together, we need to pull resources and work together. Let me know what you've got and I can get the police in our corner. I don't give a shit where the information comes from, if you can get me evidence or a lead I'll run with it I swear."

George ran his hands through his hair bringing them to the base of his head, looking towards Will he gently nodded. Taking his phone from his pocket, Will pressed the contact he needed and then placed it on speaker before holding it across the table for them all to hear ringing.

CHAPTER 30

Racing into the meeting room with the moon still high in the sky outside, the team that had helped retrieve Hayley the second time sat round with coffees in hand no doubt trying to wake themselves up to be ready and alert for the task ahead.

"Ok ok ok ok!" shouted Martin over the noise, once they had calmed down and were facing the front all bleary-eyed and ready to go Martin stood in front of the clean wipe board. "Right we're all back in, we're all tired and we all need to work our bollocks off so get over it and move on." Tapping the board, he wrote Hayley's name in the middle. "We're back to the same shit different day."

"Hayley Hallam was abducted tonight just over an hour ago; we've already lost the golden hour, so we're already behind. We have information coming in that she's been flown to Glasgow. We have officers there who understand what's going on and they have their ears and eyes open. In the meantime we need to come up with a plan of action and get on the road, so we have to be quick tonight." said DCI Walker standing in front of his team. "There's been a development." When he turned to Jesse who was slumped in a chair in the corner Jesse flicked his fingers to carry on. "Hayley didn't lose her child when she was 16, she hid it. The kid was replaced by another who unfortunately didn't survive birth. It seems someone has found this information out and has not only taken Hayley, but they've also abducted Angel Jefferson. Her uncle is ex army, and it seems we might have a vigilante crew out there trying to find the same answers we are. Now, whilst we're all working on the same side we can't allow this crew to take centre stage and whilst I wouldn't particularly like to arrest anyone trying to help us we all have to remember the law they we all serve and protect. The information we're gaining from them at the moment needs to be taken seriously, but we cannot act on anything that isn't verified, so I need to be kept abreast of everything. Now Jesse's not here in any kind of professional capacity. He is a relative, a witness and a victim of assault, he is only in this room at my discretion and if I find anyone passing on information to him without my say so you will be visiting my office at the first available moment. Do I make myself clear?" murmurs went throughout the room and Jesse looked to Martin who was smirking as if he knew something they didn't.

"It can't be the vine cross, they're all either incarcerated or dead." advised Adam swinging on his chair.

"There's not just the vine cross to contend with, there's Gemini. It's an elite club where only the rich and famous can get anywhere near it, but it's built on tradition and bloodlines run the hierarchy of it, right at the top sits a crown and while the person wearing it is the most important it the people below it who give it power. It seems we might be in the midst of some contention, only the worthy are able to access it and there's a fight to achieve that status, there's also a long waiting list to inherit it. Apparently the whole thing started with eighteen families who shared and signed a document called the Olympus pact, this pact states that each family would inbreed within the families to strengthen their heritage and purify their blood, basically with each generation the generation before it would decide which families would unite within it, thus allowing their own families to develop and strengthen in wealth. The pact would remain tight, it would work as in if you scratch my back I'll scratch yours. So if one succeeds, the success is divided into the next generation with the other family. So it's competitive and no doubt the family that seems to be doing well for themselves would have a lot of offers with marriage so their own family could unite with them and strengthen their play in the pact. In the end the 18 families would be whittled down to just one, but by then it should be completely self sufficient and in complete control of all the other families as they all would have joined it somewhere down the line, it's just pot luck who had the last name and holds the key to the wealth." explained Martin.

"What wealth? More than they have now?" asked Adam.

"Much more. As part of the pact a sum of money was entered to begin with to secure their places, this was then invested with agreement and then secured, the money was then annually topped up and topped up each time a marriage and birth took place, but only within the pact families and only with the first child. It means that over the years the pact had become a huge amount of money and if someone was to get their hands on it, it would no doubt make them the richest person in the world."

"Holy shit!" gasped Adam. "That's some motive."

"Hayley is the stepping stone to the crown, she's only one level down from that crown." admitted Martin, glancing to Jesse apologetically.

"Which means her child to Demy was supposed to be the king or Queen?" asked Rosa.

"It would have been king; it also seems to be that the first daughter is sacrificed to the gods to strengthen their bonds."

"But Hayley didn't have an older sibling, did she?" asked Rosa.

"No, not that we know of. I certainly can't find any mention of another child between Helena and Alexi Liebrev. I think her mother ran with her as soon as she could. She was probably trying to save her child's life." explained Martin.

"Yeah, which is why Frank took things into his own hands when he realised his son was infertile after he contracted glandular fever as a child." As the room silenced DCI Walker took a sip of his coffee. "Fortunately Hayley gathered something was going to go wrong when she had the baby, so when she gave birth she had it taken away, hidden and then told everyone she had miscarried. It seems they believed her and Demy was punished by his father, because he had thrown her down the stairs. That's all circumstantial, but I'd predict that Demy costing him the crown like that did not go down well. It was some time later that Hayley ran away. I've no doubt in believing that while she was on the run Demy was being made an example of, and that's why she was incarcerated on stolen property charges, it was enough to warn him without having him serve any real time. So we believe they waited, probably tracked her and watched her. Then when he was released we think he was given the task of killing the other women who were in competition with Hayley for breeding the king, hence the deaths we saw a couple of years ago. If they couldn't give birth to the king, then they weren't a threat, to ensure that happened we think Frank sent men to rape them first, get them pregnant with an illegitimate child, thus breaking the contract, we think after that they probably worked them and then their deaths were simply a message."

"I thought Game of thrones was a piece of fiction." scoffed Adam. When his eyes caught Jesse's he quickly stopped laughing and schooled his features before looking back to the DCI.

"Why do they need Angel Jefferson?" asked Adam, keeping his gaze from Jesse's.

"She's Frank and Hayley's kid." answered Martin.

"Frank?" asked Rosa. When they all turned to Jesse, he stood up and walked in front of the whiteboard. Crossing his arms he looked from Martin to DCI Walker and as they stepped back to let him have centre stage, he uncrossed his arms and tucked his hands in his pockets looking like he'd rather be anywhere but stood in front of them, explaining his personal life and that of his wife's.

"Ok. Hayley was illegally married to Demy at 14, we all know she fell pregnant at 16 but instead of what we thought we knew, she actually had the baby swapped out for a child who didn't make it. This meant she'd failed her job of producing an heir. And while DCI Walker is probably right about the burglary charge, she didn't get away unscathed. Before Demy was imprisoned Hayley was made to Honey trap a politician, that politician died while she was in the room, it seems he got too rough for one of the girls and she killed him. Hayley was there, and she was made to cover it up, but a video was taken and she's worried if it gets out she'll be accused of murder or an accessory which is why she's only just told me. I didn't know until tonight that Freya, her friend and Rob's girlfriend is the Aunty of Angel Jefferson. I think after the chest was found in the church that someone else was able to put two and two together and find her. As for Frank and Hayley being the parents, Hayley was raped by Frank when she wasn't conceiving. We found out later that he'd known from the start that Demy couldn't produce an heir put with Anatoly dying, he only had Demy to rely on, so he kept that secret and tried to pass the kid off as Demy's. Hayley told me that all was going well until Frank got drunk one night and said enough to Demy to make him rethink Hayley's faithfulness and when they argued he pushed her down the stairs which gave her the opportunity she needed to get rid of her child. Her child then became Angel Jefferson and Hayley has never had contact with her, but her father Alexi Leibrev has. He texted Hayley a few photographs that she believed was to prove the girl was happy and well. Alexi Liebrev is also known to us as Castor. Castor told Hayley that he was biologically her father and that whilst his twin brother had tricked Helena into sex, being as they were identical twins, Frank had been too late. We only have his say so on this but either way regardless of her parentage she gave birth to the person who completes the pact and I'm sure that makes both her and Angel very valuable to them."

"What happens after they crown the king or queen and the money is released?" asked Rosa.

"The pact says it starts all over again. The King decides on 18 new families and it all starts again. I imagine these families are picked from lower in the hierarchy which would buy them their loyalty." answered Martin standing next to Jesse for support.

"Ok, but what's the point of being king or queen, surely if the rat race just starts again, what's the point of winning?" asked Rosa.

"Apart from being mega rich?" scoffed Adam.

"No, I mean it's like giving everything up once you've got it."

"No, I get what you're saying, Rosa. You'd think they'd rule over everything and have a say in what happens to everyone else, even make new rules etc, rule basically." said DCI Walker rubbing his chin in deep thought. Rosa nodded.

"Ok what if being the king and queen isn't all it's cracked up to be? What if they're the sacrifice?" The room went deathly silent while they all thought about what they'd heard from Adam. "But then who would get the money?" asked Adam thoughtfully.

"The parents who sacrifice their babies, surely." said Rosa. "You'd think they'd be recompensed in some way or they'd never agree to do it, and they're clearly money orientated."

"So Hayley and Demy slash actually Frank. But Frank can't get to it cus he's in prison, and Demy's dead so who's taking her there and for what?" asked Adam, stopping again they all thought.

"Alexi" answered Jesse, when everyone turned to him his face had turned as white as a sheet. "Alexi not only carries the same blood as Frank, but he's also his twin."

"So you think he's going to impersonate Frank?" asked Adam.

"He doesn't need to, he's a member of the founding families too." answered Martin, seeing where Jesse was going with his trail of thought.

"He's also Hayley's biological father." said Rosa..

"Yeah because they're all full of morals that lot." scoffed Adam. "Sick fucks the lot of them." When Adam raised his head to the silence, he saw everyone looking his way. "What? They all are!" justified Adam. When everyone shook their heads at his outburst in front of Jesse, he shrugged his shoulders.

"But you said yourself, we only have his say so on that." advised DCI Walker looking back to Martin.

"If he has a boy with her, then her daughter could marry their son." said Rosa thinking out loud. Jesse walked over to the window; he could not be part of this conversation right now. Thinking Alexi had been an ally and to have the tables turned so violently shook him to the core, he hadn't seen it coming and that was his fault. Hayley hadn't spoken to him because she was concerned about how he handled it, and now here he was wishing he knew more in order to help her.

"That's fucking sick." said Adam "Even for them. Banging your own daughter even for an easy mill is just urggh."

"Adam!" when everyone looked at Jesse, his eyes blazed. "How about you shut the fuck up and wind your neck back in before I slam it in a door?" Holding his hands up, Adam backed up a few steps. "My wife is out there having god knows what done to her and your laughing like you're at scout camp telling horror stories. Stop acting like a prick and act your age." When Adam visibly shook and paled at the same time Martin worried he was going to leave a puddle on the floor. Adam was young, naïve and completely inappropriate at times, but he never did it from a place of maliciousness, he just tended to open his mouth before thinking and Martin knew how much he looked up to Jesse. To be verbally assaulted by him in front of everyone would have stung.

Taking his wallet out of his pocket he dropped some coins into the palm of his hand, handing them over to Adam he asked him to go and get some coffees from the sludge machine. Once everyone had taken a breath Martin looked back to Jesse who was by the window once again looking out.

"It would get him closer to the cash." Martin reminded them.

"We don't know that they don't just need the daughter?" said Rosa, looking at Jesse's ashen face. "Maybe they only need her there for the ceremony."

"If they were going to do what Adam inferred it would take them decades." said DCI Walker.

"How are they going to keep her hidden for that amount of time? She's going to have to give birth then wait until they can marry to get to the money. There's no way this has been planned too meticulously for everyone then to just sit back on their laurels and wait a couple of decades." said Rosa.

"You're right, but then that leaves this as a sacrifice." answered DCI Walker. Jesse looked around the room and felt his legs go out from underneath him.

CHAPTER 31

Eddie pushed his earpiece in and pulled on his heavy gripped fingerless gloves. Passing him a black beanie, Mac went back to his heavy duty laptop, clicking away as though his life depended on it. Rob felt entirely out of sorts, as though someone had picked him up and placed him in an ulterior universe where he was expected to just adapt.

"We're positive this is where they stopped?" asked Eddie, gripping the door handle of the van.

"Absolutely" Mac drawled out slowly as he rotated the dial on his laptop.

"Ok, Jed you go East, Smithy West, Jif South and Ben you stay here until you hear something. Do we have eyes?"

"Yes, the drones are up now, night vision on, and I have T on comms." answered Mac.

"Go." said Eddie, sliding the door open and rushing across the gravel to the building 500 yards in front of them. Thankfully, the van was hidden by some thick trees and bushes, but they had to take care not to be heard on arrival if they wanted to maintain the element of surprise. Rob sat in the van, he'd been told to hold back and he was more than happy to do so. They were a slick team, and he was a rough nut in a bag of shiny nails.

"Stay alert, you hear or see anything tell me." Rob nodded, looking at the screen that showed all three drones in the air and Eddie's body cam.

"Do the others not have cams?"

"Yeah but we lead with Jaffa's then I'll split the screen once I can rely on the drones to pick up any heat." Rob nodded again. Rob wasn't sure how he was supposed to make anything out; Eddie was bouncing all over the place and while the night vision video was good, it wasn't clear enough for him to pick anything up. Suddenly the sound system crackled and their hushed voices came through the speakers. Listening to every word they said made Mac move the drones and flick from one camera to the next. Feeling his phone vibrate in his pocket, he realised it was an unknown number. Flashing the screen to Mac, Mac nodded after flicking a switch on the computer.

"Hello?"

"Rob?"

"Yeah, who is this?" asked Rob, looking at Mac.

"It's Martin. Where are you?" Mac looked at him, shaking his head. The silence in the van allowed Mac to hear every word.

"I'm at home, what's up?" asked Rob.

"Jesse's been taken to hospital, he's in surgery." explained Martin.

"Shit! Is he ok?"

"No, he's in hospital. Look Hayley's gone missing and Jesse's riding in an ambulance, can you get to your Mum and explain what's going on?"

"Er... well... no... sorry... not really" stuttered Rob. Mac stared at him as if to warn him not to say anything that could compromise their position or extraction. "I can't really just get away."

"You just said you were at home." Mac spoke directly into his head set but Rob didn't understand a word of it. "Er... I'm not sure, Martin. I mean I'll get away when I can, you know how it is?"

"Rob, I don't even like you ok, the last thing I want to do is to be on this call with you but Marie needs to know that her son is on his way to hospital and I thought you'd appreciate doing something for someone else for a change. But clearly you're still acting like a prick, so I'll leave you to your movie and not bother you again." Rob rubbed the back of his neck and broke out into a sweat. He was fortunate Martin couldn't see him. When the line went dead Rob put his phone back in his pocket.

"That's a real fan you've got there." said Mac. "But remind me never to let you in on any trade secrets." continued Mac smirking, "you're sweating more than a fat bird at a disco."

"What do I do?" asked Rob.

"Keep them away from us, at least until we get Angel." warned Mac. "You can explain later."

"My brothers in hospital.."

"I heard." stated Mac sternly, turning the sound back up on the computer. Looking at his phone, he decided to text Freya. "If you need to call you Mum, do it, but do it now because we might not have much time."

Deciding to contact Freya, he typed, **Jesse's been attacked, in hospital. Hayley missing**

Reading it back, he wondered what she was supposed to get from that. It wasn't as though they could do anything, and Freya was already worrying about her niece. It wouldn't be fair to burden her with any more. Deleting it, he put his phone back in his pocket before making his way back to Mac and watching the screens as they popped up at Mac's command. "I'll do it later."

"A1 has visual." Mac enlarged the screen belonging to Jif and brought it into focus. "2 targets, unarmed."

"A2 on run. TOA 30."

"A3 TOA 10."

"A4 visual."

Mac showed Rob where they were on the blueprint lying across his knee. Rob looked down and saw they were practically in the middle on the first floor. "Humming bird has visual." said Mac, into his mouthpiece.

Five second later there were shots fired and movements all over the screen, Rob couldn't keep up as he heard shouting and screaming.

"Targets capped." said Eddie, breathing heavily.

"What's that mean?" asked Rob.

"He's taken them down alive." Mac explained while he shifted his head into gear again. Rob nodded.

"Where is she?" asked Eddie holding a photograph of his niece in front of the men's faces who were kneeled on the floor with their hands behind their backs while two of Eddie's teams held their heads back by their hair.

"I do not know who she is." answered the man in an eastern bloc accent.

"That's a shame." said Eddie,

Just then Rob and Mac heard a loud bang. Rob looked at Mac with wide eyes, and Mac just shrugged. As the screaming went off in the background Rob breathed a sigh of relief to know he hadn't killed him.

"Do *you* care to tell me the same shit and get a matching leg or are you going to grow some bollocks and answer the question?" asked Eddie, shoving the photograph into his teammate's face.

"I..."

"Where is she?!" bellowed Eddie.

"She's on her way to Glasgow."

"Glasgow? Why?" Looking at the bloke who was bleeding out, he watched him shake his head, when Jif saw him he whacked him round the back of his head sending him flying forward into the bare planks. "Why?" he asked again to gain his attention.

"Boss wants her." He answered.

"For what?" asked Jif.

"I do not know." said the guy shaking his head emphatically, begging them to spare him.

"Where did you take her?" asked Eddie.

"Airport."

"Shit!" Eddie's gruff voice bellowed through the speakers and Rob watched Mac run over the computer keyboard like a maniac, popping screens up everywhere.

A minute later the cool air wafted in the van as the door was flung open and the team stepped back inside, making the cramped quarters even more so. Sweat and testosterone filled the air, strangling the freshness that had come with the door opening. "Where are they?" asked Rob.

"Knocked them out, they'll be there for a while." answered Jif.

"How you getting on?" asked Eddie, tipping his head to the laptop.

"A plane left about half an hour ago. No flight plan." answered Mac.

"There must be something?" said Jif.

"There will be, just give me a second." answered Mac tapping away furiously without taking his eyes from the screen.

"How we going to get to Glasgow, it'll take ages?" asked Rob. When they all looked at him with the same look that resembled somewhere between 'no shit' and 'shut the hell up', he did so quickly.

"Got it." said Mac triumphantly. "Yeah they were right, sort of, it's arriving at Campbeltown, but if they want a quick root to Glasgow, they'll need to catch a boat."

"It's an island?" asked Eddie.

"No, but almost. If they took the road, it could take a while, they'd have to horseshoe round." explained Mac. "Much easier and quicker to just sail across."

"If that's where they're heading?" argued Jif.

"Right now it's the only lead we have." answered Eddie.

"Ok I'll drive, you keep track of that plane." said Jif to Mac as he grabbed the door handle flinging himself out so he could open the front and climb in behind the wheel.

"We're going to Scotland?" asked Rob in disbelief.

"Yeah, and it's tough tits if you've changed your mind cus we ain't got time to turn round now." snapped Eddie. Rob shook his head, there was nothing more he wanted to do than grab hold of Freya but he'd put himself forward for this now and he wasn't going to give Eddie the satisfaction of seeing him piss his pants and cry about it like a little bitch.

"Ok we've had a bit of look, someone just called in complaining about an airplane taking off and being too low causing them to drop their tea."

"What?" asked Rosa and Martin together as DCI Walker entered the room with a sheet of paper.

"I know, but this one I've just listened to because the woman was saying planes *never* take off at that time of night, they're prohibited because of how close the housing estate is. Anyway, after checking she's right, no plane should have taken off and its flight manifesto hasn't been logged, it should be being brought down at the safest available airport."

"Which is?" asked Rosa.

"Campbeltown." answered DCI Walker tapping his tech whiz's shoulder.

"Where's that?"

"Scotland." Rosa and Martin shared a look, then with everyone else they grabbed their jackets and coats and rushed out with keys in hand.

Danny sat at his computer looking at the desolate room, two chairs swinging round from how their occupants had exited so quickly. "Bye."

FEELING the plane land on its wheels then bump along the runway Hayley looked back out the window, it was still pitch black but now small lights tried to illuminate the tarmac underneath her. Her eyes were sore from tiredness and the amount of tears she hadn't been able to hold in, she wasn't sure who she had cried for more, herself, her daughter or her husband. Even the thought of him lying unconscious started a new wave of nausea.

When the sign came up to unclip, she sat still. Alexi stood up and stretched before leaning into her to unclip her safety belt, taking her hand he pulled her up and she stood. Letting go of her hand, he walked in front of her and the hostess smiled at the door as if this was the trip of her life. Maybe it was, thought Hayley, just not in the way the hostess thought. Taking the steps out of the plane carefully she was suddenly hit with how cold it was, shivering she tried to curl her shoulders up to ward off the biting wind. Thankfully, his car was waiting, so she slipped inside. When everyone was back together within the confines of the black range rover with her squeezed in the middle, she watched them move off away from the airport. Glancing to the little girl, she watched her cry quietly while keeping her eyes on the men. Hayley's heart sunk, she'd tried everything she could think of to stop this from happening and none of it had mattered, they'd found her and now she was sat in front of her terrified. Not long after Hayley felt a prick in her neck and moments later she was sleeping.

∼

"It's landed. I've got visual and a number plate, but there's no CCTV to keep track of as soon as they're out of there." explained Mac.

"Ok just look for likely routes and then keep checking and CCTV coverage that could catch them." said Jif from the front. Eddie nodded and then flicked the screen to life on his own phone.

"On it." said Mac, tapping away.

∼

"Has police Scotland been contacted?" asked Rosa over the radio.

"Yeah, they're aware of the situation and the superintendent is getting a team together. We're to team up with them first and then allow them to work the scene, but our input is invaluable so don't be fobbed off. This might be the last time we get to have a happy ending so let's make out presents known." announced DCI Walker over the radio.

"Got it sir." answered Rosa, turning to Martin she sighed.

"They're going to make us sit on the sidelines." said Martin, watching the road.

"It's their land." explained Rosa on a sigh.
"We should have been trying to find him sooner." argued Martin.
"Who?" asked Rosa.
"Alexi."
"But we didn't know." answered Rosa.
"Exactly." announced Martin.
"You think he's orchestrated all of it?" asked Rosa.
"I think father's don't kidnap daughters, granddaughters and beat up son-in-laws for nothing."
"But why? Why not take her years ago if that's what he needed?"
"I think he needed everything to play out first. I think he's far more dangerous than anyone's given him credit for. I think he's been biding his time, watching the house of cards fall before he swoops in and takes centre stage."
"How far back?" asked Rosa.
"I think he needed Demy and Frank to incriminate themselves with the sect, show how unstable they were, a threat to the bigger picture so that they had no allies. I think he maybe even needed Hayley to kill Demy, maybe even Frank because I have a feeling there is a hierarchy as far as murder in concerned and with Hayley not knowing the rules she'd only kill to protect. So he made sure she was in full protective mode." Rosa thought about it, going over everything they knew.
"Why take Daniel, I mean surely they knew that would bring hell fire on them?" asked Rosa. "It's not exactly a quiet crime."
"I'm not convinced the same people took Daniel, in fact I'd go as far to say that he was a decoy."
"But that doesn't make any sense; Hayley said in her statement that he had a video link with Daniel on the screen."
"Ok but what if one hand didn't really know what the other was doing?" Rosa shrugged, she wasn't sure what he meant. "Daniel was taken, yes, but they brutally killed Jesse's dad just as a simple warning, in broad daylight. Hayley was taken out under the cover of a supposed surgery, which is clinical, careful, manipulative but secretive."
"Just because they used different methods doesn't mean-"

"No, but it makes you wonder why?"

"Because they were trying to set up a decoy, make a distraction, loads of witnesses and then slip out the back with the goods, it's the easiest trick in the book."

"But then they took Daniel."

"To secure the hunt for him, keep us busy." answered Rosa.

"You're right, it's textbook." Martin sighed. "But something's bugging me." answered Martin.

"The whole thing's bugging me. It's shit show with a list as long as our arm and some creepy perverts in gowns using religion to admonish their guilt." said Rosa getting comfortable in her seat.

"What I don't understand is why we found Daniel where we did? He was nowhere near Hayley, but Hayley said she heard crying in the next room."

"Could have been a tape to frighten her." answered Rosa. "Make her think she was that close."

"I still don't think that woman had a clue she was holding a kidnapped kid, I mean the camera was stuffed into a teddy bear. It would have been easy to miss, and she said the bloke was desperate for childcare, maybe she was right, and maybe they were desperate to have him taken off their hands because the main prize was always her."

"But someone used your phone to tell him he was being auctioned too." said Rosa

"Which made Hayley leg it back into the room they'd escaped." Martin reminded her.

"And Jesse was taken out." answered Rosa.

"It's always him who gets beaten, isn't it?" said Martin thoughtfully.

"What do you mean?" asked Rosa.

"I don't know." Martin sighed. "I really don't know."

"You sound like you distrust him." pried Rosa.

"Sleep deprivation." answered Martin, giving her a weak smile. "Forget I said it."

CHAPTER 32

On arriving to the castle Hayley was dragged in by her arm, that was still tethered to the other at her wrist behind her back, her shoulders were aching and the restraints had started to bite into her skin a long time ago. Her feet were not only black but bare, cut and bruised. Walking was difficult, but her joints couldn't relax long enough to replenish. She'd slept most of the way due to the injection, but her head was still swimming from the effects of the drug they'd given her.

Watching the big wooden ornately decorated door open she saw the man holding it wearing a pristine wine gown with embroidered red scripture written down the lapels to the floor and what looked like a bishop's hat sat on his withered old face.

"Welcome Castor. Welcome Aphrodite." Hayley scowled at the man. What had he called her?

"Evening." answered Alexi.

"I will show you to your rooms, where you can wash up. Food will be brought and then you will be summoned." answered the man. Alexi nodded, and they followed the sprightly man up the stairs. Hayley's arm that was still being pinched by Alexi was the only thing keeping her on her feet, but she wanted nothing more than to get him off her.

Reaching a white door, the man opened it and beckoned for Hayley to enter. "You will find clothes in the armoire, you will wash and use ointment and I will have the servants bring you food and drink." Shutting the door behind her, she heard them lock it. The room was huge and looked like it belonged in a palace or a swanky hotel.

Walking over to the window, she noted the bars, so it was an overdressed prison cell. Suddenly the appeal of the room dwindled. Walking over to the wardrobe, she opened it to find three gowns and a short pink negligee. The gowns were all floor length with A-line skirts, the white one was off the shoulder while the blue one was strapless and the black one had puffy sleeves and a deep v at the front. Walking over to what she presumed was an en suite, she opened the door to a huge roll top bath. Stripping out of her clothes, she ran the water before checking the lock on the door and stepping in. Reading the labels of the array of cosmetics and lotions on the side, she grabbed a small bottle of shampoo and conditioner.

Hayley laid in the bath till the water was cold. Events playing over and over in her mind stopped her from dozing off. She'd never felt quite so desolate and all fight had escaped her. Laying her head back she stared at the ceiling, she'd just have to do whatever it was they wanted she was never going to win this. They'd been effectively taking chunks out of her for years, maybe it was time to face facts, she was theirs and they were never going to give up. At least if she did as they said, they'd leave her boys alone. At least she could save them. As the thought caught in her throat, he allowed the tears to fall silently down her face.

A knock sounded at the bathroom door, and she quickly sat up, splashing water over the sides. "Your food is ready." said an unfamiliar young female voice.

Hayley rolled her eyes before getting out and grabbing a towel that had been left on the toilet lid, wrapping it around herself as she opened the door. The owner of the young voice stood at the foot of the bed looking directly at her dressed in an old-fashioned maid's outfit. Looking around the room, she tried to see if there was anyone else with them.

"Who are you?" asked Hayley, eyeing the door behind her.

"Alice." answered the girl timidly.

"I'm Hayley."

"They said I had to call you Aphrodite." answered the girl. Hayley nodded before swallowing the lump in her throat. She wanted to ask the girl in front of her for help, but she didn't know her and she certainly couldn't risk trusting her. "Hera is getting dressed." Hayley looked at the young woman to see if she'd explain what she just said. "Your daughter." when Hayley's throat tightened, she looked away. A few seconds later her bedroom door swung open, and the girl stood before them dressed in a white Victorian style dress. Looking at her face Hayley could tell she'd not long stopped crying and the look on her face told her she was more angry than fearful, but it wasn't definitely there in the background being shielded by her pre teen attitude, it made Hayley smile a little; if she was a fighter too, then maybe they'd have a chance.

"You're not my mother!" shouted the girl. When the maid and Hayley exchanged glances Hayley took a step closer to the girl to comfort her but when she stepped back Hayley stopped.

"You're right, I'm not. But for the benefit of us both getting out of here, you might need to pretend for a little bit." answered Hayley.

"They're calling me Hera, but my name's Angel." said the girl defiantly, clenching her fists down by her sides.

"That's a beautiful name." said Hayley, walking closer to her. "It really suits you." smiled Hayley.

"They say you're my mother, that you gave me away." asked the girl quietly, allowing her bottom lip to tremble a little.

"I think your Dad must be missing you very much." said Hayley, taking the girl's hand in hers. The girl nodded sombrely. "I think we need to go with this for a short while, just until we can leave." When the girl bowed her head, Hayley watched the tears fall, not knowing what else to do she pulled her into her chest, offering her comfort. Her tiny body shook as she expelled all her upset and worry, and Hayley couldn't help but hold her tighter as she kissed the top of her head. Glancing behind her, she noticed the tray on the bed with fruit and pastries assembled on it. "Have you eaten?"

"No." said the girl quietly as she shook her head.

"Would you like some of mine?" The girl nodded and Hayley smiled while she led her to the bed. When the girl climbed up on the bed she picked up a bowl of strawberries and tucked in heartily. Looking at the girl now, she could similarities in them both, but she could also see Frank's genetics too and she shook her shoulder as a chill crept up her spine.

The girl was beautiful, with wavy dark hair and pale ice-blue eyes. Her nose was the same as Hayley's but her cheekbones were slightly more pronounced like Franks. Taking a pastry from the tray, Hayley bit into it before sitting on the bed across from her.

"What do they want?" asked Angel. Hayley glanced at the maid who hadn't moved and didn't seem to want to take her eyes off the wall across from her.

"I'm not sure." answered Hayley truthfully.

"They took me from school. I thought my Dad had asked someone else to pick me up, they told me lots of things only my Dad would know." Hayley nodded. "Then they brought me here on that plane. I just want my Dad." Her voice croaked on the last word and tears spilled from her eyes. Sitting forward Hayley took the girl in her arms and something happened, Angel melted into her and Hayley couldn't stop the wave of tears, she was holding her daughter, finally holding her and it felt good, it felt right, comfortable like somehow the caress was mending her heart.

"I love you so much." whispered Hayley, holding onto her tightly. "I'm so sorry." When the girl stiffened she let go and hoped she hadn't scared her. Taking a strawberry from the bowl, Hayley bit into it. "My son loves strawberries." said Hayley. "Now I know why, they're delicious."

"You have a boy?" asked Angel.

"Two. One's a baby, though. Daniel, he's the one that loves strawberries." answered Hayley trying to temper her emotions.

"How old is he?"

"Nearly three."

"I've just turned 8." said the girl. Hayley didn't want to tell her she already knew. She remembered every second of that day. She'd clearly already made the girl feel uncomfortable by saying she loved her, after all they were perfect strangers and she was locked in a stately home with people telling her she was someone else.

"My mum died." Hayley looked at her and watched pain cross her face before she stuck another strawberry in her mouth.

"Mine too." said Hayley, when Angel looked at her it was with surprise. "I was a little older than you. I was 9 when he died."

"Who looked after you?" Hayley wasn't sure how to answer that. Taking a bite of a pastry, she thought about how to answer. Maybe the simplest way was the best.

"My Dad." answered Hayley. Thinking back to Baxter she wished he had looked after her, instead he'd sent her right back to the wolves her Mum had tried to escape from. If he hadn't been so weak and had such a bad drink and gambling problem, then perhaps would never have found her and she'd be living like any other young woman with a family. God, did the thought of family stab her in the heart. Her family was so far away now and that image of Jesse was tattooed on her brain. Had he woken up?

"My Dad looks after me too, but he's really busy at work so I go to my Auntie Freya's sometimes." Hayley smiled. "She has a new boyfriend, he makes me pancakes sometimes."

"That's nice." said Hayley, remembering that Angel was talking about Rob made the hairs on the back of her neck stand up.

"His name's Rob. My Dad thinks he's a bit messed up, but he says he's grown to like him, but my uncle Eddie doesn't, he says naughty words."

"Why does your uncle not like him?" asked Hayley, but Angel just shrugged. "Rob says he has a brother with a girl's name." Hayley smiled and tried not to laugh or cry. She could imagine Rob saying just that. Hayley had liked his cheekiness when they worked in the kitchen, it was unfortunate their relationship had soured, she missed their friendship sometimes. "But he misses him. Rob said he was really bad, and that's why he won't forgive him."

"Maybe." said Hayley.

"But Dad says if I say sorry then it's ok, so long as I know when I'm wrong." said Angel as if she was asking for Hayley to agree.

"That's good advice." Hayley watched Angel smile, proud that her father seemed wise.

"My Baby brother died with Mummy, Dad says she'll be looking after him up in heaven, and that they look down on us and smile."

"Quite true." said Hayley although she didn't believe in religion, she wasn't about to take the girl's only comfort away from her.

"Did you have a brother?"

"I did. He died too." answered Hayley.

"So maybe my mummy and your mummy are looking after our brothers together while we're here."

"I think you might be right. I bet they're best of friends." smiled Hayley hoping she was offering what Angel needed.

"Like you and me?" asked the girl. Hayley felt her throat constrict but managed to nod. Suddenly all serious, Angel stopped eating and looked at Hayley confused. "Am I supposed to call you Mummy now?"

"No sweetheart. Not unless they ask you to, just do what they ask and you'll be safe." said Hayley hoping what she said was true. Angel nodded as though she was ok with that and thankful someone was telling her what to do. When they heard footsteps coming, they looked towards the door. A man stood in the doorway wearing a suit.

"Your presence is requested downstairs in the drawing room in 30 minutes."

"Who?" asked Hayley, looking from the man to Angel, who sat rigid.

"Both of you. You are to get dressed accordingly." when the door slammed shut and the lock clicked, Angel turned to Hayley.

"They told me to wear this." said the girl looking down at her old-fashioned dress.

"I think he meant me." said Hayley pointing to her towel. Suddenly the girl broke out into a smile. Walking over to the wardrobe, the maid pulled out the strapless bra and pants with the black dress. Taking them from her, the maid helped her get in them all the while Angel watched. Once they were on Hayley looked in the mirror by the side of the wardrobe. Turning to Angel, she scrunched her nose, making the little girl laugh.

"You can see your bra in the middle." said Angel pointing to the v in the front of her dress.

"I know, I don't think they thought about the dress did they?" said Hayley knowing exactly what they thought they'd see.

"How about the blue one?" asked Angel, getting up to walk over. Nodding Hayley tried that on, anything to make the little girl feel better; if she was worrying about dresses, she wasn't worrying about other things.

Once Hayley was dressed and she found some kitten heels, she looked around the room. Being aware of Angel watching her every move she didn't want to look worried, but the room reminded her of a honeymoon suite, she'd seen in a magazine once and that made her stomach lurch. The fear of what was to come was overbearing. Turning away from Angel, she rushed back into the toilet and flicked the tap on to stifle her cry. But it seemed she hadn't fooled anyone as two small arms snaked around her waist and then she felt a head sneak round to her chest.

"Why are you crying?"

"Because I'm very silly." said Hayley. "But I'm much better now, thank you." said Hayley as she crouched down and hugged Angel back.

"My Mum said hugs always make you feel better."

"Well, don't you have some very clever parents, now I see why you're so clever." smiled Hayley. Angel beamed.

CHAPTER 33

Not long after they were escorted to the room, she could only think was the intended drawing room. 8 men sat at a very long table at one end of the hall, with books and pens in front of them, all wearing wigs and black cloaks as though they were in a court of law and they were all judges. Angel gave a withered look to Hayley and Hayley tried her best to look unaffected by the men watching them walk forward. Suddenly to the left of the room another door opened and in walked Alexi, in a pin-stripe suit, gelled back hair and a demeanour that more suited walking into a boardroom to sign a deal he'd already brokered.

Hurrying, he stood in front of the men and bowed before standing back and showing Hayley to take the place he'd just walked from. Hayley gingerly stepped forward and looked at the men in front of her. Waiting for something she decided to curtsey and then move back. Just then Angel was pushed forward to the same spot, and with a look of anxiety in her eyes she searched Hayley's eyes. Gently nodding, she moved forward and did the same before stepping back to the man who had shoved her forward.

"We are all here today to complete the Olympus pact prophecy; this in turn opens the court up to new participants. I hope you have some people in mind; we will be taking a vote after these proceedings. Should we feel they qualify, they will then be asked to put in the recommended amounts." Hayley had no idea what they were talking about and Angel just looked ready to cry from total fear. Alexi stood tall with a smirk of complete joy all over his face. "Anyway, before we get ahead of ourselves we need to verify this union and then make the sacrifice to the Gods."

"What?" blurted out Hayley, looking from one man to the others.

"Do you have the rings?" asked the master of ceremonies.

Alexi stepped forward. "Yes, your honour I do. Also, the dowry has been set, and the release is ready to be signed."

"All marks have been established?" asked the Master. Alexi nodded before taking an envelope out from the inside of his suit blazer pocket and handing it to the Master to look over. Taking the contents out, he looked through each paper intricately.

"What sacrifice?" she asked. The man looked to his fellow companions and then to Alexi.

"Am I missing something?" asked the Master.

"I'm afraid Aphrodite wasn't brought up with her fellow gods, she is still learning our ways." answered Alexi seemingly uncomfortable suddenly.

"Well, she better learn quickly I haven't got time to create a lesson plan." said the Master sternly. "And I do not appreciate a circus."

"Of course sir." said Alexi, bowing. "She will be handled." Hayley looked at Alexi wanting to punch him full force but when she looked at Angel, she knew she had to be careful so she pushed her anger down. "As you'll see." said Alexi, indicating the paperwork he'd just given them. "I have done extensive research and you will find in your binders all the information you require, also the results of all blood tests. She is Aphrodite and as such takes hers rightful place in this ceremony to complete the pact laid down by our fathers."

"Very well, I will check this. We can't afford to make mistakes."

"Of course." answered Alexi.

"I think it would be best all round if we complete the traditions and the ceremonies listed as quickly as possible. We have the fathers flying in for tomorrow so I see no reason to delay." Alexi nodded, satisfied. "Very well, we will go through this with a fine-tooth comb, check the videos we have in stock and ring the correct authorities for their blessing to go ahead. In the meantime, you are to all stay within these walls with no communication from the outside world. Hera will stay in the nursery next door to Aphrodite and Castor will be in the men's tower." All nodding in agreement Hayley and Angel stared at one another hoping the other might know what was going on.

"All being well the wedding will take place tomorrow morning at 10am, to which you will do your duties and cement the union with the congregation as witnesses. We will then complete the paperwork and move on to the sacrifice by midday. There she will be washed, purified and laid out for the gods where we will complete the ceremony and award the prophecy and the kingdom to Hephaestus."

"Yes, sir." Alexi bowed respectfully.

"The rituals will need to be started tonight, as we do not have much time."

"Of course." He answered again.

"Ok, your servants will be with you soon, please get a good night's sleep." watching all the men stand from the desk, Hayley watched them all leave at the back of the room. The guard behind Angel walked away, leaving the three of them in the room together.

"What was all that?" asked Hayley.

"That was us getting the seal of approval." answered Alexi.

"For what?"

"A wedding."

"Are you insane?" asked Hayley, walking towards him "I'm married to Jesse. He's my husband and how the hell can I marry you?"

"I requested that they take into account the additional information." said Alexi.

"What new information?" she asked warily.

"That you're now a widow and that you didn't know about your rightful place when you gave your body to someone unworthy. I pleaded with them to give you another chance after you murdered your king. Everything I have done is to protect you. This is to strengthen your place within Gemini and to maintain your safety."

"Protect me? You've torn my life to shreds!" screamed Hayley.

"I'm building you up to the woman you were destined to be. You were meant to rule and with me guiding you, you will."

"You're my father, how in hell is this even legal?"

"You think the Greek gods cared about such matters, they didn't divide their strength they unionised it, strengthened it, unbeatable, impenetrable." answered Alexi. "Gods take what they want, they do not ask, or plead, or beg. They take."

"I'm not Greek!" shouted Hayley. "And this isn't Rome!"

"It doesn't matter. Gemini has their own set of values. You're the only woman left at your level. You should have married someone at the same level or one below to complete the prophecy. You ran before a complete marriage could take place and you gave away your heir. You're lucky they can track back your ancestry, otherwise you'd be nowhere near the crown."

"I don't want the bloody crown!"

"I do!" shouted Alexi, his booming voice echoed in the large room and the silence that followed gave him a chance to readjust his demeanour back to composed and in charge. "I have worked too damn hard, taken too much crap, done too much manipulating for the whole thing to fall apart now. You are mine by birth and you'll be mine by marriage and when you bear your first legal son, our reign will continue and cement your place within these walls." said Alexi, leaning into her. "You will do as your damn well told or you'll die." Said Alexi lowering his voice so only she could hear.

"You're sick." Spat Hayley. "I trusted you."

"Have you any idea how much thought I have had to put into this, to plan it, to make things happen, select you and keep you safe?" asked Alexi, boring his eyes into hers.

"Well, you did a bang-up job when Demy was beating the shit out of me." argued Hayley, temper flaring again.

"They found you and they hid you. I didn't even know you were alive, all I knew was that Demy had taken the only available female left and killed the others." Alexi answered, looking more embarrassed than sorrowful.

"Why did you help move my baby?" asked Hayley. "That's the part I don't understand, why help me and then do this?"

"Because I needed it to get where we are today." Alexi answered looking to Angel who stood awkwardly behind Hayley chewing on her thumbnail. "All they had to do was arrange a child to be sacrificed and the money and the crown would have gone to him, or more effectively Frank."

"You took my baby away to stop Frank being king?" asked Hayley, astounded.

"I took your baby away because you asked me to." He reminded her. Hayley lowered her head ashamed and bit back every retort she could think of, Angel was behind her and she had to be careful what she said.

"How does this even work, she's Franks not yours?" asked Hayley looking back up to his steely blue eyes.

"Keep your voice down." Alexi warned through gritted teeth. "I've told them you fell for another father, one of your standing, but you were afraid for your safety with Frank and Demy and that you ran to protect the crown. The blood tests I have given them will verify her father, they have no need to dig any deeper, so you will not give them cause to. I told them that you came to me with this knowledge so that I could protect."

"But that doesn't make any sense." Hayley said, shaking her head.

"Demy is dead; therefore, you can marry your daughter's father and complete the union." Hayley took a step back. What was he asking her to do? "If you do not do this, there will be consequences for your adultery." Shaking her head, Hayley took another step backwards. "You can fix this by getting married, but only if you complete the union."

"What happens to Angel?" asked Hayley, taking the girl's hand in hers from behind.

"Hera will be prepared and sacrificed to the gods to empower the union and your gift will absolve all sin."

"No!" shouted Hayley, gripping Angel's hand as she continued to back away from Frank. "No!"

"We're going to set her free to the gods where she will be immortalised."

"You're insane. You're all insane!" shouted Hayley, shaking her head as if she was in some nightmare and she could wake herself from it.

"You will have a good husband. You will have more riches than you could possibly dream of. You will complete your role." Alexi said, stepping towards her as she backed up.

"You make me want to stab my own heart out." Spat Hayley before grabbing Angel's hand tighter and walking back the way they came.

"What's going on Hayley?" Hayley shut the door behind her and looked at the worried face of her daughter. She wasn't sure how much she'd understood, but nothing was good. "Is your husband dead?"

"I don't know." Hayley answered honestly. "I hope not." She tried to smile, but her lips barely moved.

"Who is that man?" asked Angel whilst Hayley looked around the room she hallway they entered. Hayley wasn't entirely sure how to answer that anymore, so she just carried on looking for a weapon or a set of keys or something that could aid their escape in some way. "What does he want?"

Sighing with the knowledge that there was nothing useful nearby, and that Angel required answers she stood up tall making her way back to Angel."There's a pot of money and whoever marries last gets it, basically." Said Hayley trying to abbreviate and make it sound less menacing than it actually was.

"And that man wants to marry you?" asked Angel. Looking away Hayley spotted a camera in the corner of the hall way looking directly at them.

"Something like that." Answered Hayley absent minded while she scanned all the other walls in sight.

"So why do I need to be here?" Hayley stopped looking and stood still. She couldn't tell her that. She'd never be able to look her in the eye again, besides she'd be terrified and blow any chance they may have of escaping.

"I think they need me to have a flower girl, I only have boys don't I?" shrugged Hayley, hoping she was coming over as convincing, but the mention of her boys tightened her throat and she cracked on the last word.

"That's dumb." Angel answered.

"Tell me about it." Hayley answered.

"Can I go home to my dad after you get married?"

"Yeah." Hayley lied. Angel smiled and then ran to the stairs they'd descended earlier. "Oh-fu." Remembering she was in earshot of a little girl, she pinched her top lip between her teeth. Deciding to carry on her search back up stairs she made it to her room before pulling out all the drawers and feeling under each one. Next she checked the bed next for anything that could be easily pulled away she then felt on top of the wardrobe for anything hidden. The window had bars, so that was useless, the mirror. Looking at the mirror she thought about smashing it, she could make a makeshift knife.

CHAPTER 34

"How long?" asked Eddie from the front seat.

"30 minutes. Drones are ahead, I'll let you know if I see anything." Eddie nodded while looking out the front window, for anything that might forewarn him what to expect.

"What happens when we get there?" asked Rob.

"We'll do a recce around the perimeter. Get sights up, head up devices, sensors and anything else we might need then we'll move in on cons." Rob looked at Jif dumbfounded but chose not to ask again.

"We'll have a look around, see what we need and then try to get inside to see what's going on before we take her out." said Mac rolling his eyes at Jif as he laid it out a little more civilian style.

Jif just shrugged. "That's what I said."

"We can't just blow through the gates until we know what we're up against." Mac finished. Rob nodded. "We could put her in more danger."

"Do we have any idea why she's been taken?" asked Smithy from the back of the van.

"No. But with her mum and brother not being long dead, I'm starting to wonder there wasn't more to it?" said Eddie hearing the question.

"You don't think George has got himself into anything dodgy, do you?" asked Ben. It was the first time Rob had heard him speak, and he recognised his accent as being Welsh.

"No. George is about as straight as they come." answered Eddie turning towards the occupants at the back of the van. Besides, he'd tell me, especially if it meant getting Angel back, he loves that kid." When they all nodded and concentrated back on the task ahead, Rob decided to let Eddie and the rest of them know what he'd been told.

"I got a phone call earlier. Jesse's in hospital, he's had the shit kicked out of him and Hayley's gone missing." When the van went deathly quiet, he looked from one occupant to the other.

"You think this is connected?" asked Mac, finally breaking the silence as he looked at the back of Eddie's head.

"Two abductions in one night within the same family?" asked Jif, raising his brow to the others.

"Sounds sketchy to me." answered Ben.

"But that doesn't make any sense." said Eddie, turning for a second. "Hayley and Jesse have nothing to do with Angel."

"No, but Hayley was involved in that sick sect, what if they've tracked her and seen Angel?" asked Rob. When a sickening feeling swirled in all their guts, the van drove on in silence once again.

"Is this bird anything to do with you, Jaf?" Eddie shook his head thoughtfully. "Then they might not be related."

"No, but Rob's right, if they've watched Hayley they have been watching me." said Eddie trying to think back to anything that should have piqued his interest before now. What had he missed? Had they had followed him?

"Freya's friends with Hayley." said Rob; it could equally have come from there. Thumping the steering wheel, Eddie cursed under his breath several times. "Rob, get them up to speed with Hayley while I get us there." While Eddie put his foot down, Rob looked at the eager eyes of his team swallowing hard before telling them everything he knew and had found out about Hayley and the sect.

"Do we have anything yet, boss? Where are we heading?" asked Rosa, speaking into the radio.

"Yes, it's just come through. We think some event might be going on at Pollock house, it's a stately home but looks more like a castle, apparently it gets hired out months in advance but this had a cancellation and was snapped up the day before yesterday."

"Ok, can you give me the address and I'll stick it in the Satnav?" after their boss had rung off and Rosa inputted the new address into the Satnav, she sat back in the seat.

"What do you think's going on?" asked Rosa, looking at Martin, who was driving along the motorway nearing 120mph with blue lights flashing.

"I dread to think." Answered Martin without taking his eyes off the road.

"They're not hiding very well if it is them though, are they?"

"They don't think they need to." Martin answered. "They think they're above the law."

"Arrogant pricks." Martin laughed, he couldn't help it, she'd summarised them perfectly.

∽

On reaching the pub Mac had checked for reservations online for and then rang ahead due to the time of night they were going to be arriving, they all looked up at the dingy looking pub set back from the road. Whilst most people would be less than enthusiastic about their imminent stay, the guys seemed thrilled with what they had found. Rob supposed it was unlikely to attract much passing business, and they'd be unlikely to come across any coppers here. The last thing they needed was someone getting suspicious about why they were there and blow their cover.

Piling out of the van, they all chucked on long jackets and stalked over to the entrance. Walking into the ale and tobacco stinking pub, Eddie banged his hand down on the brass bell twice before an old man waddled towards them from the bar on the other side.

"Hoo can ah help ye?" asked the man in his thick Scottish accent.

"We booked some rooms with you, about half hour ago." Nodding, the man looked behind him and grabbed four keys. Pointing to the book in front of him as though he was bored, Eddie picked up the pen and signed them in as Mac pulled out his wallet and paid the man. Giving him his change, they watched the man walk round to their side of the bar and then lead them up the stairs. Pointing to each room as though they may be confused about what the four doors were, the man grumbled something about breakfast at eight and then left.

Slinging his bag down on one of the twin beds Rob took the other, sitting on the edge he watched Eddie toe off his own boots, before lying on the bed on his back with his hands behind his head. Taking his phone from his pocket, he held it up to his ear.

"George... No mate... not yet... we will... I'm just ringing in to see if any head ways been made by the police or if you've received anything?" Listening to Eddie talk to George made him desperately want to talk to Freya, but he wasn't sure he wanted to do that with Eddie in the room overhearing everything. Walking to the door to the side he saw it was a small en suite, closing the door behind him he took his phone out and searched for Freya. Holding it to his ear while he sat on the lid of the toilet, he watched the door to make sure Eddie wasn't going to barge in.

"Rob." Freya answered, sounding panicky.

"Are you ok?" asked Rob, more alarmed than before.

"Yeah, I've been sitting on top of my phone waiting for you to call,"

"Oh, you got it on vibrate?" asked Rob, trying not to smile. He could almost hear her roll her eyes at him and he laughed. "Sorry. It's been an eventful night. Have you heard anything?"

"No, I'm stopping with Will and George and no one's heard a thing, we were hoping you had something."

"Not really, although I'm never sure with your brother's lot, they speak a unique language. But we've stopped off at a local pub. I think they're on about looking around tomorrow for any possible places they could have gone, but I'm not going to lie, it's like looking for a needle in a haystack."

"I just hope she's ok." said Freya, sounding fretful again.

"Yeah me too. Look, I had a phone call from Martin earlier, Jesse's in hospital and Hayley's missing."

"Yeah, I know." Freya answered awkwardly.

"What do you know?" asked Rob.

"Do you want me to ring your Mum, see if she needs anything?" asked Freya, ignoring him.

"If you don't mind that would be great, just don't go anywhere. I want to know you're safe with Will and George." Rob answered protectively.

"Ok." Rob knew how much that took for her to say, for someone who was fiercely independent having to stay behind because she knew he'd worry was not something she would have found easy to agree with. But there was something else, something she was keeping from him.

"Freya what's happened?" when the line went silent he thought she'd rung off but when he heard her sniffle he knew something terrible was wrong. "Freya."

Just then the bathroom door banged open and Eddie stood in front of him breathing heavily as though he wanted to kill someone, hoping it wasn't him he quickly disconnected the call and stared up at Eddie.

"We've got a problem."

∼

ONCE ALL THE soldiers and Rob were all sitting around the one bedroom as though they were having a sleepover and sharing scary horror stories Eddie looked from one to the other before he took in a long deep breath and let it out again.

"I've just got off the phone with George. Rob's brother and another copper went round tonight and informed him that Angel was swapped at birth."

"Holy shit" whispered a few of his comrades.

"The mother who gave birth to Angel is Hayley." Pointing to Rob, he continued. "Rob's sister-in-law." With the bomb dropped, Eddie sat back and waited for them to process what he'd said and how they'd continue.

"So we're thinking this is the same people?" asked Jif "They've taken them both tonight?"

"It's a hell of a coincidence not to be." answered Eddie.

"So, you mean the whole sect thing wasn't just a bedtime story?" asked Ben.

"No, it seems these sick fucks want something and they have a woman and a girl to play ransom with." said Eddie.

"I don't think it's about money." Rob answered.

"I don't know a lot about the sect but what I heard around the house after she got back was that they wanted her to have a child with one of them. She was married at 14 and supposed to give them an heir, but she miscarried and ran."

"It seems she didn't if this bird's Angel's Mum." Mac answered. "Seems she tried to hide the fact she had a kid at all."

"Ok." Eddie said, clapping his hands together. Rob watched him a few minutes longer wondering if he would say anything else but when he didn't Rob lay back down. "Best get some kip; we'll be up early in the morning and heading out." Closing his eyes, Rob thought about Freya, and wished he was sharing a room with her rather than her gruff brother.

∼

WHEN A BAG HIT HIS STOMACH, he opened his eyes. "We're heading out, get up." Eddie said standing at the end of his own bed while tucking his shirt into his black combat trousers.

"What time is it?" asked Rob, trying to open his eyes but failing.

"0400."

"Shit! Could have sworn I just blinked." Eddie made a noise in the back of his throat that he was sure could have passed for a laugh anywhere else but with him here he didn't fancy making a big deal out of it, they still weren't mates by any stretch of the imagination.

"I'm going to grab the team, meet us at the van, in five." Nodding Eddie walked out and down the hall to the next room which it sounded like he kicked twice before moving on to the next one.

Hearing the others making their way downstairs, Rob hurried up and pulled his boots back on, pulling the laces tightly and fastening them up before running down the stairs and out the door. Piling back into the van the sky was still black, and he wondered what had been the actual point of getting a room just to put their heads down for a couple of hours, but after listening to the men in the van talk between themselves he soon realised he had been the only one to take to the bed and sleep. They had all been in another room planning, searching and pin pointing places of interest. Listening in, they had also sent out drones to scope the area around them and used the heat sensors to pick up on any movement from below on within buildings. Having scanned the areas and tapped into the police control office they were fairly certain they were in the right area they just had to work out exactly which building to storm for an extraction. All words he'd picked up from listening to them discuss plans.

Pulling up outside a derelict building, the small army jumped out and quickly but quietly made it across the field. Mac was on the computer again giving direction and Rob watched the screen for any bogies, which he now knew meant anyone that wasn't them, and quite possibly a threat.

Ten minutes later they were all piling back in, annoyed that they'd wasted yet more time on a building with no results.

An hour later, Eddie pulled up by some over-hanging trees to allow the shade to help camouflage the truck and remain out of sight. Turning to his crew he asked Mac for an update then they all exited the van, pulling on their gear before silently making their way to the house, wrapping themselves around the outside they informed each other about what they could see and any visible exits.

Deciding after some time that they had a fairly adequate head and bullet count they hooked up and came up with a plan of action.

"Are you sure about this place?" asked Rosa.

"Not really no, but we've got fuck all else to go on." Martin answered. Getting out of the car, they stretched their legs and backs before looking up at the stately home.

"So what makes you think it might be here?"

"What you said about them being arrogant pricks, they're not bothered about doing things in grand style, and they don't hide away like the rats that they are, this place would suit them down to the ground. It's prestigious and grand while away from everything else, no passer bys being nosy or calling the police concerned."

"Fair enough." Walking towards the building they looked around and tried to remain invisible to any occupants within the walls looking out.

"You have two bogies coming up on the west." said Mac into his headset. "No idea, stalking remaining in the shadows." Rob watched on the screen and tried to make out anything useful on the two figures. After a few seconds, a thought popped in his head.

"Mac, I think that's Jesse's best mate, he's a copper." said Rob, pointing to the taller figure on the screen.

"Jaffa possible police." said Mac. "They're getting too close, possible to take down?" While Rob waited for Eddie to say something he looked at Mac to watch how his face changed. "Jif move up, we need the police taking down softly." Rob wasn't altogether sure what that meant, but he hoped it wasn't what it sounded like. "They'll not kill them." Mac said, holding his hand over his headset's microphone. Rob took a sigh of relief.

Watching the drone, they followed the team take down the two coppers with accuracy and silence. Rob watched as a soldier stood behind them both with hands over their mouths while they spoke in their ears, seeing their shoulders relax Rob could see that they understood they weren't under fire. Walking back to the van, they all climbed in and Martin saw Rob.

"What's he doing here?" barked Martin.

"He's Angel's almost Uncle." said Eddie. Rob tried hard not to show any pride in how he'd been introduced to Martin and his colleague, he couldn't look smug at a time like this but Eddie had given Martin reason enough to believe that he was one of them.

CHAPTER 35

WHEN THE DOOR OPENED HAYLEY SQUINTED AT THE LIGHT SHINING through from the hallway. Standing in front of her was a young girl dressed in an old maids outfit, thinking she might be dreaming and had fallen into Downton Abbey, she looked around her until she caught sight of the young girl lying next to her in bed, sucking her thumb while she slept.

"I've been ordered to get you ready and told to pass on that if you cause any trouble, they'll be consequences." The young girl looked afraid to be saying it, but she had no doubt been ordered to give those instructions and once they were out she relaxed a little before walking out of the room and then back in with a trolley full of supplies.

"What am I supposed to be doing?" asked Hayley.

"You need to bathe and then use essential oils that please the gods, after that I will help you dress and prepare your hair and makeup."

"And I suppose you've been told how to style me?" said Hayley sarcastically. The girl just nodded before looking away. "What about Angel?"

"Hera had her own help; she'll be going back to her own room to get ready for the celebration."

Celebration, thought Hayley. Who were they trying to kid, her or themselves? They would be preparing her for her own funeral and that was all, absolutely nothing to be excited about. "She's tired, can she be left a little longer?" The girl looked unsure and rushed off, no doubt to ask if that would be possible. Rushing round the other side to Angel, she gently shook her awake. "Angel... Angel.."

When she opened her eyes Hayley smiled. "Angel they're coming to get you ready, listen to me. Yesterday I told you to do what they say, but today I need you to try to look for a way out. I need you to be really careful though and not get caught. You need to get out and you need to run ok?" Hayley knew she was scaring her but she couldn't allow them to lead her like a lamb to slaughter, she could always make a fuss and allow time for Angel to get away, she might not walk out alive after but at least she wouldn't have to live with the death of a child on her conscience. "Angel can you hear me, do you understand?" Angel nodded. "Good. When you go back to your room make sure the servants think you're getting ready but actually look for a way out, try to escape ok, when you get out, tell someone what's happened here and can you give someone a message for me?" Angel nodded. "Tell Rob to tell Jesse I love him with all my heart and tell him to tell my boys I'm sorry." Angel nodded again and Hayley kissed her forehead before moving back to where she was before the servant left. "Now go back to sleep, shush." Hayley whispered.

"No." said the servant arriving back. "The master says she is to get ready now, she'll have plenty of time to sleep later." Hayley bit her bottom lip. She knew what he meant by that. Nodding to the servant, she watched her wake Angel and then led her out. Angel looked over her shoulder just before leaving and winked.

Walking to the bathroom she decided to give them nothing to complain about until she had to, running the water into the bath she added the bubbles bath and stepped in. The warm water relaxed her muscles but did nothing to release the tension in her head. No matter what came to mind, nothing was going to get her out of what she'd have to do; she just hoped it would create enough time for Angel to escape. She hoped her boys would forgive her and one day be proud that she'd saved a little girl's life, but the thought of never seeing them again stole her breath. And then there was Jesse. Bloody and unconscious in a pool of his own blood, that was her last memory of him. Before she realised what was happening, she couldn't breathe and when she tried, she wheezed, screaming for breath, sitting up in the bath she tried to gasp for air but none made it any further than her throat.

When the door opened to the bedroom Alexi waltzed in and bent down, rubbing her back. She scowled at him but couldn't say anything to stop him as she continued to struggle for air.

"Breathe Hayley, it's a panic attack, breathe… slowly…. Breathe… slowly." spoke Alexi gently as he continued to run his hand up and down her bare back. "That's it… calm down… calm down."

"I hate you." said Hayley, shrugging his hand off her skin, once she'd managed to control her breathing.

"I know you do." said Alexi still crouched down to her level. "I know that this is what neither of us wants, but if we're to get what we deserve after all what we've been through we have to see it through to the end."

"You're sick, you know that, right? You're a sick fuck who's going to sleep with his own daughter just for a bag of cash."

"It's more money than you can even think of Hayley, this is not a bag of gold at the end of the rainbow, this is the key to the world, and this is your destiny."

"No, my world died when you beat the shit out of him in my kitchen." Alexi bowed his head and Hayley wiped her eyes.

"That was unfortunate and I apologise, but he would never have let you come."

"He was my destiny!" shouted Hayley. "He was my life!" Hayley swung, slapping him across the face. "He was mine!" she screamed, finally breaking down and sobbing. "He was my world." she cried.

"I'll see you downstairs when you've got yourself under control." standing up, he left her to cry in the bath and made his way back to his own room to finish getting ready.

Out of the bath a while later and with red puffy eyes she walked into the bedroom where her servant waited for her. "We need to get you dressed; you were a long time in the bath." Hayley didn't answer, she just walked over to the wardrobe and opened the door with a towel wrapped around her, tied at her bust. "Did you use the oils?" asked the girl. Hayley shook her head. "You must."

"I forgot. Sorry." said Hayley, feeling anything but sorry about the damn oils. When the old-fashioned looking young girl walked back into the bathroom to retrieve the oils, she asked Hayley to sit so she could rub them on her skin. Normally she'd never let anyone touch her but today felt like it was already the beginning of the end so she let her get on with it.

Once the oils had been massaged in and all she could smell was lavender, musk and honey she stepped into the white dress that had been hanging in her wardrobe taunting her. The young girl zipped up the back and then set about combing Hayley's hair that was still damp from the earlier bath.

Angel wore a pink dress that when she twirled in front of the mirror, she could see floated up around her waist. She wished she could show her Dad, he'd love it. Thinking about what Hayley had told her she had made sure she had gotten ready easily with no fuss for the girl helping her and it seemed to please the girl who then ran off to sort something else, giving Angel plenty of time to look around her room and anywhere else she might be able to search.

Looking around the room she looked for any gaps in the walls, she'd watched Indiana Jones with her Dad and there were always hiding places in the walls, but looking around she came up empty. Choosing to check the floor, she lifted the rugs and again found no hiding trap door. Going over to the door, she peeked out and around and then exited, stepping lightly on socked feet.

"You can't just barge in there like the A team, this isn't a fucking game!" shouted Martin in the van.

"Do you not think I know that? She's my niece!" shot back Eddie.

"We're hardly barging in." said Mac, pointing to his computer. "We're planning a tactical extraction."

"Tactical extraction or not, it looks like we're looking at two hostages now, not just one." said Martin.

"Then we need to join forces, not squabble." said Mac.

"Firstly, we need to find out why they've both been taken in the first place?" said Rosa.

"Bollocks to that, I don't care. We can ask questions later." said Eddie.

"But if we understand the link better, we can understand the motivation and then we can negotiate and bring whatever this is to a holt." explained Rosa.

"Well, you have your way and I have mine. Mine's quicker." remarked Eddie unswayed.

"And more risky." she countered.

"So what do you want to do? Put an ad in the paper and hope someone can explain this shower of shit write their answer on a postcard and send to P.O box too fucking late."

Martin looked at Rosa and knew Eddie was talking sense. They didn't have time to find out what was going on; they had to get in and stop whatever was about to happen.

"Ok, you're right, we need to combine resources and information and then when we know what we're dealing with then we go in, together." said Martin watching Eddie and his team glance to one another for approval when it seemed they had, Eddie nodded, taking a seat in the van while the others prepared their firearms. "You know you can't just go around shooting people right, this isn't a war?"

When no one confirmed or denied Rosa gave him a look to just go with it, they'd sort that out later.

CHAPTER 36

HAYLEY LOOKED AT HER REFLECTION IN THE FULL-LENGTH MIRROR. THE dress was beautiful and on any other day she'd be happy to wear it, but today she just felt naked. The servant girl had braided her hair like a crown and fixed flowers into it. Her diamond earring shone and her makeup was immaculate, cleverly concealing her outburst from earlier, even as her eyes popped under the mascara and pencil. Looking down at her finger, she twisted her wedding band around her finger. Taking it off, she kissed it before placing it in her bra. "I love you." she whispered.

JESSE STIRRED and Rachel sat up straight in the visitor's chair. Taking his hand, she rubbed her thumb up and down his. Feeling the sensation, Jesse opened his eyes.

"What?.."

"Jesse you've had an operation, you're in Kingsmill hospital."

"What?.. why are you here?" he watched her bristle and take her hand away. "Sorry that sounded-"

"It's ok I offered. Everyone else is out trying to find your wife."

"Hayley?"

"Yeah, she's still missing." Suddenly, the memories flooded his brain, and he had to take a breath. Rachel saw him struggling and placed her hand on top of his. "Jesse I'm so sorry." Jesse allowed tears to fall and then wiping them away, he squeezed the skin between his eyes as if to stem them. "I need to speak with Martin, there's a girl."

"A girl?"

"Yeah, give me your phone. Do you have his number?"

"Yeah, taking her phone from her pocket she found Martin's number and pressed dial before handing it to Jesse."

~

PICKING UP HIS PHONE, Martin saw Rachel's name flash up on the screen. Curious, but in the middle of trying to organise an operation with a group of soldiers who wanted to take the lead was challenging enough without being distracted long enough for them to completely push him out of the loop. Silencing it, he turned back to Eddie who was pointing at pin points on the very elaborate map they'd put together in front of them.

"Shit!" Looking at Rachel, he bit back anything further. "He declined the call."

"He's probably in the middle of something; he had to dash up to Scotland."

"Scotland?" asked Jesse, scratching his head as he tried to remember what had happened before he'd collapsed.

"Yeah, they seem to think Hayley might have been taken there. I don't know the details."

"What the hell could they want with her in Scotland?" Rachel shook her head and looked around the room uncomfortably. "This must be a bit weird for you?" said Jesse, watching her.

"Well, it was either me or Fred and I didn't think you'd appreciate the constant chewing." Stifling a laugh due to the pain in his ribs, he nodded. Fred was a notoriously loud eater and he comfort ate. Which meant any time he was anxious or even bored he would whip out a bag of Walkers and munch along while everyone around him stared in bewilderment. Many jokes went around the station about him doing under cover with Gary Lineker.

Rachel and Jesse had had a quick fling when he and Hayley were on a break and falling apart, although it hadn't meant much to Jesse, he knew Rachel had seen it differently and he had hurt her when he'd broken it off before it had really begun.

"Can I use your phone again; I'm going to text Martin. He needs to know something and you're probably right about him being busy." Rachel nodded and Jesse tapped away.

Mart it's J, phone me it's important. Passing the phone back to Rachel, he laid back down on the pillow.

"For what it's worth I'm pleased you and Hayley got back together." said Rachel.

"Thanks." said Jesse.

"I hope you get her back."

"Me too."

"I heard my name was used in a sting last year." When Jesse looked at her confused, she rolled her eyes. "Adam told me he had to use our fling to make Martin think he was working for the other side."

"Yeah." said Jesse, wondering why Adam would have divulged that. "Mart knows too much about me to be tricked so Adam came up with the story to hold Mart back long enough not to get himself killed."

"He said Martin sucker punched him." laughed Rachel.

"The DCI had thought it best to keep his inside man quiet." answered Jesse.

"Yeah, Adam says Martin still looks at him funny, he thinks Martin thinks he's playing both sides even now."

"You and Adam?" said Jesse, suddenly realising what she was saying.

"Yeah, we kinda got together."

"I'm pleased for you, both of you." Rachel smiled and any tension that had been suddenly felt a lot lighter. "He's a good bloke."

HAYLEY ENTERED the exquisite drawing room from yesterday, drapes had been arranged around the room and an altar was prominent now in the room, with chairs circling it in a horseshoe shape. Angel came up from behind her and slipped her hand into Hayley's, looking down at the girl, she gave a weak smile to which Hayley returned. Watching the men as they entered the back, she realised they were different men than yesterday. Dressed expensively and with an aura of power, they moved around the room as though they all belonged there. Taking their seats, she suddenly felt very intimidated. Squeezing Angel's hand, she tried to offer some reassurance that she wish she felt. When the Master from yesterday entered she realised he was dressed in all his finery, a cream gown with a bishop hat once again. These people seemed to swap roles like teenage girls swapped makeup tips, thought Hayley. Standing in front of the altar he beckoned Hayley to approach, looking around herself she spied Alexi doing the same, and as he walked easily forward, she attempted to walk as slowly as possible.

Reaching the self-imposed priest, she looked to Alexi who stood staring right at her. Shivering, she looked away and tightened her grip on Angel who was close behind her looking around the room and at all its threat and finery. She hoped she was looking for an escape too and hadn't taken her instructions lightly.

"We are gathered here today..." started the priest loudly, bringing the ceremony into session. As if suddenly reminded of something he turned to Alexi. "Where is he?"

"He's on his way, your honour." Hayley looked around to see what he meant. Everyone seemed to be seated and waiting, who were they waiting for? When the back doors banged opened, everyone turned except Alexi who kept his face in front.

Hayley saw a man being dragged in, barely conscious but seemingly still breathing as he mumbled something, with his head down it was impossible to see who it was, turning back to Alexi she hoped to find the answer there but he hadn't flinched.

"Uncle Eddie!" screamed the Angel. Once her voice had echoed out the man lifted his battered head and smirked at Angel as her eyes filled with tears.

"Hi Angel." Hayley stood frozen, unable to comprehend what was going on. When she felt Angel try to let go of her hand to run to him Hayley held on tighter, shaking her head to Angel. "But he's my uncle." said the girl, almost crying. Holding on firmly, she pulled the girl behind her to protect her.

"What's going on?" asked Hayley, looking back to Alexi.

"You said you had this dealt with Castor, what's going on?" hissed the Master.

"He was late arriving sir, we didn't get the chance. May we have the room for a short while?" looking from Hayley to Alexi then to the men who looked less than amused. He nodded once before raising his hands in the air.

"If you fine gentlemen will follow me, we'll have a little apéritif while these youngsters get better acquainted." Watching them all get up and leave, she wondered if this was her chance to escape somehow.

Standing barely 10 feet from her now was Eddie. Still being restrained by the thugs who were holding him on either side, he looked like he'd spent the best part of a week being beaten and buried.

"What's going on?" asked Hayley.

"This is your future husband and the father of your child." When Hayley's eyes widened, Angel's grip on her hand got stronger.

"What the hell are you talking about?" asked Hayley, watching Eddie as he tried to lift his head for more than a few seconds.

"Hayley, he's my dad." answered Eddie. Stumbling back, Hayley caught herself from tripping over Angel. Horrified and beyond shocked, she looked to Alexi who confirmed it with a nod.

"I fathered a child before they married me to Helena; it was to be kept a secret. But when you see your child take his first breath and his first steps and then he starts school, it's difficult to walk away." When Alexi flicked his wrists, both goons let go of Eddie and he almost fell to the floor, pulling himself up straight as he glared at Alexi, before walking over to Hayley. Stepping back she took Angel with her, she had no idea what was going on and who she could trust she wasn't going to allow him anywhere near her. Stopping, he realised how scared she was of him and glancing to Alexi it looked as though he blamed him entirely.

"Edith and I had to part ways, but I tried to see as much of Edward as I could. We've kept in touch, but he only knew me by my alias." answered Alexi looking directly to Hayley.

"Andrew Masterson." answered Eddie.

"Quite. Any way I lied to you Hayley and Edward and I apologise but needs must and all that. I couldn't take you away before Frank got hold of you simply because your mother never trusted me with that information. When Frank found you he kept you under lock and key. There was only one time I could have gotten you out but it would have created an all out war so I had to play the long game, the more tactical game." Hayley stood completely still, she wasn't even sure if she was breathing any more. "You attended a hospital appointment when you were 15." Alexi looked to Hayley to see if she understood where he was going with his speech, she didn't but she couldn't take her eyes off Alexi. "They were panicking you were barren. So they had an examination constructed, where I believe you were tested." Hayley nodded gently as though any movement at all might stop her finding out the answers. "I paid a gynaecologist to leave you with an implant."

"What the hell did you do?" asked Hayley, starting to sweat.

"I knew Frank would never leave it to chance, he was far too eager to get the prize and when I dug around I found out that while you were being tested so had Demy, it seemed the loveable rogue was seedless. I knew as soon as Frank found that out he would try to bury it, there was no way he could take his title if his oldest son couldn't deliver the goods and I had his youngest son killed in prison so there really was only one way he could remain in the game and that was to impregnate you himself." Hayley's stomach swirled and Eddie clasped his hand on her shoulder, feeling her tremble as she continued to listen. "I could have done it myself but that didn't seem quite right and to be honest if anyone re-checked, they'd find anomalies, so I needed to find someone who would reflect our DNA type." Hayley hadn't said a word, but her head and stomach were racing faster than they ever had. What had he done to her? "Eddie had an accident as a child which we were told could leave him sterile, or at least find it difficult to produce, we were asked whether or not we would like his semen frozen, which we decided we would, after all most men want to have a family later on in life so it seemed like the responsible thing to do." said Alexi calmly as though he was speaking about what colour paint to use in a living room, and not that he was talking about something so abhorrent.

"Oh, my god!" cried Hayley, bending at the waist while she dry heaved. Once she'd gotten herself back under control and Eddie was holding her up, she looked back to her father. Eddie looked to Angel, who looked to him equally bemused.

"Eddie is Angel's father." A scream escaped Hayley's throat, more worthy of a war cry as she ran at Alexi, punching him as hard as she could in the face. When his head rolled back the rest of his body followed. Lying on the floor, Hayley went to task. When she'd finally worn out of all energy Eddie pulled her away and held her in his arms, as her body gave out and couldn't maintain her upright position any more.

Eddie couldn't think straight, his whole world had collapsed. Looking at Angel, he could see she was scared, unable to fathom what she'd heard but not being unable to unhear it. Frozen in time, she just stared at him as if she was seeing him for the first time in her entire life. Eddie's heart beat out of his chest to know he had a daughter, but it broke to know what Hayley had been through to have her. The betrayal stung worse than any bee or nettle sting he'd ever had.

"You bastard!" cried Hayley, taking a shaky breath in. "You could have gotten me out and you used me!" Alexi sat up on the floor and wiped the blood from his mouth. He felt the side of his face and resigned himself to a nasty bruise.

"The money you'll get will enable you to start your life all over again." He assured her.

"It was never about me!" she screamed over Eddie's shoulder. "It was about what you gained!" Wrapping his arms around her, he got her to take one of the seats the men had vacated earlier.

"You still need to go through with this." said Alexi. "They'll not let you leave." Alexi smiled to Angel who just stood still, wide eyed. "You can be a family."

"And what about Angel?" cried Hayley. "What about the sacrifice?"

"It can be staged." Looking to Eddie, he looked back at her equally confused. "I was never going to let them do that. I have medication to help lower her heart rate, another to paralyse her. I can make it look real and they'd never know all you have to do is trust me."

"Trust you?!" screamed Hayley. "You let them torture me, you let them abuse me and use my like their own personal punch bag. While you set me up, treated me like a racehorse. I spent my entire youth scared out of my mind. All I ever dreamed of was someone taking me away, someone taking me out of it, and all the time you could have and you just sat back and bided your time, all to be the person who got me pregnant and for what? Money?"

"Entitlement." answered Alexi. "They tried to destroy me, so I destroyed them. I watched them take out the competition while solely relying on you to be their saviour. I witnessed them tear up my life when they told me you were his and then when I found out they were wrong I planned my revenge." Taking a breath, he looked to Angel. "I knew I could take their power, their control and their leadership as long as I stayed hidden and I instructed others to dismantle their empire bit by bit. But I knew that while they had the prophecy, they would always remain on top. So I took it away from them, that one chance they had I switched to my own advantage and then when you asked Darren to swap your child I already knew where she was going, I'd kept an eye on Eddie's family and while he hadn't been able to have a child due to being away in the army, I knew George was expecting his first. All I had to do was to ensure a straight swap, but their baby was too ill to place anywhere else and died. It saved me the trouble of re-homing so I continued with the plan, knowing I could get to Angel as and when needed. Her mouth was swabbed straight away, and I knew that my sabotage had worked, but I had to hide the real results and build up a fake identity so that the miscarriage would show up on your records. It meant they would try again, but I'd given myself time.

When you were sent to London, I paid Rihanna to get you out, but Demy must have thought something was going on and refused her entry into the room, he changed the hotel room and by the time I'd figured out where you were but it was too late, they had the video of you and the MP and I knew they would use it to blackmail you." Hayley's mouth felt so dry she was sure someone must have absorbed all the moisture in the air. Swallowing hard, she tried to collate everything in her mind and reference it. "I think they knew someone on the inside was working against them, leaking information, but they just couldn't work out where it was coming from, so they prepared little tests and tried to trip them up, but of course I had many people working for me and they couldn't stem the flow, that was when Demy started to lose his mind. That's when he started to hurt you, badly."

Hayley knew the time he was talking about, it seemed at the time that Demy had been losing his mind. He'd upped her punishments, and the violence had increased, leaving her more battered and bruised and sore than before. It was when he was beyond nasty and tore down her much too fragile self-worth. He'd torn her apart, and she wished her injuries would lead to her death, just so she didn't have to feel pain anymore. But then she'd been given an out, and she'd ran, ran faster than she'd ever ran before and she didn't turn back even when she heard how close they were not until she was hiding on the bus that took her to the nearest town and she could bunk with her friend until she worked out what to do.

"How could you not help me?" pleaded Hayley, watching him. "How could you let them do that to me?"

When the doors opened and the men filed back in laughing and joking Hayley looked to Eddie. Alexi watched something pass between them and then he stood up. "You have to go along with this." He hissed at them both. "If you want to get out, you have to do this."

CHAPTER 37

Once the vows had taken place Hayley's heart dropped, she was never going to escape this life, her soul, her body and her future all belonged to a man she barely knew, and now she was having to pretend her heart wasn't breaking and that the vows she's spoken under the supervision of the men confining her to this warped sect was real. Looking up to Eddie, she could see he was in just as much turmoil. Finding out you had a child after all these years was a shock to anyone, finding out you had one without even being present at conception was mind bending. Looking in his eyes she could see he was at war and she only wished she could read him better to construct a plan. Each time he caught her looking he tried to smile to let her know she was safe, but she felt anything but, after all she'd been through this kind of ceremony before and had the scars to prove it. This was only the beginning of things to come.

Taking hers and his hand, Alexi looked lovingly into her eyes and she had the overwhelming urge to stab them out of his head. Leaning forward, he gently kissed her on the lips and she managed to just about hold on to the contents of her stomach. Angel was still stood behind her, holding onto Hayley's dress for protection or grounding she wasn't sure but the pull she felt when she moved made her feel secure in the knowledge that she was close by, boy would that kid have questions now?

"Congratulations, you may now kiss the bride." The Master announced. Looking to one another they hesitantly came together and lightly touched each other's lips; leaning back so they were straight, they looked away. "Ok, now you two need to get more acquainted. You'll be shown to your suite where a buffet will be supplied. I suggest you get comfortable as the brothers and I will be with you shortly." smiled the priest condescendingly before topping it off with and scuttling off with the others, no doubt finding some concoction of drink to celebrate their newfound wealth that was going to be payment for assisting this shambles of a wedding. Alexi remained with them and waited until the door had closed behind them.

"I think it's best we leave Angel in the nursery for this." said Alexi, seemingly sympathetic towards his granddaughter not being present to watch. Feeling sick but knowing there was no way of successfully getting out of this, she nodded. Moving around and bending down to Angel, she took both her hands while she looked up at Hayley for a sign of what to do. The fact that she trusted her touched her heart, but she wished she didn't. If Angel couldn't find a way out, she'd be no help to her when they would take her last breath.

"Angel, the grown-ups have an important job to do, so I think it's best you stay in your room for an hour or so, okay?" When Hayley nodded, so did Angel. "I need you to do that very important job, do you remember? "Nodding again, Hayley smiled reassuringly. "Ok, you run up and shut the door, I'll collect you ok?" nodding again she ran off in the direction of the stairs. Turning back to Edward, she noted the cut above his eye and the dried blood around his left ear.

"I'll leave you to it, don't make them wait." warned Alexi before leaving.

"What the hell is going on?" asked Eddie once they were alone.

"Why are you here?" asked Hayley.

"I was setting up a task force, and I was clocked, woke up in the basement and then the next thing I know I'm being heaved in here with you."

"You didn't know about any of this?"

"What? Are you crazy? Did you hear what he said?"

"So how are we getting out?"

"Now, I have no idea. But my team will know something's wrong, they'll be putting together a plan." said Eddie walking around the room trying to find anything of use. "They'll be trying to work out how to get in and out safely." Dragging a chair across the floor, he stood on it to look out the tall window.

"They've got the whole place guarded, men and dogs." admitted Hayley. "They go across every 3 minutes, I timed them earlier."

"What about inside?"

"Every door is on a sensor and they're locked electronically as well as manually."

"So Mac can disarm the electric field." said Eddie, rubbing his chin in thought. "If they can get someone in then, disconnect the electric we might just stand a chance of getting out."

"Eddie did you not just hear what's about to happen in about 20 minutes?" panicked Hayley.

"Yeah, we've gotta be somewhere for some more shit."

"They're going to make you sleep with me!" she shouted. Turning back to her, he watched her colouring blanch. "They're going to record and watch so that they can verify consummation, they're sick but it's what we're expected to do and then when that's done they're going to drive a stake into Angel's heart."

Walking over to her, he pulled her to him and held her close as she sobbed. "I'm not going to let that happen, okay. It's not going to happen, so you just stay with me and we'll be fine."

Hayley wasn't sure who to trust anymore, but she was exhausted from having to work it out so he just nodded against his chest. Once she felt steadier Eddie stepped back and continued to look around for something to use.

"How did they know you were coming?" asked Hayley.

"I don't know, but I assume Dad knew I'd use my skills to track down Angel."

"If he knows that, then surely he'd know your team was outside too?" asked Hayley. When Eddie just nodded, she realised he'd already thought of that.

When the doors opened Hayley and Eddie turned to it. "Your room awaits." said the butler holding the doors open. Glancing at one another they followed the man out and up the stairs until they were escorted to the room that Hayley had been in earlier, only now the room was clean and tidy and had a horseshoe shape of chairs around the bed.

The huge four-poster bed covered in white silk sheets sat in the middle, looking even more imposing than before. Touching her stomach, she was sure she was going to throw up. Eddie heard the lock click and suddenly felt like joining Hayley in throwing up. Looking at Hayley, he could see the fear and the resolution. She'd been here before, and she had no hope left that they wouldn't get out of this.

"You don't have to do this." said Eddie, hoping she trusted him enough to believe it. "We don't have to give them what they want."

"And how do we protect Angel, because right now I have no idea?" asked Hayley.

"My men will come." He said sternly. Looking up at him she wasn't sure what she read in his eyes, it was a mixture of things; maybe he wasn't as sure as he wanted to be.

"The money." said Hayley despondently, why did everything come down to money?

"It's more than just money." answered Eddie. Hayley looked away. She was interested in anything he had to say, nothing could condone how she had been treated and how she was about to be treated. They were all sick perverts and deserved their comeuppance, not more riches off the back of other's pain.

"Can't say I really care," said Hayley sitting on the bed deflated.

"Do you know why they call you Aphrodite?" Turning, they saw Alexi enter the room. "Aphrodite is the Greek goddess of love, beauty, pleasure, passion and procreation." Hayley rolled her eyes. "Aphrodite was born off the coast of Cythera, she was produced by Uranus's genitals, which his son Cronus had severed and thrown in the sea."

"Marvellous." said Hayley, already bored with the mythology lesson. Eddie just stood with his thick arms folded across his ample chest.

"One of her symbols is the swan." Hayley suddenly remembered back to the case Jesse had investigated where a boy had been found with swan's wings attached to his back. "She was also the patron goddess of prostitutes. There are many stories of Aphrodite being unfaithful to her husband, at one point she is caught by Ares, the god of war. Along with Athena and Hera, Aphrodite was one of the three goddesses whose feud resulted in the beginning of a war." Hayley looked up at Alexi and saw something shift in his gaze. "Does any of that remind you of anyone?"

"So they've judged me and named me after a floosy, big wow." said Hayley flippantly.

"No, you were named at birth." advised Alexi. "I was there when your name was picked from the pool."

"What pool?" asked Eddie.

"When a child is born into our circle they're joined into our beliefs and a symbol is pulled from the pool, Hayley's symbol was Aphrodite. Yours I had to choose discreetly, and it came back with the God Hephaestus. When I took Angel she was blessed with Hera."

"When did you take Angel?" asked Hayley

"At the hospital. I visited her and blessed her, at which point I pulled a symbol from the bag and she was given Hera."

"And who's Hera? Another sacrificial lamb led to slaughter?" asked Hayley.

"No Hera is the goddess of women, marriage, family and childbirth. She is one of the twelve Olympians and the sister wife of Zeus. She is the daughter of the Titans Cronus and Rhea. Hera rules over mount Olympus as queen of the gods. She's a matronly figure serving both the patroness and protector of married women, presiding over weddings and blessing marital unions. But she has a vengeful nature against mortals who cross her."

"Marvellous, well that's made everything so clear thank you." snapped Hayley.

"Hera is important." said Alexi, continuing.

"None of this is important. It's all a huge crock of shit, stories read upon to make you lot feel better about what you know is wrong. You read this crap and think you're above everyone else, like you have some god-given right to manipulate and hurt people. Guess what? You don't. You're just a sad, pathetic man who's about to not only have his daughter raped but he's going to kill his grandchild for a pot of money, well you know what? I hope that money kills you. I hope whatever you buy with it is your demise. I hope you die a slow horrible death and think of this day when you do, because I might not be Aphrodite but if any of this crap was actually real, I'd be summoning everything I possibly could to cut you all down and destroy this stupid cult." shouted Hayley unable to kerb her anger any longer.

Grabbing hold of her chin, he pulled it up to meet her gaze. Looking directly into her eyes he saw more fire than he had ever seen in anyone and he smiled. "I'm proud of you. You live up to your name, you're a warrior. Don't regret your choices." Letting go, she dropped her gaze, confused. What was he talking about? "You are a goddess, Hayley. Remember that." Sat on the bed in shock, she heard voices in the hall. On hearing the voices himself, Alexi stepped back in front of her and took her chin again. "Please forgive me." Kissing her again on the lips she then watched him walk to the door opening it for their guests as though this wasn't the most bizarre bridal room ever.

Watching the men sit down whilst looking at her with salacious looks she felt a chill and when she glanced at Eddie, she realised he hadn't thought it would actually come to this, looking with confusion and then horror he mirrored her gaze. Standing up, she walked over to Eddie and lowered her head. "Please tell me you have a plan?" she whispered, but when she looked up into his eyes, she realised he didn't. Feeling a tear roll down her face, she wiped it away before pressing her hand to the ring concealed in her bra. "Please forgive me, Jesse." she whispered.

"Gentlemen as our guest of honour was unduly late, he has been unable to prepare for this ceremony so I would like to ask for your permission in giving them a further few minutes?"

"Yes, of course." said the Master, who had already taken his seat. Please do what you need."

"Hephaestus, go outside, you will be escorted to your room so that you can clean up and change. We will prepare Aphrodite for your return." Eddie looked to Hayley, who quickly looked away. "Hephaestus you will see you bride soon enough, you're about to confirm a holy union, you need to be cleansed." Scratching his jaw Eddie touched Hayley's elbow, and she nodded gently giving him permission to go.

Stepping outside the room, a strong feeling swirled in his stomach. He had to stop this, but with no ammunition and no allies he was outnumbered and overstretched. While his body could take out maybe a few before they got their bearings, he would ultimately lose and then he'd fail, anyway. Realising that they couldn't start without him, Eddie decided to make sure his cleaning and changing took as long as possible to give his team some extra time.

When Alexi moved behind she shuddered, waiting for what she knew was about to come. Feeling the cool air hit the back of her, she heard the zip of her dress being lowered. Deciding to stare straight ahead, she zoned out. Once the material around her hit the floor, she shivered and closed her eyes. Back there again she could get through this if only she concentrated on something else, anything. Jesse. Jesse came to mind with his smirk, looking at her like she was the only person in the world. Laughing at something she had said, a memory reel kicked in, flashing clips of their life together, their special moments and then she could smell oranges. That smell that brought out so many feelings. So many feelings that screamed at her not to let this happen, but she persevered. If she took herself back to that day, she could almost exchange Alexi's hands for Jesse's, calming her heart rate and soothing her breath.

BANG BANG BANG!!

Suddenly snapping her eyes open she saw bodies hit the floor as the firing continued around her, screaming she held her hands to her ears. Finally, when the shooting had stopped, she stepped back until her back hit the cold wall. Shaking, she saw the bodies of the men who'd witnessed her marriage slumped in their chairs with blood running from bullet wounds in their chests and heads. Her chest heaving for breath, she looked at Alexi who sat on the bed looking directly at her. Looking at the gun in his hand she could see heat coming from it like a breath on a cold frosty day.

"You're free." Alexi stated. "You started this war and now you've won. You've brought the whole establishment down."

"I don't.. I don't." stuttered Hayley.

"They wouldn't let you go. They wouldn't allow you to leave because they wouldn't be entitled to any of the dowry. I raised their reward to let me marry you off today, so that I could get to the cash and then I'd pay them from that. I had no intention of letting them have it; I just needed them all in one room. For this." He said, flicking the gun in their direction. "These are or were the rulers of Olympus. Without them Gemini and the Vine cross don't exist."

"You destroyed it?" asked Hayley, amazed.

"I promised I would." He smiled. "You were always loved, I hope you know that, please remember that." Hayley looked back at the bodies. "This was always the Coda."

"What?" asked Hayley confused.

"The concluding event." explained Alexi "The last dance."

"Wh... wh... wh?" Hayley stammered.

"The Olympians made Aphrodite marry Hephaestus, thinking that would settle her down, but that didn't work out well. Hephaestus was a jealous husband, always on the lookout for that scoundrel Ares and anyone else who might want to flirt with his wife. He was a blacksmith, craftsmen to the Gods, he was an outcast, but he had a craft which made him important." Taking a breath, he looked around before looking back to Hayley. "I was a bad husband to your mother, and I was a jealous man, it destroyed me and I in turn destroyed your mother. I may have had to get you married to get this to go the way I needed, but I had no intention of destroying you." With that he picked up the gun and before she could get to him it went off.

Screaming, she watched the blood run down the walls.

When the door flew open men ran in holding guns and she screamed more, finally the shaking of her body made her incapable of standing, falling down the wall, she came face to face with Martin.

"You're alright, we're here, and you're alright." Martin soothed, taking her in his arms as she shook. Being unable to take her eyes from her father's body, she sobbed until no more tears could come. "Everything is going to be ok."

CHAPTER 38

Two days later Hayley was sat on a park bench watching Angel running around the play area with her best friend from school.

"I still can't believe she's back." said George from beside her. Hayley just nodded, she wasn't sure how much Angel had seen, heard and understood but it was enough to addle her own brain, never mind an eight-year-olds. "I don't really know where we go from here?"

"What do you mean?" asked Hayley.

"She knows you're her Mum. We've had it explained to us about the birth switch and then Eddie went on to explain about the way you found yourself with her." Hayley lowered her head. After everything that had happened that day, she was no longer sure which way was up, never mind whether Alexi had told the truth or just tried to manipulate them.

"I'm sorry."

"No, you've no need to apologise." George smiled kindly. "To be honest, if we'd have found out our baby had died I'm not sure my wife would have survived. Angel was our rainbow baby."

"I'm sorry." she repeated.

"Then we were blessed again with my son. Angel was over the moon to have a brother."

"I'm so sorry, George." said Hayley again, wiping her tears.

"To find out my only daughter wasn't mine, was tough, is tough." explained George watching her run up the steps to the slide once again.

"George, she's still yours. She loves you; she spoke of nothing else when we were in that house."

"Thank you, but things have changed. I just don't know what you expect now?" he asked, looking at her.

"Nothing. I don't expect anything. She's your daughter."

"Then what do you want?" asked George.

"I'd like to be part of her life somehow, just to know that she's happy. I don't want to take her away from the family she loves. I could never do that to her, but I would like to be able to see her from time to time." George nodded as he watched Angel screaming and giggling with her friend.

"She tells me you have two boys." He said after a few moments of silence.

"I do." smiled Hayley. "Daniel and Michael."

"So they're her brothers?" Hayley nodded. "She loves Rob."

"I know. She spoke of him too." admitted Hayley.

"How would that work?"

"I'm speaking with Jesse again later. He needs to know what Rob did." George nodded this time. "She looks like you."

"Yeah she does." answered Hayley. "Poor kid." When George laughed it broke the tension and she smiled to herself.

"Ok Hayley, I'll be in touch."

"Thank you." Standing up, Hayley made her way to Angel and gave her a hug before leaving for the train back to Newark. Martin was going to give her a lift to the hospital, and she wanted to freshen up first.

Jesse was leant up against the pillows when they walked in. His eyes instantly lit up the moment he saw her, holding out his arms as she rushed to him, wrapping him up with her arms as he did hers. Crying, they both let go and looked at each other as if to see if they were really back together and they weren't hallucinating.

"You ok?" asked Jesse finally.

"Yeah, you?" Jesse nodded. "You don't look it; you look like you've been in a ring with Mike Tyson." Laughing, he held his ribs.

"Don't make me laugh, it hurts like a bitch."

"I best not let your comedy sidekick in then." she said referring to Martin.

"What happened?"

"You mean you've not been told?" asked Hayley.

"I've been told a version which doesn't particularly make sense." He answered. "Where are the boys?"

"With Claire, your Mum needed a break, and I needed to go somewhere this morning." nodding he waited for her to tell him the story that had led him to the hospital bed and in no state to help her.

"Alexi tricked us. He took me and made me believe we were going through with a marriage so that he could get his hands on the dowry. What he actually did was fabricate the whole thing so that he could get the heads of each family in the same room to stop the escalation of the pact. Basically, he cut the heads off the many snakes that could have picked up the mantle. Now, with none of the rulers alive, the Pact dies. The whole organisation has crumbled."

"He had to almost kill me to do that, did he?" asked Jesse

"I've no idea, other than I don't think those men worked for him I think they worked for Gemini or Olympus or whatever they called themselves."

"Why take Angel?"

"Because he needed to make them believe he was going to complete the Olympus pact, the first child of the last couple is supposed to sacrifice their child to the gods to gain the money. He needed them to believe he was doing the whole thing so that the heads could sign off on it as witnesses, which would then release the funds."

"Witness to what?" asked Jesse suspiciously.

"They were going to witness our consummation of marriage and then the sacrifice of Angel. After that they would have signed the paperwork and Alexi would have been a very rich man off the back of us. But he also took Angel to get Eddie there; it seems he knew about his extracurricular in-no-way-legal-team of operatives."

"How far did it all go?" asked Jesse.

"We got to the bedroom, the men took their seats, he undressed me and then he shot them all. He'd hidden his gun behind the curtain and pulled it out while they were distracted."

"Alexi shot them?" Hayley nodded. "Then he shot himself."

"In front of you?" Hayley nodded while she tried not to cry. "What happened with Angel?"

"She was in her room. I had told her to try to find a way out, but Rob managed to find her before the shots, he was with her getting her out when they heard gunfire and the rest of the guys piled in."

"Why the hell was Rob there?"

"It seems Eddie the soldier had a team outside working out how to get in. When Eddie had to go and wash up, he found part of his team in the room with a vast array of artillery, once they knew where everyone was they tried to get Angel out first, that was the job they gave Rob because the team behind him could clear his way and because she knew him, he kept her quite and calm. Martin got them out before the rest of police Scotland got there."

"So they know Angel is yours?" asked Jesse.

"They do now." nodded Hayley. Interlocking his fingers with hers, he realised she wasn't wearing her wedding band. "Jesse I need to prepare you for something?"

"What?" asked Jesse cautiously.

"Alexi said while I was at a hospital having checkups he paid the doctor to inseminate me." When the shock on Jesse's face kept him silent, she continued just like ripping off a plaster at high speed, she thought. "He used Eddie's semen. Eddie is his son." Watching Jesse's fists clench, she felt guilty for being the one to hurt him. "We don't know for sure if he was telling the truth, we have to decide whether we want to take a DNA test to confirm. I've left it up to Eddie, I know she's mine. So I felt that was his decision to make,"

"Where's your ring?" asked Jesse, choosing not to say anything about paternity just yet. Watching her pick it out of her bra, she held it up.

"I wanted you to be the last person to put a ring on my finger." smiling he took the ring from her fingers and slipped it to her first knuckle.

"Hayley Hallam will you promise me that this is all over and that you'll never talk about another man's spunk in front of me ever again as I feel like I'm limbering up for a heart attack and will you please continue to be my beautiful loving wife?"

"I do." she said laughing. Slipping the ring all the way down, he pulled her to him, kissing her lips as though they were his lifeline. "Jesse I need to say something."

When he stiffened she didn't know whether to laugh or cry, all she ever seemed to do was be the bearer of bad news, but straightening up and pasting a smile on she held onto Jesse's hands, she was no longer going to be that and she needed to say this. "You make me feel capable. You make me feel strong even when I'm at my weakest. You've shown me that strength comes from doing what you have to and not what you think is always right. You've made me appreciate my strengths and weaknesses and you've given me the power to see them and adapt. You've made me feel less broken and more like a human, one that feels pain, but can overcome it through love and time. I've always thought that I was broken, but you made me see that I was just hurt and needed healing. You make me whole and not disconnected. When I'm with you I feel safe and grounded like nothing can come between us, like you're my safety net and my barrier to stop me from falling. You make me want to be better but you allow me to be happy with who I am, warts and all. You have always brought me through, even in the darkest moments of my life, and you make me believe I deserve better, like I have the right to grasp for it and hold on. You make me feel worthwhile, and you make me feel good enough, and I've never had that before. I love you so much and I needed to tell you what you've done for me and how you make me feel because you mean the world to me and when I saw you there on the floor, my heart crushed and I told myself if I ever got the chance to tell you what you mean to me I would, so this is me keeping my promise to myself and to you."

"Hayley I love you more than anything, you're my world and it simply wouldn't exist without you in it. You are strong, resilient, adaptable, caring." Hayley stifled a laugh of embarrassment and Jesse took her chin, making her look at him. "You're beautiful, inside and out. You bring light and laughter and love to my life and you're sexy as hell." This time Hayley couldn't stifle the laugh. "You're my home." Smiling Jesse pulled her to him and they kissed, holding each other together as if they could only survive by being connected.

The End

EPILOGUE

"Hayley!" shouted Eddie from the back garden. Stepping over the conservatory door frame, she planted her feet on the newly constructed patio where Eddie was cooking up a storm in the barrel BBQ. "I hope you like meat because there's plenty." Laughing she nodded, sure he was aware of the double entendre, confirmed only when he winked. Walking to him he wrapped his arms around her and squeezed, being covered in charcoal smoke she stepped back coughing. "Where is he?" asked Eddie.

"On his way, I left him taking the food out the boot." Turning, she saw Jesse dumping the bags they'd brought onto the kitchen counter. "Is he coming?" whispered Hayley. Eddie looked to her and nodded knowingly.

Twenty minutes later the adults were all sitting at the garden table with food over taking every available space. Sitting back in their chairs, the women sipped on Pimms while the men drank from bottles of beer. Laughing and joking, they watched Angel play with the boys around the garden as if they'd known each other forever.

Tapping the side of his beer with a knife, the tingling told them all to stop talking. "Ok well I propose a toast at our first family BBQ." Looking around Hayley saw them all smiling at her. "Hayley I want to welcome you to the family and apologise for having to put up with me as a brother, because unfortunately there's no getting away from me now." Laughing, they all raised their drinks before drinking. "We have an unconventional bond, but it's a bond all the same and I just want you to know that you're part of us now."

"Thank you." said Hayley, feeling overwhelmed and embarrassed. Jesse leant into her and kissed the side of her head while tightening his hand on her thigh to reassure her, leaning in to him she felt blessed.

"I'd like to add to that." said George "You've not just gained Rambo as a brother, because if you have one of us, you have us all, so I just want to make sure you know you also have two more brothers and a sister."

"Thank you George." Tipping his beer, he swallowed before getting up with the doorbell. "Saved by the bell."

"You weren't gonna cry were you soft lad?" shouted Will as George made his way to the house. When George came back he had a funny look on his face but before Hayley or anyone could decipher it Rob came into view. Turning to Jesse, she watched him watch Rob intently as he neared the table. Jumping up, Freya wrapped her body around him before kissing him on the lips.

"Freya, put the bloke down or I swear I'll nail you to the fucking fence." shouted Eddie. Rolling her eyes, she let go and clipped Eddie on the back of the head while she took up her seat. Once the crowd had calmed down they all watched Rob looking at Jesse and Jesse looking at him back. Hayley stiffened and glanced to Eddie, who was also waiting with bated breath.

Rob held out his hand in front of Jesse and Jesse looked at it as though he wasn't sure what he was expected to do with it. Hayley wanted to tell Jesse to take it, but she knew the betrayal Jesse felt ran deep. Freya looked to George who shrugged and Eddie watched Hayley as though to tell her telepathically to leave it and wait.

Just when everyone thought Rob would have to take his hand back or stand there forever Jesse stood up. Taking the two steps between them, Jesse wrapped his arms around his brother's shoulders and Rob softened into him. When a gasp ran out along the table Jesse let go looking his brother in the eyes.

"You saved Angel's life and you seem to have your life on track, as long as you keep it that way I'm prepared to try, but there's a long way to go." Rob nodded; just thankful to be given a chance was something he hadn't expected.

"Thanks." croaked Rob emotionally before nodding to Hayley and making his way over to Freya. Standing behind Freya, she took his hand in hers and looked at her brothers.

"I have something to tell you." When they all groaned, she told them to shut up before slipping her hand into her pocket and pulling out a ring, placing it on her finger as she held it out, beaming. "Rob asked me to marry him and I said yes!"

I hope you enjoyed this story and if you did, please leave a review.
Thanks for reading.

OTHER BOOKS BY THE SAME AUTHOR

The Vine Cross (Hayley's Story)
The Vine Tree (Hayley's story continued)
The Vine Coda (Hayley, Rob, Freya and Eddie's story)

Path to Redemption (Eddie's story)
Thicker than Water (Will's story)
Fight for Me (George's story)